BAD COMPANY

Library of Congress Control Number: 2019908023

ISBN 978-0-9914702-6-6

10 9 8 7 6 5 4 3 2 1

Covers by Terry Fogarty
Edited by Judith Swain

www.DayZeroBook.com

Printed in the United States of America

For the survivors.

ACKNOWLEDGEMENTS

John and his team have taken on lives of their own, creating a universe way beyond any I had ever expected to experience after the first book. It may seem corny, but I have to thank the characters for allowing me to have a playground and a sandbox to build my castles in. Of course, I love to knock those castles down just as quickly as I love to erect them.

I would like to thank Judy Swain for her never-wavering support and diligence to cleaning up all my messes, bad grammar and otherwise. I know making sure I am presentable is a full-time job, so I tip my hat to you for your tireless efforts.

I would like to acknowledge my beautiful and fine baristas at the Starbucks in Duncan and Boiling Springs, South Carolina locations for keeping me in good company and in good caffeinating elixir. The energy those stores have swirling around is what keeps me going.

BAD COMPANY

Written by Charles Ingersoll

Edited by Judith Swain

Table of Contents

PROLOGUE

1

Refills

+81 Days – 0821 hours
9:01:33

We were soon laden with all the ammunition we could carry. Every pocket of our cargos and tactical vests was filled with fresh magazines and our weapons were reloaded. The comforting sounds of metal slapping against metal and breaches being checked filled the air.

The faces around me in the ward were grim. While there was something to be said for completing this objective of the mission, everyone realized we still had uncertain miles to go before we got our prize back home—even with the shuttle waiting for us at the Hillside gate.

Dwayne, Harry, Sally and several others stood outside the ward door. I hefted the three quarters full duffel and walked it over to Dwayne. He wrapped his hands around the straps. As soon as I let go, the duffel plunged to the floor and took Dwayne's hands with it.

"Shit!" he exclaimed. "That's heavy."

"Or," Sally offered, "you're really weak."

Harry brayed loudly with Sally's comment, his laugh much more comical than hers. Dwayne gave them a sideways glance, but he had just as wide a smile as they did.

"We're ready to go," I told them. "If you need more ammunition, there is still a bit in the helicopter. Just make sure there aren't any termites nested inside before you go in."

"Ok," Dwayne replied with a nod.

"I would advise getting it inside and distributed sooner rather than later. Better to have it at the ready than having to fight through termites to get more."

The new council nodded their agreement.

I hope they follow through versus forgetting everything you just told them the second we are outside the gates.

"It'll be fine," I said, answering—and hopefully quelling—Bob's concerns and bolstering Dwayne's confidence in his new position as leader of Creedmoor. "Now, let's get back to the shuttle."

2

Exit, Stage Left
+81 Days – 0832 hours
08:50:48

"How did Alisha ever find herself in charge?" I asked Dwayne as we walked up the road toward Hillside Avenue.

Sally and Harry followed closely behind us. Jude and the others were spread out behind the couple, with Westsmith bound in the middle of them. Peter, Darwin and one of the riflemen who escorted me from the padded room to the auditorium closed our ranks and protected our rear. I had my reservations about them, but they had steeled themselves for the task ahead.

It was Sally who answered my questions while Dwayne simply shrugged. "Like Dwayne said, Alisha was shoved the keys when the administrators bailed on us. She literally found herself standing there with the keys to the kingdom."

"Why would anyone follow her?" Sean asked seconds before he veered off to take out a shambling walker who had been bee-lining toward us on a gimpy bare-footed left leg.

"It's hard to say," Sally answered after watching Sean dispatch the FRAC. "She was well-liked by the patients. And the staffers staying on found her charismatic enough to follow her orders."

"And she beat that termite to death," Harry said.

"Hell, yeah," Dwayne agreed. "I think that cemented her position. No one knew what to do when it showed up in the ward… until Alisha took a broom handle and bashed the termite's head in."

"Epic," Harry added.

5

She probably let the walker in to prove herself.

Cynical much?

Me? Never. I just have my ear to the ground, so to speak.

"Why didn't you leave? Jude asked.

"And go where?" Sally answered pointedly before adding in a nervous laugh. "Most of us aren't from around here. I'm not sure where I would have run to."

"And the other staffers?" Alvarez interjected herself into the conversation. "They must be locals."

"Local enough to take two subways and a bus to get here," Sally said. "A lot more difficult when public transportation breaks down. The authorities said to stay put once things went to shit. By the time people started to seriously think about leaving, there was no good way to leave."

"Staffers care for us," Harry said.

"They do feel responsible for us," Sally added. "Some of the people here wouldn't be able to fend for themselves out there." She emphasized *out there* as if the rest of the world was a dark, mysterious and scary place.

She was right. The world *was* a scary and dark place.

Even before the end of the world.

Bob was right, too. Terrorism had grown to an all-time high with plaza and concert bombings around the world. America had continued to be embroiled in a decades-long war in the Middle East and Europe. Celebrities and A-list stars seemed to have been exposed for their predatory sexual natures by major news outlets all within the span of eighteen months. Hurricanes, earthquakes, wild fires and mudslides seemed proof the earth was rebelling against humanity's atrocities. The dead coming back to hungry life seemed the natural next step for cleansing the world of the parasites we humans were.

While Darwin moved ahead to clear our path and draw some of the herd away, I moved past Sally toward three walkers. They bumped into each other as they lumbered toward the group. The trio was comprised of two emaciated male walkers book-ending an obese woman of Latina heritage. The skinny walkers had been dark-skinned in life but now, in death, their skin was ashen almost to white.

Two Laurels and a Hardy.

I drew my tactical knife and threw myself like a spear straight into the woman. The blade went deep into her nasal cavity. Normally, the knife would have stopped up against the skull by the guard, but the bone shattered, sending the handle and my fist into her head.

The shock of having my hand wrist deep in her skull was secondary to the putrid smell escaping her crushed face. As she dropped to the pavement, my arm was pulled down with her from the suction against my hand.

The two Laurels pressed in on me from both sides, their claw-like hands scratching wildly against my sleeves. The compression shirt's material held up against their assault. They were in an agitated state, but not from my presence.

Maybe they do not appreciate the fat one's smell.

Maybe.

I wrenched back my hand. The knife caught on the edge of the skull as I tried to withdraw. Goddammit!

I head-butted the Laurel on my left, bashing in his head with a single blow. He fell on top of Hardy FRAC, adding more dead weight for me to lift against. It was enough to let me pull my hand back with a crack on bone and the suction sound of her greedy gooey innards. My other hand held the last FRAC at bay by the throat.

Dwayne's shadow fell across my back and the downed FRACs. He swung his hand down and pounded the butt of his handgun into the last Laurel's temple. He retracted and slammed the weapon down again. Then a third time. Laurel stopped struggling against my grip, instead losing the fight against gravity as he fell in a heap next to his companions.

"That's the way to be a leader," I said with a nod.

"Hopefully, not too often," Dwayne said with a triumphant smile.

I flicked my hand several times, trying to throw off the disgusting goo congealing on my skin.

Harry stepped up to me, careful not to get too close to the pile of bodies in front of me. He held out a pack of baby wipes. "Here."

I stared at the half-used pack. "Aren't those your last ones?"

"Nah." He shoved them against my clean hand until I took them.

"Thanks." It was a gesture of gratitude only me and Dwayne truly comprehended. Giving me his last pack of wipes was a heroic sacrifice to him. I pulled one out of the pack and started wiping the gore off my arm.

Harry hurried back to the safety of the group and farther away from his decision. Sally hugged Harry as he walked back. He wrapped his arms around her and buried his face into her ample chest. She obviously wasn't oblivious to his sacrifice, either.

To the victor goes the spoils.

The group was a little scattered. Heinz held his weapon on the kneeling Westsmith. The riflemen continued to take on the larger herd, their inexperience in battle showing but their determination to protect the group evident as well. Alvarez and Melissa slammed the tailstocks of their respective weapons against several walkers flanking in on the group. Jude and Sean were doing the same, one on each side of Heinz.

I whistled sharply, but softly. Twice.

Everyone collapsed back into a tight group formation. We moved as a unit toward the Hillside Avenue entrance. The white of the back of the shuttle glistened in the morning light, a stark contract to the older institutional brick columns and black-painted wrought iron fences.

In the light, it was easier to see the disrepair of the entire perimeter on this side of the property. It would hold against the FRACs who might press against it, but not indefinitely. Weeds, tall grass, and trellising vines wove their way around the posts and through the rails. Beer bottles, discarded fast food wrappers, newspaper pages and other debris littered the bottom of the fences on both sides. A single purple knit scarf hung from a low bare branch, its bright color and newer appearance looking out of place.

There were still over a hundred FRACs along the fenceline, crowded deepest around the entrance. The rest of the walkers were scattered more loosely as they spread out for several meters on either side of the main herd.

"Same plan as before," I told them.

The walkers' groans rose in volume as Melissa climbed aboard the shuttle. Sean followed and moved to the back, with Heinz pushing Westsmith inside at the end of his rifle. Heinz shoved our prisoner onto the bench over the wheelwell. Alvarez sat down in the second row opposite the driver's seat.

Jude stood in the doorway with one foot on the lowest step. She waved to Dwayne and the others. Sally waved back. Dwayne smiled and nodded. Even Peter gestured his goodbyes.

Harry, true to form, uttered simply, "Nah."

"Ready?" I asked Dwayne.

Dwayne looked at me, his eyes darting at the immensity of such a simple question. Was he ready to lead remaining people of Creedmoor? Was he ready to take on termites they found their way onto the grounds? Was he ready to see us go?

"You got the gate?" I clarified my question.

Dwayne's eyes locked onto mine, holding my gaze steadily. "Absolutely."

"One day at a time, Dwayne," I offered. "You got this."

"Thanks." He held out his hand and I took it with a firm grip. We shook on his new position at Creedmoor and on the hope for a brighter future beyond simple survival. "Get lost, huh?"

"Sure thing."

"You're welcome anytime. Keep that in your noggin, too."

"You're the boss." I gave him a wink and walked toward the shuttle. Green Eyes spied on me from the tall dry grass, sitting quietly between the separated yellowed shafts with a lazy flick of her tail. I gave her a parting nod. She blinked and started to clean her shoulder.

Fucking cats.

I climbed aboard the shuttle. Melissa turned over the ignition. The walkers snapped their attentions to revving motor and the steady beams of its running lights. She reversed the shuttle until there was a meter of space between the bumper and the gate

Moans became growls.

Swaying became shuffling.

Dwayne and the others on the road skirted the shuttle's front bumper. Dwayne pulled the keyring from his pocket and picked through them until he found the right key. He stooped over and grabbed the padlock.

Sally leaned in to assist.

The riflemen backed up a step, keeping their weapons aimed at the gate. The top of the gate was bowing in toward us from the undead weight. I hoped it would hold after we were through it.

Harry stood directly behind Sally, his hand on the back of her shirt. He succeeded in pulling Sally away while Dwayne managed to get the chains unlocked on his own. Dwayne held up the chain in one hand and the padlock and keyring in the other for our approval before scooting out of reach of the walkers and the opening gates.

"Now," I ordered.

Melissa pressed on the accelerator, urging the shuttle forward. Harry, Sally and the others side-stepped to the curbs, Dwayne shuffling out from in front of the shuttle at the last second with a big smile on his face and the heavy chain and lock in his hands.

The throng of FRACs pushed the gates toward us as a single herd, the shuttle bumper halting their progress. Melissa revved the engine and forced the gates back out toward the service street. It was a tug-o-war as the weight of the shuttle and the mass of the undead cancelled each other out.

"Gun it," I ordered Melissa.

She slammed down the accelerator, the engine roaring in response. The shuttle crept steadily forward, forcing the FRACs back. The gates were opening, with us trapped between them and most of the FRACs reaching through the wrought iron. The rest of the undead filled in the void in front of us. They clawed and pounded the grille, one going as far as slapping his bloated hand hard enough on the windshield to split the skin and smear blood and pus across the glass.

Melissa reached for the wipers, but thought against it.

"Smart thinking," Alvarez commented from the second row.

The engine red-lined as the shuttle surged forward. The nose of the bus was even with the ends of the gates. Metal gouged against glass and fiberglass as the iron scraped against the sides of the bus.

The FRAC with the burst hand disappeared, quickly crushed under the front passenger-side tire. The ride got bumpier as more undead were ground down under the weight of the shuttle's tires.

"Almost through," Heinz called out from the rear bench. "The ends of the gates are almost at the back."

"We slow down and we get stuck," Melissa advised.

"I know," I replied. "Just keep at it."

The gates scraped along the back of the shuttle, snapping toward Dwayne and his men as the bus cleared the last of the gates. One of the taillight housings cracked. Peter and Darwin rushed toward the gates as the twisting metal swung together. The men braced against them while Dwayne worked to get the chain through the bars again.

The FRACs seeped in from the sides of the gate as the shuttle moved forward. As the weight of the dead filled in the void behind the bus and threatened to push the gates inward, Dwayne clicked the padlock closed and backed away. Sally brought up her rifle as one of the walkers reached through the bars at them.

I hoped she knew better than to discharge that weapon.

She did know better.

Sally and Dwayne stood at the gate for a moment, watching it flex toward them. After a few seconds of staring at the integrity of the gate and the walkers, they retreated quickly up the road back to the Wellness Center. They would still need to fight through a few FRACs to get safely back behind brick and steel doors, but I had hope they were all capable of getting the job done. Harry may have raised a hand in a hasty goodbye, but I would never know for sure.

"Come on, muthafuckers," Melissa growled through gritted

teeth. "Come on." The shuttle's RPMs were still red-lining as it—and Melissa—struggled to get through the rows of FRACs blocking our path to the relative freedom of Hillside Avenue. Melissa shifted to S1 for more torque. The shuttle lurched forward again, bouncing over more soft bodies. The shuttle rocked up, then quickly down as the weight of the tires crushed FRAC skulls like watermelons exploding under the swing of an oversized wooden mallet at a Gallagher comedy show.

A retching sound came from the back.

Heinz covered his mouth as he doubled over in his seat. Nothing came out but the gagging of more convulsive muscle spasms. He and Westsmith were sitting on the seats over the wheel wells. They were definitely getting the full effects of the FRACs flattening under the chassis.

Finally, only two rows of FRACs clung to the edges of the front grill. One of them grabbed at the windshield wiper blades and snapped one of them off.

Well… now you will never be able to get all the goo off the windshield.

I'm surprised the wiper blade lasted as long as it did, I thought back at him.

Melissa let out a war cry as she jammed her foot down on the gas pedal. The rear double tires spun on the viscera of the dead, shooting sprays of blood up the rear side windows behind the wheel wells. The tires finally burned through the bodies and caught traction on clear patches of asphalt. The shuttle shrieked over the last few walkers as rubber burned into the pavement, fishtailing as it surged forward. Melissa compensated, steering into the slide until the shuttle stabilized and sped off in a westerly direction.

"Take that," was all Melissa gave herself as congratulations for a job well done. I patted her on the shoulder.

Jude was wide-eyed, bracing herself against the back of the seat in front of her. Alvarez sat against the window with her crossed legs hanging off the seat into the aisle. Heinz was doubled over with his head hanging between his knees. Sean held his gaze and his weapon on the now alert and smiling Westsmith.

"That was quite the little adventure, Mr. Walken," Westsmith announced. "I am sure we'll continue to have fun together. Of course, nothing compares to what the Creedmoor folks are in for now that you've taken me away from my home."

"You're full of shite," Heinz said, still looking a bit peaked.

"Am I?" Westsmith shrugged. "Maybe. Maybe not. But we all know what happens to termites."

Melissa glanced at me, taking her eyes from the road. "Change of plans?"

I looked between Westsmith's smirk and shining eyes to the others' blood caked faces and slumped shoulders. Jude realized she was rubbing the side of her neck and pulled her hand away. Alvarez tapped her fingers on the seat in front of her, no longer sprawled out. Sean continued to glare at the back of Westsmith's head.

"John?" Melissa asked, her grip on the steering wheel ready to turn us back around toward Creedmoor. "We staying or going?"

The gates were holding. Dwayne and the others had retreated to the safety and protection of the Wellness Center. They had plenty of ammunition and the manpower to use it against the undead. Dwayne would do right by the others.

Manhattan was in front of us.

I glanced at my Cobra. We had a little over eight hours to get Westsmith back to R&R, get the capsule defused in Jude's neck, and get the rest of our people back. "Keep going."

BAD COMPANY

1

Google Maps
+81 Days – 0901 hours
08:21:02

"We're here," Alvarez said, joining me behind the yellow aisle line behind Melissa. She held out the tablet-styled device from her tactical vest and swiped her finger across the aerial map on its seven-inch screen. She pointed at the street west of the Creedmoor compound. "We need to get to Midtown... here. The dark masses highlighted in green tint are walker groupings."

Manhattan Island was only a dozen miles away, as the crow flies. It was more like twenty miles using the major thoroughfares on a good day. "I'm surprised there aren't more of them as you get closer to the city," I remarked. "What are the red masses?"

"Impassable sections of expressway or parkways," she replied.

"That's a lot of red," Jude commented, looking over Alvarez's shoulder. "There's a lot more red than green."

"The National Guard tried to keep the Long Island Expressway clear, but it jams up to a snarl at the Midtown Tunnel."

"No way we're going through a tunnel," Melissa warned. "No way."

"Agreed," I said. "No tactical advantage in a confined space like that."

"Better to get to the 59th Street Bridge," Alvarez advised. "Has visibility and wider access points."

"Is that the Queensboro Bridge?" Jude asked.

Alvarez and Sean both chuckled.

"Real New Yorkers would never call it that," Sean commented.

"I guess you're a real New Yorker, then?" Jude asked.

"Closer than anyone else here," he confirmed. "That's for sure."

"You don't sound like a New Yorker," Melissa said.

"And you sound like you came from the Midwest," Sean pointed out, "not the Northeast."

"We all come from somewhere," I said, a small pang coming from my wounded side. "It may just not be where you think."

"Bridges," Jude mused. "Didn't have a good experience on a bridge when the shit went bad."

"Bridges and tunnels," Melissa grumbled. "Neither sound appealing." She brought the shuttle to a stop at the intersection of Winchester Boulevard and Hillside Avenue under a dark stoplight. One car was up on the opposite curb with its front bumper buckled against a cracked electrical pole. Its hood, doors, and trunk lid were wide open. Its state of abandonment under the glare of the morning sun reminded me of some of the war-torn towns of the Middle East. Like museum exhibits, this sedan would eventually become one of thousands of similar relics littering the landscape. Eventually, we wouldn't even notice them.

"Which way?" Melissa asked. Alvarez consulted the aerial map, sliding the image around between our current position and the R&R building on Manhattan Island.

"What's the verdict, MapQuest?" I asked.

Alvarez smiled a little, but continued to study the map. She bit her lower lip, a little wrinkle creasing between her eyebrows. "LIE is the best route," she finally answered. "We will have to reassess as we go."

"LIE?" Melissa asked.

"The Long Island Expressway," Bowers educated us proudly.

I glanced at the map. Both roads were clear of any serious wreckage what would hinder our progress. Winchester gave us a more direct route to the Long Island Expressway while Hillside gave us more outs. A twinge of worry sparked in my gut. Would eight hours be enough time to get back to the city and get everything righted again? We would just have to keep moving forward to find out. "Make a right."

Melissa turned on the shuttle's broken right turn signal and looked in both directions before proceeding onto Winchester with caution.

2

Dead Ends

+81 Days – 0929 hours
07:53:56

Winchester Blvd turned into Douglaston Parkway as we passed under the Grand Central Parkway, although we didn't spend too much time admiring it. The parkway was backed up with abandoned cars, forcing us to divert through the surface streets.

"Told you that was a bad idea," Melissa said as we sat at the fork at 241st and 242nd streets, both of which were dead ends. "Your girlfriend's sense of direction is for shit. Or at the very least, she can't read a map."

"Alvarez," I said sternly.

"The aerials are full of static and tough to read," she said in defense of her map-reading skills. "And this area has a lot of trees."

"Sean," I called to the back.

"Yeah, boss," he replied.

"You want to take a stab at navigation?" I asked. "You're the hometown boy here."

"Sure," Sean answered, getting up from his seat. "Heinz, it's your turn to shoot our guest if he gets out of line."

"I'd be chuffed to oblige," the mercenary said with a smile.

"You know you can't kill me," Westsmith spoke up. His head was still bowed and beads of perspiration had broken out on his upper lip and forehead. "I'm sure the real boss wouldn't take too kindly to that."

"Can't say I'd be gutted if my knife happened to stab you in the thigh, mate."

"And risk damaging the merchandise?"

"A nice twist of the blade will hurt like bloody hell," Heinz advised. "But I'll make sure not to nick any major arteries. Don't you worry."

"Enough," I ordered. "Sean, get up here and take a crack at it."

Alvarez stood up quickly.

She's going to slug you. Look out!

She got up close to me, her eyes glaring into mine. Her arm came up. She pressed her recon tablet into my chest, letting the device slide down my chest and into my hands. She spun about and plopped herself down with her arms folded.

"Let's go, National Guard," Melissa said impatiently.

Sean walked up the aisle and took the device I held out for him. He spun it around to have the top of the map heading north. After a minute of studying the aerials and the color codes, he looked up.

"Melissa," Sean said.

"Yes," she replied in one drawn out word.

"Turn us around back to Douglaston," Sean advised. "I'll guide you through the side streets so we come out past the jam. We're going to have to head east after all that so we can get to the on-ramp. We're still looking to get on the LIE, right?"

"As long as that's where the traffic and FRACs are lightest," I confirmed.

"Looks like it," Sean said after another study of the map.

"Alright, ladies," Melissa said. "Sit the fuck down so we can get everyone back where they belong."

3

The Great Beyond
+81 Days – 0935 hours
07:47:59

Sean quickly proved to be a better navigator than Alvarez. His knowledge of the area was more of a benefit than just the aerial video and computer-generated color-coding maps. Alvarez stared out the window, running her finger along the rubber gasket holding in the glass. Her face reflected back at her while the houses and trees on the street whizzed by.

She's sulking.

Yes, she is.

"It's a strange interchange, Melissa," Sean said. "Keep to the left or we'll end up on the Cross Island. That's a sea of bumpers like it always was. I'm sure the Whitestone and the Throgs Neck were everyone's first routes to getting off Long Island when the shit went down."

"I'm sure all those words you're spitting out mean something to someone," Melissa said, swinging the shuttle left to the Long Island Expressway, "but I don't really don't care."

"You never came through New York to get anywhere?" Sean asked.

"That's what airplanes are for." Melissa shook her head. "Otherwise, I stayed close to home for Victoria, Summer and Daddy."

"And now you're out seeing the world," Sean remarked as a bad joke, going back to studying the tablet as he remembered Melissa only had Summer left in her life. Melissa didn't say more, focusing her attentions on the road and the left lane ramp Sean had mentioned.

Heinz stared at Westsmith from across the aisle. Jude looked out the front windshield, her chin resting on her forearms on the seat back in front of her.

"Why's the LIE so clear of FRACs?" Sean asked.

Alvarez continued to study the rubber around the window.

"Corporal," I said.

Alvarez stopped tracing the frame with her finger, leaving her finger extended for me to see. "I haven't been a corporal since the Middle East, John."

"None of us are what we used to be," Westsmith chimed in from the rear of the bus.

"Shut it, mate," Heinz ordered.

"Can you truly make me?" Westsmith asked him.

"This says that I can," Heinz replied, holding up his sidearm.

"Not really," Westsmith countered. "Like I said, you need me alive. I'm sure your masters advised I be kept in suitable condition for proper presentation."

Heinz clenched his jaws.

Alvarez was still in a semi-removed state from the conversation.

She's checking out, John.

Don't count her out yet. She's still a Marine.

Fine. I will go with the always classic 'I told you so' at the appropriate juncture.

I have no doubt.

"Westsmith," I said. "My specific orders were to bring you, but nobody said what condition you were to be in when I get you there."

Other than alive.

"Other than alive," I added.

He stared at me with his too-wide plastered grin. I didn't take my eyes off of him. The longer we played the staring game the slimmer his smile became. My skin tingled and the hairs stood up on the back of my neck. It wasn't the constant grating of the rhythmic cicada warble I usually felt when FRACs were close by, but there was a palpable charge in the air within the confines of our little mobile metal tube.

I felt, more than saw, Alvarez perking up. Were the others staring at us? It was difficult to say since I couldn't see any of them in my peripheral vision. The red had crept into the corners of my vision. My heart rate increased.

Thu-thump.

I heard Alvarez's heart rate increase, matching mine.

Thu-thump, our hearts pumped in unison.

I couldn't sense anything from Westsmith. His form was a black silhouette with a fuzzy black aura. There were no sounds coming from him. I couldn't hear a heartbeat beyond Alvarez's and mine. My senses were hyper-aware, but I could only see and hear certain things.

Thu-thump.

The walls of the bus started to waver, the surface of the windows starting to weep with melting glass. The benches behind Westsmith hardened, withering as the vinyl and foam started to crumble.

Thu-thump.

The rear of the bus had disappeared entirely, a gaping dark hole filled with buzzing and swarming smoky tendrils. The darkness sensed us somehow... hungry for us... yearning for us.

It knows we are here, John.

" –damnit, John!" I heard someone in the distance.

The darkness recoiled at the voice. It pulsed tentatively toward me, but quickly gave up in favor of retreat. It faded and became

24

transparent, the structure of the rear emergency exit returning to normal. The red in my vision receded, as well. The sidewalls, benches and glass became solid again, as if nothing had happened.

"John!" Melissa shouted again.

All eyes were on me.

"Yeah," I answered.

"You gonna give me directions," Melissa asked. "Or are you gonna keep fawning over our package?"

"Sean," I ordered, glancing at a pale—maybe frightened—Alvarez from the corner of my eye, "give Melissa directions."

4

Roadwork

+81 Days – 0942 hours
07:40:37

While Melissa and Sean occupied themselves with figuring out the best options for getting into the city, Alvarez stared at me with a furrow on her brow and a questioning look in her eyes. None of the others seemed any wiser to what I had just experienced with Alvarez and Westsmith. Heinz continued to hold his sidearm on our prisoner. Jude stared out the front of the shuttle.

Westsmith's grin reappeared, wider than before. It threatened to crack his face in half, his eyes glinting with what seemed like a secret knowledge the rest of us could only guess at. Alvarez shifted her gaze from me to Westsmith and back again. I hadn't dreamt it. Something had just happened between the three of us.

Of course, she knows something. She is in Dick's back pocket, is she not?

"John," Sean said.

"Yeah?"

"We're coming up on the Clearview Expressway exits," he advised.

"What does that mean?"

"We need to make a decision on the bridge or tunnel. Figured this interchange was a good time to bring it up."

"Bridge," Melissa said simply and definitively.

"Not much safety in either option," Jude added, her voice monotone and her face a blank slate. "There's no place to run to in

26

either case."

"At least we can see what's coming on the bridge," Melissa advised.

"True," Jude agreed. She opened her mouth to say more, but was cut off by Heinz.

"Probably not any better than what we will get in the tunnel," he chimed in. "Pretty sure we're not going to go overboard into the East River if we get cornered."

"At least that would be an option you don't get in the tunnel," Melissa said. "It's going to be a fucking pitch-black tomb down there."

"Alvarez," I said.

"What?"

"You still haven't explained why the LIE is so clear," I reminded her. "Is the tunnel clear?"

Alvarez took one more look at Westsmith before finally holding her hand out for the tablet. Sean handed it over without a word. She came into the aisle next to me, using her finger and thumb to zoom in on the area of Queens next to the water.

"See this?" She pointed to a series of long rectangles on the expressway a quarter mile east of the edge of the water where the road disappeared into the water. "Those are the storage containers R&R put across all lanes in both directions on both sides of the river."

"Good thinking," I admitted, "but it doesn't explain why there are no cars on the road."

As if to countermand my words, Melissa swerved around a garbage truck crashed at a thirty-degree angle into the center concrete divider. All of its oversized tires were flat. A series of quarter-sized holes pierced the cab doors and the rear tank, made more prominent with the rising sun beaming through them.

"Christ," Melissa said with a long exhale. "Maybe just a few cars. And it's a city truck so it may not even count, right?"

"You're such a smart ass," Sean told Melissa. "Were you always this way?"

"Yep. Can't you tell?"

"Definitely," Sean confirmed. "Just getting some verification."

"That truck," Alvarez finally said, "explains why there aren't more cars on the LIE. R&R controlled the National Guard before they became ineffective. They sent them in to cordon off everything on the Long Island Expressway between the city and the Cross Island Parkway. The sanitation truck was what happened when someone tried to run the blockage."

"Shit," Jude whispered.

"That's why the Cross Island was a parking lot," Sean said. "Everyone tried to get to the outer bridges."

"Not sure I'd go through Manhattan to get out of New York," Jude said. "Not even on a good day."

"Long Island has always been a prison during emergencies," Sean said. "Every disaster effectively cuts off the island from the rest of the country. When the island lost power a few years back, the grocery stores ran out of food, refrigerators warmed up, food went bad, the gas stations couldn't pump because they didn't have generators to get the fuel out of the tanks. The stations with power to run the pumps ran out within a few hours, with lines a mile long. I remember people chasing fuel trucks trying to find where they were going next to refuel. Tempers flaring, guns waving… and that was only after a couple days. You cut off the bridges and tunnels, you cut off the island's lifeline."

"That's a pity," Westsmith said, clapping his hands together in a theatrical manner. "Oh, the woes you must have endured at the hands of your fellow man." Every utterance from Westsmith had a way of getting under a person's skin.

Always trying to stir up trouble, that one is. Always butting in to things he does not need to... just to be an annoyance.

Bob sat in the back of the shuttle. He leaned against the perfectly normal and solid rear window, looking out of place with his pressed suit and starched dress shirt. He was pristine compared to the rest of us decked out in our bloody and dirty tactical gear.

Sounds like someone else I know, Bob.

I wonder whom. Someone I know?

Yeah. You know him very well.

You have to give me a clue, John.

It's amazing how obtuse you are, sometimes.

But I am helpful, sometimes, as well.

If you want to be helpful, get me intel on the best way to get to the city.

Roger, that!

And with those words and a salute worthy of Benny Hill, Bob disappeared into whatever primordial unknown he had sprung from.

"What do you know about it?" Sean took Westsmith's bait. The kid was still too green when it came to the mechanisms of manipulation.

"Me?" Westsmith put his right hand over his heart. "What would I know?"

"You seem to have cornered the market on diarrhea of the mouth," Heinz said from across the aisle. He had his sidearm resting against his chest while his eyes were still settled intently on his charge.

"I suffer from many afflictions, my dear mercenary," Westsmith admitted. "I will certainly take that one under consideration when I next see my doctors."

"You may have more ailments to add to the list by then, mate," Heinz said.

"I will keep your threats in mind, sir," Westsmith said with a nod. "Consider me warned."

"You still haven't answered my question," Sean demanded, biting down on Westsmith's last goad like a dog with a rawhide. Westsmith sighed and ignored him, looking out the window at the concrete retaining walls of the expressway, instead. Sean sprang up, coming into the aisle behind me. I shot out my left arm out to block him from getting closer to Westsmith. He was still insistent about lunging at our prisoner. I turned around and wrapped him up.

"Enough," I whispered into his ear. 'He's just trying to get a rise out of you."

"Well," Sean said. "It's working." He looked at me, knowing I wasn't going to let him do something foolish. He returned to his seat. Thankfully.

"If you must know," Westsmith finally spoke up, "during that same East Coast blackout, I was right where you found me... a resident of the fine Creedmoor establishment." Sean shifted his stare to Westsmith. Jude and Alvarez did, too. Even Melissa looked up into the oversized rear mirror. Heinz had never taken his eyes off of him, so he was ahead of the game. Westsmith commanded the shuttle with an intangible magnetic attraction. "I was there when the lights went out. Sure, we had the generators running to keep the bare minimum requirements of lights on, not like how they lit the place up this time. Back then, things were in complete disarray. The nurses, orderlies, and staff were distracted with their own lives, making us a secondary priority. Maybe, even lower.

"It was a rare opportunity for some of the more violent residents to rise up and wrestle control from the otherwise pre-occupied staff. We had four rapes and two deaths in a matter of a few hours. I think a few of the lower risk residents even made their way out to the grounds before they were tazed into submission. Unfortunately, one of the ones making it to the expressway found out how hard it was to play chicken with the front bumper of a semi-truck. The young woman didn't really stand a chance, as you may have guessed."

Sean muttered and swallowed hard. "Bastard."

He lunged over the tops of the benches.

"Christ," Jude yelled out.

I reached out to grab him but only managed in getting a slipping fingertip on the back of his tactical vest. Melissa swerved the bus around an overturned highway patrol sedan, having been distracted by the commotion. Sean pitched toward the windows. Diving into the benches, I was able to finally wrap my fingers through Sean's tactical vest pull handle just as he wrapped his fingers around Westsmith's throat. I pulled Sean away and hurled him with force into a row away from Westsmith.

"Stay," I ordered.

Even though Westsmith's face had gone a flush red color and the sides of his neck sported a fading hand-shaped milky white pattern, he smiled. The attack hadn't fazed him. But it had unnerved me. I couldn't rely on the rationale of a man who didn't have a healthy respect for the permanence of death or the ethereal unknown of whatever comes next. Westsmith just smiled in the face of it without any concern.

Maybe because he is crazy, John. Did you ever think of that?

The thought had crossed my mind, but I couldn't imagine he was insane or unstable. It seemed more plausible he was more a

31

master manipulator then unhinged.

Don't forget he controls the dead.

Yeah. That's a problem, too.

Probably why Dick wants him so badly. He seems to want to recruit all of the test subjects he had experimented with. He had Ms. Alvarez, he chased you down, and now the two of you are charged with bringing in this mysterious 'third man'.

The question was why would Dick put two of his coveted experimental operators back into harm's way in order to bring in Westsmith. R&R had used a small army of mercenaries, firepower and transport to bring me in.

Alvarez was there, though. She was the one who brought you down. Bob added emphasis on the word 'was'. The point was not lost on me. In any event, the whole thing was all too cloak and dagger to me. I liked it better when I knew all the mission parameters. Spy games were better suited for spies, not soldiers.

You might have to learn a new trade, my friend. The benefits of brute force do not seem to get the job done, anymore.

You're right.

Bob whispered in my ear, his aura buzzing close to my bare neck. *Of course, I am. That's a perk of being your better half.*

Don't push it, Bob. You are still a massive thorn in my side. And you don't seem to have any new intel for me.

Speaking of which, you seem to be leaking, again.

I put my hand to my thigh and pulled away a palm of fresh blood. The blood was trickling out from under the compression cincher.

Wonderful.

We drove over a speed bump, making the bus shudder.

"Sorry," Melissa said from the captain's chair, swallowing hard.

"Didn't have a choice on this one."

Sean had gone into a catatonic state, curled up in the bench I had pushed him into. Heinz still had the smiling Westsmith covered as he braced himself for the bumps. Sitting over the rear wheelwell was never a good move unless you were a ten-year-old looking for a free thrill before or after school.

"Megan," Sean mumbled to himself.

I went to the front, realizing there shouldn't be speed bumps on an expressway.

Jude's eyes followed my movements, her fingers gripping the bench as we continued to bounce over debris in the road. She nodded, but didn't say anything.

"Christ," Melissa said. "Sorry."

After bouncing side to side against the edges of the benches and one painful jab into my open wound, I made it to the yellow line. I looked out the windshield. My stomach churned as I realized debris and speed bumps weren't our problem. As we moved forward, the right front tire raised up six inches before it crushed the skull of one of dozens of dead bodies strewn across the road. They were dead, but they weren't the undead. High caliber weapons fire had pocked the pavement and had ripped apart people who had been trying to get off Long Island via the LIE. Some of them still wore their backpacks while others clutched the handles of their rolling luggage in a death grip.

It had been a shooting gallery killing field, most likely from the Chinook we had used as transport to get out to Creedmoor. Its crash on the institution's grounds became more palpable and poetic in its irony.

As Melissa rumbled ahead with white knuckles on the steering wheel—a grim look on her face, and a single tear rolling down her cheek—I was reminded Melissa was just as human as the rest of us.

Well, you are not necessarily just human anymore. Neither is Ms. Alvarez. And Mr. Westsmith is certainly off the radar completely.

At least, Melissa is as human as the rest of the non-enhanced people on our team. Is that a better categorization?

Perfect.

Another lurch, to the left this time.

Roanoke and Raleigh had indeed wanted to keep the road clear of vehicle and pedestrian traffic. In this venture, however, they had only partially succeeded.

5

Tendrils

+81 Days – 1001 hours
07:21:15

The road eventually cleared of bodies, but not before I choked back the bile in my throat with hard swallows. Jude's skin had taken on a waxy pallor, her hand back to rubbing her neck. Melissa gripped the steering wheel with white knuckles. Sean hugged himself on the bench I had shoved him onto earlier. Alvarez stared through the front windshield, jaw clenched and her palms pressed against the seat back of the bench in front of her. Heinz was also staring, but his line of vision was still tracked on Westsmith and his plastered-on smile.

Westsmith's smile had faded. His facial muscles must be exhausted trying to keep his sinister Joker grin going for so long. His eyes still shone with a twinkle—a glint of the light from the interior lights, maybe—seeming to serve as a warning he knew something we didn't. It was a look saying something would keep us from getting him back to Dick at R&R. Westsmith gave me a nod, as if he concurred with the thoughts in my head as they concerned him. It wasn't possible, though.

Isn't it? Bob, the Gaunt Man asked from his seat at the back of the bus. *He did command his own little army of FRACs back at the Creedmoor campus. Why are you not more concerned?*

Why, indeed.

Creases appeared on Westsmith brow, his grin finally disappearing altogether. He looked confused, his eyes darting around for a noise he couldn't pinpoint.

Or a sound he can't hear.

What do you mean?

Have you given any thought you three may be connected somehow?

No, I hadn't given it any thought.

You hear Ms. Alvarez's heartbeat, do you not?

But I can hear other people's heartbeats, too.

True.. What about your sense of the dead?

When they are close? What about it?

Why did it not work when you were fighting them off in Building 25? Where was your FRAC radar when you were ripping their heads off their bodies?

I don't know.

The robes and gloves they wore definitely should not have been enough to cloak the fact of what they were.

I know. I get it.

I do not think you do. All of you have taken what you have seen too much in stride. It may be the end of your world, but this is a bit beyond normal comprehension.

Bob was right. Why hadn't my neck buzzed when we were cornering Westsmith? I looked from the nodding Bob to Westsmith. He had sacrificed his waning smile in favor of the look of someone working hard to drop a difficult deuce into a toilet.

Let us hope it doesn't come to that. This bus is an enclosed space.

I leaned against the bench, careful not to irritate my itching and seeping wound. Westsmith continued to adamantly concentrate on something, beads of sweat rising on his upper lip. He wasn't praying, although his lips were moving and his throat was producing an unintelligible murmur.

He is certainly up to no good.

How can you tell?

How can you not? Are you paying attention?

Maybe I wasn't. I narrowed my vision to slits, fuzzing my view of everything except for Westsmith in the center of my vision. The edges didn't seep with red. Instead, they went a dark charcoal gray. The rest of the passengers in the bus faded away. Westsmith's murmurs became more pronounced, but still unintelligible. His clothing wavered and flapped in an unfelt breeze. There was a heartbeat inside his ribcage, but it didn't have a consistent rhythm. Wait. I was wrong. The movement of his clothing wasn't from some phantom breeze. The tiniest of tendrils rose from him, surrounding him in a near transparent aura. They were wispy as smoke, but different. They seemed alive, like a symbiotic extension of him. As I concentrated on them, they grew more pronounced and substantial. Like a school of fish, the tendrils moved in swirling unison. They reached out toward me, reacting to my examination.

Westsmith looked up at me. His eyes glowed with an amber hue for a moment in this dark, pulsing in-between place where only he and I existed. As his eyes locked onto mine, the glow from his eyes disappeared. The tendrils disappeared back into his body. Or maybe they just dissipated into the heavy pulsing air. Bob nodded his approval of my feat, choosing also to fade into the ether along with the rest of the strange supernatural plasma.

The gray haze lifted, the growl of the shuttle's engine and the vibration of the tires on the expressway concrete returning to my senses. The others were still around me, exhausted and dirty. They hadn't realized anything odd had happened between Westsmith and me. But Westsmith knew.

And I do not think he very much cared for the intrusion.

6

I Can't Drive 55

+81 Days – 1010 hours
07:12:42

"Meg," Sean continued to whisper to himself in the next row. I leaned over and put my hand on his shoulder. He didn't recoil or react at all. I squeezed my fingers into him. A slight grimace came across his previously slack clammy face. I squeezed harder. His eyes snapped open as his face contorted with the pain finally fully registering in his brain. "Argh. Oww. That hurts, John."

"Good," I replied. "Means you're still feeling something."

"I felt that, alright," he said, rubbing his shoulder.

"You gonna get yourself squared away?" I asked. "I need you in one piece. We need to get back to April and Summer. Understood?"

"And Holly," Sean reminded me.

"Yeah," I agreed. "And her."

Alvarez came up to us, handing over her tablet to Sean. He took it and held it with both hands. "I'm going to relieve Heinz."

"Okay," I said. "Smart thinking."

She squeezed by me and left Sean staring at the tablet. He took a deep breath as he rubbed the corners of the device with his thumbs.

"Not sure if I'm going to be of any use to you, John," Sean said suddenly.

I had worried the same thing, but wouldn't let him know I had thought so. "Why?"

"That asshole got into my head," Sean admitted. "He shouldn't have known."

"Westsmith?" I asked.

Sean nodded. "He shouldn't have known."

"About Meg?" Jude slide across the aisle to the bench in front of Sean.

Sean didn't say anything right away, content to only shake his head and grip the tablet tightly. He looked up at Jude and her coaxing and kind eyes. He finally said, "Meg was my sister. He shouldn't have known about my sister."

Westsmith was engaged in a staring contest with Alvarez, while Heinz had retired to the back of the bus for a moment of rack time. None of them were interested in our private conversation.

"Maybe he got access to the admin files," Jude offered.

"Maybe," Sean replied, "but that is a very specific piece of info to know out of hundreds of patient files. And to know how it relates to me. I mean, she wasn't even entered under the family name. And, what are the odds he would ever meet me?"

"Maybe he didn't know," I said. "Could it be he just got lucky with his story striking so close to home? Her story seems fairly well-known to the people inside Creedmoor."

"He seemed pretty sure of how it would affect me," Sean said with a shake of the head.

"I agree," Jude said. "Westsmith was definitely baiting him."

I hated to agree, but I had to. Westsmith's grin had been too wide and his eyes too focused on Sean to believe otherwise. So, the question was, 'how did he know?' How would he be able to surmise Sean and Meg were siblings? Was it as simple as wading through stacks of in-patient admin files and venturing a guess with the hopes of goading Sean into attacking him? How would he know there was any connection between what had happened to a patient named Meg and one of the men R&R assigned to retrieve him?

"John," Melissa called out. "Can I have Sean back now, please? If we're heading to the bridge, all the signs on this road ain't reflecting it."

"You up for it?" I asked Sean. He nodded, gripping the tablet like a security blanket and headed to the yellow line at the front of the aisle to assist Melissa.

"We are going to the bridge, right?" Melissa said, pushing all the emphasis on the 'are'. "Because I'm not going to drive if you all decide to get to Manhattan under the river."

Sean hugged the pole behind Melissa's seat while he looked at the tablet for more information. "Usually I would get off at the cemeteries."

"You shitting me?" Melissa said.

"No," Sean replied. There are lots of big cemeteries in Queens along the LIE. Calvary, St. Marys, Cedar Grove." He looked out ahead as we crested a highpoint in the road. The sun was big and bright in the sky, casting its rays down on several tall structures to the right of the expressway. "See? That's the Unisphere and Flushing Meadow Park."

"What?" Melissa asked. "That big globe?"

"Weren't those two towers in that Will Smith movie?" Jude asked, having joined Melissa and Sean below the yellow line.

"Leftovers from the '64 World's Fair," Sean said. "And, yes they were in the movie."

"We're all leftovers now," Melissa muttered.

"Ain't that the truth," Jude said.

As we drove closer to the park, the Unisphere seemed so close and shiny had backed down to a smaller, less inspired version of itself.

"I love when it does that," Sean admitted.

"What?" Alvarez asked, coming up the aisle behind me.

"The size of the Uni–," I started. Alvarez plunged her tactical knife high into my back. I screamed as I lurched forward past the yellow line, drawing my Glock. "Aaaah!"

She stabbed you in the back? Again?

"What the hell?" Melissa exclaimed. She swerved the steering wheel, distracted from the road by the tactical knife sticking out of my shoulder. I slid into the metal pole, banging my wrist against it and losing my grip on my sidearm. The blade was into my shoulder up to the hilt. Melissa stared at the knife. "Shit... shit... shit..."

Jude and Sean fell onto the bench behind the driver's seat. I felt Alvarez standing above me. She reached for the knife. Muscles tore as I twisted away, my breath a wheeze as my left lung deflated.

"Fuck!" Melissa overcorrected the skidding shuttle.

We hit something solid. A guardrail? A car?

The shuttle tipped onto two wheels.

"Weee," came from a cackling Westsmith in the back.

The shuttle slammed onto its right side. The tempered glass of the windows cracked against the pavement. I landed in the door well. My side was bleeding profusely. Blood drenched my back. I couldn't catch a breath.

Alvarez fought her way out of the tangle of an unconscious Jude and Sean.

I got up to my right elbow. The Glock was wedged in the leg supports of the bench behind the driver's seat. More muscle ripped in spite of me nursing my left side.

Alvarez grabbed the handle of the knife and pulled it out.

I hissed in pain.

Alvarez raised the knife.

"Don't," Melissa said, still strapped into her seatbelt.

Her words were followed by a familiar clicking sound of a Benelli shotgun.

7

Hey, Hey,... Hey... Goodbye

+81 Days – 1011 hours

07:11:44

Everything hurt. My back stung. My side wept with its own heartbeat. Blood trickled out of me onto the bi-fold doors from both wounds.

Alvarez stood above me in the overturned shuttle. Her feet were braced on the side of the post supposed to support the roof. Melissa hung from her driver's seat, tight against the seatbelt. The barrel of her Benelli pointed at Melissa's back.

"What fun!" Westsmith exclaimed from the back.

"Shut your hole, mate," Heinz said with a growl.

At least he was okay. I couldn't see Jude or Sean. They were still tangled up somewhere between the benches.

"I said get away from him," Melissa warned Alvarez.

The corporal's only reaction was to glance over her shoulder, and raise her arms slightly with her palms out and fingers splayed.

"Such a good show." Westsmith clapped.

"You need to shut it," Melissa ordered him, the barrel of the Benelli wavering toward him. Alvarez grabbed the barrel and ripped it out of Melissa's hands. She spun it around and clocked Melissa in the forehead with the butt of the tailstock. Melissa's arms went limp and her head drooped down against her right shoulder. Alvarez spun the shotgun around at me, her cold eyes glaring at me from behind the barrel.

"Don't shoot him," Westsmith said good-naturedly. "Let's take him outside."

Holding the shotgun in one hand, Alvarez grabbed me in an iron grip to the throat with the other. Both of my hands went up to her wrists trying to break her hold. She lifted me easily out of the doorwell and dragged me toward the back of the shuttle in the space above the seats. Jude and Sean were wedged between the first and second bench—both unconscious, but still breathing and without bleeding or any limbs in odd directions.

"What're you doing, Boss?" Heinz asked, propped up against the bench in the back row with his tactical knife in hand. He had lost his gun in the rollover. Alvarez raised the shotgun and pointed it at him

"Get out of the way," Westsmith ordered as he stepped in behind Alvarez. "We have business to attend to."

"Can't let you through, mate," Heinz said, his eyes darting to the emergency exit hatch.

Alvarez said nothing, speaking volumes by holding the Benelli unwavering at Heinz's chest. Her viselike grip against my throat hadn't relaxed at all. Even my strength seems futile against hers.

"Ah," Westsmith said. "The proverbial 'knife to a gunfight' scenario. And here I thought that was only for the cinema."

"Get your head on correct, Boss," Heinz said, trying to reason with his commander. "We all have stakes in seeing this mission complete. We need to crack on."

If Alvarez was registering his words, it certainly wasn't being relayed to her slack face or the tightness of her grip. My efforts to twist her grip away only served to make me more lightheaded as both my windpipe and carotid artery were being compromised.

"Last chance, mate," Westsmith said, mocking Heinz with his use of 'mate'. "You don't want to stand in my way."

Alvarez extended her arm even further, closing the distance between the business end of the shotgun and Heinz's chest by a few inches.

"Stand aside," Westsmith ordered Heinz again. Even though he seemed to have the upper hand, he wiped the sweat from his brow and lip with his sleeve, looking a bit worse for wear. Car crashes tended to do that to a person.

Heinz squared his jaw and shoulders, hefting the knife. "No."

"Very well," Westsmith said. His shoulders slumped down while a tired smile tilted up. "Ms. Alvarez... if you please."

The inside of the shuttle erupted in a blast of booming sound. Heinz slammed against the rear emergency door, blood bursting from the edges of his chest and back. His tactical vest protected his vital organs, but not enough at close range against the raw power of the Benelli. To his credit, the knife stayed in Heinz's grip as he fell into the last bench.

"No," I croaked.

"That answers that," Westsmith confirmed, ignoring me. "Knife, 0. Gun, 1." Westsmith turned the lever for the emergency exit. The heavy door banged open as gravity did its job. He climbed out, but not before he pried the knife from Heinz's slackening fingers. Alvarez, unfazed by the shooting of her last teammate, dragged me through the exit hatch to whatever fate they had in mind for me.

8

Thunderdome

+81 Days – 1013 hours
07:09:29

The sun continued its climb up from the east—always serving as the harbinger of a new day—as Alvarez tossed me to the pavement at Westsmith's feet. Debris from the burnt-out shells of several wrecked vehicles littered the road—what Melissa had crashed into. Some of the passenger cars had collided into each other, but the telltale signs of weapons fire were evident through their windows and sides. One had even been opened up into a jagged steel blossom from the explosion of an RPG.

"My dear Mr. Walken," Westsmith said, squatting down to my level. "You certainly are trouble, aren't you? Trying to understand what goes on in my mind." He leaned in close and put a knee on the side of my face, tapping me on the temple with the point of Heinz's knife. With a thoughtful, almost empathetic look, he traced the edge of the blade along my cheek down to my chin. The blade drew blood, dripping hot fluid down my face. Westsmith pulled it away, waving it in front of me like he was about to cast a spell over me with a blood-tipped wand.

The knifepoint drew closer, again.

"What're your thoughts about having me administer a lobotomy right here on the expressway?" Westsmith asked, his smile in full bloom again, the knife centimeters from my eye. "That would be interesting, right?"

"Doesn't really work for me right now," I replied between

painful wheezes. "I'll have to take a pass. Plus, my insurance is for shit."

"That's the country we live in now," Westsmith said. "a sad truth."

"And," I said with effort, "it doesn't seem fair I go out like that. I figured you would want to put me down in a grander fashion. This seems a bit anti-climactic."

With the knife almost touching my right eye, Westsmith's own eyes went elsewhere in thought. His tongue poked against the inside of his cheek before he made clicking noises with it against the roof of his mouth. "Right you are," Westsmith announced. "A true battle of wills is what you demand? Then you shall have it."

He stood up, the weight of his body no longer pressed against my skull. He backed away with his hands out and his palms up. I lifted myself to my hands and knees, having difficulty breathing and hearing a worrisome rasp from my left lungs.

Blood stained the concrete under me.

My Glock was in the shuttle with the others.

The knife was in Westsmith's hand.

We all saw what happened to the last person who held a knife on Westsmith and his lovely puppet.

"You prefer to share the same fate as Heinz?" Westsmith asked, amused at the pensive look on my face.

"I don't... have a choice," I replied between ragged breaths.

"Marines," Westsmith said. "A strange breed."

I raised my closed fists.

"That's the spirit!" Westsmith exclaimed.

Are you up for this, John?

I've survived worse, right?

Maybe. The gauntlet you ran at the museum had you starting out in much better health, though.

Alvarez held the shotgun even with my chest. I didn't know what the fuck was going on with Alvarez, but we didn't have time for this.

I told you. She is a puppet. Like the guards in Building 25.

I rose to my feet, my fists still clenched.

"Good man," Westsmith said, beaming a very pleased smile. He held a hand out to Alvarez. "The gun, please."

Alvarez slowly handed over the Benelli to him. As soon as the gunstock left her hands, she lunged at me. She made no sound. There were no screams or war cries—just lightning fast reflexes.

Alvarez led with a straight kick. I got my forearms up in time to take the brunt, still getting pushed back a few steps. She swung a left hand, catching the side of my neck.

She had never led with her left when we sparred.

I swung an elbow as the arc of her punch brought her face closer to my reach. She blocked with her right arm, slipping her hand behind my head. Grabbing my hair, she pulled my head down as she slammed her knee into my face. I took the hit, lacing my hands behind the leg she was balanced on. I lifted her off the ground and drove her into the concrete.

She didn't lose her breath. Was she even breathing?

She is. She is still alive.

I punched her across the jaw. Alvarez absorbed the punch, staring at me with cold eyes. I swung again. She caught my fist and squeezed.

Argh!

Her fingers were like a vise. She twisted her hand, turning me along with it. Catching me off-balance, she wrapped her legs around my waist, arched her back and squeezed. More of the expanders in

49

my slowly knitting stomach wound failed, new wet warmth escaping down my hip. Luckily, the body restrictor was still holding together as a last line of defense for keeping my insides on my inside where they belonged.

I punched her wrist repeatedly, trying to break her grip on my other hand. She batted at my swinging fist with her free hand, but I was able to land enough blows to crack her ulna. Her grip didn't lessen in spite of the fractured bone. She pulled my arm down toward her shoulder, scissoring her leg over it and around the back of my neck. Alvarez locked the back of her other knee around the ankle of the one around my neck. She had me in a constricting choke hold.

Shit!

The day darkened. Wavering tendrils, like maggots or squirming worms, burrowed out from her temples. The capillaries in her eyes pulsed.

Thu-thump.

Her pupils dilated so wide I could no longer the color of her irises. The red mist tried to envelope my vision from the edges, but was no match for the gray wispy curtain taking up residence.

"Too easy," Westsmith's voice echoed from somewhere in the murky darkness.

The darkness did sound inviting.

Don't you give up, John.

Just a moment without pain…

You were designed to take pain.

Why do I have to carry everyone's weight?

Because you were built that way.

I'm tired. I have been since coming home.

You pick yourself up, soldier!

I'm not a soldier. I'm a Marine.

Then act like it!

With a deep wheezing breath, I got my legs under me.

I grabbed Alvarez with my hands wherever I could get purchase. With a scream, I lifted her off the ground. She was still locked into the triangle chokehold, her legs squeezing with increased pressure. I drove her into the ground. She didn't budge. I lifted her up again. And drove her into the ground. Again. The pressure around my neck increased.

Fuck!

With my last bit of failing strength, I lifted her up one more time. Carrying her toward the steel edge of the fighting pit the semi-circle of wrecked cars had made for us, I made one final plea.

"Rosalita," I whispered. "You're better than this."

All I got in return was a crushing pressure from her legs. And, her blank dark stare. The wispy charcoal worms wriggling from her temples had grown in size and number. I slammed her on the hood of the RPG-wrecked sedan. She was still locked on.

My muscles quivered as I slammed her down again. Nothing. I lifted her up one more time, knowing this was all I had left before I passed out. I slammed her onto the ruined frame of the windshield. The peeled-back steel impaled her through the center of her back. Her tactical vest kept the jagged metal point from coming through the front of her.

Her legs loosened and her breathing returned. She let out a rush of ragged, watery air. I finally twisted out of her grip, leaving her hanging on one of the vehicular spikes the RPG had produced.

Carnage breeds more carnage.

"You are certainly more resourceful than I gave you credit for." Westsmith said, hefting the Benelli. "But I can't let you walk away from what you've done."

Rosalita stared at me, luckily—through whatever hold Westsmith had on her mind—not seeming to feel the metal impaled through her lungs and torn through her heart. I had sentenced her to death in order to save myself.

And to save the others.

Not sure any heroic thought was going through my mind when I impaled her.

Westsmith stepped forward with the Benelli pointed at my chest. My hands went up in surrender, almost involuntarily.

Not surrender, survival.

Westsmith loved his grin, as it was plastered on his face again. He loomed between the shuttle and me. If he fired, I would take the brunt of the shot. Hopefully, I could keep Rosalita from taking any more damage—even if she was already dying.

No gun.

No knife.

Not a single luxury.

"Goodbye, Mr. Walken," Westsmith said with what seemed like genuine sincerity. "You've been an interesting man to get to know."

A gun blast erupting in the warming day was followed by a painful scream. The scream wasn't from me. The Benelli barrel wavered and dropped toward the ground as it fired its own round into the pavement. Westsmith clutched his thigh and fell to the road.

Heinz hung partially out of the shuttle's rear exit. He had found his sidearm, although it was too heavy for his failing strength to keep holding it up. He dropped his arm, clanking his weapon against the side of the vehicle.

I retrieved the shotgun and held it on Westsmith. He put his own hands up in surrender, his left palm covered in his own blood.

"Definitely more interesting," he said through gritted teeth.

Rosalita screamed. Westsmith was down, so I rushed to her side. Her breathing was hard and panicked. She made strange whimpering noises as she looked at the bulge in her chest armor.

"John," she cried. "We crashed?"

"Yeah," I lied, sweeping a stray lock of hair out of her eyes and off of her forehead. "Yeah."

"It hurts," she breathed. "Hurts to breathe."

I put a finger to the side of her neck. Her pulse was thready and uneven. I couldn't even hear her heartbeat in my head. The pounding of my own blood was way too loud. Her face clenched up. I wasn't sure if she could come back from this like I had from the Chinook crash. In the back of my head, I might have thought she could recover from almost anything... as long as I could incapacitate her enough to break Westsmith's hold over her.

"Christ," she said through hisses of pain. "I'm not going to make it, John." She grabbed at her vest pocket, but her fingers failed her in opening the flap. She was finally going to give him the off-switch for the explosive capsule in Jude's neck.

The last gesture of a Marine.

I opened the flap and reached into the pocket for her. Rosalita held my wrist gently. I frowned, pulling out some sort of leather wallet and a thick plastic card.

"Show me," she whispered. "Open it."

I did as I was asked. Inside the flap was a picture of a dark-haired boy of four or five years of age. Rosalita burst into tears as she reached a finger out to the photograph. She smiled at the boy in spite of the pain she was experiencing.

"Sorry, baby," she said. "Mommy tried."

Mommy?

She dropped her hand to her chest.

Thu-thump.

Her heartbeat was light and fluttery. Rosalita looked at me with those sharp eyes I had once fallen in love with. "Sorry."

"For what?" I asked.

"For getting you into this."

"Nothing to be sorry about, Rose," I said. She smiled weakly. She had always liked when I called her Rose. It was a special name I only uttered to her in extremely special circumstances. She looked at the laminated photograph, tears welling in her eyes. She had no strength to even lift her arms.

Thu-thump.

"Get to...," she whispered.

I leaned in, still holding the photograph up for her. "What?"

"...get back to city... only they can undo... undone to Jude."

She didn't have the off-switch for the device in Jude's neck?

"... only there..."

I put the wallet back into her jacket's breast pocket and pocketed the plastic card. I would have to deliver Westsmith as promised. For Summer and April... for Holly... in order to fix Jude.

"...by..."

I put my ear to her lips. No more words came out. Only a long light exhale carrying with it the last wisps of her spirit.

Thu-

There was no more. Her heart was empty of life.

I lifted Rosalita off the metal and lowered her gently to the concrete of the Long Island Expressway. I took one last look at the boy who she kept close to her heart throughout everything we had been through lately. Folding her hands over her heart, I placed the photograph between her fingers so she could gaze upon his dark hair, dark eyes, and smiling innocence whenever she chose to. A single photograph serving as a reminder she had been human. A reminder she had been something more than just a killer of men and of the undead.

She was a Marine, but she was also a mother.

Semper Fi.

9

Assessment

+81 Days – 1017 hours
07:05:21

Rosalita was gone. She was really gone. There was no mistaking her death this time.

"A shame about Ms. Alvarez," Westsmith said. He stared up at me from his bloody and oily spot on the concrete. His smile had faded—probably from the pain of the gunshot Heinz had inflicted to his thigh—but there was still a faint upturned line to his lips. "I'm sure you did what you thought best."

My answer was a swing of the Benelli across his jaw. It wasn't meant to render him unconscious, but I hoped it would wipe what remained of the fucking smile off his face and shut him up for a few minutes. The strike dazed him. I grabbed him by the collar of his shirt and dragged him closer to the shuttle. A line of blood trailed off behind him. There was a second set of tracks as the blood from my wounds had found its way to the soles of my boots.

Why are there two tracks? I thought there would be one set of tracks because Jesus carried you there.

I slammed Westsmith against the side of the shuttle before I checked Heinz for a pulse. It was thready, but it was there. The question was whether it was a good thing for Heinz or not.

Don't forget what is best for the group.

Not now.

Heinz's eyes fluttered open and his shooting hand instinctively came up. I grabbed the slide of the sidearm so he couldn't fire it, even if he had the strength. "It's me. Good shooting."

"Anytime, mate," he said, nodding before returning to semi-consciousness.

I took his weapon and put it in the back of my waistband. The skin of Heinz's chest, arms and shoulders was punctured with small round red stipples. Luckily, the vest had taken the worst of the close-quarters blast. He needed to be patched up before any FRACs in the area caught his scent. Westsmith also had a bloody dinner bell seeping from his thigh.

And you.

Yeah. I was still bleeding, but the seepage of blood was slowing.

Another miracle of who you are.

I looked at Rosalita, the photograph clutched between her fingers.

She was a miracle in her own right, only not meant long for this world.

Heinz grunted in pain from the rear fire door, but didn't stir. Melissa still hung from the driver's chair, her arms and body pressed against the seatbelt holding her in. A small hand grabbed at the edge of the first bench seat. Jude pulled herself out from the tangle she had found herself in with Sean.

"You good?" I called out.

Jude's eyes searched the interior before locking in on me at the rear door. She shrugged, but gave me a thumbs-up.

"Sean?" I asked.

Jude looked down behind the bench. "Unconscious, but breathing."

Scraping noises came from my right. Westsmith had managed to crawl halfway to one of the wrecked sedans. I walked over and grabbed him by the collar, just to drag him back to the shuttle's rear axle. "Where you going?"

In spite of the rhetorical nature of the question, he smiled and answered, "Wanted to find a bit of shade."

"I don't think so," I said, pressing my boot into his thigh. He yelled out, all remnants of upturned lips gone. "That's what I thought. Move, and you'll be on the receiving end of way more hurt."

He raised his hands and bowed his head in surrender.

I went back to Heinz and pulled him out of the shuttle. He grunted a bit when I put him down on the pavement. I went back to the door to see Jude dragging Sean under his armpits toward me. Sean's boot heels thudded against the window frames. When Jude got to me, I took over and pulled Sean out.

"There's no way I can manage Melissa," Jude admitted.

"I know," I replied. "Grab the first aid box and see if you can stop some of the bleeding on Heinz's arms and neck.

"Oh," Jude said, realizing Heinz had been shot while she had been unconscious. "Uh. Okay."

I retrieved my tactical knife and put it back in its sheath.

In the meantime, Jude pulled the first-aid kit from the wall—now the floor—came back, and lifted herself out of the shuttle. After she knelt down next to Heinz, I took her place inside the bus and made my way to Melissa.

My Glock was on the floor. I retrieved it, wondering how many more times I was going have it taken from me before it was lost to me for good. It went back into its shoulder holster and got snapped in.

Melissa was still, her arms dangling toward me. The buckle was mangled. I drew my knife and started cutting. It only took a few seconds before her weight spilled onto my shoulders. I adjusted her into a fireman's carry and side-stepped her to the rear of the shuttle.

Jude was still administering to a now conscious and muttering Heinz. I slid down the open emergency door and carried Melissa over next to the just stirring Sean. As I lay Melissa gently to the pavement, Sean roused enough to whisper something I couldn't hear.

"What, Sergeant?" I asked.

His eyelids fluttered and his eyes darted around before he was able to focus on me. "...all okay?"

"No," I replied honestly. "We're not all okay."

He looked around. Melissa lay to his left. Jude was using the last of the gauze to wrap up Heinz's shoulder. Spots of blood were already blotting through her efforts. Westsmith, knowing better than to attempt another escape, had managed to strip his own belt and wrap it as a tourniquet high on his thigh. Rosalita lay in repose on the road in the center of the circle of wrecked vehicles, her hands crossed over her heart.

"Shit," Sean muttered, slowly getting up onto his elbows. He rolled over to his side and breathed deeply, trying to shake the cobwebs of a possible concussion from his head. "Shit."

"We're way too exposed out here," I said. "How far is Flushing Meadow Park from the city?"

Sean closed his eyes and started moving his lips as he searched for the answers in his rattled brain. "I don't know... probably nine or ten miles if we keep straight on the LIE through the tunnel."

Even with a straight shot and no obstacles, the injuries the group had sustained would put the hump back to Manhattan at probably a few hours. More, if we encountered any resistance.

It has been very quiet since we left Creedmoor.

I would say *too quiet...* but I hated such cliques.

The fact we have not encountered any FRACs since we left is disconcerting.

It *was* disconcerting. The last leg to the city may be the worst part of the mission. Sean was still shaking out the effects of the crash. Jude, who probably had used Sean as a landing pad during the rollover, had escaped anything worse than bruising and a few scrapes. Melissa was just starting to stir. Heinz was a question mark. And Westsmith would be trouble no matter what his condition.

Jude didn't have enough time. We would burn at least a quarter of it getting to the tower. Heinz probably needed medical assistance. Westsmith needed bandaging up, too, although I wasn't opposed to cutting the belt off his leg and letting him bleed out.

No man left behind.

I highly doubted he was a man. Or ever had been.

The same could be said for you, John.

I know.

A faint whiff of something flowery hit my nose, making my repairing lung itch with each inhale. Everything hurt as I wheezed out a rattling breath. I was sure I was slowly bleeding out, too. It could be I would end up being the one the others would have to leave behind.

10

Repose

+81 Days – 1027 hours
06:55:59

It took over twenty minutes before we were ready to travel. When Melissa finally came to and found enough strength to get to her feet, she stormed over to Westsmith and slapped him across the face.

I think he knew not to smile at her. Maybe he was smart instead of crazy.

Oh, he is still insane. I have no doubt.

The way he followed our movements with his eyes; the way he stalked us in an almost predatory way was certainly not of the crazy variety. More like a caged panther.

More sociopathic in nature, I would surmise.

Sean handed the Benelli back to Melissa's capable, but deadly, hands. She cradled the weapon like it was a squirming untrained puppy trying to escape.

Jude lifted Heinz to his feet, having done as good a job as she could bandaging him up with the limited first aid supplies. Then she looked at the small pool at my feet. "Jesus, John," she said. "You need to be taped up, too. Why didn't you say something?"

"I'll be fine," I said. "He needed it more than I do."

"Not from the look of things," Jude replied.

"We'll find a pharmacy on the service drive, somewhere," I said.

"That may be more difficult than you think," Sean added,

tossing the dark screen of the broken tablet to the ground. "The last time I checked, the Horace Harding service drive was crawling with deadheads."

"Why aren't they down here?" Melissa asked.

"Because R&R did a bang-up job of closing off the exits to the expressway," Heinz answered, wincing in pain. "The neighborhoods were left to fend for themselves."

"Odd that FRACs didn't made it through the barricades," Sean said.

"R&R is a thorough lot, mate," Heinz said. He grimaced through a flash of pain to his chest.

"Come on," Jude coaxed, hesitant to hold him anywhere other than under the armpit. He was a stumbling billboard for shotgun safety. "What can I do?"

"I'll survive, lass," Heinz replied in a most Scottish way. "I'm made of sterner stuff."

"Still strange about the FRACs," Sean said. "Just sayin'."

He was right. Where were all the FRACs? R&R may have done a superior job cordoning off the expressway, but I couldn't believe the service road or the overpasses above us weren't overrun with the undead.

It was New York City, for Christ's sake. The City that never slept. The mecca for artists, musicians, and aspiring performers. A city boasting over 8 million people. Sure, there had been plenty of FRACs around the Creedmoor property, but the streets we had driven past had been too quiet and devoid of the walking dead. I looked up the concrete walls to the elevated service streets on both sides of the expressway. If the undead did decide to breach the ramps or tip over the guard rails, we would be trapped down here like ducks in a shooting gallery.

It may not be a good omen, but it is fortunate.

We'd better make the best of it.

"You going to make it, soldier?" I asked Heinz, still propped up by Jude.

"Don't worry about me, mate," Heinz said, cocking his head toward his fallen leader. "I'll crack on. I've been shot by worse turncoats than this one."

What could I say?

I wouldn't be able to adequately explain the smoky worms burrowing out from Rosalita's temples nor the unblinking dead stare and lack of emotion she exhibited during our fight. I couldn't tell him my speculation Westsmith had something to do with it, even after we all had witnessed first-hand his army of undead followers back at Building 25. How would I defend the honor of the woman and Marine who I had impaled on a twisted shank of steel? She was just another person in a growing list of people under my charge who were now dead.

I grabbed Westsmith around the arm and dragged him up to his feet. He hissed in pain as he put weight on his injured leg. He shuffled until he found a balance tolerable for travel.

"Suck it up," I said to our prisoner and to the rest of my weary group. "We have miles to go."

11

Dark Skies

+81 Days – 1035 hours
06:47:33

We walked westbound on the eerily empty Long Island Expressway. There were faint FRAC moans on the flowery scented breeze, but they were far off and isolated. A dog barked. A series of intermittent pops from light firearms followed. There was even the rev of a motorcycle. Even at the end of the world, New York City could claim to be noisy in comparison to other places.

Six wounded and tired people trudged toward the silhouetted skyline of a city no longer powered by electricity or the kinetics of millions of citizens. Melissa and Sean walked point, leading our column with weary determination and a loaded Benelli. Heinz and Jude walked with Westsmith limping between them, both giving him a two-meter berth like he was the predator we all believed him to be. I covered our rear flank.

We passed another trio of vehicles—two Mercedes SUVs and a Chrysler minivan—parked tightly together in the breakdown lane. Melissa peeled off from Sean to investigate. She stopped short and put a hand over her mouth. The doors were open, but passengers still sat inside. They were all dead, shot twice in the chest and once in the head. The shooters hadn't distinguished between men, women and children during the executions.

The driver of the lead Mercedes clutched a stack of one hundred dollar bills in his left hand. A few bills had escaped and lay on the ground under the open driver's door, one sticking to the back of the front tire. The love of money was the root of all evil, the bible once proclaimed. In this new age, the shooter or shooters either had deeper pockets or the allure of cash had dulled in favor of food, shelter, and bullets. Regardless, this group had misjudged the reach of their own wealth for getting off the island alive.

Roanoke & Raleigh had substantial reach.

The last stars dotted the outline of the dark Manhattan skyline. Two red lights blinked below the heavens. Several windows of the R&R tower burned bright, serving as a beacon and a warning to anyone who gazed upon them. It must be a good life to lord over all one could survey. Roy had believed he lorded over all he surveyed, too. His kingdom had reached as far as the sidewalks around a local museum in Massachusetts. How quickly his fiefdom had fallen into disarray.

You had a hand in that.

Maybe. But I was just the last stone cast at the glass house. Its windows had cracked long before I set foot inside.

True.

Was Dick just another paper king content to sit on high in his ivory tower? Was he like Nero who played the fiddle as Rome burned around him?

I assume we will just have to ask him when we see him again.

Several of the building's lights winked out. Only the deep red of the lights marking the perimeter of the helipad continued to pulse. I guess even gods needed their rest.

I thought there was no rest for the wicked.

No. Only for us.

12

Processional

+81 Days – 1038 hours
06:44:12

The morning breeze continued to puff toward us from the west, carrying with it the smell of oil, salt, and rotting flesh. It wasn't overpowering, but it was distinct. Under the powerful concoction of odors was another scent. The smell of flowers.

There were no sirens. The dogs had stopped barking. There were no blaring car horns. Thankfully. But something else replaced it. Every so often came the far-off pop of weapons fire. Usually it came as a single shot. But, sometimes there were more. I could still hear the faint and soft hungry chants of the undead. The others, while perking to attention with the gunshots, didn't react at all to the moans and growls.

It was probably better they didn't hear the FRACs. It was unnerving enough to be the only one to hear it in the first place. I was surprised, though, Westsmith didn't cock his head to listen to the undead warble since he considered himself to be so much more in tune with them. He simply shuffled along between Jude and Heinz, our ragtag column wandering itself forward with the destination of Manhattan in mind.

Heinz's limp was almost as pronounced as his prisoner, more from blood loss, fatigue and weakness than from pain. He was a warrior, never slowing. There was no doubt about that.

None whatsoever. The Gaunt Man walked beside me, his hands clasped behind his back. His white dress shirt and pale waxen skin seemed to float inside the darkness of his black jacket.

What shall we do when we deliver our dear Mr. Westsmith?

What else? Deactivate the bomb in Jude's neck. Get back the rest of our people. It would be a welcome feeling to put Westsmith, Dick and the R&R corporate building to our rear.

Miss the ocean?

Yes, I do.

Ah. The simple pleasures of life.

Weren't you supposed to find us the best route to the city?

The intel was scarce. I did find out some info, but... not everyone is going to like it.

13

Bridge and Tunnel Crowd
+81 Days – 1041 hours
06:41:12

"No fucking way," Melissa told all of us, the barrel of the Benelli bouncing around as her arms moved around as adamantly as her words. "There is no goddamn way I'm going to step foot inside that tunnel."

I knew Melissa wouldn't be pleased with the decision to go through the tunnel. Bob's intel described the bridges – 59th Street, Brooklyn, Manhattan, Williamsburg – all as impassible steel and concrete mezzanines of stalled vehicles and streams of undead making a stumbling exodus from Manhattan island. With eight million people in New York City at the last census, there was no way there weren't FRACs walking around.

"You claustrophobic?" I asked.

"No," Melissa said with a shake of her head. "Just don't like being in tight spaces under a river." Sean opened his mouth to correct her, but a wave of the shotgun in Melissa's hand and the slightest glare from me stayed his words. Like Sean, I wasn't sure if she was kidding or if she really didn't know the meaning of the word.

"Taking the exit to the get to the bridge will definitely have deadheads around," Sean advised. "The LIE to the Midtown Tunnel is our safest route."

"Plus," Jude added, "we have three injured."

Three?

You are one of those people, John. And she counted Westsmith because she's that kind of woman.

The blood had dried on my back and pant leg, but I guess I could still be considered one of the walking wounded. Jude counting Westsmith as one of the injured could make her complacent. Too much kindness could get her killed.

"Sean," I said.

"Sir," he replied.

"How much farther until we're at a point of no return?"

"That's a trick question," Sean shot back. "The point of no return would be the dead center of the tunnel. No pun intended."

I was going to say that!

"Barring that?" I asked.

"It's actually the truth, John," Sean said. "We can always backtrack out of the tunnel to the toll road back to Van Damme or just climb up over the abutments to get to the service road. Then it's just a matter of getting to Northern Blvd to hook onto the bridge."

The others looked on at our conversation, waiting for the final word. Melissa smiled thinly at me with the hopes her pleas wouldn't go ignored. Heinz stood up razor-straight, not letting the visible pain on his face dictate the control over his body. Westsmith, on the other hand, focused on cleaning out the dirt and blood collected under his too-long fingernails. He looked worse for wear, a sheen of sweat covering his exposed skin.

After her comment on the group's condition, Jude had wandered several meters away to look west toward the red twinkling lights of the R&R corporate executive tower. Her slim figure was outlined in silhouette, the eastern sun casting her back into a panel of black. She was skinnier now. Not scrawny yet, but another couple months of light eating would quickly change that assessment.

We were all less than we had started.

Yet some of us are a bit more, aren't we?

Yes, some of us had been hapless victims of unsigned deals with the devil. When I lay on the cot in the desert, I hadn't been given the luxury of reading the blood-inked fine print at the bottom of the R&R contract. I had to wonder how many human skins had to be tanned and stretched out in order to make the parchment itself.

Morbid, are we not?

Maybe a little.

"We at the cemeteries yet?" I asked Sean.

"Not yet." He shook his head. "Another mile or two."

"Melissa," I said firmly.

She snapped her head toward me, reacting to the tone of my voice. The others held their breath for a moment, feeling the rising tension between us. "Yeah?" she asked cautiously.

"We have less than seven hours to get Westsmith to the tower," I said. "The city may be only a few miles away, but I don't want to watch the seconds tick down to zero when we deliver him. Do you understand what I'm saying?"

"I told you I don't want to go in there," she whispered, the barrel of her Benelli drooping toward the pavement and her eyes drifting to her boots.

"We're all doing something we don't want to be doing," I reminded her. "Remember Summer."

She swallowed hard in the silence after my words. Her eyes didn't come up to meet mine. Her chin and shoulders were working their way closer to the pavement.

"We'll be with you," Jude said to Melissa, returning to stand with the group, "all the way."

"What she said," Sean agreed.

"Without a doubt, luv," Heinz said.

I nodded.

Westsmith looked up from the work of his roadside manicure and shrugged.

The barrel of the Benelli came up. Melissa pointed the shotgun at each of us in a slow sweeping semi-circle. "If something happens to me, I'm going to kill you all."

"I'll take that as consent," I said, not overly concerned with her proclamation of the promise of pain. In my career, I had more destructive weapons pointed at me.

And by more sinister trigger fingers.

14

Full of Grace

+81 Days – 1045 hours
06:30:22

Cemeteries littered gravestones on both sides of the expressway as we approached the Hunters Point exit.

"We can still redirect to the bridge from here," Sean reminded us.

The hairs on the back of my neck stood on end. The sounds of cicadas filled the inside of my head. On top of that, I could still hear the faint distant sounds of the undead looking for fresh meat. We were safer on the expressway—with the walls, guardrails, and barricaded ramps working in our favor.

"Thanks," I said. "The tunnel is still the better play."

Melissa knew I was right, but hung her head as she trudged forward. She was still adamant in her reluctance to going into the tunnel, but she showed trust in the group to get her through. They all knew I was right. What they didn't know was I was taking intel from a voice in my head. A specific tidbit of knowledge to possibly sway the entire group against me.

Mum is the word.

The road rose out of the earth as it became the concrete ramp of an interchange. We crested the top of the roadway, rows and rows of headstones dotting gentle hills radiating out on both sides of the expressway. The Manhattan skyline had taken on a gray silhouette as if out of a painting. To our immediate right was some sort of production or reclamation facility, with three tall red and white striped smoke stacks rising out of it.

Was someone processing the dead?

Shut up, Bob.

Maybe the corpses are being used for fuel. Like the British did when they explored Egypt. Used the mummies to power the railroad.

I said shut up.

That factory definitely has a look of menace, does it not?

Bob was right. The smokestacks were out of place next to the cemetery, allowing my mind to conjure all sorts of reasons for its existence next to a field of the deceased. I saw pictures of hazmat-suited aliens carrying the dead like carrion to huge open blazing furnaces, the roar of the bellowed flames engulfing the screams of those still clinging to life. The smokestacks billowed dark ash into the air, sending souls as tributes to their respective makers, the headstones serving as a reminder to the mass of destruction the furnaces had capacity for.

I shook my head. It was a macabre notion, but one not too off-center from the reality of a world where the undead roamed the countryside in search of the living.

As we walked west, the sea of cemetery plots and the uncharacteristic factory stacks receded behind us. We also passed the Hunter's Point exit leading to the 59th Street Bridge.

Melissa soldiered on alongside Sean. In another life, she would have made an excellent Marine. Sean raised a fist from the front of the column. We all stopped, except for Westsmith who had to pulled up by the back of the collar by Heinz.

"Wha-what?" Westsmith asked.

"Shut up," Heinz warned him in a low voice.

We quietly took a knee with our rifles at full draw in a semi-circular position as Sean made his way to the next rise in the road.

He stood at the crest of the road with his arms folded. After a moment, he waved us forward. With Heinz giving Westsmith a shove, we joined Sean at his position. Beyond the ridge were the cash tollbooths and the purple designated EZ-Pass lanes leading to the tunnel. Eight lanes disappeared into a dark cavernous void under the East River with the city looming above and beyond it.

Melissa started shifting her weight as she stared at the mouth of the tunnel. Her grip went white on the stock of the shotgun. It was a good thing her hand wasn't on the trigger or she may have inadvertently shot one of us. "Hail, Mary, full of grace,..." she whispered, repeating the prayer as a mantra to herself.

"We got you, Melissa," Jude told her again, careful not to startle her with any errant touches or sudden movement. Melissa nodded, continuing to speak to her God in the way best comforting her.

"We all good?" I asked Sean.

I didn't get any strange feelings about the tunnel, only a low-grade dread from its dark maw generated by the mere nature of its architectural design. Maybe Melissa was rubbing off on me.

"We're good," Sean confirmed. "Thought I heard something."

As if to confirm his senses, the Midtown Tunnel let out a long low sigh. Melissa's chants to Mary, Jesus, and the Catholic God grew louder. "...Hail Mary, full of Grace, the Lord is with thee. Blessed art thou among women and blessed is the fruit of thy womb, Jesus. Holy Mary Mother of God, pray for us sinners now and at the hour of our death. Amen... Hail Mary, full of Grace,..."

"Looks like we have found the source of your angst, Sean," I said.

"Yes, sir," he replied.

"That's Sergeant," I reminded him.

"Yes, sir," he joked. "Sorry, sir."

"Asshole," I said, knowing the return of jokes meant the return of Sean. His previous comatose state with the breath of his sister's name on his lips was a memory. Melissa, on the other hand, may have become our new internal problem.

"Hey, Melissa. Let me tell you about how fucked up life is." Sean walked through Tollgate #3 of the westbound tunnel without correct change or an EZ-Pass device. "I had a sister once…"

15

Meg and The Deep Blue Sea
+81 Days – 1052 hours
06:30:24

"Before I was even six-years-old, my sister had already been at Creedmoor for a few years," Sean said, his words echoing off the concrete ceiling. "The doctors told my parents Meg was bipolar and had some dissociative disorder I don't think they totally understood or had documented. Probably didn't even have a clinical name for it yet, whatever was ailing her."

"And then she ran off and was hit by a truck," Westsmith added. We ignored him and let Sean continue.

"I remember visiting her in Building 25 back when it was still kind of a nice facility. Although, the whole institution was already feeling the effects of budget cutbacks, even back then. Staff was overworked and undermanned. The doctors were churning through patients like it was an assembly line. At least from what my dad said, anyway.

"I was too young to understand. All I knew is me and my sis would run the halls and play games. She always had the best hiding spots for hide-and-seek. I guess she got a lot of practice when I wasn't around."

"Probably learned all the tricks from the other patients who had been there longer," Jude said. "All that info gets disseminated like state secrets. Sometimes the patients end up knowing more about the hospital than the orderlies do."

"That's what Meg said, too," Sean confirmed.

"And then she was hit by a truck," Westsmith said again.

Heinz jabbed Westsmith in the thigh with the butt of his gun. Sean gave Westsmith a grim smile as our prisoner staggered off to the right to walk off the new pain. He wasn't being baited by Westsmith's words like he had in the shuttle.

Good man.

"I don't think the doctors ever really had a handle on her condition," Sean said with a shake of his head. "My mom would get her hopes up every time we visited the hospital, chasing down the doctors and nurses for new information on when Meg would be released and able to come home. Every time my parents would say their goodbyes. Every time I would give my sister a big hug and kiss on the cheek. Every time my mom would cry for the entire ride home. Just like clockwork."

"So, what he said is true?" Melissa asked.

"The stuff about the blackout?" Sean replied. "Simple answer is yes."

"See?" Westsmith said, still walking off the new pain in his leg, "Sean's big sis was hit by a truck. She should have known her hundred and twenty-pounds were no match for a Mack truck."

"And you should know," I interjected, "I can give you a few more openings to add to your throbbing thigh."

He put his hands up and closed his mouth.

At least for the moment.

"I'm not sure how he knows the details," Sean said. "Most of it wasn't made public. But he's right. Meg got outside the building and off the grounds. I don't think she ever saw the truck on the expressway. Maybe, she was over-medicated."

"Maybe, she thought she was invincible." Apparently, Westsmith couldn't help himself. Sean walked over to him.

Westsmith beamed him a fresh broad smile. Sean smiled back, swinging his fist into our prisoner's jaw. The punch, plus an unsteady leg, dropped Westsmith awkwardly to the ground. I did hope Dick wasn't expecting an unblemished prize.

"Yes," Sean said as he stood over Westsmith. "She was invincible."

"And she always will be," Melissa offered. "Just like my Victoria." That was the first time Melissa had uttered her sister's name since Victoria was killed on the front steps of the museum. A night from what seemed like years ago. A distant and faded memory from when the world was simpler.

If you consider a time when a fake king of a fake castle trying to have you executed was a simpler time... then sure.

Maybe simpler was the wrong word. Maybe, straightforward was better?

Maybe. Still does not seem like appropriate.

Heinz lifted Westsmith up to his feet, our human bargaining chip still struggling to find a balance on his wounded leg. A fresh thread of blood dripped off his chin, courtesy of a split lip from Sean's roundhouse. He spat out some blood mixed with saliva at Sean's feet.

Then he smiled again. This time, his teeth were stained red. I wasn't sure which was worse... the too-white veneers or the blood-soaked version.

"Very nice," Sean said. "I hope you enjoyed that."

"I did," Westsmith replied.

"Good," Sean said with a smile on par with Westsmith, but not quite as practiced. "Because I enjoyed the hell out of it."

16

Bottom of the River
+81 Days – 1102 hours
06:20:40

After ten minutes of walking, we were still heading at a downward angle. The two lanes were eerily empty of vehicles, whether passenger, civil or MTA. Our footfalls sent up faint echoes against the formerly white ceramic tiles. Rivulets of water streaked down the walls, cutting through the thin film created from decades of car exhaust. There came also the periodic sound of dripping water. With the darkness trying to invade our small and uneven pools of tactical lights, it was impossible to determine where the water was falling from. We weren't at the middle of the tunnel yet, but the angle of the roadway started to level out.

"Shit," Melissa whispered, her voice deafening in the cool, damp air. "Shit."

"You okay, Melissa?" I asked her, wishing there was something to distract her from her misery of being in the tunnel without her consent.

"Do I fuckin' sound okay to you, Walken?" Melissa said with a growl. My name echoed back at me from the dark ahead of us—and behind us.

"Pull yourself together," I advised. The tunnel was no place to lose one's shit.

"How 'bout I shove this barrel up your ass and pull the trigger?" Her breath was ragged, on the verge of hyperventilating.

"That's the spirit," Sean chimed in. "That's the Melissa we

know and love."

"A kinder and gentler Melissa," Jude added.

"You all can go to Hell," Melissa yelled at us. Her words echoed through the darkness. Good. I wanted her mad. Her anger tended to be both blinding and clarifying. I hoped it would serve the same purpose now.

A low murmur came from our immediate right. Sean and I spun our lights toward the sound. Westsmith's skin had taken on a waxen and sweaty pallor. He lumbered along in a stupor, mumbling the same unintelligible thing over and over. I walked up to him and shined the Glock's tactical light in his face. His eyes dilated, but not down to the pinpricks they should have in such dark confines.

He continued to smile—the man most likely to succeed—like a lunatic. The blood flowed freely down his chin from his split lip. He didn't even bother to lick it away, simply muttering and limping forward. But it wasn't the muttering, his crazy grin or his comatose shuffle bothering me. All of those things I had gotten more or less used to.

There was something else… a buzzing under the muttering. Like the constant vibrations I felt in the base of my neck. I craned my neck. Yep, definitely like the painful throbs running into my brain stem like a railroad spike. "Watch him," I ordered Heinz, a headache forming at my temples.

Heinz nodded and put his pistol barrel against the back of Westsmith's neck while holding a fistful of shirt. I walked past the alert Sean and panicked Melissa.

Jude joined me. "What is it?"

"I don't know," I said, my stomach clenching. "As cliché as it sounds, I have a bad feeling."

"Is it FRACs?" she asked.

"I don't know. It seems different."

"How?"

"It doesn't feel like FRACs. It just feels like I am getting sick. Like there's a vise closing on my stomach and bowels."

"Is it your side?" Jude looked into the darkness, the beam of her light managing to point out the lowest point of the tunnel and its slow incline ahead.

"I don't know," I admitted. "I don't think so. But, I've never been impaled through the belly before, so it's hard to tell. I feel like Westsmith looks."

"That must be pretty shitty, then," Jude said, elbowing me in the arm. "See what I did there?"

"I saw," I said, smiling in spite of the wave of nausea bubbling up in my throat. Apparently, Westsmith's grin was infectious.

Like the Joker. Bob did not materialize, or say more. His voice carried to my ears alone. But as quickly as I heard him, his words drifted away.

I walked several meters forward, truly at the bottom of the tunnel under the East River. I cast my tactical light around to assist with my heightened night vision. The tiled walls and ceiling were no less grimy here, the dotted stains of antifreeze, oil and water run-off to the grates easier to see on the roadway. The raised walkway to our right—the north wall of the tunnel, if my directions weren't all twisted around—was built a meter above the road with its too-often painted-over steel tube pipe railing. We had already passed several PlexiGlas enclosures separating the pathway, primarily for the attendants to rest their lungs from the pollution-filled rush hour tube. Now, they served as silent steel coffins to a world no longer needing them.

At least they have office chairs as creature comforts while they wait out eternity.

A puff of air hit my face. It was cool and refreshing for a moment, a tinge of saltiness mixed with the rot of seaweed and foam. Another breeze swept through, stronger this time. The smells of the ocean were replaced with a stench far more sinister.

The moans came a moment later.

"Shit," Jude said.

I didn't sense them, but I could hear them fine.

"How many?" Melissa asked as she joined me, her neck snapping toward the sound of every drop of water.

Sean and Heinz corralled the smiling, but semi-comatose Westsmith. He had stopped walking. Instead, he swayed back and forth in place rocking from foot to foot. The barrels in Sean and Heinz's hands swayed along with him to keep him centered in their sights.

"Can't tell," I said, "The problem is we're really at the point of no return, Melissa. We're at the bottom of the tunnel. It's all uphill from here, no matter which way we go. The only difference is this way forward involves less miles."

"But more FRACs," Melissa said.

Decisions. Decisions.

17

Let's Play a Game...

+81 Days – 1105 hours
06:17:33

The moans didn't seem to get any louder or closer, although the acoustics of the porcelain tiles made it almost impossible to know for sure. The FRAC groans pressed out to us from the darkness.

"Forward or back?" Melissa asked, switching the Benelli from one hand to the other. Now she was focused on locating the FRACs in the dark, instead of her issues with tunnels and being under the East River.

You said you wanted a distraction.

Walking through a tube with the opportunity for one or more of the undead to lunge out of the darkness certainly qualifies as a distraction. Thanks.

Not of my doing, I assure you.

You know what I mean.

Do I?

Yes. You do.

"We go forward," I told Melissa and the others. "It's the most direct route."

"Then let's go," Melissa urged. "It's not going to get any better with us standing here."

"Copy," I said. "Ooh rah."

"Ooh rah," Sean and Jude replied.

Melissa gritted her teeth and nodded.

Heinz shook his head. "Marines and their war cries."

"Ooh rah," Westsmith mumbled. "Ooh... fucking... rah."

"Let's go," I said, taking point with my Glock drawn and the beam of its tactical light trying to push back the black farther than just a few meters.

Westsmith continued to bastardize the United States Marine Corps battle cry as I walked past him. Heinz saw my look of disgust and shrugged.

"Ooooo..." Westsmith's lips took on the shape of a large mouth bass as he formed the words. "Raaaa..."

18

...It's Called, 'Scary Noises'

+81 Days – 1110 hours
06:12:11

I wasn't sure what was worse, the steady rhythmic moan of the unseen FRACs or Westsmith's continued chants. Heinz had nudged him in the back of the neck with the business end of his rifle several times, not dissuading Westsmith from being an annoyance.

"Ooh rah, ooh-oh, ra-ra..." Westsmith sang, his warbles bouncing off the walls, ironically melodic. In any regard, I disliked its source. He didn't chant the battle cry out of respect for what the USMC stood for. He did it to entertain himself and to get a rise out of the rest of us.

Mostly, me.

And is it working?

A little bit, yeah.

We were climbing out of the bottom of the tunnel. Whatever her rational or irrational issue was with this specific claustrophobia, I was sure it would make Melissa happier to know we were walking toward a promise of open skies.

It is always darkest before the dawn.

Right.

There is a light at the end of the tunnel.

Not yet, even with my enhanced vision. We would continue to use the tactical lights for now.

Wise choice.

Bob, my constant spectral companion, drifted ahead of me. He stopped after several meters, clasped his hands in front of his waist and bowed his head. As if needing concentration or exertion to do so, he started to shine more brightly. His luminescence expanded out several meters, brightening the off-white tiles and quadrupling my visibility downrange. I wasn't sure if being able to see the dozens of bodies littering the roadway was better or worse.

"Hold," I called out to the others, thankful they were oblivious of the bodies ahead. "Hold!"

"Roger," Sean called back.

"Copy," Heinz added.

I stepped forward. Bob continued to stand still with his head bowed and his eyes closed.

"Thanks, Bob," I said in a loud whisper. The tunnel was very unforgiving about suppressing the human voice. I wasn't sure if the Gaunt Man had nodded in response, but I could see for certain he held a thin strained smile across his lips. Was he expending effort? Could a phantom sweat?

I dismissed the crazy thought and went to the closest body. Turning it over, I saw two shots to the chest. The young thirty-something woman's face was ruined, but not by weapons fire. Her cheek was a pulpy ground up mess of muscle and skin, the white of her skull reflecting brilliantly against the beam of my tactical light.

I shined my light to the other nearby bodies. Each had seen a world of hurt before they were executed with the double-tap to the heart.

A hand grabbed my wrist. The woman's eyes snapped open. She snarled and bared her still-white teeth.

Stop!

I pressed her down against the pavement with my forearm, my Glock in the same hand. She growled, snapping her teeth and lunging her mouth at me as far as her neck allowed. Something pressed down on my boot. A man dragged himself hand over hand up my leg. His spine had been ripped open by a .50-caliber round. The MTA worker's irises were a brilliant gold and red, the whites now a bloody canvas of burst capillaries.

He snapped his teeth.

Stop!

He kept coming. The woman fought against my forearm. Other movement. Several of the other bodies started twitching and wriggling up to their hands and knees.

"Stop!" I yelled.

"What is it?" Sean called out from the darkness behind me.

"Stay there!" I ordered. "Keep them there! Copy?"

Sean didn't answer.

"Copy, goddammit?"

"Copy," he finally called back.

The FRACs weren't listening to me.

And they saw me... as food.

I pulled my knife with my left hand and drove it into the soft tissue under the FRAC humping my leg. The lines in his forehead smoothed out and he dropped his dead weight on my thighs. I rolled him away, using the knife handle as a lever. After his weight was off my legs, I pulled out the knife blade and swung it into the woman's ear still under my forearm. She finally listened as her muscles relaxed and she dropped her head back to the ground.

Three others were close enough to snag their fingertips on the leather of my boots or the canvas of my black fatigues.

And crimson.

I kicked the teenage boy who was trying to gnaw through my boot. I helped him along by driving the steel toe of my other boot into his mouth. Teeth cracked off as he continued to chew on it. I dropped the heel of my left boot into his skull. He died with a mouthful of my boot still between his teeth.

A girl of no more than fourteen bit her teeth into my arm. All she managed to do was to bite into the nylon of my Cobra watch's wristband. I pulled her off by her black ponytail. Saliva and one incisor were left behind on the nylon.

I swung her like a rag doll into the path of a slovenly older gentleman, his suit jacket crumpled and wrinkled beyond office presentation. It bore two entry wounds on the left lapel through the chest like the others. He climbed over the girl like she was a human speed bump. She wriggled and struggled under his weight, reaching her fingers out to me.

I rolled away and came up to one knee.

Bob's aura still pulsed its light twenty meters into the darkness ahead of us. All of the bodies were now stirring.

"oooo…" Westsmith's singsong drifted in the air. It multiplied as it echoed off the tiles. "raaaa…"

Stockbroker FRAC continued to crush the young girl as he rolled over her. He opened his mouth. "…oooooo…" Was the sound coming from the FRAC? Or an artifact from Westsmith's singing? "…rhhhaaar…" The sound definitely came from the man in the thousand-dollar suit. The growl deteriorated into a guttural slurry of semi-paralyzed vocal cords and a gurgle of blood and saliva.

He may have some meat stuck in his throat.

My answer to Bob was to shoot Wallstreet in the top of his head. Skin and bone imploded, the wisps of his graying comb over ruined. As blood oozed out of the top of his head, Wallstreet served perfectly as a meat weight for the young girl he pinned down. She twisted her shoulders but didn't have the muscle mass to break free from his dead weight.

Two at my three o'clock.

BOOM!

The retort was deafening in the enclosed space.

BOOM!

The muzzle flash acted as a strobe, giving a sepia tone to the cold luminescence Bob's light produced.

On my six.

My next headshot snapped the walker's neck back a moment before the body realized it had no choice but to follow. Each squeeze of the trigger dropped one of the undead. But, like a Hydra, two more seemed to take its place.

"...ooooo..." Westsmith sang.

"...rhaaar..." The walkers joined in with their own butchered version of the battle cry.

It was no longer parody.

It was disrespect.

It was dismissal.

It was red.

BOOM!

Three rounds left, plus one in the pipe. The FRACs kept coming into the pool of Bob's light. But Bob was gone and the space was still washed in a cold illuminance. The radius of light was now coming from me?

Over thirty FRACs.

Four rounds, plus three full magazines of the explosive-tipped, burrowing rounds. New York City had boasted millions of people when society was still buzzing. I didn't have enough bullets for that kind of campaign. I emptied the Glock into the walkers. Twenty-four shambling FRACs zeroed in on my location.

Reload.

The Glock fired with a deadly precision with every squeeze of the trigger. Each walker's head erupted in a spray of gore, brain and skull evaporating with each shot. A couple shots decapitated the walker I aimed at, plus took out the undead unlucky enough to be directly behind it.

Thirteen FRACs in range.

The magazine slid out and clanked against the road.

"Keep back," I yelled. "Stay ready!"

Reload.

"…oooooo… raaaaa…"

The bodies continued to drop to the pavement.

One hit the ground with such force his ruptured head literally cracked open. Another FRAC stumbled through the fragments of skull, its feet squishing through the liquefied brains. My body convulsed as my throat tried to retch up the contents of my empty stomach.

Three FRACs managed to get within striking distance before my Glock did what it did best.

It is also what you do best.

Four rounds left.

The ground was as littered with bodies as it was when Bob had lit up the tunnel. Blood speckled the white tiles, burning ghostlike Rorshach afterimages in my vision when I blinked.

That is why hospitals painted the corridors green. To keep the surgeons from having to relive the procedures on the wall from the patients they had just stitched up.

Bob didn't make an appearance, content to be only a tired voice in my head with his trivial knowledge.

"…oooo…" Westsmith laughed. I could imagine his shit-eating

grin as he cackled.

"Shut the 'ell up," Heinz said.

BANG!

An athletic walker had managed to find himself on the raised catwalk, unsure how to climb the railing to get at me. With a bullet in his head and cast-off brain matter splattered on the wall behind him, he pitched forward over the railing and landed face first against the road's gutter. His body wedged against the poured wall, his feet now dangling against the steel tubing.

The echoes of my last shot finally faded away, leaving a terrible void of sound in the tunnel. Westsmith had stopped singing, which was a vast improvement.

Were there more FRACs ahead of us? I strained to hear for more groans or snarls. There might have been something in the distance, but I couldn't be sure. Maybe, it was just a trick of sound on the wind.

The light faded around me. Apparently, it had served its purpose. As the aura dissipated, the beam from the Glock's tactical light became more apparent. Its beam had all but been forgotten in the supernatural light during the firefight.

"John!" Jude called out, her voice edged with uncertainty and concern. It was for the best her vision wasn't enhanced like mine. The carnage around me was still something the human brain was desensitizing to. It might be something we never got accustomed to. Why would anyone want this scene to be considered an everyday occurrence?

It is an everyday occurrence. Surely, you realize that.

"John!" Jude took a chance to break the silence again.

"I'm ok," I replied, surrounded by bodies. "Hold tight."

"Copy," Sean acknowledged.

"Copy," Westsmith mimicked with a laugh to finish it off.

"I told you to shut it," Heinz advised.

"So, shut me up," Westsmith dared him.

He was much more awake than earlier. I guess he found his second wind.

He is definitely a windbag.

Agreed. What was the deal with the light?

That's called an LED tactical light.

Not this. I waved the Glock away. The light you created before so I could see?

I am not sure of what you mean.

Are you shitting me right now?

I am not 'shitting' you, John.

You're a pain in the ass, Bob.

True. But you may want to get your eyes checked if you are seeing bright lights.

Seriously? You got jokes?

Don't go into the light, Carol Ann!

"I can see light!" Melissa exclaimed.

Shit.

The other tactical lights clicked off.

"Oh, crap!" Jude agreed. "I see light, too."

I looked at my Cobra. The girl's tooth was still embedded into the military-grade nylon. I pulled it out with my thumb and forefinger. It was white and sharp.

It was also high-noon.

19

Eureka Moment
+81 Days – 1115 hours
06:07:37

The others' eyes hadn't deceived them. The tunnel was brightening with the zenith of the sun high in the sky.

"There's bodies here," I called back.

"Huh. Is that what all the gunfire was about?" Melissa asked, her response dripping with sarcasm.

I guess my comment had been a stupid thing to say. Apparently, three months into the End of Days was indeed enough time to desensitize people concerning the walking dead, the fall of government, and having to resort to violence and killing to survive.

The others came up in a tight formation, their weapons up. Heinz led Westsmith a meter behind them with his hand on the back of our prisoner's shirt and the barrel of his weapon in a modified Harries hold against his neck.

Even with the knowledge of what to expect, Jude and Sean's already solemn faces fell and their eyes averted when they saw the bodies. Melissa stared at the corpses, her jaws clenching and unclenching. Looking at their faces, I knew there was still hope for us.

"Christ, John!" Jude punched me in the arm. "Don't ever tell us to hold us back when the shit gets this deep. What the fuck is wrong with you?"

I opened my mouth to respond but Melissa beat me to the punch with her own comment about my behavior. "You're an idiot. I totally agree with Jude on that."

"Yeah," Sean chimed in with a glare. "Not cool. We got firepower, too, you know. We weren't able to help at the hospital, but we still have your six."

"Well done, John," Heinz complimented me, unfazed by the bodies as I was sure he had seen plenty of death in several theaters of operation around the globe. "Looks like you had some good hunting."

"Thanks," I replied with a nod, acknowledging his professional assessment of the wetwork.

"Ooh rah, Sergeant," Westsmith said with a wink and a smile, not bothering to look at the remains. "You have a natural talent, without question."

"And I would advise you stop your desecration of my Corps," I warned him.

"And what will you do if I do not?" Westsmith goaded. "I am too valuable to the corporation to be delivered in a more damaged state."

I stopped within a half-meter of him, searching his eyes. As he grinned, his crow's feet gave away the harder existence he had led way before meeting us.

I didn't smile... or blink.

"And what terrible thing will you do to make me tremble before you?" he asked, his smile plastered on his face.

A moment of clarity flashed across my mind. Just as quickly, my tactical knife jabbed into his right shoulder between the clavicle and the shoulder joint before he could react. His smile was replaced with a scream. Jude and Sean gasped. They shouldn't have worried. I had made sure to miss any major arteries or bones. I pulled out the blade and returned it to its sheath.

Heinz smiled and nodded.

"Nice work," Melissa commented.

Westsmith's scream dialed down to a whimper, his left hand covering the wound. He tried to smile, but the pain had contorted his face too much for any part of his lips to tilt upward. "Was that the terrible thing?" Westmith managed between painful breaths.

"No," I said with a shake of my head. "But I just realized I don't need you alive to get my people back."

His face fell. "What about the capsule in your girlfriend's neck?" He smirked the last part, as if he was catching me off guard with an unsolvable puzzle. Westsmith had certainly been paying more attention to our conversations then he had let on.

I smiled back at him, hoping the grin was on par with one of his. As I stared at him, I could see in his eyes he was unnerved by it. Leaning in, I whispered, "Truthfully, I was only told to bring you in. Like it or not, no one mentioned you actually still had to be breathing. Maybe, Alvarez had been told something different. Maybe, not. No worries, though. Death is underrated."

20

My Condolences
+81 Days – 1119 hours
06:03:39

Whether from fatigue, the litter of bodies strewn across the roadway, or my unexpected rage and the resulting sinking my tactical knife into Westsmith's shoulder, the others remained silent as we walked westward and upward toward the City That Never Sleeps. Westsmith managed to keep his whimpers to an almost inaudible whine as he limped and held his seeping shoulder. Even Bob had lit out for the territories, content to leave me to my thoughts and the consequences of my actions.

It was a strange optical phenomenon to see the tunnel slowly brighten even with the dead fluorescent bars in the ceiling. Stranger still was the knowledge electricity would likely never flow through the ballasts again, remaining dark for all long as this tunnel remained passable. Ironically, we couldn't see the light at the end of the tunnel yet. The real sky remained just outside our sightline in spite of the tunnel's upward climb. After another minute, the road's incline leveled out again, but there still was no direct sunlight to greet us. Finally, the road curved to the right and a stronger breeze washed against our skin.

Again, there was a faint scent of flowers. The others didn't wrinkle their noses up at it, so I assumed I was the only one lucky enough to have a heightened olfactory sense. Yeah… lucky me.

The white tiles on the outside curve of the tunnel wall was washed in gold light a moment before we saw the actual sun again.

Sunlight streamed between the buildings, brightening our surroundings and warming our skin, finally finding full strength after hours of dragging itself out of the Atlantic beyond Manhattan Island.

"Thank you, God." Melissa hugged her Benelli tight in her arms and took in a long breath. "Thank you, God."

Even as the sun welcomed and coaxed us out into the daylight, the world beyond the tunnel wasn't necessarily an improvement. Bodies littered the roadways in both directions outside the tunnel, most cut down by large-caliber weapons' fire. Abandoned cars and small trucks sat bumper-to-bumper in their owners' desperate attempt to escape Manhattan to Long Island.

"Jesus," Sean said, breaking the awkward silence instituted since the bottom of the tunnel.

"Aye. They were serious about keeping the islanders out of the city," Heinz said, nodding to the large storage containers blocking the westbound lanes leading to the rest of the island.

"Why aren't there more walkers?" Jude asked. "The Cross Island was a parking lot of cars and the dead. There was no way R&R could keep an entire island from turning into FRACs."

"Alvarez said there were rumors R&R had a contingency plan already in place for this," Heinz said.

"'This', what?" Sean asked. "The end of the world?"

"Something like that," Heinz answered.

"R&R has a contingency for every scenario," Westsmith muttered quietly. "The end of the world is just one of many." Westsmith's words caught our attention. For once, he wasn't trying to bait any of us, cackling uncontrollably, or butchering battle cries he had no business uttering in the first place. We waited for him to say something else. He shuffled his feet, put weight on his wounded leg, and rolled his painful shoulder before meeting our stares. "What?"

"How do you know?" Jude countered.

"About R&R?" Westsmith replied. "Why do you think you could find me? I had the doctor cut the tracker out from under my skin. They do the trackers with all of their high-value assets."

"You're a high value asset?" Sean asked with a snicker.

"If I wasn't," Westsmith answered, "why would he send in an entire goon squad to retrieve me?"

"Maybe Dick misses you," Sean said.

"Dick?" Westsmith asked.

"You don't know Dick?" Sean said. "You know... the big boss?"

"I have no idea who's in charge at R&R these days," Westsmith admitted. "I've been *in the field*, as they say, for quite a few years."

"I'm not sure what being an inpatient at Creedmoor means, mate," Heinz suggested.

"Maybe." Westsmith shrugged painfully. "Doesn't really matter now, does it?" He walked forward toward the carnage of decaying bodies and twisted metal. Heinz drew up his weapon.

"Let him be," I ordered. "He doesn't have anywhere to go."

I let him study the bodies as he passed them, each receiving a slight nod before he moved on to the next.

"What the hell is he doing?" Jude wondered aloud.

"Maybe, he's finally paying his respects," I said. "Doesn't matter. We move out in one minute."

21

Down the Shore
+81 Days – 1127 hours
05:55:16

Steel rungs were welded on the edges of the shipping containers, making for an easier climb to the top. It was better then wading through the rotted dead and burned out sedans in front of them. One young boy's hand still clutched at the second rung, as if in defiance against the tyranny of the R&R mercenaries who had cut his life short under a hail of gunfire.

When we had finished helping Westsmith and Heinz get to the top, we stood and looked west to the rest of the city. Second Avenue and 36th Street were clogged with a snarl of Yellow Cabs, mini-vans, and buses. They were parked bumper to bumper going into the eastbound tunnel toward 34th Street. In many cases, the doors of the vehicles hadn't had enough room to open far enough to allow the driver or passengers the ability to squeeze out. Many of the windows had been rolled or powered down.

One particularly obese man had tried desperately to pull himself out from his Audi's moon roof before his massive gut decided upward wasn't going to be a successful method of egress. Scratches on the roof's paint in front and on the sides of the bloated body were only partially obscured by the thin splatter of blood sprayed on the silver-painted steel from a self-inflicted gunshot wound under his chin. The weapon was nowhere to be found, possibly taken or falling to the pavement and bouncing under another car. The man would bake under the summer sun until he withered away enough to fall back into the front seat again.

Or, maybe the crows will enjoy feasting on him.

Maybe, Bob.

"Funny," Sean noted.

"What?" Jude asked.

"Look at it," Sean said, waving a hand at the sea of steel, rubber and tempered glass.

Melissa shrugged and stood next to him. "What are we missing?"

"I see a few things," Westsmith announced.

"This should be good," Heinz said with a snicker.

"First off," Westsmith said, ignoring Heinz, "the cattle tried to take everything with them they owned." A few of the pieces of luggage had ripped open when they hit the ground. The ground was littered with sweaters, t-shirts, and other clothes. There was even a little fuchsia tutu for a child who would never see it again. "When that failed, they left the important things behind. I'm sure those mountain bikes would have served someone well getting across the Manhattan or Brooklyn bridge." Minivans and sedans with roof racks were filled to overflowing, with barely enough room to be buckled down. Expensive touring bicycles hung off the trunk rack of a nearby Range Rover. There was even a souped-up Chevy pickup with a kayak sticking out of the bed. "And, even as the ramps backed up with traffic, the people still tried to get through the tunnel," Westsmith finished. "As if they could use the power of their collective minds to will the cars forward like any other afternoon rush hour."

"And all stacked up going eastbound," Sean added. "Not a single car pulled over or abandoned in the westbound lanes, all going to Long Island." It was a strange sight to see the seemingly endless line of cars trying to escape New York. People desperate to get off one island just to figure how to get off another island.

"Should have tried to get to Jersey," Melissa said.

"Even at the end of the world," Sean said. "No one wants to go to Jersey."

22

Waste Management
+81 Days – 1136 hours
05:46:00

The light and warmth of the sun we had enjoyed after emerging from the tunnel had been short-lived. Clouds rolled in over the dark city skyline from the west as soon as we moved to 2nd Avenue. Only the red flashing lights from the top of the steel, glass and concrete of the Roanoke & Raleigh corporate world headquarters stood out among the rest of the towering buildings of Midtown Manhattan.

On the skeleton of the old Metlife building, the Roanoke & Raleigh tower was a re-imagined 140-story modern monument. It rose above the lower office buildings, apartments and townhouses like the monolithic fortress it was, even as mist wrapped around its upper floors like a shroud. The pulsing blinking lights winking on and off at its pinnacle could still be seen against the underside of the low forming clouds. Black onyx-colored steel material raced up the building in vertical strips, mirrored glass surfaces between them. There were currently no interior lights visible through the highly reflective windows. It was an impressive and imposing sight from the street, even from several blocks away. The Empire State Building may have been a universal symbol of the city's engineering ingenuity. The Chrysler Building may have been erected as a nod to an Art Deco representation of wealth and decadence. But neither of them compared to what R&R's military contracts and bio-engineering had built.

Here, at ground level, the sidewalks and streets were empty

except for heaps of trash and haphazardly abandoned cars. Something rotten drifted up from the black bags and cardboard boxes, but it was a dry smell from a summer sun baking away the more pungent odors. Sheets of the New York Times, The New York Post and the Village Voice slapped against overflowing trashcans, light posts and Siamese water connections—any place where the wind could carry the paper.

We were in the more residential area on the East Side. I knew every corner of Manhattan Island had a name, but I was only familiar with Midtown, Chinatown, SoHo, TriBeCa, and the more popularized areas. I was sure Sean would know what section of town we were in, but he was a little too busy to be asked as he was leading us in a tight column up Third Avenue.

Jude and Melissa followed next. They worked in perfect tandem as they cleared each open shop doors or rusty diamond plated basement access doors they came across. Heinz kept watch on the now quiet Westsmith, seemingly unfazed by the wounds in his arms and shoulders. He was a hardened war horse, trudging on without complaint. I was sure his burning hate for Westsmith over what had happened to the rest of his team kept him going, too. I was thankful he didn't remember what happened after he was shot by Alvarez. He might think differently about his current alliances if he had seen me impale Rosalita on the twisted frame of the car.

"This shit is spooky," Sean said.

"Really? Spooky?" Melissa mocked him, swinging the Benelli right to clear a street corner bodega. Much of the newsprint scattered on the sidewalk was from the almost empty racks in front of the corner convenience stand. The candy bars from the rack and the beverages from the dead refrigerator were long gone. "Who are you? Shaggy?"

"More like Scooby-Doo," Jude interjected. She expertly cleared the broken glass window display of a fashion boutique, the naked mannequin staring at Jude with painted eyes and a lipstick smirk.

"Rhutt-rho," Sean said at the curb of 40th Street, raising his closed fist in the air. "Dead heads halfway down the block." We moved to Sean's position, Heinz keeping Westsmith in a doorway close to the corner of the building. A dozen FRACs were milling about, interested in something in a dumpster in the middle of the street. One FRAC slapped at its top with her arms, while others used their shoulders to move the garbage bin a few inches at a time.

"They're occupied," I said. "Let's leave them to whatever has their attention."

"Agreed," Jude said, cringing with each bang of the lid.

Sean nodded and moved slowly across 40th Street to the cover of the building on the north side. The FRACs paid him no mind. I gestured for Jude and Melissa to do the same Still, the FRACs didn't look up from their attention at the dumpster.

"Heinz," I said.

"Right-o." He nodded. "Move, Westsmith. And, not a peep out of ya."

Westsmith put his hands up, the right one unable to reach the same height as his left. He looked tired again. They trudged through the crosswalk and joined the others several meters into the next block. Sean and Melissa scouted ahead, careful not to let anyone— or anything—flank us. The FRACs had slowed their attack of the dumpster with a WM logo emblazoned on its green side. Had they heard us? None of them looked this way, so maybe not. I waited until the majority of them faced the other end of the block.

Too many of them still had us in their periphery. Walk away, I thought at them. I envisioned them moving toward the next avenue.

They looked confused—as if the undead were still able to pull off human expressions. Some bumped into each other as they shambling away down the street, while others stood their ground and stared at the hunk of green-painted steel in front of them. Walk away, I thought. They reacted too slowly to my commands.

Finally, I was saved. A large New York City sized subway rat scurried across the street from the alley. It had grown as large as a scrawny cat, apparently finding courage or desperation in the hot sun to forage for something to eat. It sat up on its back legs and sniffed at the dumpster. A FRAC in a red nylon windbreaker—still fixated on the bin—shuffled toward the lid, effectively kicking the rodent in the process. It squeaked and scurried off to the west, capturing the walkers' attention. As the FRACs craned their necks to follow the rat's egress, I crossed the street with the barrel of my Glock sighted on Windbreaker FRAC until I disappeared behind the northwest corner of the building.

One block down. Several more to go.

23

Chicks Dig Scars

+81 Days – 1143 hours
05:39:47

Westsmith stumbled, careening hard enough into one of the first-floor store's front doors to make the pane rattle. Heinz grabbed him under the arm to stabilize him.

"What's going on?" Melissa asked. "He better not fuckin' die before we get him there."

"Don't know," Heinz said. "He's gone all pale and sweaty again."

"Christ," Melissa exclaimed, raising the shotgun. "Let me put him down."

"Nah," Heinz said with a shake of the head. "I got 'im."

Melissa and her shotgun spun about and went back to where Jude and Sean watched Westsmith's episode from the intersection of 42nd Street.

"You got him?" I asked Heinz.

"Aye," he confirmed. "I got 'im."

"Okay," I said. "Let's g–"

I screamed and dropped to the sidewalk. The pain in my abdomen was excruciating, forcing me into a fetal position. The pain was too much. People ran toward me. Someone said something about *wrong* and I distinctly heard the word *blood*.

My belly expanded under a vast internal pressure. Something escaped through my wound—my insides were coming out.

"Jesus," I heard.

Hands grabbed my face.

"…it off," Jude said.

"Wha…?" I asked.

"…take…off…," she said again.

"…uh…" I replied, the light of the day starting to fade.

Slap!

"Focus, Marine!" she ordered, her face directly in front of mine. My eyes fluttered, the lights of the world outside strobing in and out of existence. "Goddammit," Jude yelled. "Stay with me John."

Even with the daylight pulsing, I put all my effort into mapping the contours of her face. The laugh lines around her mouth and eyes. The way her eyes were predominantly one color, but with their own flecks—those of a living soul. Not the gold of the undead. The living.

Shooting pain.

A gull screamed from the distance.

"You can take it," she told me.

The gull called again. It wasn't a gull, though.

The pressure disappeared from my belly and sides. It was replaced with something wet. I smelled something ancient and metallic. Jude leaned down to my belly. A crowd of people had joined her.

Where had these spectators come from? They swayed back and forth trying to get at me. Look out, Jude!

I reached for my Glock.

Steady on, mate." Heinz put a hand over mine. Where had he come from? He sounded funny.

More pain. More words I didn't understand.

Hello, John.

A young blonde girl knelt beside me. The others' frantic words drifted away, all but mumbles in my ears.

Hello, I said to her without moving my mouth. She smiled at me and cupped her soft small hands on my cheeks.

You have seen much, haven't you?

Yes, I agreed. The gossamer sleeves of her flowing white nightgown fluttered in a breeze I couldn't feel. I longed for another puff of cool air on my face.

Are you ready to give up?

What? Why?

If I am here, then I assume you want to go?

Go where?

Back to the sea.

I don't understand.

Remember the screened-in room by the water?

With the dark skies?

Yes. Her sleeves flapped and pulled back from her arms. Two faded scars ran parallel with her forearms, the scar on the left arm deeper and longer than the one on her right. When she saw me staring at them, she pulled down her sleeves and folded her arms across her belly.

Ready?

Will it hurt anymore?

She looked to the west for a moment before answering

No. Not in the same way, at least.

My mom had once told me, 'a life without pain and misery is not a life lived with any risk'. I don't know, I told the little girl.

Oh? You have things to do? The young girl in the nightdress— who one who had visited me during my fevered dreamstate at the museum and whose physical arrival in the plaza of Rainier's Island marked the beginning of the end of the world—returned to the inside of my brain with the whispered promises of comfort and peace in a room by a fierce and powerful sea. But, even with the incentive, clouds formed behind her. She looked up at the rumbling skies before bowing her head, a pout on her lips. *I have to go.*

Why?

The Man in the Black Suit is coming.

So?

He doesn't like me meddling.

A flash of lightning.

See you soon, Mr. Walken.

She winked before disappearing.

The skies were blue and clear again.

Jude and Melissa had moved to my arms.

The buildings and streetlights moved above me. Was I floating? The blue skies disappeared, replaced by the speckled and water-stained tiles of a formerly white drop ceiling. One of the brown stains seemed very interesting, looking like the face of a bulldog.

I leave you for a minute and you bleed all over the place.

Hi, Bob. I looked past my feet. I had indeed left a trail of blood in my wake. It was deep red, laid out on the dirty laminate tiles like it was freshly brushed on bright red paint.

Westsmith was corralled on the other side of a half-filled fish tank, several small Koi floating sideways at its green and murky surface. A tri-fold dividing wall made of balsa and rice paper was propped against the wall next to them.

My stomach was no longer held in place by the restrictive brace cincher. Blood covered my compression shirt, the tactical vest cast off onto the floor. My shoulder holster with my Glock was draped over the back of a chair. I reached down to my belly. The skin was scarred and pocked, but I didn't find any gaping holes. Another wave of cramps hit, involuntarily constricting all of my stomach muscles and forcing me to curl up on the floor.

Like a baby.

I stared at Bob, wishing he would go away in favor of the little blond girl. She had a better bedside manner.

The pain was akin to hundreds of mining drills spinning under my skin, trying to get out instead of burrowing deeper. Blood bubbled out of my skin where the pain was the worst. A mass of whitehead pus oozed out of my pores like an erupting zit. When it had escaped, it fell off my belly and onto the bloody tiles. It wasn't pus—more like marshmallows. The expanding foam in my side had decided to exit my body all at once. "Christ!" I yelled out in pain as more of the expanded pellets forced their way out.

"What the fuck?" Sean exclaimed. "Why is that shit coming out? Lee said it would dissolve."

"The foam ain't supposed to do that," Heinz concurred, shaking his head. "Never saw it happen in the field before. Crazy-ass military toys."

Jude grabbed my hand and squeezed. Her voice was bordering on shrill. "I don't know. I don't know."

"Sorry," I croaked, knowing I squeezed back harder than intended as her face contorted into a grimace of her own pain.

"It's okay," she said, her eyes darting at the foam seeping from my skin. She tightened her grip on my hand in spite of her discomfort. I didn't realize why until the next wave of cramps came. It felt like I was being stabbed repeatedly.

"Fuuk." I tried to curse, but it ended up more a ragged hiss. Pellets, like marshmallows, erupted through my skin. They gathered on the surface to soak up a bit of the blood pooled on my belly before they rolled off.

"Look at me," Jude ordered, her eyes glistening with tears and her jaw clenching. Her own eyes betrayed her as they darted to my side. "Look at me."

Melissa stared out the door to the street.

It felt like I was being stabbed repeatedly with a sharpened tooth brush in the side. Then, suddenly, the pain disappeared. My body relaxed and my breathing steadied.

"Better?" Jude asked. I searched her face. She nodded so slightly I almost missed it. "Your face is smoothing out. I think the worst is over."

The cramps were gone, replaced by a dull muscle ache with each deep breath. It was like the pain you get the day after suffering a 3am charlie horse. "I think I'll be okay," I said.

"Good," Sean said. "You're scaring the shit out of us."

And by *us*, Sean meant him.

I lifted myself up to my elbows, the cramps in my abdomen feeling like I just finished a five hundred sit-up marathon. But the amazing news was the gaping hole in my belly from the helicopter crash had healed over completely. My side was still laced with a ragged series of hard scars, but I was whole again.

"There's something seriously wrong with you," Melissa muttered, looking at all of the foam pellets on the dirty tile floor around me. "Seriously wrong."

24

Hungry Thirty Minutes Later

+81 Days – 1156 hours

05:26:25

We sat for a while in the Chinese take-out restaurant. The others deserved a breather.

No rest for you, of course.

We were burning daylight.

Always so gung-ho, my boy.

Ooh-rah.

Yes...yes... ooh-rah.

We had humped a few miles since the shuttle crash. It was only a few hours since we left Rosalita behind with a picture of her boy in her hand, even though it already felt like a lifetime ago.

You cannot blame yourself. She was beyond saving.

If that's true, then the same could be said for me.

You're a special case, Sergeant.

My parole officer said the same, too.

Oh? Do tell.

Melissa stood guard at the door, her eyes darting up and down the Avenue for anything out of place. Sean and Jude huddled at the counter. They didn't say anything to each other, Jude content to lean against the Formica while Sean punched the buttons of the cash register in the hopes of opening the till. Westsmith sat in a chair at one of the three tables in the front of the restaurant. He still looked feverish as sweat beaded on his forehead. It was hard to imagine an establishment was considered a restaurant when only six people were able to eat in its dining room at the same time.

Maybe he has an infection from all the knife and bullet wounds.
One could only hope.

We might as well still be at Creedmoor. Even though the R&R corporate tower loomed above us a few avenues away, it seemed as if it was painfully out of reach. Heinz pulled the remaining napkins from the dispenser sitting on a shelf located above the trash bin and pushed them into our prisoner's hands. Westsmith took them and dabbed at his brow. Heinz ran his meaty hand across his scruffy chin, attempting to rub some life back into his body through his face. Everyone looked like they could drop from exhaustion at any moment.

Except Melissa.

She held the stock of the shotgun against her thigh as if she was desperate for it to be part of her. She continued her vigil while the rest of us recovered. She was an unstoppable superwoman.

Except, just like Superman, we have found her kryptonite.

Yeah. Tunnels.

Wet tunnels.

I'm sure there was a story behind the phobia.

Maybe she was doing her laundry in the basement of her off-campus apartment in San Francisco when an earthquake caused the building to collapse on top of her. Maybe it burst a water main and she was trapped in the rubble with the water rising all around her.

I shook my head at him. He shrugged and smiled at me through the grime and water of the fish tank. The Koi drifted in the still water, one of their tails and fins slowly pulling apart from the rest of its body. Bob tapped on the glass, making no sound but somehow causing minute ripples on the surface of the water.

Or, maybe I just imagined it.

Bob tapped the glass again. More ripples cut across the top of the water. The floor vibrated under me. Melissa felt the doorframe for a moment before backing into the restaurant with the rest of us. There was an audible rumble from the empty avenue.

"Motorcycles?" Sean asked, his interest torn away from the cash register. He went to the window while Jude helped me to my feet. It was still difficult to stand up straight, but my core was intact. "Definitely cycles," he confirmed. "Damn buildings make it sound like it's coming from everywhere."

"We go out?" Melissa asked.

"Wiser to let them pass, yeah?" Heinz said. "In my opinion."

"I agree with Heinz," I said, calculating the supplies of our firepower. "We aren't in any shape to take on whatever's coming."

"Maybe they're friendlies?" Jude offered.

"Whoever they are," Sean said, "they have numbers and the run of the streets."

"And we don't need to take any chances," I advised. The rumble got louder in the otherwise silent air. I went for my shoulder holster. Westsmith shot from his chair and flipped over the table.

"What the blood–?" Heinz yelled.

Westsmith side kicked Heinz in the chest, sending him flying off his feet into the edge of the counter and the restaurant menus on racks there. Our prisoner grabbed the back of his chair and hurled it at me. It cracked against my wrist. The shoulder holster fell to the floor. Westsmith charged at me with the second table in his hands like a battering ram.

BLAM!

The tabletop splintered from Melissa's shot before Westsmith drove it into me. He shoved it—and me—into an empty wire snack bag rack. Jude fired off-balanced over my shoulder. Her shot went high. Westsmith swept up my holster and Glock.

There it goes, again!

He slammed into Melissa's ribcage, sending her against the doorframe. Her Benelli fell from her hands to the tiles. Westsmith grabbed that, too, as he fled to the sidewalk. He bolted to the right across the plate glass window, his injuries not slowing him down at all. Melissa got to her feet and stared with rage at her empty hands for a second before she ran out after Westsmith.

"Wait," I ordered.

She either didn't hear me or didn't care. Sean helped Jude to her feet. Heinz bumped me as he ran out after Westsmith and Melissa. The others did the same. We were leaving the restaurant in worse condition than we had found it, a trail of blood and strange gooey puffs like marshmallows on the tiles between the overturned furniture and displays.

The rumbles of the approaching motorcycles grew louder. The possibility of a new threat didn't make a difference, though, as everyone was in pursuit of our escaped quarry.

25

Anarchy

+81 Days – 1204 hours
05:18:41

It only took a block before we caught up with Melissa and Heinz. She had already tackled Westsmith to the ground, her knee pressed into the middle of his back. Heinz had disarmed him, the Benelli barrel to the back of Westsmith's neck. I could see my Glock shoved into Heinz's waistband. When I approached, he promptly handed it over.

"Gotta keep a better watch of your sidearm, Sergeant," Heinz advised. "Never know what hooligan is going to run off with it."

I shrugged into my shoulder holster and put the Glock back where it belonged. "Thanks."

The rumble continued to get louder.

Someone was hollering along with it.

"We need to get off the street," I said.

Sean tore open a garbage bag with his knife, spilling its greasy contents all over the curb. Maggots feasted on the rotting remains, swimming and wriggling their engorged bodies around with the disturbance. Sean shook out and twisted the plastic enough to tie it several times around Westsmith's wrists. After he was secure, Melissa and Sean pulled him to his feet. His face was bleeding, scraped up from the collision with the sidewalk.

Heinz reluctantly took the shotgun barrel away from Westsmith's neck, but gave the weapon over to Melissa where he knew it belonged. He drew his own sidearm and put Westsmith's head in its steel sights.

"The motorcycles are still coming," Sean said.

Where would we go? We could retreat to the United Nations Building or try for the R&R Building while we still had room to maneuver. I pointed and started walking uptown. We hugged the buildings as we jogged single-file toward 43rd street. I peeked around the granite block corner of a Nike Store. Seven bikers stood astride their motorcycles.

So much for having room to maneuver.

The bikes were a mix of BMWs, Harleys, and Suzukis, but all were accessorized with the vestiges of the dead. There were FRAC heads on pikes, their jaws still snapping slowly. One of the Harleys had what looked like a length of intestines wrapped around its handlebars. The riders were as eclectic as their rides. Ranging from a bespeckled nerd to tweed vested hipster, to an actual 1970s era metal-spiked, leather-clad, porn-mustached muscle head, they were an odd assortment. The end of the world did indeed bring people of all walks of life together.

"Don't fuckin' believe it," Heinz complained as the bikers revved their cycles and howled into the air like a pack of wolves. "It's only been three months into the fuckin' end and its already an off-Broadway production of *Road Warrior* out there."

Warriors... come out and play!

Wrong movie.

Is it?

I waved the others back, glad the store didn't have windows on both corners. The last thing we needed was the bikers to see us. The rumble on 43rd street wasn't loud enough to include the entire contingent, so more riders must be out there terrorizing the streets— just not visible yet.

We were too exposed.

Bad sightlines.

No cover.

Were the walkers still on 40th Street? It would seem the dumpster FRACs should have been distracted enough by the mufflers and cycle revving to investigate. I waved everyone back the way we came. "Move,"

What were our viable options? We weren't a match for men on motorcycles. It would be like an infantry going against a cavalry. We needed a choke point. 42nd Street was a wide thoroughfare, but even filled with abandoned cars it wouldn't be enough to keep the riders from running us down. We moved across the street—passed the Consulate General of Brazil residence and office—cutting west on 41st Street until we returned to the westbound tunnel exit ramp we had come up from. If we got back to the barricade containers, we would have ample cover. I looked over my shoulder at the R&R tower. All the time we had spent getting closer to the R&R tower had been a waste.

"What the fuc…?" Sean's words were drowned out, motorcycle exhaust bellowing as three bikers raced straight at us. They yelled like Apache warriors riding into battle. The lead bike had a steel tube welded to its bitch seatback. At its top was a long-haired female FRAC head with its mouth agape. The biker's tongue stuck out the side of his mouth as he leaned into the handlebars for greater aerodynamics. He wore vintage brown leather aviator goggles with a matching leather jacket, his spiking hair swept back in the windstream. Lucky for them the new world didn't have pesky helmet laws or noise ordinances.

I swept the others behind. The Glock was in my hand and my finger felt the smooth composite material of the trigger. Sean pulled

Jude close. Heinz grabbed Westsmith's garbage bag restraints, forcing him to his knees. Melissa seethed with anger, her Benelli coming up.

The bikers were thirty meters away. The leader had an oversized yellow button pinned to his jacket. In the middle, in a red scrawl, was a capital A.

The universal symbol for anarchy.

The motorcycles slowed, exhaust lazily rising into the air from the puttering mufflers. The bikers' rebel yells elongated and drew out like playing back a video tape at half speed. The breeze stopped. I heard the leader's heartbeat, slowly racing with adrenaline. I heard the other bikers' heartbeats, too. All of them were elevated, even in this slowed-down moment of time.

Five heartbeats thudded behind me.

The man in the lead—Goggles—was twenty-five meters away. His gang flanked either side of him, trailing back a bike length. The hammers of Melissa's Benelli clicked. Endless seconds later, vaporized gunpowder blew out from the end of the barrel. I could see the individual swirls of vapor and smoke as the gases expanded. Goggles slowly reacted to the blast when he was twenty meters away, his expression changing from drug-induced elation to mortal concern. Melissa's buckshot glinted like balls of silver as the sunlight hit them. It seemed like a full minute had gone by before the shot had traveled between us and Goggles.

In what seemed like an eternity, the two opposite and opposing forces tested a couple of Newton's Laws. Goggles straightened up when the buckshot tore through his jacket. While his bike still lunged forward, he pitched backward off the bike. I stepped left and grabbed the motorcycle's welded pike with my right hand, using its own momentum to swing it away from my people. It careened into

Goggles' right-hand man. They collided hard, crashing into the concrete rail.

"Down." Sean's voice dragged out for several seconds. I dropped to one knee as he fired at the remaining biker. The bullet ripped through his right eye socket, spattering blood and matter across the white stars of the Confederate flag waving behind the seat. His death grip pulled the bike to the left, crushing the front suspension and flipping over the concrete divider and propelling the rider completely out of sight.

"Arghh," came a scream to our left. Goggles' right-hand rider strained against the frame of the bike tangled on top of him. When he saw us staring at him, he stopped his attempt to escape the wreckage and tried to reach for the gun holstered at his hip. "Fuck." He groaned, his arm pinned and his fingers failing to get around the grip. "Cock-a-doodle-doo, fuckers."

"How many are you?" I asked, the world revving back up to normal speed.

"Infinite, man," he said, laughing until his bruised or broken ribs turned it into a cough. "We fucking own this city. It's time to get up and collect."

"Not anymore, you don't," Sean added.

The rider spit at us, managing to hit my boot. "Cock-a-fuckin-doo."

I watched it a moment as it dripped off the toe. When I looked back at him, his smile of many missing teeth collapsed. He mistook what he saw in my eyes with what I felt in my heart.

He sees rage.

What I felt was sorrow.

"Do we leave him?" The biker's eyes darted from me to Sean.

"Seems cruel," Jude replied.

"Guys." Melissa's voice registered.

"So does killing an unarmed man, mate," Heinz offered his opinion. "Or, at least to say he can't get to his gun."

I pulled my Glock and pointed it at the trapped biker.

He puffed out his cheeks in hyperventilation as he realized his last day would be today. The Glock in my hand would make sure of it. "Cock-a-doodle-doodle-doo."

"Guys!" Melissa's call was more insistent. We turned as one to Melissa. Even the dentally-challenged biker cocked his head in her direction. She stared at a trail of blood. It followed the path the biker with Sean's bullet in his brain had taken. The red trail swiped against the concrete rail and spread out at the top.

Goggles had survived. Now, he was gone.

"Oh, shit!" the tangled rider exclaimed. "You gonna get it now. Doodle-doo! Anarchy loves company."

26

Rio Grande

+81 Days – 1217 hours
05:05:44

Now we had two prisoners.

"Fuckin' cock-a-doodle fucker." Rooster spat at me, his hands bound like Westsmith's.

Should have left him.

Probably would have been the smart play.

Or, should have killed him.

It's done. I'm not looking for more input on the matter.

He is going to slow you down.

I needed leverage in case Anarchy returned for his man.

Sean had a hand on the leather vest of our new biker prisoner, while Heinz continued his vigilance with handling Westsmith. Jude and Melissa walked side by side in the middle of our now growing column. Jude had tucked Rooster's revolver into the back of her waistband. Her clothes were a bit dusty and the soles of her boots looked a little thinner. She looked thinner, too.

As do you, John.

Do I? I know some shit just oozed out of me a while ago, but I don't feel lighter.

Make no mistake. You carry the weight of the dead across your shoulders. And, the albatross will only get heavier with every step you take.

Thanks, Dr. Phil.

What were you thinking?

I chuckled out loud at Bob's surprisingly spot-on southern twanged impersonation. I covered my mouth with my forearm and faked a cough as Melissa turned her head.

It would be strange for you to be happy in the apocalypse.

Wouldn't want that.

Nope. Would not want them to add more to a list supporting their belief you are, indeed, crazy.

I'm talking to you, aren't I?

We walked west on East 37th Street, passing the aptly named Tunnel Exit Street. A grid system, coupled with obvious street names. New Yorkers did try to make it easy for themselves to get around.

You should see the subway system. It is anything but simple!

At the next intersection, 3rd Avenue, we stopped under the tattered awning of a neighborhood market across the street from the El Rio Grande on the northwest corner. The roll-up security grille had been ripped off the header. The doors to the market themselves were wide open, their tempered glass shattered.

Jude wrinkled her nose.

Melissa covered her mouth and made a retching noise.

"Shit," Sean muttered.

"Worse than that," Melissa said between gulps.

The strong odor of spoiled meat and fish drifted out to us on a weak, but hot current of air. The shelving had been ransacked and overturned. There wasn't one can or box of non-perishable food left in the store. The rolling aluminum bins, usually filled with ice and wheeled to the sidewalks with fruit or fresh meat, sat inside the doors. They were filled with the disintegrating sludge of what some may have guessed to be fish.

I listened for the rumble of motorcycles.

Jude tapped me on the shoulder.

"Yeah?" I whispered.

"We gotta keep moving," she advised nervously. "You know guarding two people is going to get flakey, fast?" She almost hissed out the word *people*, as if to classify them as such was close to being painful.

"I know, Jude," I replied. "Nothing feels right."

"I don't think anything is ever going to feel right again," she admitted.

"I hear you," I said, "but, I mean the city is all wrong."

"What do you mean?"

"No people," I explained. "Is it actually possible there aren't any survivors besides these bikers? Eight million people and all we get are wasteland scavengers and a few dumpster FRACs?"

"The food was taken," Jude observed for herself. "Maybe everyone left is holed up somewhere to keep away from the gangs and the dead heads."

"Maybe," I said, assessing the windows in each building above us. Jude's assessment was correct. We needed to get downrange.

Or uptown, as the locals would say.

I was used to Middle Eastern towns where villagers would stay indoors. Of course, the opposing side's snipers would usually use the same buildings for cover, too. Those streets had been deserted and too quiet. Those towns had never felt right.

And time is winding down, is it not? No time to settle into an overwatch. Chop! Chop!

The Gaunt Man stood in the middle of the next intersection, at East 38th and 3rd Avenue. He looked almost human under the dead streetlights, the avenue running straight into the distance until its edges started to converge toward a single point.

Rooster started grumbling in a low voice. Westsmith muttered some unintelligible chant under his breath. His hands clutched at the wound in his chest where I had stabbed him.

"Cocka-doodle-doo," Rooster sang, as if he hoped he and Westsmith could start their own singing group.

A hammer clicked. Sean held the barrel of his sidearm against one of the biker's nostrils. Rooster raised his bound hands and stared cross-eyed at the gun, stopping his rant as quickly as he had started.

It was almost too comical to interrupt.

Almost.

"Let's move out," I ordered, only the slightest upturn of my lips giving away my amusement.

27

The Rooster Says...
+81 Days – 1225 hours
04:57:13

The top of the single black spire of the Roanoke and Raleigh Corporate Tower was still visible from this angle at street level. The rest of the massive obelisk was partially obscured by a thickening cloud cover and the 600 Third Avenue property ahead of us. A FedEx office and packing center occupied its first floor, but the less-than-extraordinary 1970s architectures paled in comparison to what the R&R engineers had erected on the ashes of the former Metlife site a few blocks away.

I didn't know much about the Manhattan cityscape besides the obvious landmarks, but I remembered the day the tourist helicopter had crashed on the Metlife rooftop. It had caused a multiple-explosion, multiple-story collapse leaving the property owners and Metlife to wonder whether to rebuild or abandon the property. The massive loss of life from the incident—and the billions of dollars paid out from the ensuing lawsuits—clinched the final decision of the company to abandon the idea to rebuild their New York headquarters.

"We should cross," Sean advised, pointing across Third Avenue. "We need to go that way."

We moved in a single file across the avenue, making our way along 39th Street. The street was eerily empty, not just of pedestrians but of the congestion of vehicles. Parking in the city would forever be easier. We passed a pristine 1982 Cutlass Ciera parked at the curb next to an alley. It was definitely my grandfather's Oldsmobile.

Westsmith coughed and suddenly doubled over.

"Quit fuckin' about!" Heinz grabbed him by the collar and dragged him upright.

Rooster started laughing.

Sean struck the biker in the ear with the butt of his sidearm.

"Owie," Rooster said, although he didn't seem to feel much pain.

Groans erupted from the alley. A flash of red lunged at Heinz. He swung his rifle around toward it, managing to get the barrel between him and the nylon jacketed FRAC from earlier in the day. Heinz let go of Westsmith in order to face the walker straight on, purposefully dropping his guard to let the FRAC get closer. The merc rammed his forehead into Red Jacket's nose, driving the shambling walker back enough for him to pull his rifle up into a full draw. Red Jacket lunged again, moaning loudly. Heinz thrust the barrel of the M4 into its gaping maw and pulling the trigger. The back of Red Jacket's head blasted open in a mist of blood and skull fragments. The gore sprayed itself onto the face of two other walkers shuffling out of the alley's mouth. They paid it no mind as they snarled at us with their lips peeled back to show their blackened teeth and gums.

Red Jacket's herd had grown substantially. With him lying on the sidewalk with his brains oozing out onto the concrete, the others shambled around and over him to get to us. One of the younger FRACs stepped directly in the pool of Red Jacket's blood. The soles of his once-expensive Nike Air Jordan's left their familiar circular patterns on the ground as he walked. In an act of defiance, his baggy jeans defied gravity as the waistband clung to his top of his scrawny hips. In the hopes his hip-hop fashion style would end, I shot him in the forehead. BaggyPants' head snapped back. His body twisted and his pants dropped to his ankles a moment before he dropped to his knees. Typical.

We fired into the marching horde.

Melissa notched her Benelli's barrel to a cylinder choke and fired a wide spray into the three walkers closest to her. The middle FRAC took the majority of the shot, its head shearing clear off from the jaw line up. The others took enough shot to the head to stop their brains from having any further ideas. They collided together, looking like two friends who were propping a drunk friend up as they hailed him a cab.

He does seem to be a bit light-headed.

Not now, Bob. He stood between me and the herd in the alleyway.

And I do not think they are going to find a cab at this time of day.

Shut up, Bob. I fired through his heart. Bob covered his chest with his arms.

How rude!

A FRAC, whose head barely came up to the Gaunt Man's armpit, fell through Bob's spectral form to the alleyway apron. Low Altitude FRAC skidded to a stop on top of the debris and runoff in the gutter.

You saved me! My hero!

Jude and Sean stood side-by-side, taking out the walkers with practiced precision. One headshot equaled one dead walker. Heinz squeezed the trigger of the M4, smoothly pivoting at the waist to center the next forehead and squeeze the trigger again. He was indeed a seasoned operator. Melissa moved to flank the alleyway from the left side. She stood behind one of the yellow-painted steel pipe bollards. A FRAC cleared the corner of the building. Her Benelli blew out both sides of its head. Chunks of muscle and bone burst from its ear to embed into the side of the face of the one next to it, shutting down the second walker, too.

I hopped up onto the hood of the Cutlass, scuffing what had been a shiny pearl white paint job. My grandpa worked for General Motors for forty years before he retired to Florida with a fantastic pension and a love for the products he had helped produce.

Shit.

From the higher vantage point, I saw the alley was a quarter full of moaning FRACs. They slowly bunched together in an effort to get around the bodies piling up at the mouth of the alley. I fired at the walkers in the middle of the pack, pulling the trigger until the magazine was empty. At this rate, we would run out of ammunition long before we mowed through the alley FRACs—assuming any more walkers attracted to the gunfire didn't pour in behind them from the other end.

I checked my six. Two FRACs walked toward us from Third Avenue. I holstered the Glock and unslung the M4 to a full draw with the tailstock tight to the pit of my shoulder. I had always felt comfortable with a weapon in my hands. Center the sights. Adjust for the angle and any wind, even at close range. Breathe. Squeeze. Center next target. Adjust. Breathe. Squeeze. All this occurred in less than two seconds.

Melissa and Heinz continued to shoot into the ongoing FRAC herd. The biker was on his knees between Jude and Sean, clapping his hands together nervously as much as the bindings would allow.

I pivoted toward Lexington Avenue. There were no FRACs coming flanking us. Someone was hobbling away, though. Westsmith was trying to use his teeth to get out of his garbage bag restraints as he ran.

Sonofabitch.

I rested the M4 on the palm of my hand, settled the weapon into my shoulder again, and breathed out before I squeezed the trigger. The report from the muzzle echoed through the urban canyon. A quarter second later, Westsmith screamed and tripped over his feet as he fell to the street. It was most likely from the bullet graze through the meat on the outside of his left calf. As the echoes faded, it was replaced by something else. The rumble of motorcycles had returned, louder this time.

As Westsmith struggled to get up to his feet—with Heinz's bullet wound through his left thigh and now mine through his right calf—the first Harley Davison came around the corner of Lexington Avenue and 39th Street from the south. Goggles, with his brown leather jacket now sporting holes in addition to his Anarchy button, led a convoy of seven other riders. Some I recognized from their revving session earlier, while three others were new to the patrol. Goggles—or maybe I was supposed to call him Anarchy—kicked out the Harley's stand, dismounted and approached our escaping prisoner.

Westsmith put up one hand in a warding off or surrendering gesture, speaking to Anarchy and shaking his head. Anarchy—nope, I was going to stick with calling him Goggles—nodded and put his revolver away. Goggles waved to his other riders. Two of them revved their engines, spun their back tires and accelerated toward us.

Breathe.

Squeeze.

The left rider, with human ribcage bones around his own chest, took a bullet to the helmet visor. His front wheel shook for a moment before the Yamaha slid out from underneath his now dead body. He still held onto the clutch, the momentum of the bike dragging him for several meters across the street.

The other rider, distracted by the loss of his companion, clipped the front tire of his bike over the debris from the housing of a downed streetlamp. He jettisoned over the handlebars like an equestrian rider being tossed off a horse during a failed steeplechase obstacle, landing face first into a pothole. Even from this distance, the sickening crack of his neck could be heard. His body flipped over to a skidding stop, his shirt catching on the ground and tearing up the meat around his spine.

"Get the fuck off me," Melissa yelled. I pivoted, shooting a walker who had managed to grab the barrel of Melissa's shotgun before she had been able to pump a new shell into the breach. His brain matter splattered against the brick. As he slumped against the wall, the FRAC dragged the shotgun down with him. Melissa gritted her teeth, the muscles straining in her shoulders and neck to keep possession of the shotgun.

I fired again. This time, the walker's hand separated from the rest of the arm at its wrist. Melissa staggered backward, her efforts to pry the gun back now meeting with zero resistance. She slammed against a roll-up door leading to an underground parking garage.

I continued to pull the trigger, thinning the herd coming out of the mouth of the alley. The bodies were stacking up, forming a helpful low barrier to keep the awkward FRACs from getting to us as quickly. More walkers filled in the alleyway from the other end.

You did love your grandfather's Oldsmobile, didn't you?

This wasn't working. I jumped down from the hood and opened the driver's door. The interior was pristine and still had a new car smell. The owner had loved his car, probably crushed he had to abandon it. Ripping out the steering column cover, I re-familiarized myself with the wiring. Nothing had changed since my days of misspent youth. I pulled two of the wires out, shaved the exposed ends with my tactical knife and touched them together. I heard the sizzle and smelled the ozone of electricity, but nothing happened. I tried again. This time the dashboard lit up and the motor turned over. I tied the wires together and revved the engine.

The others looked back at the Cutlass. I pressed on the horn. Melissa backed up another couple steps, still firing at the FRACs passing into her line of sight. Jude and Sean grabbed Rooster under his armpits and dragged him into the middle of the street. Heinz followed them in his retreat, still firing at the wall of undead. I revved the engine until it red-lined. Jamming my left foot into the clutch, I put the sedan in first gear. Popping the clutch, I sent the front wheels of the Cutlass spinning and smoking. The car jumped the curb as I aimed it directly at the mouth of the alley. The American-made steel bounced over several rotting bodies before it crashed into the wall where Melissa had been standing.

I extracted myself from the formerly classic and well-maintained car, not bothering to close the driver's door. I pulled the Glock and shot two FRACs in the side of the head who were still trying to get through a small opening between the wall and the back fender, now effectively plugging up the gap.

I looked toward Lexington Avenue. Goggles and the other riders were gone. And, worst of all, Westsmith was gone right along with them.

"The rooster says," our remaining bargaining chip told us, "cock-a-doodle-doo!"

28

Rage Against the Machine

+81 Days – 1237 hours
04:45:16

With the FRACs unable to escape from this end of the alley, we raced down to Lexington Avenue. Goggles, Westsmith and the gang of bikers were gone. Their revving engines were a distant and fading rumble.

"How the fuck did they disappear so quickly?" Heinz asked. "The only thing I hear are the goddamned walkers in the alley."

"Why didn't they hit us from other angles?" Melissa asked.

"I shot two coming in from Second Avenue," I said, "but I think they were strays from somewhere else."

"Westsmith brought them," Jude surmised.

"What?" Sean asked.

"Come on, mate," Heinz said. "Remember the army of robed undead back at Creedmoor?"

"Yeah." Sean nodded slowly. "Seems too surreal to be real."

"Every time he's ready to drop," Jude mentioned, "the shit and the FRACs start hitting the fan. And whenever we distract or knock him out, things go back to normal."

Westsmith controlled the FRACs. Why didn't we connect those dots before?

Maybe, because Westsmith did not want you to remember.

So, Westsmith was able to cloud our minds?

Seems likely, does it not?

"Shit," I said. "Westsmith's able to control the dead and made

133

us forget about it."

"Seems obvious now, doesn't it?" Heinz remarked.

"Something Dick should have warned us about," Sean added.

"Maybe he didn't know," Heinz speculated. "Alvarez never mentioned anything after her briefings. Can't ask her now."

And what about Ms. Alvarez?

Westsmith controlled the dead. Alvarez wasn't a walker.

Wasn't she?

Stop the riddles, Bob.

She died in the desert. And was brought back.

She *had* died. I had been helpless to save her. She had died on the gurney in the medical tent with the wind spraying sand against the tent flaps and the smell of copper, salt, and diesel fuel in the oppressive stagnant heat of its interior.

He controls the dead.

My thoughts went back to the shuttle bus.

The emergency exit becoming a black void. Tendrils, like some inter-dimensional horror straight out of a Lovecraft story, slithering their way into our world. The maggots burrowing out from Rosalita's temples. Westsmith controlled her? He made her shoot Heinz and fight me?

You know he did.

Yes. Westsmith had expended a lot of his energy making sure none of us remembered how to connect the dots about his abilities. Rosalita had been under Westsmith's control and I had killed her. Rosalita would still be alive if I hadn't let her get shot in the mountain foothills of the Middle East.

You continue to miss the point.

Do I?

You cannot redirect the path of a bullet.

I could have shot the shooter before he squeezed the trigger.

Lay your blame and anger at their rightful feet.

Westsmith was responsible for at least three deaths. Dick, sitting in his plushy ergonomic executive office chair in his high castle, was responsible for countless others.

Focus on that.

"If Westsmith pulls any mind control shit after we find him, shoot him." I looked at my Cobra, the one incisor puncture in the nylon catching my attention for longer than it should have. "We have less than five hours."

Melissa circled the intersection, alternately looking at the road or far off into the distance as far as the street or avenue allowed.

"We going to be able to hunt them down in time?" Sean asked. "We have no idea where they went off to."

"It was maybe thirty seconds after I got the car running," I said.

"And they obviously didn't go past us," Jude added.

"Don't think they went off straight the other way, either," Heinz said. "We would've caught a glimpse of 'em."

"They retreated downtown or went up Lexington," Sean surmised.

"And they're close," I said.

"How you figure?" Sean asked.

"The mufflers," Melissa answered for me. "They faded into silence way too quick."

I nodded.

"Parking garages?" Sean said with a shrug.

"Makes sense." Heinz nodded.

"Hate to tell you," Sean said, his hands out in surrender. "I would need a phone app to figure out where all the parking garages are. Impossible to memorize them all."

"That's not going to be a problem," Melissa stated with confidence, crouching down with her shotgun across her thighs.

"Oh, yeah?" Sean asked in disbelief.

"Yeah," Melissa shot back.

I walked over to Melissa. A pothole was a few feet in front of her. Fresh flakes of chrome had scraped on the lip of the concrete depression. On the road beyond were tiny streaks of fluid. Not a lot, but just enough to form an intermittent trail.

I checked the street heading downtown.

No fluid.

I extended a hand to Melissa. She took it and allowed me to help her up. I squeezed her hand for a moment before letting her fingers go. In response, she gave me the widest smile I had ever seen on her face since meeting her. It wasn't much more than a slight upturn of the corners of her lips and a show of teeth, but she understood how important her discovery was.

In the distance, not more than five streets and two avenues to our northwest, the black and silver of the R&R tower glistened in the daylight. The sun absorbed into the building's onyx surface, using the window's silver surfaces to reflect razor sharp and blinding glints of light.

At least we were going to be moving in the right direction.

"Looks like we're heading uptown," I said.

29

24-Hour Parking

+81 Days – 1242 hours
04:40:28

The trail took us to north for one block on Lexington Avenue before it cut over the sidewalk and continued leaving drops west on 40th Street. We stopped at the southwest corner so I could peer around the edge of a building toward Park Ave. On the opposite side of the street—mid-block—was a huge black aluminum sign with the words PARK emblazoned across it in large white capital letters. In addition, a tall sign with the same letters stacked vertically was affixed next to the first sign. In case any tourists were still unsure about how Quik Park managed to handle so many cars, white circles with red down-facing arrows were included on each sign to advise all vehicles would be parked underground.

Three of Goggles' men milled about in front of the entry, each outfitted with a rifle, sidearm, and knife. One of them bummed a cigarette from the second guy before demanding a light from the last. In spite of the cigarette bandit ordering the other two around, they made fun of the fact he was so ill prepared. Cigarette Bandit man lit up the bummed cigarette with the borrowed Bic lighter before the lighter disappeared into his own pocket. His eyes were dark and his brow heavy, giving off a much different tone than his smiling face.

I backed away from the corner.

Sean's stomach growled. "Sorry," he said, holding his belly with both hands. "I had a great breakfast here once." The menus from the restaurant were still readable through their glass cases next to the wide-open double doors. Unlike the market, the scent coming from the restaurant smelled of coffee beans and stale pastries. A decided step up from rotting fish.

"Shit," Jude whispered. I looked back at her, tears streaming down her face. Jude caught me appraising her and dried her tears with the sleeve of her shirt.

"What?" I asked softly.

She nodded in the direction of the other side of the street. On the northwest corner was a Starbucks Coffee. I was surprised we hadn't passed several more before now. Maybe we had and hadn't noticed. Biker gangs and herds of the undead tended to draw one's attention away from Seattle's finest caffeinated export. Jude had found April and Lenny shacked up at a Starbucks.

The lovebirds.

Scarce time had passed since Lenny's death. April hopefully had begun to process her grief while she waited for our return. The rest of us would be forced to gloss over our need to grieve with the death constantly occurring around us and within our midst. Dick had seen to that.

"Plan?" Heinz asked, now concentrating on keeping Rooster from giving away our position with a pistol barrel to his tattooed neck. "Shoot them?"

I shook my head. "We need surprise on our side."

"Sightlines are atrocious for sneaking past the guards," Heinz said. "Even for idiots like these."

There were no cars on the street to crouch behind. The sidewalks were clear, with no cover. Guns were too noisy for us. Even if we all selected a target and killed them with one shot each, the reports would most likely bring the rest of the bikers out of the woodworks.

Even if we back-tracked to Park Avenue to flank the parking garage, we still wouldn't be concealed before we needed to engage the enemy.

Paper slapped against my leg.

Then, another. Two twenty dollar bills pressed against my calf from the light breeze. The Bank of America, across from us on the southeast side of the avenue, was missing most of its windowpanes. Its doors were wide open, too. Someone had tried to extract an entire ATM, managing to crack it open but leaving the money behind because the opening hadn't been wide enough to get much of it out.

Maybe FRACs scared them away. Or, maybe it had been the gangs.

Maybe. None of that mattered.

Just needed a bit more time and muscle.

The contents in the ATM were worthless. Currency had changed. At this point, Dead Presidents were going to be relegated as footnotes to storytelling, not a person's wallet.

Money has gone the way of the dinosaurs ever since electronic payments were born.

Maybe it was time for paper currency to make a comeback.

30

Makin' It Rain

+81 Days – 1256 hours
04:26:56

Rooster tapped the sidewalk with his leg. His wrists and ankles were hog-tied to a railing in front of a store a few doors away from the corner using another sacrificed garbage bag. Heinz had reluctantly handed over his bandanna to be used as a gag. I wasn't at the point where I was going to force someone—even Rooster— to have to taste the remnants of rotten city trash sticking to plastic.

Such a humanitarian.

Jude held her weapon on the biker, just in case he proved more resourceful than anticipated. I couldn't have Rooster go all MacGyver on us. Our plan was tenuous already. Heinz had positioned himself on overwatch behind an open window on the second floor above the Bank of America lobby. The barrel of his rifle was hidden from my vantage point at the café's corner. He had made sure to set up deep inside the room. Good man. Melissa was sitting on the single step of the café with her Benelli in her lap. Her eyes were closed while she ran her fingers lightly over the black composite stock. She hadn't been a fan of the plan, not because of its absurdity but because it involved another go at dark underground places.

The three sentries at the entry to the parking garage continued to smoke, having gone through at least three cigarettes each since we hatched our plan and got it underway. Goggles and his gang must have hit every bodega and liquor store in the city to make sure they could support their habits. The wind was picking up, blowing the smoke back in the boss's face as the second guard exhaled it from his nostrils like a fuming dragon.

Another twenty-dollar bill slapped at my arm in the light breeze. Another stuck to my chest for a moment before the wind plucked it away and carried it toward the parking garage. Suddenly, denominations of fives, tens, and twenties rained down into the street from above the bikers. Taking on the look of a ticker tape parade or the moment after the ball dropped in Times Square on New Year's Eve, the money floated down in a swirling cloud. Finally, after Dragon Breath sent up another plume of smoke, he noticed the money coming down. He slapped Cigarette Bandit in the arm and pointed to the sky. The last guy turned around on his own.

"Now," I whispered to Melissa.

She sprung to her feet and followed me out from the safety of the corner café, the fingertips of her left hand on my shoulder. Smaller target.

Or, at least, she is.

We moved quickly down the sidewalk opposite the bikers on the north side of the street. I had holstered the Glock in favor of the tactical knife. Rushing through the thickest downpour of raining cash, I caught sight of Dragon Breath's back as he reached up for the money. I thrust the knife blade into his side under the armpit. He gasped for a moment before I cupped his mouth with my other hand. Dragging him back to the other side of the street, I dropped him in the gutter before pulling out the knife and stabbing him in the heart with it.

I rushed across the street, the downpour of money turning into more of a drizzle. Cigarette Bandit and the other biker were more tangible than the obscured currency-hidden versions they were a minute ago.

"Ain't this the–"

The blade went into Cigarette Bandit's ear. When he started falling away, I pulled out the knife. The cast-off blood splattered onto the last guy's face. He felt the wet warmth at his face with his fingers and pulled away a red stain with it. He looked at his fingers in disbelief, trying to figure out where it had come from. He touched his fingers to his face again in search of seeping holes for a moment before I gave him a new one under his chin. The biker made involuntarily clicking noises with his tongue as he focused at me. His fingers were still smearing blood onto his cheek, never to find the new slit in the soft palate under his jaw I just gave him. His eyes closed and he dropped to his knees in front of me.

Like declaring his fidelity to you.

I kicked him over to his side, the money only coming down a few bills at a time now. I looked up at the roof of the building across the street. Sean waved at me from the parapet, showing me the last empty paper bag he had taken up to the roof with the cash from the cracked ATM.

Good thing you know your own strength. It would have taken days and the Jaws of Life to open it otherwise.

I waved for Sean to come down. He gave me a thumbs up and disappeared from the edge.

Melissa knelt on the sidewalk next to Dragon's Breath, just pulling her own tactical knife out of his eye socket. "Had to take him out," she said, blowing a stray strand of hair off her face. "He was starting to come back."

Heinz trotted up along the sidewalk against the building next to Starbucks, his rifle in a half draw. It still had the Poland Springs bottle taped to the end of the barrel. The makeshift suppressor would have been mangled and useless after the first shot, if it had been needed, but we had taken all precautions. I pulled the other two bodies over to Dragon's Breath and lined them up next to him. I patted them down, distributing the weapons to Melissa and Heinz.

I ejected the magazines of their AKs and held them up.

"Seriously?" Melissa said with a mix of disbelief and disgust. "Two each?" While they seemed to have an abundance of liquor and cigarettes, a check of the rifle magazines uncovered they were woefully lacking in the firepower category.

"Makes it a might easier, I would say," Heinz commented.

"Not for the first couple of rounds," Melissa retorted.

"Aye, true," Heinz agreed. "But their penchant for the drink will definitely keep their aim off."

The entry was still clear. The money, emptied from the ATM and from Sean's grocery bags, lay on the asphalt like a carpet. It nearly covered the entire area immediately around the parking garage entrance. Sean and Jude came up onto our position.

"What?" Melissa asked. "No asshole biker to babysit?"

"Better to leave him back," Sean answered.

"He's not going to be any use, except to be in the way," I said.

"Well, human shield is an admirable career," Melissa said with a snicker. "Maybe I should go get him. I never liked bullets much, anyway."

"He would definitely be more a handful than a help," Heinz advised. "Better to leave him for the dead."

I chose to gloss over Heinz's comment. I wondered if Rooster would encounter any walkers while tied up. The FRACs from the alley had probably dispersed by now. Some of them might come across Rooster in their search for fresh meat.

"We ready?" I asked instead. We weren't prepared for what

could be waiting for us beyond the curve of the ramp under the streets. The others knew, too, nodding in agreement anyway.

Even Melissa nodded, her eyes a bit too wide and her mouth twitching without knowing. "Only one way to find out, I guess."

31

Make It Quick

+81 Days – 1305 hours
04:17:33

We entered the Quik Park parking garage. The two lanes immediately descended on a steep angle, curving to the left after five or six meters. A convex mirror was mounted on the outer curved wall, providing visibility to any obstacles on the ramp ahead. Luckily, Goggles didn't have more men watching us through the reflection from the other side of the curve.

In single file and hugging close to the inside wall, my M4 and I led us down to the bottom of the ramp. Like in the Queens/Midtown Tunnel, the sun faded quickly as we lost more and more direct light from the street. We didn't lose complete visibility, though, as a construction light had been erected in the vehicle drop-off area. It was tied into one of several car batteries with emergency roadside jumper cables, the hope for electricity through wall outlets long gone. With the artificial light, it was easier to see inside the cashier's booth and the small adjoining waiting room. The vintage chairs had seen much better days, the paint on the tube aluminum flaking off, and the seat cushions flattened from years of overweight Midwest tourists' asses.

Otherwise, the area was empty.

"It doesn't make any sense," I whispered. It was too quiet. There were no motorcycles lined up anywhere. Goggles should have stationed more sentries here.

Heinz tapped me on the shoulder and moved past to take up the point position. There was an open bay with a freight elevator lift to take vehicles down to the lower levels.

"How do they take the bikes downstairs?" Sean asked in a low voice from over my right shoulder. "I can't imagine they got enough car batteries strung together to run the elevator."

"Maybe they have power," Heinz said, "and we just don't know it."

"Seems too obvious a dead end," I said.

"Too neat," Melissa added.

"And too organized," Jude pointed out. "These guys don't seem to be the most on-the-money bunch."

I tapped the trigger guard of the M4. There was a stairwell next to the freight elevator bay. Its door was propped open with a wood wedge. Faint light illuminated the interior of the concrete block enclosure, not as bright as the construction light in the drop-off area, but bright enough.

Heinz peeked inside, moving the barrel of his rifle in sync with his eyes as he cleared the first and second landing. He waved us forward. I moved to the point position, quickly descending to the first cutback landing. The steps to the next floor were clear, plastic caged automotive worklights strung around the inside railings with green extension cords beakoning us to journey deeper.

Faint voices drifted up from below. They weren't in the stairwell itself but from one of the main garage levels. I hugged the outside wall as I took each step, careful to keep a wary eye on each door as I approached it, the rifle's end site always leading the way.

The doors to the second and third subbasement level were closed. I wedged the side of my boot against each door as I pressed my ear against the gray painted steel. The voices were too faint to be behind either of them. I continued down to the landing between the third and fourth sublevels. The lighting was scarce here, the extension cord and string of worklights abruptly coming to an end on the railing in front of me.

I crouched down to where the walls met, and listened. Water dripped onto a hollow metal surface in triplicate before pausing. They came again in another series of three weak thumps.

The voices were louder down here, but still subdued. It was more conversational in its rhythms than the ignorant juvenile jabbering of imbeciles.

Maybe they are more sophisticated than you assumed.

The notion seemed to be a stretch, especially with Rooster and the three entrance sentries as our examples. Goggles, though, did seem to be resourceful, clever, and somewhat resilient.

The conversation waned, the humming cadence gaining longer pauses between them. There was the sound of a low long breath, labored like the final death rattle of a man with the life choked out of him. It softened, quickly replaced with quick heavy pants coming from the other side of the heavy fourth floor door.

A single sharp whistle came from the third-floor landing. Sean gestured for me to come back up. I took another look at the fourth level door before returning to the third-floor landing. Sean had a tense expression on his face, his brow furrowed and the corners of his mouth downturned and twitching. Heinz was crouched on the other side of the landing, keeping an eye on our rear.

Jude sat on the third step of the next flight of steps, rubbing her hand in a circular motion on the small of Melissa's back. Melissa sat with her head between her knees like she was battling a bout of nausea. The first real indication something was wrong was the fact the Benelli was propped against the inside railing instead of across her lap was the second. Regardless, neither of those things was as

147

distressing as what I saw when she looked up at me.

Tears streamed down her cheeks. A snot bubble was forming in her left nostril. She didn't seem to notice or try to wipe any of it away. Her pupils were dilated, even in the low light. She inhaled in shallow short bursts. Her chest didn't expand enough to let in enough oxygen. It was like her lungs didn't want to keep the CO_2 or replace it with any oxygen, either.

She was hyperventilating.

I knelt before her. Wiping a stray hair stuck in the stream of tears on her cheek, I placed the palm of my hand on her belly before putting my cheek to hers and whispering into her ear. "Just breathe." I pressed my hand into her diaphragm. "Listen to my voice. In and out. Deep breaths."

Her stomach muscles clenched and fought against me, while her brain was fighting against her body's need for oxygen in its self-preservation. Ironically, her hyperventilation was a form of her body trying to protect her. Sometimes, the mind can be fierce in what it thinks is best for the rest of the system.

"Don't think," I told her. "Just breathe. In… out." I continued to press my hand into Melissa's belly under the ribcage, forcing her to take deeper breaths. "In…out."

Relaxing my hand, I was relieved to see her taking deeper breaths all her own. I sat back on my heels. Her eyes dried a little. Or, to be more accurate, they weren't actively leaking. The snot bubble had receded. Her muscles softened.

"Deep breaths," I said again.

She complied, squeezing my hand.

"Better?" Jude asked.

Melissa continued to take deep breaths, nodding her reply.

"What's happening here?" I asked in a low voice.

"Can't take enclosed spaces," she answered between inhalations. She cringed when the water dripped again in its triple rhythm several times before tapering off again.

"Like I said before," Sean muttered, "claustrophobia."

"It's not fuckin' claustrophobia," Melissa answered with a hiss. "It's being underground. With water."

"No idea what that even means, lass," Heinz commented.

Melissa recoiled at the sound of the three drips of water thumping against metal, the water letting her know they understood what she meant.

Drip. Drip. Drip.

"It means I was trapped in an apartment laundry room when the upper floors collapsed over me," Melissa explained through gritted teeth. "It means when the pipes burst, the water flooded the entire basement and I almost fuckin' drowned. Now, do you know what I mean?"

"Aye." Heinz nodded. "I 'spect I do."

Sean also nodded. "Shit. Sorry."

"I don't need your pity," Melissa said, as if by merely giving life to her angst in words allowed her to change her paralysis to anger. "Let's get this shit done so I can get my niece back."

How did Bob know?

"Easier said than done," came a voice from below. Goggles and three of his men had their weapons trained on us from the landing between the floors. They had taken advantage of Heinz and Sean being distracted by Melissa's story.

Fuck.

"You can come quiet," Goggles said with a smile, "or me and my boys can light this here situation up. Your choice."

32

Level Up

+81 Days – 1310 hours
04:12:50

I slowly stood, my hands in the air in front of me. Heinz and Sean had their rifles up in a quarter draw, their shoulders and arms tense. Jude's hand was on Melissa's back with Melissa's shotgun still leaning against the handrail. They were both partially hidden by the stairs they were sitting on.

"You need to drop those weapons, pretty boys," Goggles said, waving his weapon between Heinz and me. "You put me in a shitty mood today. Where is your lovely girl with her boom stick?"

"Where's the hitchhiker you picked up?" I asked.

"Which one?" Goggles said with a chuckle. "We pick up so many."

"The last one," I elaborated.

"Oh! Xavier!"

"That's the one."

"He's doing fine," Goggle confirmed. "He's about as happy with you as I am, unfortunately for you. We've been comparing notes about how much we have grown to dislike you. Of course, he's had much longer to despise you. I only have the one shotgun blast to the chest."

"You seem no worse for wear," I said.

"Yeah, I clean up pretty good."

I walked closer to the edge of the landing.

Heinz spotted me in his peripheral vision, not taking his eyes off

Goggles and his goon squad. He stepped closer to the wall to give me room to work. He was the most professional mercenary I had ever met. One day, after all of this bullshit, I would have to hear more of his story. Find out on what soil his boots had landed.

"Are you going to make me shoot you, Sergeant?" Goggles asked.

"I would rather you not," I replied. "I see you've really bonded with Mr. Westsmith in the short time you've been together."

"Yes," Goggles said with a nod. "He's very chatty. Told us all sorts of interesting things about you and the big boys in the black tower. All very interesting stuff, I must say. Some of it almost too unbelievable." One of his men snickered. Goggles gave him a sideways glare. The man's expression fell quickly. "Joe here is going to come get your weapons. If either of your men raises their barrels an inch, we will lay waste to this stairwell. Do you understand?"

"Yes," I replied. "Heinz, do you understand?"

"Roger, mate."

I raised my hands a little higher and stepped down three steps to meet Goggles man. Heinz was now behind me. Jude and Melissa were still hidden behind the steel and concrete of the steps on the flight above me. Sean was in the middle of the landing, in the open.

Joe, the goon who had snickered at Goggles' words, ascended the steps. He held his sidearm on me, the sights on the center of my face. The other two bikers had their guns raised. Their barrels moved from Heinz to Sean to me. Joe slung his Winchester rifle to free up his hands. He reached for my Glock.

Nope.

I grabbed his wrist. Bent back his hand. Spun him around and crouched behind him. Goggles fired, true to his word. The Man Who

Snickered became the Man without a face. I flung him down the stairs. Heinz fired, taking out the second of Goggles men with a practiced headshot.

Sean fired. He clipped the last goon high in the shoulder.

I drew my Glock. Goggles launched himself down the flight of stairs. My first shot ricocheted off the steel railing. The second caught Sean's biker in the cheek. My third shot buried itself into the concrete wall at the back of the landing. The retorts were deafening in the stairwell, but I still heard the fourth level door slam shut.

"Chase?" Heinz asked.

"We have to," I said with a nod. "Now, before they get organized." Heinz moved smoothly down the stairwell. I followed. "Sean," I ordered as he moved in behind me, "stay here and guard our flank."

He opened his mouth to protest, but snapped it shut again when he saw my eyes and the shake of my head. He moved back up to the cutback landing.

Heinz was already at the door to the fourth level. I moved to the other side and put my hand on the lever. He shifted his weight, bending at the knees and waist to make himself a smaller target before nodding.

"On three," I whispered. I counted off with my fingers on the door, my Glock drawn in my other hand and resting against my thigh. On three, I swung open the door and slipped inside to the left.

A bullet sparked high off the door. I shot at the muzzle flash. Somebody cried out in the dark. Another round fired, this time into the doorframe a couple inches above my head. I fired back. A body thumped onto the floor.

"Go!" I ordered.

Heinz, protected by the steel of the door, slipped inside the garage and flanked right. A full automatic weapon sprayed bullets all around us from behind a parked car. Heinz and I both squeezed off a single shot each.

The bullets stopped… for a moment. A crossfire erupted. Heinz pivoted right and squeezed off two rounds toward the flashes. The biker's gun thunked off the hood of the car as its owner slid to the ground behind the fender. I squeezed off three rounds. Two of the shooters fell to the concrete. The third shot embedded itself in the driver's side frame of an Escalade SUV. He made the mistake of flinching, moving away from where the bullet sparked off the metal. I easily picked off the better profiled target. His hands squeaked against the hood before he slipped out of sight.

The parking garage was dimly lit by bare LED lightbulbs strung up in no particular fashion. Heinz and I flanked the outer rows, slipping along the cars and clearing each possible hiding spot between them. We met at the rear of the garage.

"Clear," he announced.

"Clear," I responded.

One of the bikers we shot lay a few meters away.

Heinz went over and picked over his body.

"Not much here," he said.

"I don't think they have much left in their armory."

"Agreed. The question is where did the boss go?"

As if on cue, the hum of an elevator came to life. We turned with enough time to see a slim shaft of light strobe past the slats of the closed bay door. Goggles had left his men to be fodder for us. More important was the fact they still had electricity enough to run the elevator. Definitely needed more than a daisy-chained array of car batteries to operate it.

"Bloody 'ell," Heinz said. "Now we're at the bottom of things."

We moved quickly back to the stairwell, checking the bodies for ammo. They were indeed running on empty. They might have depleted all they had defending the garage—and Goggles—against us.

Three shots came from inside.

We cleared the fourth-floor landing and moved up to the next landing. Sean fired off three suppressing rounds above us, the bullets pinging off the railings.

I tapped him on the shoulder. "Report."

"Somebody was shouting from up there on the second level," he said. "They shot off a couple rounds. Nothing direct."

"Goggles went up the elevator," I told him.

"They've got enough juice for that?" Sean asked, keeping an eye for any movement or shadows from the stairs above us.

"Yeah, mate. Go figure."

"We need to hunt down Westsmith," I said. "We don't have time for this shit."

"We don't have ammo left for much more of this shit, either," Heinz advised.

33

Wind Sprints

+81 Days – 1319 hours
04:03:05

We made it back to the surface in time to hear the rumble of retreating motorcycles. A back tire and muffler jetted out of sight onto the street as we ran up the ramp toward the sidewalk. I stopped in the middle of the street to see nine of them, plus Westsmith on a motorcycle of his own, rounding the corner and speeding north on Park Avenue.

I fired three rounds.

One caught the trailing rider in the bicep.

The second caught his rear tire above the chain.

I don't know where the third shot landed. He careened out of control, his bike running onto the sidewalk and up a series of steps at the base of the office building. He crashed into a massive concrete planter with a withered tree growing out of it.

That's when I ran. I don't know if the others were behind me. Didn't care. I couldn't think about it. The key to my freedom was riding north. My legs carried me to the intersection quicker than I realized. I cut through the plaza just as the crashed biker extracted himself from his motorcycle. I kicked him without breaking stride. His helmet cracked open and the visor popped from its pins. He staggered back and tripped over the scraps of metal and plastic previously known as his mode of transportation. He landed hard, his helmet clunking off the ground and splitting open completely.

I left him behind.

The other nine riders had accelerated down a ramp into a split in the road where the center of Park Avenue became a tunnel. I skidded to a stop, brought the rifle up and squeezed the trigger. The shot sparked off a green road sign downrange. I had lost the sightline.

Suspended in the dark skies was a black monolith. The Roanoke and Raleigh corporate tower. It was an imposing architectural testament cutting straight across the avenue, indifferent to the rest of the island's midtown grid pattern. Was Dick staring at us ants from his top-floor office windows, watching us scurry around with our pop-guns and two-wheel toys? Did he actually care if we succeeded or was this mission just something to distract him from the blandness of a broken-open world?

The building mocked me.

Dick mocked me.

Do you want me to do so as well?

Not now, Bob.

Why not? It is always a treat to get under your skin.

The Gaunt Man walked out from the Park Avenue tunnel, a phantom wind slapping at the crease of his slacks. The tails of his suit jacket flapped in the same way.

Yet, there was no breeze.

The rumbling of the motorcycles had stopped. It was replaced with another rumbling, this time sustained but off from the west. The steel and glass canyons amplified the sound of rolling thunder. The city was in need of rain. Maybe it would wash away some of the filth from the streets. Maybe it would wipe clean the smell of death.

34

Captive Audience

+81 Days – 1323 hours
03:59:22

By the time I walked back to the corner of 40th and Park, Heinz and the others were crowded around my clipped biker. At least we managed to drop their number down by one.

"You were haulin', Walken," Heinz said. "Christ almighty."

"He was a track star before he was a sharpshooter," Sean said.

"Sniper, mate," Heinz corrected him. "Don't get those two confused."

"Don't worry about it, Sean," I said, sensing his embarrassment. "Labels don't mean much these days."

Melissa was sharper and more alert being above ground and in the fresh air. Jude, on the other hand, looked tired. Her eyes had dark circles and her face was covered in a thin film of dust.

Someone had propped up the biker against a massive granite column. His helmet was now in two pieces beside him, his stripped weapons in a small pile two meters to his right. His eyes were just now fluttering open.

"Shit," he said in one long drawn out breath. He put his hands up to his head. When he realized his arm was grazed, he lowered his arms down and covered the seeping wound with his hand. "What did I ever do to you?" he slurred, looking up at me with glazed eyes. "You like going around killing people you don't even know?"

From his perspective, he was in the right. We had been the ones taking the first shots at them as they raced at us at the

Queens/Midtown Tunnel. We took out their three guards outside the parking garage, and quite a few more underground.

"Where were you going?" I asked him instead.

"You mean, before you shot me?"

"Yes," I said without hesitation.

The tone he heard in my voice made him hesitate, but only for a moment. "I don't know."

"You were just playing 'follow-the-leader'?" Sean asked.

"I guess so," our biker friend replied.

"So, you follow Anarchy wherever he goes?" I asked, using Rooster's name for Goggles. "Without question?"

"It's as good a plan as any," he said with a shrug.

"Good to have family," I agreed. "People to watch your back. People to depend on."

The biker looked at me, without answering.

I pulled Heinz aside, making sure I was out of earshot of our newest prisoner. "We need an incentive."

"Aye, Sergeant." Heinz looked at me and nodded, his eyes seeming to know exactly what I was referring to. He trotted off down 40th Street, his weapon at half draw.

The biker watched as Heinz double-timed up the block. "I ain't got nothing to say to you," he said, his cheek starting to swell. By saying those words, he had already said volumes.

35

One-Eyed Willy

+81 Days – 1328 hours
03:54:45

We waited a few minutes before engaging the biker again. He felt his cheek, hissing when he touched where the swelling was most pronounced. He tapped the tips of his boots together as a way to pass the time, also serving to take his mind off the hot pain pulsing in his face.

"You got a name?" Jude asked.

He looked up at her, checking her out from bottom to top. He mostly lingered on her hips and chest. He licked his lips. "Yeah, I got a name. You got a name?"

"Jude," she said without hesitation.

"Well, Jude," the biker replied. "Pleased to meet you."

"And you are?" Jude coaxed him again.

"Willy," he said.

"Pleased to meet you, Will–," Jude started. She clamped her mouth shut as the biker started rubbing his crotch, grabbing a handful of bulging denim in his left hand.

"Disgusting," Melissa commented, the business end of the Benelli coming to rest with the barrel aimed at Willy's crotch. "We can always call you by another name. I'm thinking something more like Linda. Seems like it will be more appropriate in a minute. Or, maybe, Bloody Mary."

Willy smiled at Melissa for a second until studying her face made him realize she wasn't bluffing. Her finger tightening—and her knuckle whitening—against the trigger probably was a good tip-off, too.

"Stand down, Melissa," I said gently, knowing full well ordering her to do so would have a less than desirable effect. "Please."

Melissa raised the shotgun to Willy's face and left it there for several seconds. Willy's eyes went cross-eyed staring at the end of the barrel.

"Don't even look at her or me sideways," Melissa said, nodding toward Jude. "I have zero tolerance."

Willy nodded, his hands raised at chest level.

Melissa snapped the shotgun back toward her body and walked away. She grabbed Jude by the crook of her arm and led her away toward the intersection, descending the steps to the sidewalk.

"Crazy bitches, right?" Willy asked aloud, but mostly to himself.

I dropped to one knee, my kneecap crushing into his privates. He started to howl in pain but I put my arm around the back of his neck and the other cupped across his mouth. The holler was stifled. I locked my arms together, tightening my grip. Willy could breathe through my cupped hand, but I was putting a dangerous amount of pressure against his neck. It wouldn't take much more before he would slip into unconsciousness.

Or, you will just snap his neck. Like you did with Randy.

An accident.

Are you going to tell everyone this time is an accident?

Willy's wide eyes searched my face for any sign of amnesty. I knew for a fact he would find none there.

Cannot get blood—or information—from a stone.

I released him and stepped away. It was pretty pathetic when the

Gaunt Man was the voice of reason.

Happy to assist.

Yeah. You're a lifesaver, Bob.

Well, I did help to save this life.

For now. Willy coughed and rubbed his hand on his windpipe. His fear had been replaced with anger. His fingers got caught on a gold chain with a crucifix on the end of it.

"Keep your perverted thoughts to yourself, Willy," I advised, realizing the irony of his actions versus the cross he carried. "None of us would hesitate to pull the trigger."

"Especially that one with the shotgun, by the grace of God," Willy agreed.

"I'm sure you don't want to lose your balls," I advised, pointing the business end of my Glock in a semi-circular motion around his still aroused parts, "and everything in the blast radius around it."

Looks like he is a fan of erotic asphyxiation. I guess the world is getting harder every day.

You're disgusting, Bob.

"You sure you don't have any info for us?" I asked Willy. "Any ideas on where you were riding off to?"

He grabbed his junk again through his jeans and stuck out his tongue at me. He laughed. "Answer enough for ya?"

It was an answer, but not the answer we needed to get Westsmith back. No matter. Sean, who had been keeping watch from the southeast corner of the intersection, trotted back over to our side of the street. He met up with Heinz as the Brit pushed Rooster forward up the steps. They cut across the plaza. Both looked a bit worse for wear than when I last saw either of them. Rooster was out of breath and his jeans had a huge tear in them. Luckily, there was no blood. Heinz's clothes were the same as before, but he was flushed and panting.

"Lil fucker tried to get away," the mercenary said when he finally sat Rooster down next to Willy. "He's your problem, now."

"You cocka-doodies killed them," Rooster whimpered. "Got 'em laid out like meat for the rats."

"You want to join them?" I asked.

"No," Rooster answered meekly. "Although you left me tied up for the subway bums."

"Didn't see any homeless around," Sean pointed out.

"Not bums, idiot," Willy corrected him, looking at me through the corner of his eye to see if I would smack him for talking to Sean out of turn. "The dead people."

I let it slide. Things were going to get a little bit dark in a minute.

"Sean," I said. "Go keep Jude and Melissa company back by the sidewalk."

"Uh," Sean replied with a cock of the head. "Okay."

He walked off in the direction of the women. Once they were engaged in conversation, I turned my attention back to Willy and Rooster. It seemed pointless to ask them for their real names now.

"Where were you going, Willy?" I asked.

He smiled with my use of his joke moniker. "I don't know."

"Well," I said. "Your friend doesn't know."

"Cockie-doodie-doo," Rooster sang, and then cackled. "I said cock... and doodie!"

"Your mate's been out of the loop," Heinz said.

"Way outside the loop," Willy confirmed. "For as long as I've known him!"

"You go back a ways?" I asked.

"Farther back than this shit storm," Willy said. "Worked MTA together."

"Yep," Rooster confirmed. "We did clean-up."

"You did clean-up," Willy said, emphasizing the 'you'. "I was an engineer, by the grace of God." Willy puffed out his chest in spite of the fact his face was taking on a distinctly splotchy bluish and yellow tone. Rooster looked at the swelling on his friend and, without thinking, poked it lightly with his finger, "Owwww," Willy cried, pulling away and protecting his face with his hand. "Why'd you do that? Christ!"

"You're getting weird colors on your face," Rooster commented, his finger still floating in the air level with Willy's cheek.

"Keep your fucking finger away from me," Willy warned him. I put the barrel of my Glock on his forehead. Willy shut up and looked cross-eyed up at it.

"You talk to me and we let you walk," I said.

"I doubt it," Willy replied. "How many of my people have you murdered?" I didn't have a good answer for him. We had shot at them first. Took out their guards. Wounded Goggles.

You do have Mr. Rooster.

"Your friend here is still alive," I said. "We could have left him on the road with his bike on top of him."

"Or shot him in the head," Heinz added.

"Was heavy, too," Rooster said with a nod. "Heavy-doodie bike." He smiled with how clever he was.

He said 'doodie' instead of 'duty'.

Yes. I got the play on words. Thank you, Bob.

"We just need the hitchhiker back," Heinz said. "He's the cause of all of our problems today. He's already killed five of us."

"Wait," Willy said. "So, you're bounty hunters?"

"He's been directly responsible for the deaths of two of us, and indirectly for three more," I explained.

"We need to mete out some justice, mate," Heinz said. "Eye for an eye. Old Testament style, if you hear me."

Willy seemed to be interested in the idea of B.C. retribution. He nodded slowly.

"We aren't looking to take any more lives than necessary," I said, pulling the Glock away from his face. "We just need Westsmith."

"Is that his name?" Willy asked. "He didn't mention it to me before getting chummy with the Bossman. Only talked about where to get more weapons and ammo."

Shit. I knew where there were plenty of crates of weapons, ammo, and explosives. A black shiny building towered north of us only four blocks away. It loomed over the avenue, standing directly in our path. All roads led to the black monolith—obscured by fog—dominating the Manhattan Midtown skyline.

All roads led back to Roanoke & Raleigh.

36

Split Personalities
+81 Days – 1337 hours
03:46:09

I hadn't needed to use Rooster as an incentive after all.

True to my word, we allowed them to part ways. Rooster hoisted Willy to his feet and put an arm around his waist. As they hobbled away toward the parking garage, probably to get Willy stitched up, the rest of us stared up at the fortress of the Roanoke and Raleigh tower.

The sun had lost the battle for supremacy against the angry dark clouds coming across the Hudson River. They were low and threatened rain. From far off came the quiet build of thunder, starting off low but quickly gaining enough in volume to shake the glass. But as quickly as it roared, it would retreat to a whisper again.

"Ain't gonna be easy, mate," Heinz said, looking skyward. "They have the lower floors locked up tight."

"Didn't think we were going through the lobby," Sean added.

"We aren't," I said. "There's more ways than the lobby to enter a building, especially for an operation so keen on transportation of military-grade weapons."

The rumbling came again.

"Wouldn't that make the building more secure?" Jude asked, her hand to her neck.

"You would think," I said. "But big cargo needs big entry points."

As we walked up Park Avenue, Melissa walked backward

behind us to keep an eye on our six. "You sure it was smart to let them go? They were creeps."

"I don't think they will be a problem," I assured her.

"One's a deviant and the other's crazy," Melissa advised. "Those ain't personalities allowing much in the way of predictability."

"Yeah," Jude agreed, deciding to hang back with Melissa.

"Fucking great," Melissa said, putting her hand out to catch the first fat raindrops from the saturated storm front.

Just as the sprinkle of rain became more insistent, I led us into the Park Avenue underpass where it ramped down from the service street. It wasn't a tunnel under a river, but the water from the rain was already starting to trickle downhill in the gutters on either side of the roadway. I was just happy we were out from under the weather. It would make the next part of what we needed to do a bit easier. Not easy, but easier.

37

Potpourri

+81 Days – 1341 hours
03:42:41

The Park Avenue tunnel wasn't as glamorous as the name might have implied. It was built with limestone blocks, a simple utility thoroughfare instead of an ornate set piece.

"Used to be used for the railway," Sean said. "Lots of history in these walls. Didn't even have the granite roof on it until 1850."

"Fascinating," Heinz commented. I wasn't sure if the mercenary was being sarcastic or was truly interested.

The beams from our tactical lights bounced off the curved ceiling. Melissa and Jude tightened rank on our rear flank, slightly less worried of ambush by Willy or Rooster with the protection from the elements. Rainwater trickled past us into the drainage grates in the gutters. The sound of thunder echoed off the hard walls. Melissa still moved her Benelli from one hand to the other, as if it was too hot to hold against bare skin for too long. Neither did anything to calm her already frayed nerves about wet enclosed spaces.

"Where are we going?" Jude asked from my left.

"I'll know it when I see it," I replied.

She rolled her eyes at me. "Not the best laid plans, sweetie."

"Maybe." I shrugged my shoulders. "But we haven't done much in terms of planning since we started this mess."

"Yeah," Jude said. "There's definitely that."

"Where are the goddamn FRACs?" Sean blurted out. "Not having them around is more unnerving than when they're swarming all around us. Jesus!"

It was true.

Midtown Manhattan was woefully underrepresented by the undead.

No taxation without representation!

Really, Bob? Don't let Heinz hear you. He may still be a little touchy about how Britain lost their American colonies.

I suppose so.

You have any helpful information to share?

I am afraid not, John. There is no network to tap into here.

We finally approached what I had been looking for. The end of our lights pooled on three motorcycles. One was Goggles' Harley Davison. Another was a Suzuki crotch rocket. The third looked like a chop-shop special, comprised of parts and pieces from several models of bikes. All were adorned with some matter or degree of twined bleached bones, stretched tanned skins or some other rotting parts of the human body. A string of fingers was tied to the headlight of the Suzuki. Several ribs of varying lengths were built into the back of the rear seatback of the chop-shop bike, layered to resemble a fin. The other bikes were parked farther away in a cut-out alcove in the wall.

Two sets of stairs—one on each side of the road—had been built in recessed cutouts of the sidewalls. Graffiti and huge swatches of peeling paint covered the walls. One tag showed an explicit phallic appendage shooting dotted-line piss at a snaggle-toothed head with crosses for eyes.

"That's the spirit of New York I missed," Sean said.

At the top of both stairways was a wrought iron footbridge—also covered with too many layers of clumpy and peeling black paint. Sean, Jude and I walked up the stairs, making our way up from the left while Heinz and Melissa used the stairs on the right. The footbridge led to a single stairwell centered above the roadway.

Heinz scanned the enclosure and the steps leading upward. "Clear." I tapped him on the shoulder and took point up the next set of steps.

A landing separated the lower flight from the upper one. The ceramic tiles reflected my light back to me in sharp and harsh angles. Even after several months of disuse, the corners of the landing reeked of old urine, sour sweat and urban decay.

"What's that smell?" Sean asked. "Lavender?"

"Think so," Jude replied, swallowing hard.

I didn't bother to mention I had been smelling it since the shuttle bus crash. It would never overpower the pungent rot of the city nor the abuse afflicted on it by its indifferent people, but it still lingered. Maybe the perfume served as a sweet reminder of a world re-attainable, amid the undead.

So poetic.

I ignored Bob. Staying close to the wall, I ascended to the top of the stairs. The lavender was much more evident here. I cast my light around. The limestone was finished and smooth. A line of boutiques and shops occupied each side of the wide hallway, the shop doors heavy leaded glass with gold trim. Each of the shops was protected behind closed and locked security grates. It was as if I had arrived minutes after closing to find everyone had gone home for the evening.

Just another day at the office.

My boot knocked against something.

I shined my light down.

A woman in her thirties, wearing a black dress with a gray long-sleeved sweater wrap, lay curled up at my feet. The handles of her

Coach purse were locked into the crook of her elbow. Her eyes were wide open and glued to the screen of her dark iPhone laying half a meter from her outreached fingers.

I crouched down. The lavender was drifting up from her body. Her skin was taut without looking mummified. If was as if she had used a tanning bed for too long without using moisturizer regularly afterward.

Footsteps clomped on the stairs behind me. The added tactical lights illuminated the shopping corridor further, giving the wide hallway a dim wash of color. More bodies lay on the marble floor where I knelt. The entire corridor was littered with the dead! I stood and walked along the storefronts with my M4 drawn. There were no pulses or thumping of heartbeats. There was no buzz of cicadas or itch at the back of my neck. These people were dead, never to return in any form.

The flowery smell assaulted me as I stepped over the bodies deeper into the corridor. The smell was overpowering, making my throat close up. I coughed in an effort to combat it. The others covered their mouths with their sleeves or by pulling up their shirt collars, looking like a poor imitation of Dracula or a kid getting ready for an impromptu convenience store robbery.

"Christ," Jude muttered. "Shit."

"Could be God." Heinz shined his light around the floor, assessing each body. "No obvious trauma. No bullet wounds."

"Like they dropped all at once," I assessed.

"Except her," Melissa said, pointing to a woman still clutching at one of the shop's door handles with a frozen look of terror on her face. "It wasn't immediate. At least, not for her."

"Smells like essential oils," Melissa commented, and then choked up on her next words. "Victoria loved lavender."

"Coming up from the bodies," Heinz said. "They reek of it."

We moved along the wall toward the next intersection, stepping over the bodies when necessary.

"Dear God," Sean whispered.

The main atrium opened up to several stories, glassed in with interconnecting angles and a criss-cross of steel supports. Eight massive steel and concrete pillars supported the hundred floors above it. The day had become night with deep black rolling and roiling clouds outside. Rain pelted the glass at a severe angle, blown in from the west on gale force winds. Jagged lines of lightning flashed in the sky around the tower, casting the impressive commons area into brilliant white for a moment.

I wished to Sean's god the modern architecture of the R&R atrium space had been worthy enough of his exclamation. Hundreds of bodies lay on the granite and marble floor of the atrium. They huddled together with pained looks on their faces, their eyes frozen open in terror and pain as they wrapped their arms around each other. Several people, before succumbing to the effects of the lavender, had been crushed against and inside the revolving doors on each compass point egress from the building. Hundreds of men, women and children had died here, clinging to each other and to their last moments of painful life.

"What a waste," Heinz whispered.

A mother lay across the steps in front of me, her toddler daughter in an Oshkosh romper pressed into her chest in a too-true-to-life death grip. She had fallen against the edges of the risers, most likely breaking a rib before dying. She had sacrificed herself for the safety of her child.

Retching sounds from my left. Jude was doubled over a waste receptacle. Unfortunately, the rotting smell coming from the trash can, coupled with the heavy odor of lavender and the sight of such a massive display of sudden death, made her dry-heave even more. Melissa went to her, put an arm around her waist and led her away to an unoccupied wrought iron patio chair still upright in the food court area.

"It all happened right under my feet," Heinz said with disgust, spitting on one of the only vacant marble surfaces. "Motherfucker sat up in his ivory tower looking out over the world. With all this ruin at his feet." He walked away, crossing his arms and cradling his weapon.

"It all happened early on," Sean pointed out, watching as Heinz kicked the same trashcan Jude had been doubled over. The crash of the lid was resounding, startling both Melissa and Jude. Another flash of lightning and an immediate rumble of thunder quickly overshadowed Heinz's ground level disturbance.

"What did you mean, Sean?" I asked.

"What?" He looked a bit confused, still keeping an eye on Heinz as the mercenary walked the perimeter of the atrium like a caged tiger.

"Knowing when this happened," I reminded him.

"Oh. Yeah." Sean caught on. "Look at how everyone is dressed. Definitely looking a cool spring day based on the jackets and boots."

"And the colors," Jude added, still sitting with Melissa massaging the small of her back. She swallowed hard before finishing. "Spring colors."

I looked back at the little girl in her mother's arms. She had completed her ensemble with a pink hoodie with fur trim and Disney characters embroidered on the back in a high energy, dancing ring around Walt's logo. A mouse spinning a dog. A princess twirling around a lion. A wolf with a funny hat dancing by himself with a banjo full of broken strings.

"What's the plan, mate?" Heinz said.

He handed a sealed bottle of Gatorade to Jude. She broke the seal and slowly sipped a quarter of its contents. She passed it to Melissa who wasn't as delicate in her gulps. After Sean was able to take a swig and hand it back to Heinz, I spoke. "We go down."

We moved through the maze of bodies toward the north end of the atrium. Behind two of the eight massive pillars the elevators were divided into two banks. Four cars lined each wall, a three-meter wide corridor between them. The doors were decorated with onyx and bamboo. R&R had spared no expense.

So many people had suffered broken bones and trampled spines trying to escape the building. Dozens more had piled up against the doors and walls of the elevator banks. One of the elevators slowly slid open, the light from the interior of the car inviting. The door futilely continued to close against a pile of people who had tried desperately to be whisked away from the carnage in the atrium. We didn't speak, leaving the rationalization of what we were witnessing for a time where we weren't so steeped in the dead.

"Why did they try to go up?" Jude asked, still swallowing hard.

"The same reason they tried to get to the streets," I answered. "To get away from what was happening here. Rats fleeing a sinking ship."

"Or eating their way through someone's stomach when the bucket they are trapped in gets too hot," Sean said.

"First... morbid," Heinz said. "Second... unfortunately true torture tactics in some parts of the world. Even today."

The elevator at the far left had the least number of bodies stacked against its doors. I pulled the corpses away and dragged them into a line on the sidewall of the elevator bank.

Jude had one hand over her mouth and nose and the other hand on her neck over her injection site. Her eyes were wide, a film of wetness threatening to spill past her dark thick lashes to her cheeks. She shook her head so slowly it was uncertain whether she realized she was doing it at all.

Sean and Heinz pulled a couple bodies each away from the elevator, giving us enough room to get to the doors. I stepped up and put my hand on the metal. The hum of the motors and of the electricity running through them tingled through my fingertips. All the while, the doors of the elevator next to us continued their vain attempts to rattle against the bodies blocking its closure.

Sean pointed a finger and stabbed at the up button next to the elevator. "Sorry. Couldn't help it."

"You have OCD," Melissa said. "No other explanation makes sense."

"Yeah," Sean said with a grin. "Uh oh. Fifteen minutes to Judge Wapner."

"Really?" Melissa asked. "A *Rainman* quote?"

"Hey," Sean said in defense of himself. "Dustin Hoffman won the Oscar for that one."

"Kmart sucks," I said, smiling a bit myself but tracing my fingers along the edge of the doors.

"The Marine's got jokes," Sean said in surprise. "Who knew?"

Yes. Who knew?

There was a lot people didn't know about me.

Not everyone can be in your head like I am.

Not a very comforting thought.

It is what it is, I am afraid.

While the call button had lit up with Sean's push, nothing happened. No bells dinged. There was no whirr of motors or resonance of cables. No breeze escaped through the cracks of the frame to denote the descent of the car. We were going to have to do this the hard way.

38

Lift Up Your Hearts
+81 Days – 1348 hours
03:35:34

The elevator doors had proven much more difficult to pry open than anticipated, even with my enhanced strength. The security measures Roanoke & Raleigh had employed to keep out the undesirables were still operating in full effect. I stood in the doorway, leaning against one door while propping my foot against the other. The elevator car was locked in place, suspended dozens of meters above me. It was probably on the fourth or fifth office floor, taking into account the height of the atrium itself.

The shaft was an almost entirely white enclosure of poured reinforced concrete, framed in red primed steel girders and I-beams. The greased cables were a charcoal black, with tight braiding straight off the factory spool. The shaft continued down for another several stories, even though there was only one more set of elevator doors leading, most likely, to the atrium security offices and janitorial supply closets in one of the higher sub-basements.

"How did Westsmith get in?" Sean asked, peering over the edge of the threshold. "This is way more work than it should be."

"He must know something we don't," I said. "Heinz?"

"Aye, mate."

"How did you get in and out of the building?"

"The Chinooks," Heinz answered. "We always deployed from the roof. Never did any boots on the ground in the city. Not until this operation, anyway."

"We gonna be able to get you where you want to go?" Sean asked.

I thought back to the dark concrete block storage closet where I had been held when Alvarez first brought me to the tower. It was a strange irony since I had been squirreled away to a sub-sub-basement in one of the tallest buildings in Manhattan to recuperate from my wounds. Even the height of the World Trade Center building down in the Wall Street area looked puny in comparison.

We needed to stop Westsmith, and stop Goggles and his men from powering up with more weapons than they could possibly haul away with a hundred men. We needed to get Westsmith back into custody and delivered to Dick's desk. Jude needed to get the capsule deactivated. Summer, April and Holly needed to be returned unharmed.

We needed to get to the freight elevator bank via the sub-basements in order to get to the upper floors. Rosalita, in her last moments, had given us what we needed to get into the elevator with a direct ascent to the man in charge.

As the thunder rumbled and the sky lit up with an angry god's ire, I wondered what could possibly go wrong?

39

Getting out of a Jamb
+81 Days – 1352 hours
03:31:10

Elevator shafts aren't like what people see in action movies. We didn't have to tear off strips of our shirts to bind our hands against the sharp braids of the cables. We didn't need to lower each other down hand over hand to huddle on the slim profiled ledge of each floor's doorframe. In reality, once the doors were pried open, it was just a matter of reaching in and grabbing a slim steel access ladder and climbing down. It was a descent of several stories to the bottom, but we made quick work of it.

There was no conversation on the way down. Melissa didn't say a word about being forced into another task inside an enclosed space. The shell-shock from witnessing hundreds of bodies in the R&R main atrium affected all of us. It was an image permanently burned into my brain, like those blinking spots in your vision after a photo is taken with the flash set to ON.

We crowded around the locked service door. Behind us, massive brakes—designed to slow a runaway elevator car's descent—were set into the poured concrete floor with four-inch nuts. Four six-foot hydraulic springs were positioned under the elevator car to stop it in case the brakes didn't do their job sufficiently. From my point of view, if the brakes didn't do their job I wasn't sure the springs would do much good, either.

"Blow the lock?" Heinz asked, ready to get into some shit.

"Gimme a sec," I said.

I went to the door. It had a keyed lock and deadbolt lock. A quick test verified the door wasn't budging without a key or extra assistance. I listened for a moment. Laughter drifted over to me through the crack between the door and the frame. I doubt if the others heard it, although Rosalita might have caught the sound had she been here.

Regret has no place in the here and now, John.

The laughter continued, a series of whoops and clapping peppered into the cackling for good measure. Sounded like Westsmith and his new friends had found the Roanoke & Raleigh arsenal.

Shit.

I pressed my shoulder against the door. Leaning in, I braced my legs and pushed. I could feel the deadbolt resist, its solid steel bar resting against the frame it was set into. The deadbolt wasn't going to fail. It was designed to withstand unauthorized access.

"We can always blow it, Heinz reminded me, his weapon at the ready. "Just give the word, mate."

"Give him a second," Sean insisted. "I'm sure he has it all figured out."

I didn't have anything figured out. This whole plan was unfolding with each obstacle we encountered. I knew the main objective and had faith in my training and quick thinking to achieve it. My gut said going into the sub-basement with our lighter version of shock and awe would get most of us killed.

The deadbolt didn't relent. But the door started to move, anyway. The sound of softly squealing metal filled my ears. My muscles flexed in my back, thighs, and calves. I dug in my boots against the rough concrete floor. The squeak grew louder. The others stood beside me in anticipation. Suddenly, the door flew outward, my momentum taking me through the threshold with it.

"Shite!" Heinz exclaimed in a low voice even as he hurried through the door behind me, pivoting right to cover my forced entry. Sean moved left through the doorway once I let go of the door handle. I got to my feet, unslung the M4 and followed Heinz. Sean stayed close behind me. Jude and Melissa came through the door last. Melissa covered her as Jude shut the door, having taken on the job of serving Jude as personal security. Melissa's head was back in the game. Thank god for small favors. Jude traced the distorted and twisted metal of the jamb around the door handle before looking at me with a wide-eyed mix of what looked like disbelief and...

What?

Fear? Or something akin to it? Something changing her opinion of me forever?

Now who is being melodramatic?

Did you see the look in her eyes?

Stop projecting, Marine, and get to business.

Ooh-rah.

40

Spin the Barrels
+81 Days – 1358 hours
03:25:38

Emergency lights lit the corridor in a dim wash of low voltage red. To our left was a dead-ending concrete block wall. The corridor led away to our right, turning right turn after twenty meters. We passed several storage units and a janitorial management office as I had expected, plus separate locker rooms for men and women, an exercise room, and a lounge boasting a full kitchen, two sixty-inch flatscreens, and plenty of comfortable seating.

"I should have gotten a job here," Sean noted in a low voice. "Looks a lot swankier than the military."

"The private sector is swankier than the military," Heinz confirmed. "That's the same worldwide. It's better than being skint after serving your country. I needed to pay the bills. And, I had plenty of bills, if you know what I mean."

I peeked around the corner of the intersection. After ten meters, it opened up into a huge space. I recognized the rows and stacks of crates, interspersed between several brightly lit medical bays. This was the sub-basement where Rosalita had brought me to antagonize me and dig the museum shrapnel out of my back.

The hollering was much more audible now. It was followed by the shriek of large nails being pulled out from hard wood. Wood clattered against the floor. More hoots of delight.

Pulling back against the wall out of sight of Westsmith, Goggles and his new biker friends, I faced the others. They looked at me with

181

expectation, their faces betraying they were all relying on me to carry them through to safety. Even Heinz, the hardened soldier of fortune, looked hungry for orders.

"They're halfway across the basement," I said. "We can hide in the perimeter shadows but we will have to show ourselves eventually... hopefully at the last couple seconds. Plus, they're distracted."

"Since we don't have silencers or suppressors," I advised, "once we light it up we have to go in hard and fast. And still keep Westsmith in one piece. Heinz and Sean will follow me along the left side. Melissa, you and Jude will go right. But, trail back far enough to stay out of the crossfire."

"What the fuc–" Melissa argued.

"Enough," I ordered. She shut her mouth and clenched her jaw. "This isn't about any misconceived notions about men being better at this sort of thing, Melissa. The three of us have professional training... which is needed right now."

She looked at me with fierce hard eyes. Jude put her hand around her waist and whispered something to her ending in, "...need you." Melissa softened a bit a nodded.

"If the shit goes sideways, Westsmith and the bikers are going your way, Melissa," I advised. "Then you can do all the shooting you want."

"Except for Westsmith," Sean reminded her. Melissa shot Sean a look, to which Sean shrugged his shoulders and raised his hands in surrender. "Just sayin'."

Westsmith's laughter grew louder and more continuous.

"We go now," I said. We all moved low and fast to the end of the second corridor. I signaled for Heinz and Sean to move to the left. They moved silently against the wall where the shadows were deepest. I tapped Melissa on the arm and pointed to the right. She nodded grimly and moved to the closest concrete support column. Jude squeezed my arm and followed after Melissa and her Benelli. When they were several columns away, I followed to the far corner of the basement where Sean and Heinz had set up position. I passed them and worked my way along the sidewall toward Westsmith's laughter.

"Holy fuck," Goggles exclaimed, his vulgar statement of disbelief echoing through the cavernous space. "You weren't fucking around, Mr. Westsmith."

"I am a man of my word," Westsmith's voice answered with a laugh.

"That you are," Goggles agreed. "That you are! Look at these beautiful guns. We can live like the Lords of Flatbush with toys like these. Right, boys?"

There was an enthusiastic roar of approval from the other bikers as they pulled out brand new M4s and AK-47s from their foam cutouts. Three of Goggles' men had opened boxes of modified M67 rounds and were loading a stack of empty magazines, tossing each into olive green duffels when finished. The duffels looked half-full from the wide sag of their canvas.

"And we can get in whenever we want?" Goggles asked.

"You saw how easy it was, right?" Westsmith replied. "It wouldn't make any difference if I was with you or not at this point."

Goggles drew his sidearm and pointed it at Westsmith's head. Westsmith stepped forward toward the barrel and smiled. Squinting his left eye and sticking his tongue out the side of his mouth, Goggles starting making robotic radar pinging noises as he targeted points on Westsmith's face. Westsmith simply clasped his hands in from of him and laughed cheerfully. Goggles filled his cheeks with air and expelled it in a gun-firing noise, like a kid playing cowboys and Indian with his plastic six-shooters.

"Well done," Westsmith commended him. "Well done."

Goggles grinned and went back to scouring through the contents of some of the other crates his men had pried open. "Play-doh?" he exclaimed. "That's dumb. Next!" Goggles walked away—toward us—to the next crate and marveled at his luck of finding it full of Beretta 9Ms. "Fuckin' Christmas!" he shouted with delight.

They were still distracted. Now was the time. I nodded to Heinz and Sean before moving out the shadows. Standing tall, I drew the M4 tailstock against my shoulder and started hunting.

Thirty rounds.

Take out the closest first. First shot caught a biker trying to pry into a rocket launcher crate. Blood from his heart splattered through his back against a larger stack of crates behind him. The pry bar fell from his hand and clanked on the ground. A second shot found his forehead as he fell forward.

Twenty-eight rounds. Eight targets. Westsmith.

Two others spun around with their new AK-47s and pulled the triggers. They had forgotten to load a full magazine into the rifles. I guessed they didn't realize weapon systems weren't delivered fully loaded.

"Idiots," I said, firing a round into the one on the left.

My second shot was deflected off a rifle stock as the other biker raised his weapon in an effort to shield his face. I shot him in the stomach. He screamed and lowered the rifle as he hunched over to hug his belly with it. My next round went into the top of his head.

Twenty-five rounds. Six targets. Westsmith.

The remaining bikers fired back. I ducked between two tall crates, one of them holding something more substantial than ammunition or sidearms. RPG7 was listed on the barcode label. Removing the firing pins and the safety caps were the first things you needed to do to make the shaped charge deadly.

Would it explode if shot at the right way?

I rolled away from the crate to the next aisle, just to err on the side of caution. Heinz passed me and fired at the bikers, catching one of them in the cheek. As the biker fell, his hand contracted and he wildly sprayed the rounds of his entire magazine. Rounds tore into wood and the concrete ceiling.

"Ugh!" Heinz cried, dropping to his knees as more rounds rained around us.

Sean took cover on the deck, his body pressed to the epoxy-painted concrete. Heinz held his belly, hissing out air and pulling up his tactical vest and shirt. The shot was dead center in his abdomen, an inch above his belly button.

"Fuckin' twats," he said through a grimace of pain.

"They're over there," Goggles yelled.

"Sean!" I yelled.

He looked up.

"Suppress," I ordered.

He got to one knee and fired three-round bursts above the crates at the approaching men. I slid over to Heinz. He looked at me with a pained grin on his face. "Less severe than a tree branch through the side, right?"

He wasn't going to make it. I knew it. He knew it.

"Can't say I'm chuffed about being gutted." His bloody hands clasped mine. "Get it done."

He didn't utter any other movie dialogue clichés. He was too much the professional. He simply nodded and pushed me away.

I crouched and waited for Sean to stop firing before I stood up.

One of the bikers, a burly, hairy-chested man, had managed to get to within one crate of us. The three-round burst from my M4 to his face at almost point-blank range had sickening, meat-pulping results. All of his facial features were gone in an instant. He slapped against the crate with what used to be his face, leaving a gory slop of meat and blood behind on the lid.

Twenty-two rounds. Four targets. Westsmith.

The world flashed into a brilliant fiery yellow. Hundreds of rounds ripped through the crates, forcing Sean and me to our bellies again.

"Jesus Christ," Sean yelled.

After several seconds, the room went dark red again and the gunfire stopped. Three of the crates literally splintered and split apart, their contents spilling out on the floor. Metal clacked against metal.

Sean and I stood up at the same time as the last of Goggles' men. While the three were distracted by Goggles who was struggling to re-feed the Dillon Gatling Gun he had uncrated, I squeezed two three-round bursts into the side of two of their turned heads. The spray from the second one blinded the third long enough for Sean to double-tap him in the chest. He added the headshot like a practiced expert. The end of the world was a great place to practice one's marksmanship.

Sixteen rounds. Goggles. Westsmith.

"You might want to stop now," I said as Sean and I moved toward the struggling bike gang leader. Sean moved between the crates to flank Goggles on my three-o'clock. Goggles continued to fiddle with the gun, knowing I was directly in front of its barrels. He panted with exertion, trying desperately to get the gun running again.

"Stop," Sean ordered.

A single gunshot retorted. Goggles face went slack and a tiny drop of blood and saliva dribbled from between his lips before he slumped over the massive gun.

"Thanks for letting me finish what I started," Melissa said, the smoke still rising from Goggle's pistol—the same one Jude had been carrying around since the Midtown Tunnel.

Sixteen rounds left. Goggles' biker contingent was no more, unless you counted Willy and Rooster out there wandering the streets of Manhattan. I looked around the sub-basement.

It didn't matter how many rounds I had left in my M4.

Westsmith, and one of the duffle bags, was gone.

41

Funeral for a Friend

+81 Days – 1412 hours
03:11:01

We stood around Heinz, still wary of Westsmith coming back to ambush us.

"Whataya all bloody staring at?" he said between pants. "Ain't you got someplace to be?"

"In a minute," I said through a closed-up throat, getting down on one knee beside him. "It'll keep."

"Don't let me hold you up," Heinz said. "Shite. I'm just gonna lie here and paint the floors a little bit before I take a well-deserved nap." Heinz shot out his hand and grabbed my wrist, still surprisingly quick and strong.

"It's been an honor," I said I putting my hand over his.

"You stealing my thunder, Marine?"

"Maybe just a little."

"Well," Heinz said with a hard swallow. "I know the R&R docs ain't gonna want to patch up a turncoat… and I don't think it would matter. I've seen what these gut shots do to a man."

"You're hell of a fighter," Sean added.

"Almost as good as Melissa," Heinz chuckled, meaning every word. Melissa nodded her head and bowed slightly to accept the compliment, wiping away a tear in the process.

"Go deliver that fucker," Heinz said as he squeezed my arm, the pain evident in his voice and the ebbing of his life evident in his eyes. "Finish, and get… get the hell as far away from 'ere…"

His hand slipped off of my arm, his fresh blood slick on my skin. I reached for his hand, but knew it was a wasted effort. The thump of his heart softened, the time between beats agonizingly drawn out as his eyes closed. I put his hand on his lap with the other. He let out a thin slowly evaporating exhale as his life left his body. We stared silently on as Heinz died. His aura dimmed to a hazy gray, fitting of a man from the typically overcast British Isles.

Sean stepped forward and drew his tactical knife.

"Wait," I said, watching and waiting for Heinz's aura to drift into a smoky black. It stayed gray. "Leave him."

"What if he turns?" Jude asks.

"He won't," I promised her. "Let him be."

42

Out of Service

+81 Days – 1420 hours
03:03:46

We decided to place Heinz to rest someplace more suitable, even if the circumstances and conditions failed to fit a man of his caliber. Goggles had been trying to lift the Gatling Gun out of its crate. I finished the job by moving his body and the gun aside. Sean and I lifted Heinz's body and placed him inside the crate amid the packing straw.

Jude came in behind us and placed his hands across his lap again. Melissa stepped up to the crate and looked at Heinz with a thin smile. She put the fingers of her right hand on his chest. Before she turned away to follow the rest of us, she slipped a shell from the Benelli and stood it on his chest. "Death before dishonor."

She followed behind us after those words. True words. Deserved words, even if death wasn't. All warriors feared death, not because it was unwarranted or unexpected but because to surrender to death meant a failure to protect people, property, or mission objectives. To die on a great battlefield may be the most honorable way to perish, but it still meant the bloody battles would carry on without them.

So poetic.

The death of a warrior is always deserving of poetry and odes, Bob.

I understand that. Bob walked in front of us, leading the way to the freight elevator. As we passed the remaining duffle bag of filled magazines, I picked it up and slung it across my shoulder.

"Swap your M4s," I told the others, discarding the rifle I was assigned at the start of this operation in favor of the Russian-born AK-47. The others did the same, filling their vests with any stray filled magazines not in the bag.

"Should take the Gatling," Melissa commented.

"It *is* pretty epic," Sean admitted.

"Leave it," I said, knowing Melissa was just keen for its destructive capacity as opposed to its closed-quarters practicality.

"Whatever." She shrugged.

Long spools of wires lay scattered across the floor. The spools had rolled away from the crate they had been stored in. An array of flat rectangular electronic devices was still in the box. They looked like smart phones, with flat touch screens.

"Probably for recon," Sean commented. "Like the tablet we used at Creedmoor."

R&R had their hands in plenty of pots, but none of them seemed to be interested in furthering humanitarian efforts. Bob waited at the elevator, leaning against the wall and picking at something under his ethereal fingernail. Above the call button and a black square glass tile, a metal panel had been opened to reveal a numeric keypad.

"I hope you know the code," Sean said hopefully, pressing the call button without it lighting up. "Because it's a dead stick."

"No," I said.

"Westsmith figured it out," Melissa said.

"I think he always knew it," I said.

"Typical," Melissa griped.

"So," Jude asked, "what's the plan? I'm sure you had a better plan than getting us here with no way to the top."

"You kidding me? We've been flying by the seat of our pants since we left the rooftop," Melissa said. "No offense, John."

"None taken." I shrugged. "You done?"

Melissa mulled it over for a moment. "Umm… yep. For now."

"Good," I said, fishing around my front pocket. "Cause, like a Boy Scout, I'm always prepared."

I pulled out the electronic keycard I had found in Rosalita's pocket along with the photo of her son. I held it up between my index and middle finger for a moment before I pressed it against the glass tile above the call button.

My triumphant grin soured as nothing happened. No dinging bell responses. The call button didn't light up. I pressed the card against the glass again. Still nothing.

Fuck.

"Yep," Melissa proclaimed. "You're batting a thousand, Captain America."

43

Hope Floats

+81 Days – 1424 hours
02:59:33

I stared at the card, oblivious of what to do next. I slumped against the brushed steel elevator door. This one wasn't gold and shiny like the ones in the main atrium. The door paralleled my life in recent days—drab and unwilling to open for any positive result.

"We could try to crack the passcode," Sean offered, taking a look at the numeric keypad for any clues as to what digits had been pressed.

"Can we get up another way?" Jude asked.

"Climb up like we did to get down here?" Melissa added.

I shook my head. "Not a hundred stories. We wouldn't make it."

"You could, John," Sean said.

"Not sure even I could drag Westsmith to the boss if we found him."

"What about the stairs?" Jude asked.

"The stairs don't come all the way down here," I said.

"Ain't that against code?" Sean asked.

"When you control the world around you," Melissa said, "the rules don't apply anymore."

"Basically," I confirmed.

Stuck in the sub-sub-basement with only hard options to get to the upper floors. Westsmith was roaming freely around the building and we were now working against a three-hour deadline.

"Can't we go back to the lobby?" Jude asked. "I'm sure the

stairwells will get us into the towers."

"The executive floors are separated from the main office spaces," I said. "They made sure to disassociate themselves from their underlings. The freight elevator was the only direct access to all floors."

"Ain't you a fount of knowledge?" Melissa said with a sad smirk.

"Yeah," I answered. "For what good it's doing me."

"Us," Jude said.

"What?" I asked.

"Us," she repeated. "We're all in this together, remember?"

"Right on," Sean added.

"And this," Jude said with a cracked voice, pointing to her neck, "isn't all on you."

If she knew she had been used as an incentive after I had turned down Dick's first request to be a part of the Westsmith exfil operation, she might have a different opinion of me. She carried on like everything was guaranteed to work out at the end. She was a fool if she believed that. Everything we had tried to do while chasing Westsmith had turned into a shit show.

But she has one thing going for her.

Yeah? What?

She has hope.

Hope will eventually kill us all.

Or it could serve as our salvation.

How did having hope work out for Heinz? For Lee? Damon?

They were soldiers. They understood what they had signed up for.

How about Rosalita? The picture of her little boy—how she looked at him—didn't make me think she had willingly signed up to be one of R&R's thugs.

Perhaps not.

So, tell me again how hope is going to lead to our salvation? Bob didn't have an answer for me. Of course, he didn't because he knew I was right. The others stared at me with expressions of expectation, looking to me like little children waiting for the next chapter of a new book. They had all made the mistake of following me. I wasn't anyone's hero. And, I certainly was nobody's savior.

Well, you are definitely in the fail column for acting like a Christian deity.

I never asked for this.

But here you are. So, you are only good at taking orders… and killing the enemy from a mile away?

I'm not sure if I take orders all that well, either.

"John, we'll figure this out," Jude said, barely above a whisper. She paused, the wetness returning to her eyes. "We have to. I don't want to die."

I didn't want her to die, either. What could we do? Westsmith could be anywhere in the building. No way to get to the upper floors from here without the pass card.

You're right, Bob, John thought. Hope was a good thing. Maybe the best of things.

And no good thing ever dies. I believe your Stephen King wrote those words.

Stephen King wasn't here to write us out of this situation, was he?

We do not need him. We have you.

And hope?

Some people may consider those one and the same.

Well, let's hope your faith in hope saves the day, because I am out of anything useful to contribute.

From above us came the quiet addition of static, followed by three quick muffled taps. "Welcome back," Dick announced clearly through what I assumed was a building-wide public address system. I could vaguely make out the circular pattern of holes disguised within the field of the actual pores of concrete. Truly, a sophisticated broadcast system. "If you have had a nice respite after your firefight with the locals," Dick continued, "I would appreciate you rounding up Mr. Westsmith for me now, please." His voice was unassuming and easy to listen to. But his words carried with them a savagery bubbling just under the surface. The use of pleasantries didn't mask the fact Dick was still pulling our strings.

"If you please," Dick repeated.

A familiar double chime announced the arrival of the freight elevator. Its doors opened on quiet and expensive hardware, the recessed lighting brightly shining on the diamond plating and thick wood paneling. Smooth jazz horns, bass and percussion quietly serenaded us. We looked at each other and shrugged before filing into the elevator. The freight elevator was decked out in a nicer decor than most regular apartment elevator interiors. We turned around to face the doors as they slid closed. It was proof we had all been trained to "face front" when using this crazy vertical lift contraption.

Dick's voice was just as clear inside the elevator. "Mr. Westsmith is currently rummaging around on the 32nd floor. I would appreciate you collecting him and bringing him to me." The square button on the console marked with a 32 lit up, another chime rang, and the elevator smoothly started its ascent. We stared at the numbers with Pavlovian precision, listening to the music.

See, John? Hope. Ask and you shall receive.

44

Smooth Jazz

+81 Days – 1431 hours
02:52:49

"*Morning Dance*," Sean said.

"What the hell are you talking about?" Melissa asked.

"The music." Sean pointed to the ceiling of the elevator. "Spyro Gyra's *Morning Dance*."

"Is that who this is?" Jude asked. "I never knew."

"It is a good tune," I commented.

We were just us again, whittled down to the core group who had traveled together across Massachusetts, suffered and fought against a self-proclaimed king, and made it out of the asylum in one piece. The elevator chimed as we passed the tenth floor. I checked the AK-47, verifying a full magazine and a round in the breach. The others did the same. I handed out four magazines to each of them. They filled the empty slots in their tactical vests. I turned my rifle on an angle for the others to see. "This lever is the safety. When it's all the way up, it keeps the bolt locked out. Middle position is full automatic. I don't want any of you using the middle position. All the way down is single and semi-automatic."

They each looked at their own weapons, walking through the safety levers positions in their heads.

"What's the top?" I asked.

"Safety," Melissa chimed in quickly.

"Where aren't you going to set the lever to?"

The elevator chimed the arrival and passing of the twentieth floor.

"The middle position," Jude recited.

"Where's the single shot mode?" I asked Sean.

"Lever to lowest position."

"Outstanding," I said.

"Plan?" Melissa asked.

"I lead," I said. "Sean and Jude go to the left side. Melissa, you're with me to the right. It's probably the same layout as the floor where we had our sit-down with Dick."

Another chime signaled the thirtieth floor. I approached the doors with the AK at a quarter draw. I wasn't going to be able to raise it much more with the others in the car with their own weapons at the ready.

"Get to the sides," I ordered. The others quickly moved against the side walls offering protection from stray weapons' fire.

Thirty-one. Ding. The elevator decelerated and came to a smooth stop with a final ding at the thirty-second floor. As soon as the doors opened, I raised the AK to a full draw and stepped out into the lobby.

My rifle barrel was grabbed, pulling me forward. A fist swung at my face. I ducked, still not avoiding the punch. It landed against my temple, a grazing shot catching me enough to daze me. My grip loosened, but I hung onto the AK enough to squeeze the trigger. A single shot erupted from the barrel. The tension on the AK was gone.

Westsmith darted away through the lobby. Damn. He was deceptively quick. I held my position at the elevator bay, waiting for the starbursts to diminish from my vision. I held my arm out to keep the others from stepping out of the elevator.

"Let's get him," Melissa said. "What are we waiting for?"

"One goddamn minute," I ordered, still shaking the last of the cobwebs out of my head. "He has hell of a haymaker."

"Still keeping to the plan?" Sean asked.

"Yeah," I replied. "But he may not come quietly."

"You think?" Melissa retorted. "I'm not sure why he wouldn't want his head delivered on a silver platter to the dreaded Wizard of Emerald City."

"I just want to go home," I let slip out, my bones feeling brittle and my muscles weary.

"Well, buttercup," Jude said, "we're definitely not in Kansas anymore."

"Ain't that the truth," Sean agreed. He and the others looked out from the elevator's softly-lit interior, keeping an eye out for another sneak attack from Westsmith.

When the last of the flashes of light dimmed behind my eyelids, I dropped my arm and turned to face the lobby and the uncertainty of another day at the office.

45

A Day at the Office

+81 Days – 1436 hours

02:47:33

We fanned out in two columns along the marbled lobby, Melissa behind me and Sean and Jude lined up along the opposite wall.

"Remember," I said in a low voice, "the layout curves out like the upper floors. Offices on the outer wall and conference rooms in the middle." All those hours memorizing the floorplans in the concrete sub-basement cell were finally paying off.

"Copy," Sean responded with a nod.

Jude put a hand lightly on Sean's right shoulder. Melissa was doing the same with me. Within a period of mere weeks, we had become more and more like a well-oiled four-man assault team. I would go into battle with any of them.

"Go," I said softly. Almost in unison, Sean and I moved forward toward the reception area where the marble tiles transitioned to a tight-weaved swirling patterned carpet suitable for everyday office traffic. At the receptionist's desk, we split off into our two-man teams. Sean cleared the space behind the waist-high counter before he and Jude disappeared into the right-side corridor. I led Melissa down the left side corridor, thankful for the added silence the carpet provided our footfalls.

The closest office door was open, the first of a series of executive suites with floor-to-ceiling windows between them and the hallway. The outer glass wall provided a million-dollar view of Manhattan and the separated lanes of Park Avenue trailing north to the base of Central Park. The sky was still dark and angry with clouds.

I led the AKs barrel inside, my eyes inspecting the room with the rifle's front sight directly in the center of my vision. Behind the door. Clear. Behind and under the desk. Clear. I backed out of the office, dropping the barrel of the AK on the way out so it didn't catch the doorframe. Melissa took point as we moved in tandem to the next office.

Through the next set of interior windows was a huge oak desk with a black multi-extension phone with the receiver sitting on a desk blotter. Next to both was a flatscreen monitor. The door was closed. Melissa checked the doorknob and shook her head. I kicked the door in. The hardware snapped off and bounced off the side of the desk support, leaving an indentation. The windows separating the space from the hallway shuddered from the force.

We weren't relying on stealth anymore.

Melissa moved inside with her new AK, quickly pointing the weapon at the other side of the desk. The Benelli swayed across her back from the makeshift strap she had made from my discarded M4. "Clear."

I nodded and we made our way back to the corridor. The next three offices were easily accessible and dismissed as empty, as there was no office furniture. Westsmith couldn't be lurking in any of them. The curved opaque glass wall to the conference stood to our right.

"Stupid smart glass," Melissa whispered.

The glass was frosted so not even a shadow showed through. It was brilliant technology. PDLC glass—Polymer Dispersed Liquid Crystal tech—allowed for excellent privacy. The CIA used similar electrochromic windows at their Langley campus and in other locations around the world.

"Not even a window in the goddamn entry," Melissa complained under her breath as she stopped at the solid conference room door, although I heard her with perfect clarity. "A perfect spot for accidents to run rampant." Melissa twisted the doorknob and let it swing open into the conference room. I followed the motion of the door and put my boot against the heavy steel.

The glass went from frosted to clear. A heavy ergonomic chair sailed across the room at me, hitting me square in the chest hard enough to knock the wind out of my lungs. The rifle barrel was tangled between the backrest and the armrest frame. I flung the chair away, crashing it against the other door just as another chair flew at me. I deflected it on top of the other one, but not in time to ward off Westsmith as he followed it in with a kick to my sternum. Whatever oxygen I had inhaled blew out with a hrumph.

He grabbed the barrel of Melissa's AK and snapped it out of her hands. The grab was so deliberate and sudden the tailstock caught her under the chin. She went down hard to the floor, lost to unconsciousness. Westsmith came at me hard and fast, weapon in hand and a backpack strapped tight to his back. He swung Melissa's rifle at me like a baseball bat. I leaned back out of its trajectory but he caught me again with a kick, this time to the jaw. The world went dark for a moment—this time not just from the black clouds swallowing up the sun's rays all afternoon.

I thought I heard someone call my name. Maybe.

Another pointed object crashed against the back of my neck. The floor rushed up to meet me. My forehead stopped the carpet's ascent. Hard. I tried to shake out the cobwebs, but the world went darker than it should have. My vision cleared enough to see the underside of the massive conference table.

The smart glass was still transparent to the corridor we had come in from, letting in the darkness from the storm outside. The other wall of the conference room was still frosted over. Two chairs were piled against the opposite side door, keeping it from being opened more than a few inches. Melissa was sprawled out on the floor, half inside the conference and half in the corridor. Metallic sounds. I heard the rattling of a botched breach check. Westsmith was trying to inspect Melissa's AK, but he didn't understand how to operate the weapon.

Good for me.

My AK was across the floor out of reach. I rolled up to a crouch as I pulled the Glock. Westsmith swung the AK toward me, not able to fire it. I squeezed the trigger. The front of the AK's stock sparked. Westsmith howled and dropped the weapon. He held his left hand in his right, blood squeezing out from between his fingers. His shoulders were rolled forward and his footing wide apart in a low aggressive stance. He glared at me, his breathing heavily and his skin beaded in sweat.

I heard voices calling my name again, but they were much farther away than they were before. The door was still struggling to open against the chairs pinned against it. The smart glass went opaque again. They didn't turn into the frosted white like before, but a deep onyx black. It had the look of smooth obsidian. The bank of monitors at the other end of the room popped into life. Instead of lighting up, the flatscreens took on a darker and deeper black. The surfaces of the monitors buckled and swirled, looking like they were broadcasting the storm clouds above Manhattan. The turmoil on the screens pressed against the glass of the monitors until each panel bubbled out into a convex shape. The glass split open, sending spiderwebs of cracks across them to the edges of the thin frames.

Chunks of glass fell from them, the video still playing in the space behind it.

Was that even possible?

More glass fell from the screens. One monitor fell from its wall mounts. The clouds continued to display on the wall behind it, even without the monitor to broadcast it. The tendrils of smoke—the same as the ones in the shuttle bus—crawled along the wall. Its tip probed where the wall met the ceiling before it ventured along a new horizontal path toward us.

Someone called out my name. From somewhere far away.

Westsmith hadn't moved, but his shirt was soaked in perspiration. The muscles on his neck and the veins in his forehead were pulsing with exertion. He had forgotten all about his missing fingers from the ricochet of my gunshot, both of his hands down at his side. A pool of blood stained the carpet next to his left leg.

The cicadas chirped in the back of my head. Dull daggers plunged between my shoulder blades, sending heat and pain up my neck into the middle of my skull. My temples pounded. It felt like something was trying to burrow its way out each side of my head.

"Ahhhhh!" I screamed. The pain inside my skull was unbearable. Had to release the pressure. It was the only way. The Glock was still in my hand. One bullet. It was all it would take to relieve the pressure. Someone had drilled a hole in the top of my skull and poured in smelted iron. The searing gray matter dissolved any rational thinking in its way.

A bullet was the only way.

My hands went up to my temples, my Glock along for the ride. Something was trying to get out of my head. The buzz of the cicadas inside was joined by a rampant scurrying sensation. I could feel thousands of tiny legs and pinchers trying to burrowing out from behind my eyeballs. Their tiny shadows flitted across my vision.

There was tingling in my temples. My head was threatening to split open. One round to the side of the head. I would take as many of the bugs with me as possible. The 9mm round wouldn't rattle around enough to kill them all before they escaped.

The Benelli was on the floor still strapped to Melissa's back. I holstered the Glock and crawled toward the door. Westsmith was still there, but more transparent somehow. The tendrils of smoke had enveloped the ceiling, slithering over each other as they thought to venture back down the walls.

The shotgun was only a meter away. I pulled my tactical knife. Westsmith made no move to stop me. Odd. Something erupted from my skin. Did one of the bugs crawl out? The chirping was louder. I heard several whines before I realized they were coming from my lips. Something else poked its head and pinchers out of the growing gashes in my skin.

My right hand found the shotgun strap and cut cleanly through it with the blade. I dropped the knife and dragged the shotgun into my hands. Had to vaporize the bugs before any more found their way out from the confines of my skull. I quickly swiveled the gun around and jammed the barrel directly under the soft tissue below my jawline.

The buzzing got louder. The pressure against my temples increased. The rest of the bugs were ready to burst out like an angry enflamed whitehead pimple ready to pop.

With a final yell, I pulled the trigger.

46

Suicide Prevention

+81 Days – 1446 hours
02:37:22

Nothing happened.

What?

The bugs were on the verge of erupting from the stretched and bubbling skin at my temples. I couldn't think of what was wrong with the shotgun so I pulled the trigger again. It still didn't fire. More whines slipped from my throat. Tossing the shotgun away in desperate frustration, I reached for my Glock again. Did the sidearm still have the modified rounds in the magazine? Maybe. I knew it would fire, at least. It always had.

The ceiling was a frothing sea of swinging limbs, the tentacles slapping against each other as if they were battling for supremacy. The animated mist in the corners where the ceiling met the walls was less concerned about claiming the field of battle around the recessed lights, content to work its way down the rippling black smart glass walls.

I raised the Glock and put the barrel in my mouth. The taste of minute traces of blood, grit and gunpowder lay on my tongue. There was even a minute trace of gun oil, even though I hadn't been able to clean it properly for weeks. The metal clicked against my teeth.

The cicadas' antennae and forelegs poked out from my face. Their hindlegs skittered as fast as they could to find enough purchase to push their hard-shelled bodies all the way into the real world.

Someone called my name. Again. Closer this time.

Westsmith and his backpack had all but disappeared. The smoke had enveloped the conference room's walls and ceiling. The tendrils tested the floor, exploring around the baseboards and furniture. I could just make out Melissa's body where she laid unconscious half in the doorway, a sliver of light still penetrating into the room from the corridor.

Pop.

A faint noise from far away, but insistent.

Pop. Pop.

The smoke tensed. The ends of its exploring fingers perked up like attentive cobras, swaying side-to-side hypnotically for a moment before retreating up the walls en masse. The smoke sucked back into the empty space behind the monitors, leaving the walls and ceiling as it had found them. The black of the smart glass walls returned to a milky frost color.

"John!" The same voice was now in the room with me. Sean appeared, now holding the barrel of the AK-47 directly against the base of Westsmith's neck—who had reappeared. I could smell the singe of skin and body hair from the hot barrel. He had returned to holding the stumps of his fingers in a tight grip.

"John," Jude said in a compassionate soft voice. She approached me slowly with her arms out in front of her, fingers out and palms down. "It's okay, John."

I looked at her with puzzlement. Of course, it was going to be okay. Westsmith was back in custody. We still had time to get Jude fixed. Even Melissa was coming around, even if she was gingerly testing her swelling jaw with her fingers. The cicadas chirping in my head had stopped. The pressure in my head had dissipated. The monitor bank had returned to its original state, the glass intact on all of the screens.

"John." Jude spoke to me in the same soft even tone. Her eyes betrayed her worry. "Give me the Glock, please."

I still had the barrel of the Glock in my mouth. And my finger was still putting pressure on the trigger. What the fuck? I returned my finger to the trigger guard. Slowly, I removed the gun, the front sight clicking against my top teeth. I spit on the carpet twice to rid myself of the taste of metal still on my tongue. The Glock went back into its holster. I retrieved my tactical knife and did the same with it. The Benelli was still in the corner where I had tossed it. I picked it up and returned it to Melissa who had propped herself up to a seated position against the doorframe.

"Thanks," she said, laying it cross her lap and stroking the stock absently.

"What were you trying to do?" Jude asked, her voice cracking at the end.

I didn't know. The idea cicadas were trying to escape from my skull seemed absurd. To say it out loud would make Jude and the others more certain I should have stayed at Creedmoor for a long-term evaluation. The chirping was gone. The burrowing had ceased. All I felt now was exhaustion. My muscles ached. It hurt to concentrate. I could only shake my head and shrug my shoulders in response.

"You gonna make it, boss?" Sean asked, never taking his eyes off Westsmith or letting the barrel slip from contact with his skin.

"I'm okay," I replied to everyone, staring at the side of Westsmith's bowed head. He also looked spent, the sweat clinging to his clothes and only starting to dry on his forehead. The blood still dripped from where his fingers used to be, but it had tapered off considerably. "Let's get this asshole to the boss."

Sean and Jude nodded in agreement, but still looked at me with furrowed brows and sideways glances at each other. Great. Now, they thought I was suicidal.

"I'm good," I tried to assure them. "Really."

The looks on their face told me they didn't really believe me. How could I explain the tendrils of twitching mist or the sudden thoughts of having to keep the bugs in my head from getting out. It was a ridiculous notion.

"Ooh-rah," Melissa said with groggy commitment from the doorway, taking the focus off of me for the moment, at least.

47

Penthouse, Please
+81 Days – 1453 hours
02:30:21

We marched the silent Westsmith back toward the elevator. Melissa had bound his hands with the remainder of the strap I had cut off the Benelli. She had to sling the AK-47 in favor of holding the shotgun, but I think she preferred it to the rifle anyway—for comfort, familiarity, nostalgia, or, maybe, a combination of all three.

"You know you'll never make it out of the building, right?" Westsmith warned us, still holding the stubs of his fingers tight in spite of the bindings. "The Powers That Be would never allow it."

"Powers That Be," Sean muttered. "I don't think people still say that."

"You're missing the point," Westsmith insisted.

"He always does," Melissa spoke up, giving Sean a wink.

"You think he'll fulfill his contract?" Westsmith asked. "He's never been a man of his word."

"And you're any better?" Jude asked pointedly.

"Cut from the same cloth," Westsmith said with a shrug. "So, it's difficult to say."

"I don't trust Dick any more than I do you," I said. "If there's a double-cross coming, it won't end pretty."

We arrived at the elevator and I pressed the UP arrow call button. It lit up and the elevator let out a ding before the doors slid open. Since we were the only ones using the elevator today, it had nowhere else to be. I leaned his chest against the lobby wall and patted down his legs, waist and the flat backpack

"In," I ordered Westsmith. He moved inside and stopped in the middle of the car. Grabbing the back of his shirt, I pushed him into the right back corner until his forehead was touching the expensive wood paneling. "Stay."

Sean drew up his AK into his shoulder, braced out his elbow and settled the front sights on Westsmith's heart. Under the shoulder blade and left of the spine based on the angle Westsmith was standing. The others filed in, each taking up a vacant corner. Melissa and Jude held their weapons up in a half draw, partially in case Westsmith decided to try something and in preparation of reaching the upper floors of the executive suites.

I pressed the ES button for the top floor. Nothing happened. It didn't light up. No chimes sounded. The doors remained open to the 32nd floor lobby.

"John?" Jude said, sporting a raised eyebrow.

"Dunno," I said as I stepped back out onto the marbled floor of the office lobby. The reception desk was empty, the space quiet and growing dark. Not like whatever had occurred in the conference room. There were no fog-formed probing tentacles trying to advance toward me. It was more mundane, if not less awe-inspiring. The storm clouds had dropped from the sky considerably, forcing the darkening shadows to lose their sharpness in favor of a fuzzy fade into a gradient black. The whole scene seemed to be a muted painting of realism, only punctuated by the occasional flash to white and the following low rumbles from the rapid change in air pressure and temperature. It had gotten cold in the office, too. With the sun hidden above the clouds, and no heat being pumped into the space, the glass, steel and marble had nothing to warm it up. This level was as dead as the rest of the world.

"Did you ring?" a familiar voice crackled through the elevator's intercom. "Do you have what I asked you for?"

I didn't remember the request being a favor. He had used plenty of pleasantries, all the while making demands using threats of death and abduction. I stepped back into the elevator. "We have Westsmith," I said. "We can't deliver if you won't let us up to do so."

"I must admit the security cameras have been blacking out intermittently on various floors," Dick said.

"And do you see us now?" I asked.

"Yes," Dick confirmed.

"Good. So, let us up so we can conclude our business." I stared at the circle of holes in the brushed aluminum panel above the call buttons while I waited for Dick to respond. A minute amount of charcoal-colored mist dropped lazily out from the lowest openings. I backed up to the middle of the car and watched as the smoke drifted down past the rest of the panel to pool on the floor.

The others either didn't mind it or didn't notice it. Melissa was the only one looking directly at the speaker along with me, a glare in her eyes instead of wonder or curiosity about the smoke. She didn't see smoke, but she was smoldering a burning rage in her heart for the man whose voice was coming through the PA system.

I glanced at Westsmith. His forehead was still pressed into the corner. He didn't show any new sweat or tremors. The only movement was the expansion of his chest with pained breathing and a slumping of his shoulders.

"So," Dick said, his voice dripping with arrogance and confidence. Of course, I was sure those qualities were a prerequisite in the work he did. "You say you're ready?"

"Yes," I answered simply, waiting for Dick's next move. It was like a chess match. The question was how many moves ahead was Dick contemplating. And, of course, we didn't have the advantage of seeing the board at all. I'm sure Roy had been an amateur compared to the level of calculations and manipulations in which Dick operated.

The elevator chimed. The doors closed slowly with a quiet click.

"Then, it's time to present me with a tribute," Dick announced.

The dark vapors were gone. The elevator was just an elevator again. We occupied each corner of the car, with me at the center. Sean was poised to execute Westsmith if he moved any more than it took to breathe. Melissa continued to stare at the speaker, stroking the stock of the Benelli like a Persian cat. Jude held her AK at her thigh in her right hand while her left hand was cupped over the side of her neck. She leaned with her back against the wall with her chin to her chest. We had traveled so far, just to return to where we were forced to start. Was this the reason why so many hated New York City in favor of New England?

Maybe. I was more a Midwest boy, anyway.

The ES button winked off. The low whirr of motors and cables lifted the elevator—and us with it—skyward. Even though it was a freight elevator, the ride was smooth. Another Jazz tune played in the background. This time, Sean didn't offer any suggestions to its origins. The electronic attendant chimed with every floor we passed. There were a lot of chimes. The good thing was this miserable operation was coming to a close. I let out a sigh as we passed the one hundredth floor.

I checked the AK and tapped how many magazines I had in my vest. The Glock was still comfortable in its holster. The tactical knife sat securely in its sheath. I measured my breathing as the attendant chimed again.

110th floor.

The women and I looked at the digital display over the door. Even Westsmith had turned around to watch the numbers. Sean darted his eyes after each ding, quickly returning to watch our prisoner for any sudden moves.

Ding. 120th floor.

Be prepared. We were close to being done but weren't out of the dark forest yet.

Ding. 130th floor.

Next stop, the top floor. Dick's executive suite. The elevator slowed to a stop, chiming again. The call button ES was lit again, as was the button with 136 on it. The digital reader above the sliding doors still displayed an LED ES with a series of animated chevrons moving in in an upward direction next to it. The doors opened.

Twenty AK barrels pointed at us from the relative safety of this new red granite themed lobby. The team Rosalita had headed up apparently wasn't made up of the only operatives on Dick's payroll. Before I could do more than raise my hands to chest level, the doors to the rear of the car opened.

BLAM!

Blood splattered from the side of Sean's head as the gunshot reverberated inside the elevator. He fell dead to the floor. Jude screamed out his name. I was shocked into disbelief—and paralysis. Melissa swung up her shotgun.

A flash-bang grenade exploded, blinding and disorienting us. Being trapped in the enclosed space made it worse. The world was white with a steady ring in my ears. Vague shadows swept in and spirited someone away.

"Walk–" Westsmith yelled out. His voice was cut off as all of the elevator doors closed at the same time.

The car started to ascend, smoke from the flash-bang swirled around to the ceiling with nowhere else to go. The air at ground level was heavy and hard to breathe in without burning the lungs enough to start coughing fits. We covered our mouths behind the collars of our shirts, for what good it did. The taste of aluminum and potassium coated my tongue.

The ringing faded, replaced by a whirring of a small motor. The haze cleared through a hidden exhaust fan, the vapors whisking away along the corners of the ceiling. Quickly, the elevator returned to a normal atmosphere as if nothing had happened. Everything was the same as before. Well, except the fact Westsmith was gone and Sean was bleeding out on the floor, offering up the last of his lifeblood for a lost cause.

48

Even Trade

+81 Days – 1459 hours
02:24:54

I slid to the floor beside the elevator panel. The 137 and ES buttons flickered alternately. A low steady buzz could be felt through the walls. Dick had locked down the elevator between floors, trapping us.

Sean continued to stare at me with a slack jaw. His cheek was pressed against the floor in a pool of blood of his own making. His face reflected back up at him, the blood still wet enough to serve as a deathly mirror.

Sobs filled the car. Melissa had propped herself in the corner on the other side of the doors, her arms around her shotgun and her wet cheek against the cold barrel. Jude had crawled over to Sean and put tentative fingers on his leg. She stroked his calf and mumbled something behind the cupped hand over her mouth. It could have been a prayer, but my hearing was still compromised from the flash-bang. She grabbed a handful of his pant leg and twisted it up in her fist.

"John?" Jude asked, dropping her other hand into her lap. I could only stare back at her. As a hot tear sliced down my face, I realized I had added to the choir of lamentation. "Are we done fucking around?" she asked.

I looked at Sean's face, another person killed under my command. He was dead because of me. His lifeless eyes stared up at me with accusations of my guilt. Vengeance was what was required for Sean… for Heinz… for everyone we had lost along the way. Damon. Lee. Rosalita. Victoria. Seemed stupid to rattle the names of the dead so quickly after their demise. It wasn't like we had forgotten them already. Plus, I could list dozens of others who deserved to be on the list. People who needed to be on the list.

We were Stateside. There shouldn't be this much death on American soil. I had been trained to take death to others in foreign lands so the same death wouldn't be meted out here. And I had seen so many people—good and bad—be taken out by FRACs or a bullet to the head. Sometimes, both.

Jude let out a woeful moan as her tears flowed freely onto Sean's pant leg. The two of them had connected on a level she and I hadn't. They were like brother and sister, except better because they weren't fighting over mom and dad's attention. Jude had already lost her brothers… and parents. Of course, Melissa had lost her parents and her sister. No one was immune to what this new world had brought with it.

"Thank you for the delivery, Mr. Walken," Dick said through the intercom. "You have done me a great service."

"Where's our people?" I asked, through gritted teeth.

Dick answered after a moment of awkward silence. "I have them."

"We delivered," I told the speaker. "It's time you delivered."

"Well," Dick pondered, "you did come back much lighter than you left. Several hundred pounds, by my estimation. I can convert into kilos for you if you want. I know how Marine snipers like to measure in metric." He chuckled at his own joke.

I was sure he was patting his own back at his cleverness. He certainly did have me—or my kind—pegged as it related to thinking about the world in terms of meters. "So, what does that even mean?"

"You owe me more lives," Dick calculated. "You brought me one. You lost four. You owe me three."

This wasn't going anywhere good. Melissa slowly shook her head as she grasped what Dick was talking about. Jude's tears had dried up. She still kept a hand on Sean's leg, but not in the same desperate way from a minute ago. Even with her head down and her hair falling over her face, there was a look of grim determination in the way she clenched her jaw. Her head cocked slightly with Dick's every word.

"I just happen to have two people in my possession to serve nicely in an even exchange," Dick told us. "And I will throw in the animal to make it an even three. Seems fitting as your former spotter was really just a trained dog for me."

"Fuck you," I said under my breath.

"We may have a bad connection, Mr. Walken," Dick said. "What did you said?"

I didn't answer. It was obvious the intercom system was state of the art equipment, allowing for perfect clarity and tone. Roanoke & Raleigh wasn't in the business of sparing expense to sacrifice quality. Of course, Dick had no qualms about sacrificing other things. Human lives to him didn't hold the same intrinsic value. Fodder was still fodder, regardless of the form it took.

"And the capsule in my neck?" Jude yelled. The elevator went silent for a time, so quiet the hum of the recessed lights became more obvious.

I wasn't sure if any of us had exhaled before Dick spoke up again. "I'm sorry. I was distracted with bureaucracy. Always dealing with incompetence and endless red tape. It is exhausting."

"Well?" Jude asked, not concerned about Dick's administrative difficulties.

"Incentive, Ms. Sawyer," Dick said. "Mr. Walken has two hours to decide how he would like to pay his debt. Plain enough for you to understand?"

49

Blast Radius

+81 Days – 1504 hours
02:19:23

We sat in silence for several minutes after hearing Dick's proposal. The hum of the bulbs in the recessed lighting housings seemed overly loud. The fan motor behind the ceiling panels whirred as it sucked out the stale air in the elevator.

"How many shells do you have left, Melissa" I asked.

"For the Benelli?" she confirmed the request. "Five rounds in the extension and another six in my pocket. Why?"

I got to my feet, despite the firmly entrenched exhaustion. The standing was an effort in and of itself. Not because I was at the limits of my body, but because of the emotional weight on my shoulders. Sean wouldn't stop staring at me from the floor.

I walked over to Melissa and put out my hand. She looked at my hand and then at my eyes. "What?"

"The Benelli," I ordered. "Please."

She turned the weapon over in her hands and presented me with the tailstock end. I took it and nodded my thanks. Chambering a round, I pushed in the safety button behind the trigger guard and settled my index finger on the trigger.

"Cover your ears," I ordered.

Both Jude and Melissa did as they were told as I swung up the barrel and squeezed the trigger. The blast was deafening... and satisfying. The intercom speaker disappeared and roughly a meter diameter hole replaced it on the gold colored panel above the buttons.

"Ouch," Melissa cried out as a couple sparks and a stray piece of heated metal singed her arm. "Damn!"

I pumped another round, the spent shell spinning out of the breach. Swinging the shotgun around, I took aim at the hooded security camera in the same corner where Westsmith had spent his time. I squeezed the trigger again. The blast left a massive gaping hole, exposing some of the backing of the paneling and steel framework. The ringing dissipated after a moment, leaving only a few errant sparks to mark any surveillance or communications had existed at all. Jude and Melissa lowered their arms. Melissa looked at her singed skin but said nothing about it.

"Feel better?" Jude asked.

"No," I replied honestly, worried I might never feel better again. "I'm just tired."

"You ain't alone on that front," Melissa commented. "Gimme."

"Thanks," I said, returning the shotgun to her outstretched hand

"No problem."

"So now what?" Jude asked.

"Now we get our people back," I said.

"How do you intend on doing that?" Jude scooted back into the corner, brought her knees up to her chest, and pointed at the mangled metal above the call buttons. "You blew up our communications. What the fuck, John? I don't have much time left!"

This was the first time Jude showed this level of fear about her own mortality. She was right to worry. Here we were in a locked elevator with no communications, and two hours to get our people back. I somehow had to fight through Dick's men, get to April, Summer and Holly, and then force Dick to deactivate the explosive in Jude's neck.

Another impossible task.

I had made shitty decisions since coming to New York. From letting Rosalita call the shots at Creedmoor to making emotional decisions in the field when I finally did take charge, all I had succeeded in doing was losing Rosalita and her entire team... and now Sean. Summer and April had to be found, Holly included.

I had cut us off from the rest of the building, now facing the real possibility of losing Jude to death... or worse. Fuck. *Way to go, hero*, Sean's gaze screamed. I averted my eyes to the ceiling.

Think, John. You have been in worse scrapes. The Gaunt Man took up the corner under the obliterated security cameras, his arms folded and his shoulder against the wall.

I can't think.

When have you ever been a thinker?

So tired. Everything hurts.

So? I've never seen you give up.

But, I'm too–

Too, what? Too exhausted? Too weak? Caught with too many variables and not enough options? Quit being a pussy and start being a Marine.

I've lost so much.

You are not terminally unique in that regard.

You're right.

One of my more excellent qualities. Stop miring yourself in your despondency and start working a solution!

I started to object, but Bob had disappeared again. My constant hallucination was always my most adamant cheerleader, never falling into my nihilistic musings.

Where did we go from here? Thinking back to the blueprints I had occupied my idle time with during my sub-basement storage room recovery, the configurations of the floors between 130 and 138 were different than the rest. Instead of the typical corporate offices and conference rooms, those floors included a series of observation rooms, labs, and medical theaters. Westsmith must be there. It made the most sense. Westsmith was one floor away, so we needed to get there, too.

50

Behind Door Number One
+81 Days – 1508 hours
02:15:17

The majority of the R&R security force had come from our left during their raid to take Westsmith from us. The mercenaries who had grabbed him through the other doors at the back of the elevator only had a couple hired guns in tow. The assault I was planning on this floor was made a little more feasible.

My memory of the blueprints showed the only connective corridor on the experimental development floors was through the elevator itself, an interesting and clever way to keep unwanted visitors from accessing the more highly secure medical wing. The concrete poured around the elevator shaft and the adjoining walls cleanly separated the floor into a 30/70 percent split, with Westsmith in a room somewhere within the smaller percentage of the floor's layout.

I put my hand on Sean's chest before taking the AK-47 from his grasp. Jude pulled the full magazines from his tach vest and handed one to each of us, taking two for herself. After securing the magazine, I jammed the AK's tailstock into the seam between the doors. Using the wedged rifle as a crowbar, I pulled to the right with all my strength. The AK started to bend.

Come on. Come on.

The two doors suddenly slid open, just enough to get my boot between them. I leaned the rifle against the corner and wrapped my fingers on the edges of each door. Even with my enhanced strength, it took an amazing amount of exertion to open the doors enough to get my back and legs sideways in the gap. I pressed between the doors and pushed them open all the way.

Past them was another locked set of steel doors to thwart my attempt to access to the rest of the floor below us. Only the top half of the doors were visible, but it was enough. It wasn't a typical set of elevator doors but the mechanics were the same, designed to withstand attempts to breach from the lobby side, not from inside the shaft itself.

I flipped a mechanical lever disengaging the locking bars. The doors parted a few centimeters, allowing for me squat down to wriggle my fingers between the seals. I pried the doors apart until I could peer through the widened crack enough to see into the vestibule on the other side.

From the shiny marble floor to the large white ceramic tiles on the walls, the vestibule was almost too bright to look at for too long. The white was broken up with gray and red swirls in the marble and a six-inch black band of plastic or glass running horizontally along the walls at waist height. The bands led to a set of black-framed steel doors opposite the elevator. Two sentries dressed in black tactical gear were posted next to them. The sentries were black blobs in the too-white lobby, looking bored. They hadn't noticed the elevator doors had opened, probably lulled into a false sense of security from too many weeks of having little or nothing to do. They hadn't realized I would have enough strength to escape the locked down elevator. Heinz would have known.

Taking a knee, I quietly drew the Glock and aimed it through the slit. The others covered their ears. After taking a measured breath, I squeezed the trigger. The report was loud in the elevator car, but muffled in the lobby. Blood splattered against the white wall of the sentry on the left. As his knees buckled and he pitched forward, the other sentry reacted by reaching out to his falling partner.

Another shot.

More blood marred the white walls. The second sentry continued his forward momentum; his hands outstretched to his partner. They collapsed into each other, sliding to the floor in front of the black double doors.

I waited, listening for any indication we were going to be overrun. No alarms went off. There were no sounds of the slapping boots of reinforcements. A minute went by. All I heard was our breathing.

A thin rivulet of blood ventured toward me in a ragged line from the pool gathering between the two guards. Its path seemed deliberate as it traveled across the smooth marble, only diverting minutely when it encountered a vein in the otherwise smooth surface.

Pun intended?

I opened the heavy steel doors wide enough for us to slip through to the vestibule, being sure to sidestep the blood as I hopped down to the marble floor. I turned around and helped Jude and Melissa to the floor.

We fanned out. There were no cameras here. We seemed to have escaped detection. Other than the dead sentries and the Jackson Pollack relief of blood on the floor and walls, the vestibule was still a disorienting and blanched stark white. Behind us, the interior of the elevator—with its wood, gold trim and warm tones—seemed completely out of place. It looked like a chamber from another world altogether. The interior of the elevator was warm and inviting while the lobby was stark and cold. What tied the two spaces together was the dead littering the floors.

While both Sean and the security guards wore black tactical gear, Sean's body was weighed down with more gravity. As if the cables above the elevator would snap at any second from his ever-compounding density. At least Sean had been killed in the line of service for us... for his friends... not in compensated service to the manipulative head of a multi-billion-dollar corporation. He had more than redeemed and separated himself from his naïve decision to follow Wallace before I had met him on Rainier Island. He had died with honor, even if his death had been unnecessary.

He had been a much better man than me. All I knew was death. It followed me wherever I walked or with whomever I came in contact with, as evidenced by the armed men at my feet.

"John," Jude said, having caught me staring back at Sean and the elevator. "We have to go." She leaned against the wall, her AK at half-draw and a thin film of sweat glistening on her neck and arms. The way she carried herself made her look all the more beautiful to me. She looked like a woman with everything to lose, but with the perseverance to continue on at all costs. She was better than me, too.

"We'll mourn later," Jude advised. I took one more look at Sean's prone body before focusing on the task at hand in the sterile white room.

Melissa and Jude pulled the soldiers' bodies away from the black doors. They tried to keep their own feet and the bodies from tracking the pooling blood with them, without much success. I approached the doors, stepping over the smeared pool. From this angle, the gore on the marble looked like a distorted Seussian tadpole. My reflection was just starting to fade in its hardening viscosity.

The doors leading deeper into the private labs and operating rooms weren't as heavy duty as the outer elevator doors. Other than a deadbolt, the steel of the doors was more decorative than structural. The posting of two armed soldiers had been more of a deterrent than an additional set of heavy-duty locks.

I pressed my shoulder into the left side and gave it a measured bump. The glass shuddered and the lock assembly cracked from the focused impact. The doors swung in, revealing a long empty corridor as white, stark, and brightly lit as the lobby. It was still amazing R&R had power running throughout the building. The horizontal black chair rail height strip continued along each side of the corridor, giving it the illusion it was longer than it really was. The only elements to break the illusion was a series of evenly spaced solid white doors.

Jude and Melissa stepped into the corridor on either side of me, their rifles tight to their shoulders like they had undergone months of formal military training. We walked quietly along the left wall, Jude on my shoulder and Melissa bringing up our rear flank.

You are Jack Tripper.

What the hell are you babbling about now, Bob?

Janet. Crissy. Jack.

I'm a little busy at the moment, Bob. Do you have a point?

You just reminded me of the characters of Three's Company. I have not seen that show in a long, long time.

I'm so glad we can provide you with entertainment. Now, shut the fuck up so we can work.

Sorry, John.

We moved to the first door to our left. Jude stepped to the other side of the doorframe and tried the door lever. She nodded and unlatched the door. I pressed my thigh into the door as it swung open.

The room was dark, allowing a rotting smell to be the first thing assaulting my senses. Even with the HVAC circulating the air, it couldn't draw out the stench of the slowly deteriorating bodies. The air was heavy and filled with the pungent odor of death, underlined with copper and a familiar lavender scent.

My throat closed up.

I sipped in air through my mouth and forced it out through my nostrils. Several seconds passed before my senses decided blindness to the smells and tastes was better than trying to take in all of the stimuli of carnage in the confined space. Dried blood was splashed all over the floors and walls. The windows and light ballasts were covered with arterial spray, too, giving the room its darker crimson tint. Four bodies were scattered around the private hospital room, tortured looks on their faces and huge gashes and bites on their necks and shoulders. One more body in a hospital gown was on the hospital bed, strapped in with wrist restraints.

That looks famili–

I blocked out Bob's voice. I was too close to dry-heaving to listen to his voice. Instead, I stepped out of the hospital room and closed the door.

"Jesus Christ," Jude said from behind me.

"You're sweating," Melissa said with concern, not having a chance to see the room in its full gory.

"You don't want to see what in there, Melissa," Jude said with a gulp. "What the fuck, John?"

"I don't know." I replied. "Maybe someone turned too fast?"

The lavender seemed to cling to my clothes. My throat threatened to close up. With the door closed again, I concentrated on my breathing until the HVAC switched out enough of the air in the corridor to dissipate the rot of meat and the sickly flowery scent.

Melissa took the lead to check the room directly across the hall. She opened the door and swung the barrel of her rifle across the room. "Clear," she announced.

Luck of the draw.

We moved to the next set of rooms. I found myself hesitant to turn the doorknob, but I did finally open it. I was rewarded with an empty post-operative suite. Jude was rewarded with the same on the other side of the hallway.

"This is bullshit," Melissa said. "We're never going to find him at this pace."

I started explaining to Melissa the importance being cautious and thorough when clearing structures in urban operations. I never had the chance to get the words out because of the screams.

51

Unlawful Entry

+81 Days – 1509 hours
02:14:44

The rest of the rooms were ignored as we rushed to the far end of the corridor. At the intersection, the left corridor ended in a set of more of those black-framed double doors. A black gloss metal placard was mounted right of the door with Kubrick Auditorium written on it in raised brushed stainless steel letters. The other corridor looked like the one we just ran through, complete with those black lines and its own series of evenly spaced doors. The fluorescent bars in the new corridor weren't as bright in this section of the building—unlike the steady cast of light in the previous corridor. Some of the lights worked, but flickered intermittently. A closer inspection revealed bullet graze marks on the tiles and holes in the ceiling. While the corridor was still a sterile white, it had seen at least one firefight.

"Seems too clean for an outbreak," Melissa said to herself.

Maybe the FRACs turned on their masters.

"Maybe," I replied to the both of them.

We cautiously stalked the length of the corridor, tensing for more screams or an ambush with R&R forces. The fluorescent lights ticked as they flickered. Streams of air from the circulation system hissed quietly. Our boots tapped softly against the marble. The same hint of flowers drifted through my nostrils. Jude and Melissa's breathing filled my ears. The hairs stood up on my arm, attuned to a change in air pressure.

Thump... thump...

It wasn't my heartbeat or Jude or Melissa's pulse.

Thump... thump.

It came from farther away.

Thump... It was softening, pumping slower with longer pauses between beats.

"This way," I whispered, pointing toward the dark end of the corridor. Once at the intersection, I put up my fist to stop our advance before I cleared the corners. There was only darkness in both directions. I paused for a moment until I heard the thump coming from my left.

I went into a lower walk, pivoting my body to more of a profile. In any closed quarter operation, as the enemy threat becomes more viable, it becomes more natural to decrease the cross-section of the target you present to them. The Glock led the way.

Thump... thump...

At the end of the corridor was another set of black double doors.

At least they kept to the same aesthetic.

This entry had an electro-lock accessed by a card reader, complete with a ten-digit keypad and a black smudged scanner screen for a thumbprint.

"Must be the place," Melissa said.

Thump...

It was. I didn't wait to finesse the card reader. Taking a step back—forcing Melissa and Jude out of the way to keep me from bumping into them—I put down my shoulder and slammed directly into the seam between the doors. The doors shuddered and the frame bent where the locking pins extended vertically into the frame.

I stepped back to the others. A pain erupted in my side, causing me to grimace. Pain was always temporary, so I ignored it. I launched myself at the doors again. This time the locking pins didn't stand a chance. They burst open, the left one swinging in so hard it cracked and dislodged the tiles where it slammed into the wall. The right door was now curved enough its top and bottom edges were visible, its pins pointing toward us.

I slid into the lobby, leaning back on one bent leg across the slick marble. Six sentries were stationed behind the furniture of a large round reception area. They fired over me and into the doors, not anticipating my low entry.

As their movements slowed to a crawl, I took practiced and patient aim at their heads. I exhaled and squeezed the trigger of my beloved Glock. The eye protection of one of them cracked. A rush of red spray misted on the face of the soldier behind him. As his hand involuntarily went to his eyes and the first soldier fell, I had the next perfect shot. The next round went through his hand and then through his cheek left of his nose. He jerked the trigger of his rifle. It erupted in a semi-automatic hail of bullets tearing through the side of another member of his team. The strafed man barely had time to grunt before I landed a round into his forehead. His head snapped back and he fell into an overstuffed cream-colored chair. The chair pitched backwards to the floor with him in it.

Even distracted, the remaining soldiers had enough discipline to continue firing at me. The one standing behind the overturned chair, though, was suddenly riddled with rounds to the upper chest and face. His rifle dropped onto his dead partner and he fell like a stone to the floor next to him. Melissa and Jude fired from the corridor, partially protected by the walls on either side of the doorway. With the security force in the open and the barrage of bullets from our AKs, it was sickening how quickly the guards were put down.

Thump… thump…

"–eeeaaaar!" Melissa said.

"Clear!" Jude answered, the world spinning back up to normal speed.

"Clear," I said as I got my feet under me and surveyed the rest of the lobby.

"Christ," Jude said with a pant. "My heart is racing."

Adrenaline was a very good thing. Until it bled off.

Thump… thump…

It wasn't Jude's heartbeat I was hearing at the moment. The one I heard came from deeper inside this medical suite. We were in the right place.

52

Pre-existing Medical Condition
+81 Days – 1515 hours
02:08:51

We positioned ourselves behind the reception counter in the lobby for another few minutes, expecting to be met by more of Dick's security forces.

"Maybe the rest of his goon squad is trapped on the other side of the elevator," Melissa offered. "There were quite a few of them on that side."

It was possible. Anything was possible. It seemed odd Dick wouldn't have re-deployed his forces from other floors or have re-directed the forces we came into contact with against us by now. The elevator wasn't as big of an obstacle for someone who controlled the security locks and other ways to move from floor to floor. The schematics I stared at for all those days in captivity had showed the medical wing as designed and built to be isolated from the rest of the tower.

There had been no more screams. The heartbeat I had been following had diminished to an almost unperceivable level, or at the very least, too quiet to divine a direction from it.

"They must know we're here," Melissa said. "There's no way everyone on this floor didn't hear the gunfire. No fucking way."

Jude nodded. "We're running out of time."

We *were* running out of time for both whatever Dick had in store for Westsmith and for the countdown of the capsule detonation in Jude's neck. It was time to move out.

Only one corridor led from the lobby into the medical wing. I swiped a keycard from one of the dead soldiers. Going to yet another set of black doors, I waved the plastic at a black raised square on the wall right of the entry. A red LED light turned green and the doors hissed open, the left door swinging toward us and the other door swinging back into the rest of the wing.

I didn't hesitate. Moving inside quickly, I cleared the white tiled hallway before it ended in a plain white door. I heard Jude and Melissa step in behind me before the doors hissed closed again. There were no markings on the door. There were no placards next to it or numbers screwed into it to denote what it was for. There was no keypad or card reader. It was just a plain white steel door. I tried the doorknob. It was locked.

"Looks like a janitor's supply closet," Melissa observed.

It was a very nondescript door. No frosted glass inset. I couldn't recall the plans describing this door as anything other than ordinary. In fact, I didn't remember this door being on the plans at all. All I remembered was there was no door on this wall. I grabbed the doorknob tight, the metal squeaking in protest. Pushing down with my weight, I could hear the long high groan of the assembly bending, and then breaking off in my hand. I tossed it to the ground where it skittered and spun until it bounced off the wall.

"John," Jude said, "you're bleeding again."

The wetness on my side had returned, soaking my shirt around the previously closed entry and exit wounds and trickling down to my fatigues.

"Figures," I said, looking at the fresh blood staining my hand. I didn't even feel the pain anymore. Was it an indication I wouldn't feel anything soon? Except the steady misery in my head? I shook my head and pushed the thoughts away.

A single kick to the door broke off the latch assembly, the force swinging it wide open quickly enough to slam against the wall on the other side of the hinges. The interior was dark, but, for some reason, it was warm and inviting. I pulled the Glock and stepped inside to the left.

The room wasn't a supply closet or a windowless concrete room. Warm bamboo paneling framed a semi-circular tiered room with a sloping stucco ceiling. Several rows of overstuffed brown leather theater seats descended to a seamless curved wall of tempered glass. Besides the ultra-modern aesthetic of the space, it strangely reminded me of the mezzanine at the Rainier Island Town Hall. Only Sebastian sitting with his feet propped up on the bottom railing was missing to complete the picture.

Melissa and Jude moved inside the room behind me and flanked to the outside aisles as I walked down the steps of the center aisle. We met up at the crosswalk running along the observation window and railing. Through the panoramic window were more of the stark ceramic tiles. This time, they were in a pale mint green lining an oval operating theater.

In the middle of the room was an operating table, covered in green sheets. Around it, several nurses, doctors and technicians were busy rushing around various equipment and monitors, frantically preparing for a procedure. I couldn't see who was on the table. The surgeons, with their gloved hands up, looked bored. One leaned in to another. His face mask moved. The other shook his head. The third man, having heard the conversation, shrugged his shoulders before his eyes squinted and he held his hands to his belly.

It is better to have a good sense of humor at the end of the world, I always say.

You've never said that.

But my actions support it, do they not?

My mind went back to Bob's pantomimes of an orchestra conductor and a marching bandleader of the undead, as well as his excitement and eagerness to play a teenage detective at the museum.

One of the technicians rolled a heavy monitor out of the way of the operating table and our line of sight.

"Shit!" Jude spat out.

"What the fuck is going on now?" Melissa asked with a shake of her head.

Xavier Westsmith was on the table. He was on his side, his hair covered by a cap and his body covered by the green sheets except an exposed area on his chest. I realized now why Dick wasn't concerned about our whereabouts. He was too busy directing the surgical teams from the other side of the theater.

53

Kept Under Observation

+81 Days – 1526 hours
01:57:00

I stood at the center of the curved glass in the operating theater's gallery. The glass must have been tinted or mirrored with one-way film as Dick looked up at the ceiling of the operating theater above us several times without slowing his gaze to rest on my glare.

"He's got Westsmith," Melissa said through gritted teeth. "Where's my niece?"

"And April and Holly!" Jude exclaimed. She didn't mention the bomb lodged next to her carotid artery, although her hand had gone back to cupping her neck over the injection site.

"Didn't mean anything, Jude," Melissa apologized. "Sorry."

"I know," Jude replied, putting her palms on the glass. "How do we get down there?"

"Us against Dick and a bunch of medical staff," I said. "I like those odds."

We hadn't passed any stairwells accessing the operating theater. As far as I was aware, the elevator might have been the only way to move between the 130th and 140th floors.

Dick was right there, oblivious to our presence. We could sit back and watch the trio of surgeons and their support personnel cut into Westsmith without the threat of discovery. At least, until Dick' security team stationed on this floor failed in check in.

"That fucker's right there," Melissa pointed at Dick through the glass with the barrel of the Benelli. "Right there, John."

"I know," I answered quietly.

"I want Summer back," she insisted, a rare tear falling down her cheek. "I want this to be done."

I looked between Jude and Melissa. While neither would say the words, I could see their fatigue and pain in every smudge of dirt, splatter of blood, furrow in their brow, and wrinkle around their eyes and mouths. Their eyes searched mine for a solution. Their slumped shoulders and body language pleaded for me to do something.

I raised my AK and pointed it at Dick, lining him up to its front sights. Mock-pulling the trigger, I let out a sound like I would have used as a kid when playing Cowboys and Indians with my silver colored plastic six-shooters. After a moment, I climbed the steps to the rear of the observation suite.

"Where are you going?" Melissa asked, stalking me up from the side aisle. Jude did the same from her side. "Don't walk away from this! What are you doing?"

"Don't worry," I said. "Nothing stupid." I knew my last comment was possibly the farthest statement from the truth.

54

Manhattan Standoff

+81 Days – 1556 hours
01:27:31

Melissa and Jude chased after me from the side aisles as I reached the rear doors. I turned and faced the glass while they cut through the rear cross aisle, both of them mad and disappointed I was abandoning an opportunity to take out Dick.

"We gotta do something," Melissa said.

I pressed the AK solidly into my shoulder. Melissa and Jude both stopped their advances, putting their hands up to ward me off. I flipped the lever to the middle position and squeezed the trigger. The observation suite lit up from the muzzle flashes, giving the warm paneling and plush seats a strobing jaundiced look.

The gun went silent and the gallery went dark.

The window was filled with pock marks. Apparently, the glass was tempered and bulletproof.

I released the magazine and let it fall to the floor as I reloaded with a fresh one from my vest. As soon as it seated in the stock, I squeezed the trigger and emptied it in the same concentrated area of glass. The pock marks were joined by a series of lengthening cracks.

Not bulletproof after all, but still very bullet-resistant.

"Stay out of sight," I ordered. Both of them stared at me, wondering what hare-brained scheme I had going on in my head.

I dropped the second magazine and reloaded again. As soon as I slammed the magazine home, I charged down the middle aisle steps and launched my shoulder at the window. The damage from the gunfire had been enough. When I hit the glass, it shattered and my momentum carried me through it with a cascade of thick chunks of tempered glass. I figured it was six meters to the floor of the operating theater below.

Dick was farthest away, observing me with a cocked head. The surgeons stared as I fell, their hands still held up. White shimmering twinkles surrounded me as the bright lights of the operating theater reflected off the tumbling glass falling with me. It would have been beautiful if not for the fact I was plummeting twenty feet.

I landed on the hard tiles, using my momentum to spring forward into a roll. I came up on one knee with the fully-loaded AK pointed directly at Dick's chest. His look of puzzlement dropped into a wide grin.

"Bravo!" He started clapping. "An amazing entrance, Mr. Walken. Simply brilliant!"

I didn't bother to listen to what he was saying. I ignored his arrogance making him believe in his own immortality. The front sight of the AK moved from his chest to his forehead.

A quick glance at the center of the operating theater confirmed the medical staff and surgeons had no intention to rush me. Hippocratic Oath, I suppose.

"Where are the girls?" I asked in a booming voice.

"And I'm sure you want the dog, as well?" Dick answered with his own question.

"Yes."

"Well, I did mention you owed me three lives for the ones you lost, did I not?"

"I didn't lose them." I stood and stepped right two steps to make sure the heart monitor didn't get in the way of a clean shot. "Blame the man on the table if you are looking to collect debts."

"He counts as one, already, if you recall," Dick pointed out. "As you can see, he is more than doing his part in all of this."

"And what the hell is that?"

Dick shrugged. "He has something I need."

"The girls," I ordered.

Dick waved his hands in a sweeping gesture over my shoulder. I glanced back at the wall occupying the structure under the observation gallery. Except, it wasn't a wall. It was another observation gallery. This one was almost identical to the one above, but in lighter tones and missing the glass enclosure.

Dick hadn't lied. April and Summer sat in the first row of seats, left of the center aisle. April waved, but said nothing. Summer held Holly on her lap with her arms tight around her, the mutt squirming to get closer to me.

"Stop," I said forcefully.

Holly dropped to Summer's lap but continued to pant and whine. Summer buried her face into Holly's curly white hair, hot tears streaming down her face.

The girls weren't the only people in the gallery. A dozen armed men in full tactical riot gear were deployed throughout the gallery, their weapons pointed either at the girls or directly at me.

"As you can see," Dick stated, "they are safe and in good health. I treated them as if they were my own in anticipation of your return."

I calculated whether I could get to the girls without them becoming causalities. The quick answer was no. Even at this range, I wouldn't able to take all of Dick's men down without the possibility of losing someone.

"You have Westsmith," I said. "Give me the girls."

"You are not in a position to negotiate."

"What use do you have for them? We brought you Westsmith as promised."

"Maybe, Mr. Walken. But I have it on good authority you've killed several more of my men since entering the building. The exchange of life you owe me continues to steepen." As if on cue, a voice crackled through on one of the soldier's earbuds. He put his finger to his ear and nodded to Dick. "See?" Dick's grin widened. "Good authority."

If Dick's men found the bodies, it was only a matter of time before Jude and Melissa would be discovered in the upper gallery. With the one-way tempered glass still intact on the outer edges, they would still have a good view of the standoff between me and Dick without being spotted.

He had no fear of me... of any of us. Why would he? Dick had all the leverage he needed. He had the girls and the dog. He controlled the device in Jude's neck. We all had something to lose.

What does Dick have to lose?

We'd already decimated his security forces, although there was no telling how many more men and resources Dick still had at his disposal. If the sub-basement was any indication, his resources were vast. The presence of a surgical team of over twenty-five doctors, technicians, and nurses ready to perform a procedure on Westsmith was staggering enough.

Westsmith.

I pivoted at the waist, drew the rifle's tailstock tight to the shoulder and fired. The casing on the top of the heart monitor sparked and peeled back. Dick's smile didn't falter but his eyes sharpened as they narrowed. I heard guns tightening up and slapping against tactical gear from the gallery.

Westsmith is the key. He was always the key.

Dick's smile faded slightly as I felt a smile curl up from my own lips.

"That is expensive equipment, Mr. Walken," Dick said in a monotone. "I would appreciate you showing it some respect."

"Why?" I asked. "You mean you don't have twelve more lined up in the basement? You know… where you had me patched up? Not a nice swanky operating theater like you have here for Westsmith, though. If you don't have another one, maybe you can get a replacement at the CVS pharmacy."

I fired again. This time, when the monitor was hit, the cart rolled around. Only one of the cart's wheels had been locked while the nurses and technicians had been racing around to prep for surgery.

"Are you enjoying yourself?" Dick asked, his smile returning bit by bit.

He is calling your bluff.

I don't want to start shooting unarmed civilians. Especially when it came to people with medical expertise. And I can't shoot the guards with the girls in the crossfire.

You could shoot him.

If I shot Dick, I was certain there were standing orders to kill the girls and me immediately. It was a contingency I would have put in place. I could take a few soldiers with me but I don't think I would survive long enough to get April and Summer to safety.

The seconds seemed to stretch into hours. I preferred Melissa and Jude stay hidden… and safe. I hadn't thought any further in my planning.

Yes. Your strategic planning has suffered a bit since your resurrection.

That's for damn sure, I thought. I had become way too impulsive in the last few months. My training had been superior to what I was currently demonstrating. I was disgracing the mantle of the United States Marine Corps with every poor decision.

Enough.

Bob appeared at the far side of the theater, leaning against the pale green tiles. It was surreal to see Bob in the same space as Dick again. They were dressed in almost identical suits. But while Bob had a pale luminescence about him, Dick's mere presence darkened the space. It was ironic my ghostly shackle was the lesser of the two evils in the room.

You need to do something a bit more dramatic, I'm afraid.

I pivoted ten degrees to the left and squeezed the trigger.

A hole appeared six inches away from Westsmith's head, making one of the technicians jump back away from the operating table. Dick's smile faded again. This time, when his cheeks fell and his eyes narrowed, he took on the look of a shark sniffing blood in the ocean. It was predatory and single-minded.

"Do I have your attention now?" I asked, keeping pressure on the trigger and the sights on Westsmith's head. "And keep your men frosty. It would only take a flick of the finger to fire my next round if I was suddenly found myself shot in the back of the head."

Dick looked over my shoulder. He shook his head slightly. The sounds of weapons filled my ears as tailstocks loosened from shoulders and soldiers relaxed their bodies. They sounded seasoned and capable.

Heinz had been capable. He had been a good man. Lee and Damon had been good soldiers, too, even if they had been a bit green. An image of the soldiers in the elevator lobby lying in their own blood as it pooled on marble flashed behind my eyes. It wasn't an impossibility Dick's security force was filled with good people trying to do the best they could under the circumstances. Rosalita had been blackmailed into working for R&R, Dick dangling the safety of a young boy in front of her as motivation to keep her in line and on task.

How many of these men and women had similar stories?

How many had I killed in the pursuit of my own goals?

Did it matter Dick was playing with all of our lives, not overly concerned about what happened to us as long as his objectives were reached?

"If you attempt what you are thinking," Dick advised, "none of you will make it out of this room alive." He nodded up to the observation gallery. "That includes the children, the dog, and your women upstairs."

"I'm no child," April muttered in protest. Her defiance made me smile, in spite of the jeopardy we faced.

"We just want to move on," I said.

"Aha," Dick pondered. "Just like the world has moved on."

"What's the point of keeping us here?"

"The billion-dollar question, isn't it?"

"It's the answer I'm most interested in."

"I'd assume it would be."

Can we just shoot him and be done with it?

And if his men start shooting up the place, how do you think things will turn out for us?

Unfortunately, there are always casualties in war.

I'm trying to avoid more death.

Some soldier you have turned out to be.

I straightened up and stood taller.

I'm not a soldier. I'm a Marine.

"What do you want?" I asked him, keeping the AK pointed at Westsmith's head.

"Isn't it obvious by now?" Dick admitted. "I want you!"

55

Deal with the Devil

+81 Days – 1629 hours
00:54:44

Dick's words rattled in my head longer than its echo survived against the hard tiles. Nobody spoke or moved, the only noise coming from the monitors and the respirator taped to Westsmith's mouth. I flexed my fingers and re-sighted on the back of the patient's head. It would be so easy to take him out of play. A quick pivot and I could take Dick out of play, too. If this had been a Search and Destroy op, I would have taken both shots and singlehandedly faced head-on the maelstrom guaranteed to follow.

"Explain," I said.

"Are you truly so dense you do not understand your status here?" Dick asked. "You are wholly the property of Roanoke & Raleigh. We have sunk millions of dollars into this program and you."

"And?"

Dick pondered my question before answering. "And… if you come quietly without any fuss, I will let your friends go."

"The capsule in Jude's neck?"

"Oh, yes. We will deactivate the module in Ms. Sawyer's neck." He glanced at his watch and then at the digital display on the wall between the observation galleries. "She does seem to be bumping against the clock, doesn't she?"

"The girls go free." I rattled off my list of demands. "Ms. Sawyer has the capsule deactivated permanently."

"Yes," Dick agreed.

"The Russells', Ms, Sawyer and the dog walk out of here unharmed with as much weapons, food, and supplies as they can carry."

"Yes."

"You equip them with a suitable all-terrain vehicle with as much gas as they can carry."

Dick didn't answer right away. He looked up and did some quiet calculations on his fingers. Shaking his head from side to side, he made a series of clicking noises with his tongue against the roof of his mouth. He answered, "Fine."

"And you and your men stay away from them. Let them leave without stopping them or hunting them down."

"You are very paranoid, you know." Dick nodded, his smile returning. "Yes. And, in return, I will own you. You will carry out my orders without question. I need a man like you in the field to represent R&R and my interests."

"Aren't they one and the same?"

"I guess you could say that," Dick said. "I am essentially all R&R is these days."

"And what makes you think I will follow your orders after my people are safely away?"

"I suspect we will just have to trust each other. You would have to trust me to leave your people alone after they leave, and I will have to trust you to not shoot me in the back at your earliest opportunity."

Dick clapped his hands together.

A flashbang grenade exploded above us. The light flashed through the broken part of the curved window. It was followed by wisps of smoke escaping through it to the front of the gallery. The expected commotion followed. Men shouted orders. I held my breath. After several seconds of scrambles and more yelling, there was silence. There were no gunshots. I finally exhaled.

Nobody in the operating theater moved. I stared at Dick and his stupid smile. It was more sinister than Westsmith's, making me actually miss our former prisoner's antics. Most of the medical staff stood around their patient, the surgeons still with their hands partially raised. They didn't want to put themselves into the line of fire. The security team was wary of me, standing in the gallery, stalking me with their eyes even though they no longer pointed their weapons at my head.

I looked at each of their faces, cataloguing them. Most of the men and women carried themselves like experienced ex-military or local police. The rest looked at me nervously with minute twitches, repositioning their weapons as if this was their first assignment—ever.

At least Roanoke & Raleigh is an equal opportunity employer.

I tried to gauge their commitment to Dick's cause. Were they just hired hands happy to bolt as soon as the money dried up? Did they have a deep connection to R&R and the company's success? Did Dick have leverage against them as well, like he had on Rosalita?

A door opened at the back of the observation theater on the first level, the current group of security now joined by another dozen armed men and women. Melissa and Jude—stripped of their weapons—were escorted to the front of the gallery.

"Auntie!" Summer yelled.

Melissa—her hands zip-tied in front of her—still managed to give her niece a long hug with her arms looped over her shoulders. She showered Summer with kisses in her hair, and on her neck and cheeks. All the while, Holly was hanging from Summer's crossed arms by the armpits, trying to get her own licks in. April put her hands around Jude's neck, burying her face in Jude's shoulder. She mumbled something I couldn't quite make out, but Jude nodded and said, "Yes."

"Wonderful," Dick said in a booming voice. "Wonderful. Please take your seats and we can return to our currently scheduled procedure."

"What about our deal?"

"The deal holds, Sergeant," Dick said through gritted teeth and an annoyed tone. "You were the one to barge in while we were prepping for surgery. You will show me patience. Gentlemen, please take his weapons."

The majority of the security team who had originally been guarding April, Summer and Holly moved from the tiered seats toward me. I relinquished the AK to the closest soldier. When a green recruit tried to disarm me from my holstered Glock, I punched him square in the face. He fell backwards—just as I realized I probably shouldn't have struck him. One of the more seasoned soldiers cracked me on the back of the knees, making me collapse to the floor. I put my hands up, palms out.

"Ok," I said in surrender. "Ok."

I reached into my shoulder holster with the thumb and forefinger of my left hand to pull out the Glock just I felt the tip of a gun barrel against my neck. I grabbed the Glock by the barrel and handed it over my shoulder to the soldier with the gun to my skin.

The Glock was taken away.

The guard who I had punched was on his feet again, blood gushing over his lips and mouth. He grabbed my tactical knife and added it to his empty sheath, then spat blood on the tiles in front of me. The man with the gun to my neck tapped my right leg. I crossed it over my left ankle.

"Hands on your head," someone with a deep burly voice said.

I complied. The soldier grabbed my right hand and twisted it around to the small of my back. He slipped a plastic zip-tie around my wrist like an overly tight bracelet. He repeated with my left hand, interlocking a second zip-tie through the first and tightening it around the left wrist.

My stomach churned. I glanced at what remained of my group. We were now without any way to defend ourselves. I hoped Dick was a man of his word. Of course, trusting Dick at all could end up being the dumbest decision I've made to date.

Only time would tell.

56

Dead Man's Hand
+81 Days – 1650 hours
00:33:31

We had lost our weapons, but at least we had each other. We sat together in the front row of the lower gallery. Melissa hugged her niece and kissed her hair. Summer pressed into her aunt and hugged Holly tight—the furry critter more than happy to be nestled in the girl's arms for the duration. Jude held April's hands, their temples touching and their eyes closed.

I sat alone, watching Dick and his associates. The doubled security force had fanned out in a semi-circular line along the perimeter of the operating theater. Their ranks ended even with the table. If they needed to deal with us, it was best to not deploy where you would have to fire through the surgical staff.

Nurses and technicians bustled about again, recalibrating their equipment. A female nurse delicately touched the holes I put into the housing of the heart monitor. She shook her head as she rolled it back toward the other equipment, locking the wheel brake. One of the surgeons argued with the technician who had been closest to Westsmith when I had shot the gurney. The technician looked at his watch and shook his head. The surgeon poked a gloved finger into the technician's chest, physically demonstrating his authority and superiority over him.

I concentrated on listening to what they were arguing about.

"…we need to get this procedure started now," the surgeon said from under his mask.

"And I told you I need to wait to administer the anesthetic," the technician—correction, anesthesiologist—replied. "I was halfway through the dose when that asshole shot the table. Now, I'm going to wait until the patient stabilizes again before starting again. I'm not going to get killed because I'm in the line of fire for someone..."

Asshole? Me? Harsh.

Yes. I am sure you are crushed by the news.

We had barely a half hour before Jude's time was up. And it sounded like the procedure on Westsmith was having its own delays.

Thanks to you.

"Let's take care of this capsule if the procedure you are trying to get off the ground is taking too long," I demanded.

Dick looked over at me from the far wall. "In good time, Sergeant."

"Now is a good time," Jude called out, her voice cracking the tiniest bit. "We held up our end with Westsmith. And you got John." She choked on her last words.

"You asked for trust," I said. "Now, I'm asking for good faith."

Dick pushed himself off the wall and approached the lead surgeon and the anesthesiologist.

He spoke to them in a low voice. "...long due to this holdup?"

"...we need twenty minutes," the anesthesiologist replied. The sound of thunder finally reached inside the theater, its thick walls and lack of windows keeping its rumble at bay up until now. Dick looked at him with narrowed eyes. Daggers would have physically shot out of his pupils had such a thing been possible. The anesthesiologist withered, his shoulders slumping and his head turning a few degrees away from Dick's glare. "If you want him to still be alive during the procedure, I need for him to come up from the general in order to know what's needed to put him back under."

"Firestein?"

"Yes?" the imposing surgeon replied to his name.

"Do you concur?"

After a moment's thought, he replied with a simple, "Yes."

Dick exhaled loudly, his glare getting sharper. He looked between the two members of his medical staff for a moment, the tendons tight in his neck. Without another word, he turned away from them. In response, their body language lost a bit of the tension Dick had inflicted upon them.

"Williams!" Dick called out.

A slender woman in her mid-thirties came over from the other edge of the operating room. She looked like one of the staff, yet carried herself like a soldier. Maybe she was a military corpsman. "Yes, sir?"

"Please bring Ms. Sawyer over and prepare for her procedure."

"Yes, sir." Williams turned and walked across the theater toward us with purpose.

"Here you go, Jude," I said.

"Ms. Sawyer," Williams said as she stopped in front of her with her hand extended. "Would you join me, please?

Jude let go of April and hoisted herself out of the comfy observation chair. She looked back at me with a thin smile, mouthing the words, 'Thank you'. Williams took her hand and they walked back to the center of the theater.

The other technicians were still busy going through their own checklists. One of the monitors—not the heart monitor, thankfully— flickered. The technician raised his hands in surprise for a moment before the screens and lights returned to normal. To the right side of the equipment two technicians wheeled over a massive chair. It resembled a dentist chair, complete with padded arms and a headrest. As the techs locked it into position, Williams motioned for

Jude to sit. Jude turned around and slid herself into the chair.

"I will need to restrain you," Williams said in a soft professional voice.

"Okay," Jude said with uncertainty.

"It's a precaution only, Ms. Sawyer," Williams assured her. "We cannot have you moving during this procedure as there will be some discomfort."

Jude nodded with understanding and consent. Williams bound her wrists with padded restraints. Once done, she placed a palm on Jude's forehead and eased it into the headrest. Once Jude's neck muscles relaxed, Williams buckled a strap around her forehead.

The lights dimmed a little. I had been surprised Dick had enough juice to keep the lights on for as long as he had already. And I was thinking both in terms of executive and literal power. Even Dick looked up at the exposed light ballasts until they returned to their previous brightness, as if his will alone powered them.

"Comfortable?" Williams asked with a smile.

Jude tried to nod, but the strap kept her head immobile. She tittered with a small nervous laugh and answered, "Yes."

"Great," Williams replied, talking to Jude and everyone who may have been listening. "Great. We are all set here."

Jude closed her eyes and tried to breath with a measured rhythm. She turned her fingers into fists, the tight restraints not doing much to alleviate her instinct for fight or flight. Williams put a hand on Jude's arm and squeezed lightly. Jude smiled, even while she continued to breath with her eyes closed.

Dick walked over to the reclined chair.

"Just a few more minutes," Williams told her boss.

Jude squirmed and twisted away from him as much as her restraints allowed, basically thrusting her hips to the other side of the chair.

"Once this is done, John," Dick said, "I expect you to fall in line without any more blustering or strife."

The rumbling continued from outside the walls of the theater.

"Why did you do all this?" I asked, thinking back to Felix's house on Rainier Island. The Hammermill box under his sink had been full of incriminating evidence concerning Roanoke & Raleigh's involvement in the development and weaponization of whatever serum they had concocted to create enhanced soldiers for the United States military. Or, maybe as a product to sell to any other government body or organization willing to pay the price.

He chuckled. "I can't take full credit or blame for what has occurred."

"But, yet, you've been developing this shit since Korea."

Dick's head cocked to one side. "For someone who just came in off the streets, you do have a surprising amount of knowledge of the history of our program."

"I like to stay informed."

"But, I doubt you were informed," Dick pondered aloud. "The idiocy of one redneck country bumpkin caused the spread of the virus."

"That's hard to believe," Melissa said with a snicker.

"I incinerated an entire complex in an attempt to contain it."

"Wyoming?" I thought back to one of the last broadcasts in the Oceanside Diner. They had reported on an R&R facility fire out west. "That was you?"

"Yes," Dick confirmed. "But the same bumpkin escaped several thousand pounds of Thermite and managed to carry the virus out with him. Once he was outside the perimeter, it was less a matter of containment and more of damage control."

"Is that why you killed all your employees?" Melissa spat out. More flickers of the lights.

"Ms. Russell," Dick said, "there were eight million people living and working on this island. Do you understand the magnitude of chaos if the infection had taken root here?

"What does it have to do with your employees?" I followed up Melissa's question.

"In and of itself? Nothing." Dick shrugged. "I did not target my employees. My concern took place on a much larger scale."

"So why are there hundreds of people in your lobby curled up in agony, stinking of fear, rot and lavender?" Melissa demanded to know.

"Did you know most New Yorkers are proud to claim New York City water has the best water in the world?" Dick asked. "New Yorkers are very proud people... and stupid... and hypocrites. They claim to love their water, but spend millions on bottled water from Poland Springs, Evian and Deer Park."

"Fascinating," Melissa remarked, her response dripping with sarcasm.

"With all their bluster and chest-thumping, they say one thing and do another," Dick continued, ignoring Melissa's comment. "Luckily for us, New Yorkers are as predictable as they are stupid. Easy enough to swap all of the bottled water before it reached the bodegas, convenience stores and supermarkets."

"How did you get the bottling distributors to go along with the switch?" I asked.

Dick let out a bellowing laugh. "What makes you think we negotiated with anyone? Sometimes a sledge hammer can still be used to open a can of peas."

"So you introduced your own supply of all types of

258

contaminated bottle water in Manhat–" I started.

"Manhattan?" Dick laughed. "We are not an upstart tech company in someone's garage, Sergeant. We distributed the water around the world."

R&R's reach was indeed worldwide, but the idea of the sheer immensity and audacity of the global genocide the company had perpetrated was enough to make one's brain stop thinking and to sap one's will enough to stop soldiering on. I also thought back to the case of bottled water we found during our scavenging at Melissa's apartment complex.

"Unfortunately," Dick said with a genuine sense of disappointment, "we couldn't redirect enough water distribution centers to keep the virus from spreading. A true epidemic acting like a pandemic."

"So, you're disappointed you couldn't kill more people before they became walking corpses?" I asked.

"Essentially, yes," Dick said with a nod. "But, we did manage to distribute water here in mass."

"Sick fuck," Melissa muttered, continuing to serve as a shield for her niece from the relaxed coverage of the security detail.

"That very well may be, Ms. Russell," Dick agreed, "but had I not done so, the entire eastern seaboard would have been overrun with the walking dead and you would have never made it ten feet outside your apartment. That, my dear, is the reality."

The fluorescent lights flickered and ticked, making Dick's words more dramatic. Unfortunately, I found I had to agree with Dick. The New England countryside had been eerily devoid of the walkers I had expected after returning Stateside and stepping into a landscape of the undead.

"I guess bottled water is off our list of must-haves," April said, finally joining the conversation and pointing out a serious and practical issue.

My vision started to blur. I was suddenly very tired. As my eyes watered, the walls wavered.

"Can we take care of this bomb in my neck, please?" Jude called out impatiently from her bindings in the recliner.

Dick glanced at Williams who nodded back at him. "Oh, of course."

Williams approached with a metal tray. Dick turned his back to us and pulled off the green sterile surgical towel covering it. Williams walked back to the rest of the surgical team with the empty tray and towel. I couldn't see what the device was designed to extract the capsule from Jude's neck.

Dick faced us, extending my Glock to Jude's temple.

"No!" I yelled, leaping from my seat. The guards rushed me, grabbing my arms and wrapping me up around my waist. I shrugged two of them off.

"Stop," April screamed, either toward me or to Dick.

Guns clicked her into silence.

"Leave her alone," Melissa warned.

Rifle butts banged against my jaw, ears, and neck. Someone kicked me in the face. Arms wrapped around my legs. The sheer weight on me forced me to my belly. Once I was pressed against the tiles, someone grabbed me under the jaw and by the hair. My face was pulled up enough to have a clear view of Dick and my sidearm pressed against Jude's head.

I spat out blood onto the floor.

"As I said previously," Dick reiterated, "I expect you to fall in line after this. Because I still have plenty of beautiful bargaining chippies to work with."

Dick looked to Jude. He braced his arm and shoulder and put pressure on the trigger.

"Mutha—!" I screamed, just as the lights flickered, extinguished, and left us in darkness.

57

Fog Bank
+81 Days – 1700 hours
00:23:23

People were yelling out orders. Boots slapped and squeaked against the tile floor around the blackened room. In the confusion, the weight pressing down on my extremities and torso disappeared. My arms were freed altogether as those soldiers spread back out to the rest of the room. My enhanced vision made out flitting dark shapes. The only light in the sealed windowless theater came from the screens of the various monitors from their battery backups. Suddenly, choppy beams of light bounced to life. Around the room soldiers switched on the tactical lights on their rifles and the mounted lights on their tactical gear.

Dick stood next to Jude, the Glock still aimed at her head. The cords in her neck stood out as she fought against her restraints. Luckily, the tip of the barrel was no longer against her skin as even Dick was distracted by the commotion.

Sonofabitch.

Dark smoke poured in from the lower air vents. It sank to the floor and spread out in all directions, wrapping itself around the operating table, and the legs of the personnel and the equipment. The surgeons and staff took no notice. It must have been a safeguard suppression system if the power was ever interrupted—maybe similar to the chemicals used in a clean-room decontamination cycle.

The rumbling of thunder rattled the remaining glass on the

observation gallery above us enough to dislodge and rain down more chunks of the tempered material around me.

"What the fu–?" the man holding the back of my thighs shouted as a brick sized piece of glass dropped on his head. Blood spurted out from under his visor. The glass had completely crushed his helmet, and his skull under it. He fell to my right, dropping his weapon. The last man assigned to pin me down lifted his knee from my shoulder blade in order to check on his downed squad mate.

With his weight now off me and his attentions elsewhere, I twisted my torso and shoulders toward my remaining captor. I grabbed the barrel of his AR and pulled. He sailed into the squad mate trying to assess the condition of the man with the crushed skull. The force knocked both men unconscious. I flipped the AR around, shouldered it, took aim and squeezed the trigger. My heart was pounding in my ears as the muzzle flashed and the retort echoed off the hard walls of the room.

The Glock sparked.

Sorry, old friend.

Dick's hand snapped back with the impact. The Glock discharged.

No!

The bullet went into the padding of the headrest. Dick spun around and ducked behind one of the pieces of beeping equipment, firing wildly twice in return. I fired again. The lights on the monitor went black as Dick raced behind the equipment. Another shot whizzed past my face. I pivoted and shot the soldier who fired at me. He slumped against the wall.

Beams of LED light swept through the room. The entire surgical staff, including Williams, was prone on the ground around the operating table with their hands protecting their heads. Melissa and the girls were still guarded.

I fired again, hitting more of the equipment Dick was using as cover. He was a quick little bastard. Sweeping right, I took the soldiers' crossfire away from Melissa and the others in the lower gallery. The last thing I needed was bullets whizzing past me and ending up in one of them.

Jude struggled to slip her restraints.

I needed a better sightline on Dick's retreat.

The nearest flanking soldier shined his tactical light into my face, a look of wide-eyed surprise on his face to see me so close. His eyes got wider—and crossed—as I punched him in the middle of his face. He sprawled into the man behind him, the second man's rifle pinned between them. I surged forward, grabbing them as human shields as I fired at the next three men on the right flank. One got a bullet in the bicep before he could even swing his rifle up. The next managed to get his rifle up to his shoulder, but got a round through the palm of his trigger hand. The last soldier caught a bullet in the chest under the collarbone. All five of them fell to the ground, writhing and yelling out in pain.

The soldiers on the other side of the operating theater were sweeping along the perimeter toward me from both sides, having enough presence of mind to not shoot at me through Westsmith and the prone medical staff in the center of the room. Jude was lucky enough to still be strapped to the chair, out of the line of fire.

I didn't see Dick... or my sidearm.

Instead, I pulled a tactical knife from one of the downed soldiers and rushed over to Jude. Without a word, I quickly sliced through her left wrist and head restraints. Pushing the knife into her freed hand, I opened up the rifle to full-automatic mode. Shock and awe— just the way America liked it. Keep them disoriented and off-balance.

A muscular woman—in as much tactical gear as her male counterparts, ooh-rah—moved silently around the perimeter, the fog swirling up to wrap around her knees and thighs. I hesitated. She reminded me of Rosalita. As she drew up her weapon, she disappeared into the mist altogether. A scream echoed through the theater. She appeared again for an instant, a second scream barely escaping her lips as the charcoal smoke took quick advantage to jam itself down her throat.

"Blake," one of the other soldiers called out to her. There was no answer. Another soldier gurgled out a strangled sound, more guttural and pained than a battle cry. "Regroup!"

Jude cut her other hand free and pulled herself from the chair. She bumped next to me. She probably wasn't aware of them yet, but I could already see the bruising rising around her wrists. "We're not getting out of here, are we?" she asked rhetorically. Her eyes had taken on the look of a cornered animal. She reversed the grip of the knife, her thumb covering the end of the handle. "Might as well do some damage, right?"

I had to smile. No matter what, Jude was never going to lose her inherent defiance. It didn't matter there was a gruesome end waiting for her in next few minutes.

The soldiers' tactical lights tried, and failed, to cut through the mist. Those pinpoints were all I needed in order to hunt. I fired off three rounds, pivoting in a smooth motion. Muffled cries of pain came from two of them. The third went down without a word or grunt. I must have hit him in the heart.

More of Dick's men were spread out along the other side of the theater, plus those guarding Melissa and the girls. The surgeons and their staff were still crouched low behind the equipment or prone on the tiles. I knew Dick was gone, even with the mist obscuring my sightlines. I just knew it as a fact, not knowing why.

He always has a Plan B.

I'm sure he thinks ten steps ahead at all times, I thought.

Assessment. Fifteen soldiers. Maybe sixteen? Melissa and the girls were still hostages. Jude, with only a few minutes left, was at my side with the knife in hand. Dick was gone. The mist and equipment were good for cover. Rifle had a half-full magazine. The unconscious and bleeding men against the wall behind us had more magazines strapped to their vests.

A three-round burst flashed from across the room, the bullets embedding in the wall tiles behind us. Another several rounds whizzed over us. They weren't aiming high with suppressing fire. The rounds were just missing us. Luckily, the fog still concealed our position.

Movement from my left. A cart with an oversized defibrillator unit rolled toward me. One of the soldiers lunged at me from behind it. His knife embedded into my shoulder at the seam of my tactical vest. Both of the soldiers' hands were on the handle pushing the knife in to the hilt.

I looked at him, annoyed. His eyes widened with surprise. The fact I didn't react to being stabbed in the chest perplexed him. He mustn't have been fully briefed on my abilities. I restrained him by the wrists and drove my forehead into his riot gear visor. Blood splattered on the inside of the now cracked plastic. I released his wrists as he became dead weight. He dropped to the floor, leaving the knife behind.

More muzzle flashes.

Jude answered with her own spray of semi-automatic bursts, having pulled a weapon from one of the fallen soldiers.

"Christ, John," she exclaimed. I pulled the knife out and sheathed it, replacing the one I had given to her.

"We need to take them out," Jude assessed. Bullets sparked off of the seat Jude previously had occupied. She pivoted and squeezed off another burst, keeping away from the operating table and the lower gallery. Unlike the security force, she laid down a suppression line of fire. "Because they're trying to do the same!"

Drawing up the AR, I fired several single shots into the mist, picking likely locations of the soldiers. Only one yelp sounded as a reward for emptying the magazine. I let the magazine drop out of the stock. It dropped and clanked off the floor in slow motion. When it hit the floor, the mist swallowed it for a moment before the impact cleared the fog away and sent ripples out in all directions. Even the floor tiles seemed to waver and pulse under the smoke.

Jude held out a spare magazine. I went to grab it.

"Shit," I said with a hiss, hot metal boring through my bicep. The bullet ripped through the compression shirt and tumbled out the other side. I dropped the magazine, my fingertips forgetting how to apply pressure. I curled my arm to my chest, tightening my grip on the AR with my left hand.

Jude slid to my side and slammed the magazine into the AR's stock for me. I set the barrel on the top of the defibrillator unit, squeezing off rounds with my left hand. There were screams, but not from any members of the security force. And they weren't screams of pain, but of fear. And panic. More rounds went off. This time the muzzle flashes weren't pointed at us. The remainder of the security force coordinated in loud voices.

"On your 3 o'clock!"

"Against the wall!"

"Blake? Fuck!"

A sustained retort of gunfire came from several weapons.

We dropped to the deck but none of the shots whizzed by or ricocheted anywhere close to our position.

I tapped Jude with my spasming arm.

"What?" she whispered.

I pointed in the direction of the observation gallery. "The girls."

She nodded and followed closely behind me as we crouched our way toward where I believed Melissa and the girls to be under guard. The mist swirled ahead of us, enveloping our bodies and line of sight as we passed through it.

A single shot and flash came from ahead of us, ricocheting off the tiles to my right and puncturing the bottom of a waist-high storage cabinet. Either they saw us or were shooting blindly in the dark. I hoped for the latter.

At least I knew which direction to go. Vague figures came into focus. Several weapons fired ahead of us, dozens of rounds being expended before magazines had to be swapped out. The mist instantly solidified into a six-foot mass to our right, the tendrils spinning in tight rings around a slender column of stationary smoke. As quickly as it started, the column of smoke dropped to the floor and spread out in all directions as it dissipated. Before new mist could fill in the area, I caught sight of perfectly formed bullets standing on end in a tight circle. Then, the mist swallowed them up, too.

Magazines were slammed home with metallic clicks. Lightning suddenly streaked through the space. The sudden flash blinded the soldiers, their night-vision goggles over their eyes. Even as they tore the equipment off their faces, they fought against the spots in the middle of their vision. I took advantage of the swap and charged forward through the haze, lunging right into the middle of the blind spot.

In the center aisle of the lower gallery, I swept my arms wide, and tackled two guards under the barrels of their weapons before they had a chance to fire a shot. Even though the hole in my right bicep kept my arm from extending all the way, I slammed my shoulders into their stomachs to force the air out of their lungs. We crashed into the steps. A sick crack denoted the severing of one of the guard's spine. He went limp. I used my right forearm high on the other guard's chest to immobilize him. I moved my arm up to his throat and pressed all of my weight on him. He gurgled trying to get oxygen into his lungs. His eyes widened, his lips turned a darker color to match the charcoal mist, and his tongue lolled out of his mouth.

Jude found her way to the gallery, tapping me on the leg before coaxing Melissa, April and Summer out from the row of seats where they cowered away from the gunfire. Holly trotted after them, finally finding herself free of Summer's hug. I fired at the confused and blinded sentry in the left aisle, then quickly pivoted to the armed man on the other side of the gallery trying to get a bead on the retreating women. Both received a clean single shot to the head.

Time was short. There was no more time to worry about the value of life. Red, pencil-thin beams of light suddenly formed dots on the seat backs.

"Get down!" I heard.

"Don't move!" another voice demanded.

I hoped I had been lucky enough to incapacitate or kill the squad leaders. The remaining guards were in disarray, shouting out contradictory orders at my back. I slowly turned around, the AR held by the barrel and my hands raised. The dots gravitated to my chest in a tight circle around my heart. Someone moved in from the side to disarm me, staying away from the laser pin-lights. When he grabbed my wrist to twist it behind my head, I couldn't help but wince from the shooting pain of the bullet wound through my bicep. He kicked me behind my knee, forcing me to the wider landing between the runs of steps. The dots followed me, never straying too far from center mass. With his weapon pressed against the back of my neck, the soldier pulled a zip tie restraint from his vest with his free hand.

I couldn't see where Jude and the others had gone, hoping they were still hidden from the soldiers on the side of the observation gallery in the thick smoke. I couldn't even see past the soldiers and their tactical lights and laser sights. The rest was just a hazy swirling backdrop. The entire operating theater was shrouded in darkness, but I could hear and feel the thunder. And underneath the rumble was something else, like long drawn-out bowstrings from an orchestra of out-of-tune violins.

The soldier fumbling to zip tie my wrist, only having one free hand to work with, wore a patch embroidered with Sinclair on his tactical vest. "Munez," he said, "get over here and cover this asshole."

None of the beams of lights moved from the front of the gallery railing.

"Double-time it, grunt," Sinclair, my would-be jailer, ordered. A vest-mounted tactical light beam bounced over from the side through the fourth row of seats. "About time. Cover him."

Munez's gun came up. Sinclair shouldered his own rifle so he could focus on binding the zip tie around my wrist with two hands. A shot rang out over my shoulder. I instinctively ducked, my one zip tied wrist still caught in Sinclair's fingers. He put all of his weight on my shoulders to cover me from the gunshot. A second later he fell to the landing beside me.

"Who fired that shot?" someone yelled. "Sound off!"

Sinclair's blue eyes stared at me as he lay awkwardly on the steps in the aisle. A streak of hot blood ran across his eyes from one temple to the other. I looked back at Munez. A bullet had entered through his hairline, ripping away part of his earlobe. It had been administered by my own hand moments ago. His eyes were quickly glazing over with a white haze; the remains of his brown irises speckled with gold and red. The whites had become bloodshot with burst capillaries.

Munez was one of the walking dead, wielding a rifle his twitching thumb suddenly set to the full-automatic position. Swinging the barrel of the AR over my head, Munez pulled the trigger and let loose a spray of the entire magazine in a spit of muzzle fire at the soldiers at the front railing of the gallery. Laser sight dots careened toward the ceiling. Tactical light casings burst and their lights fizzled out. Screams in the dark were followed by thuds of bodies hitting the deck. Munez's weapon was empty.

The few remaining steady laser dots found their way to Munez. Rounds burst through his chest. Munez looked down at the holes in his vest with a strange cocked-head interest before he took a round to the top of the head. He dropped to his knees and slumped against a seat with the gun still in his hands.

"Munez is down!" a new voice called out. "Secure the prisoner."

Five soldiers approached me—the remaining five soldiers. Gunfire erupted from the right aisle, bullets ripping through their chests, necks and cheeks. Red spray spat from their mouths as they choked on the blood pouring down their throats. They fell to the floor in front of me.

The mist swirled and poked at Munez's body for a moment

before it receded down the carpeted steps. The lights in the ceiling started to flicker, popping back into life. A limping form drifted through the mist, its form solidifying into a stark dark silhouette. The smoke lightened and dissipated. I reached for the gun Sinclair no longer had use for and swung it around at the figure.

"There is no need for that, John," a low husky voice said. Westsmith appeared, his fist gripping a surgical sheet around his shoulders, only wearing his pants. "I think the worst is over."

The fluorescent bars came on one at a time until the theater was bathed in bright white lights. The mist had retreated completely back to wherever it had birthed from. Bodies of soldiers littered the room. The surgeons and staff were slowly getting back to their feet.

"Yes," Westsmith said, "the worst is over."

"John!" Melissa yelled out from the railing at the far end of the observation gallery. Summer and April hugged each other.

"She just collapsed!" Summer shouted from under April's arm. "Help her!"

Jude lay prone on the floor, Holly licking her face. Her eyes were wide open, the irises completely rolled back. Time had run out.

58

Clear!

+81 Days – 1721 hours
00:02:11

"She's dying!" Summer cried out. "Do something!"

I stared at Jude as she lay motionless on the floor. I checked my watch. She still had two minutes.

Maybe the capsule detonated prematurely. Bob, with the battle over, had returned. *Dick was never one to be trusted.*

But I had trusted Rosalita. If the device had a chance to be faulty, she would have told me.

Unless she did not know.

R&R didn't seem to be the kind of company producing substandard products, especially with Dick at the helm.

Anything can be faulty, John.

"Where's that fucker?" Melissa cursed, waving her Benelli around. She had quickly retrieved it from the dead soldier who had disarmed her in the upper observation gallery.

I pointed at the surgeons and the rest of the staff. "What do you know about these capsules R&R uses?" The surgeons all raised their gloved hands and shook their heads. The technicians and nurses averted their eyes, doing the same.

I lunged forward and grabbed Williams by the throat, lifting her off the ground. She batted away at my forearm, trying to break free. "How do we take out the capsule?" I demanded, watching as tears of pain fell down her cheeks.

"I don't know," she croaked, struggling to shake her head. I tossed her away, sending her arcing into the restraint chair where she had held Jude before Dick's botched procedure.

Westsmith grabbed my arm with his uninjured hand, dispensing of the surgical sheet to reveal his smooth naked chest. "Get Jude up. Now!" He had a look in his eyes more earnest than I had ever seen from him before. Not quite sane, but definitely more genuine. As a result, and because we had no other options, I scooped Jude off the floor. Holly woofed her annoyance for taking her away from her tongue.

"On the table," Westsmith ordered, pointing to the operating table where he had been sedated with his bandaged mangled hand. "Quickly."

I rushed Jude over to the table, the surgeons and staff shrinking away toward the far wall. Firestein, the surgeon who had been ordering the others around, tripped over the leg of one of the soldiers and skidded headlong onto the tiles with a squeak of palm meat against porcelain. I pulled over the rolling tray with the scalpels and forceps.

"No!" Westsmith said. He grabbed clumsily at a cart, its sides riddled with bullet holes. Flipping switches with his good hand, he stared at the monitor. "Come on," he whispered. Finally, a low whine started from the machine. It got louder as Westsmith turned a dial to its highest setting.

"Do what you're going to do." I glanced at my Cobra. 1722 hours. "We only have a minute left."

"No worries, John," Westsmith said, his familiar grin plastered onto his face. He laughed as he pulled the defibrillator paddles out of their cradles, fumbling the one paddle in his less than complete hand.

"Come on!" Melissa yelled. "Come on! Do it!"

Thirty seconds.

"Take these," Westsmith ordered me. I took the paddles and held them out in front of me. Westsmith coated one of the paddle faces with gel. "Rub them together!"

I did as I was told.

"Against both sides of her neck," Westsmith ordered. "Now!"

I pulled the paddles over to Jude, the spiral cords stretching out from the machine in long bouncing low-hanging arcs. I went to the head of the gurney and placed a paddle on either side of Jude's neck. Gripping the paddle handles tight.

Westsmith closed his eyes tight.

Fifteen seconds.

The whine of the defibrillator was loud and even. "What are you waiting for?" I yelled.

Westsmith ignored me, his eyes still closed. "Shut up," he finally advised.

Ten seconds.

Summer rocked with April in her arms. Holly paced in tight circles in front of them, whining in sync with the defibrillator. Melissa gripped her shotgun with white knuckles, glaring at Westsmith.

Five seconds.

"Please," I plead to Westsmith.

Four seconds.

The whine from the machine was burrowing into my head.

Three seconds.

"Wait for it," he said with a laugh.

Two seconds.

One sec–

"Clear!" Westsmith slammed the edge of his hand into the defibrillator shock button. Jude's body convulsed, her back arching off of the gurney. With the charge delivered, the defibrillator returned to its low recharging tone. Westsmith grabbed the paddles from me and tossed them back at the cart. They both missed, slapping against the side and falling to the floor. The cords stretched and bounced like bungee cords before they recoiled into a more constricted state. "Viola!" Westsmith said with a deep bow, his hands swept out to the side. "My work here is done."

"Nothing's happening!" I yelled at him. I couldn't hear her pulse amid all the other adrenaline-fueled heartbeats in the room.

As if to placate me, Westsmith stepped forward toward the table and pressed his index and middle fingers into Jude's neck. What he discovered wasn't what he had expected either, his grin dropping to a frown. "Gimme that!" he said, pointing to the anesthesiologist's neck. The specialist handed over his stethoscope and Westsmith put the buds to his ears and the diaphragm to Jude's chest. His facial expression was blank, giving me no indication whether he was finding what he was hoping for.

"Well?" Melissa demanded.

Summer and April were crying, loose snot flowing as readily as their tears. They still clung to each other as if their lives depended on it. Emotionally, their lives probably did depend on it. Holly trotted over to the table. She sat down and raised herself up onto her hind legs. With a whimper and a shake of her front paws, she urged the motionless Jude to pay attention to her.

"Enough of this bullshit!" Williams shouted, pointing a recovered AR from one of the dead soldiers at us. Melissa brought her Benelli up. My rifle was set to my shoulder before I even realized it. Williams eyes widened, stunned at the speed of my reflexes. "I see why R&R so desperately wanted you, Sergeant." She approached the gurney and Westsmith. He stepped back a step, the stethoscope dangling from his ears. With the AR still pointed at my chest, she stopped at Jude's side. With a glance at each of us and a slight waver of her weapon, she pulled out a syringe, stabbed it into Jude's chest, and thumbed in the plunger.

My finger pressed against the AR's trigger. Melissa stepped forward for a better shot. The girls bawled and the dog whined. A blood-curdling moan filled the room. Jude's back arched, the syringe still sticking out of her chest.

Williams backed away, her rifle now pointed at Jude. The medical staff huddled into the far corner, trying desperately to be forgotten as they pressed themselves against the wall. One was wielding a pair of scissors, but held it at her thigh instead of pointing it at any of us.

Another moan filled the room. The hair on the back of my neck stood on end, even as an itch started tickling under the skin between my shoulder blades.

No. This can't be how it ends.

I approached the table, never taking my front sight off of Williams.

"Face it, Sergeant," Williams said. "She's gone."

Jude reached out her hands at me, her eyes still rolled back to white. She let out a guttural groan.

"You need to put her down," Williams advised. "It's over."

"Don't listen to her," Westsmith countered. "She doesn't know shit."

"And you do?" Williams said with a hiss. "You're only here because you have something R&R needed."

Westsmith barked out an unexpected booming laugh. "So true." He stepped back to the table and the writhing Jude. "But who do you think designed these nano-capsules, sister?"

It was obvious from the look on Williams face she hadn't known. None of us had. Westsmith pressed his good hand into Jude's chest, pushing her still arching spine back flush with the table.

Williams recovered from her shock. "Doesn't matter. Kill her."

"Don't." From Westsmith.

"Kill her! Do it!" Williams roared.

I reposition the rifle, exhaled slowly, sighed, and pulled the trigger. The report was deafening in the too quiet theater. A thick spray of brains, bone and fluids exploded from the back of her head.

"Wha—" It was all Williams managed to get out, a shocked expression on her face. It was as if she was surprised I would actually go through with the act. She didn't know me as well as she had thought. The dime-sized hole in Williams forehead dripped with blood before her legs collapsed under her and she fell to the floor.

"Bravo, Mr. Walken," Westsmith clapped.

I swung the rifle toward him. He stepped away from Jude and the operating table with his uneven hands up. Jude was no longer convulsing with spasms, her back and arms having relaxed enough to make it look like she was just tuckered out from a long walk on the road. Her eyes were closed and a thin smile creased between her lips. Melissa joined me at the gurney, stopping at Jude's feet. Holly continued to whine, still standing on her hind legs. Summer and April came up behind me. They stopped at the perimeter of the surgical platform, not wanting to walk closer than any of the medical equipment.

Maybe they have seen enough death for one day?

The surgeons and techs murmured at the loss of Williams, the back of her head lying in a pool of her own blood. Bob walked past them and stopped at the gurney opposite me. He looked at Jude with sympathy, reaching out to—but not quite touching—her cheek.

We had all seen enough death today. No matter what I did, I couldn't escape the harsh realization I had become its harbinger. When I looked at the healers in the corner, each of them averted their eyes from my glare.

I set the rifle against the gurney and took Jude's warm hand in both of mine. Life hadn't left her body yet. I squeezed her hand, wondering what could have been different if we had stayed at the Howard Estates instead of continuing across the state and ending up here in New York.

Sean would be alive. Melissa would have her father and sister back. Jude wouldn't have had to carry around an explosive capsule in her neck for days, only for it to be too late to keep the charge from detonating.

Jude stared past me, no longer having her eyes rolled back into her head. The pupils didn't dilate, but the new silver flecks peppered across them did reflect the overhead lights like tiny diamonds on a felt at a jeweler's counter.

Had Jude completed turning? She had made those terrible sounds—gruesome noises the human larynx shouldn't be able to reproduce. She had arched her back so violently; she may have broken her spine in the process.

"Westsmith," I said.

His shoulders stiffened as he heard the edge in my voice. "Yes?"

"Is she going to turn?"

"I don't know."

"You said you designed the fucking thing in her neck."

"I did," Westsmith confirmed. "I designed the device and delivery system. But I have no idea what version of the serum the old man decided to put inside it."

I closed Jude's eyelids, not wanting to keep looking at her terrible, but beautiful silver-laced irises. My shoulders slumped. I was tired. Maybe my body would soldier on without sleep because of the new genetics R&–

And Diggs. Do not forget him.

And Diggs. I'm sure Dick didn't know dick as to why I am the way I am. He may have plunged in the first experimental dose, but whatever Diggs scooped into his playtime syringe was what actually killed me. His secret ingredient. A secret Diggs took to his death.

I remember. I was there.

You always are, aren't you?

"John," Melissa said more softly than I had ever heard from her. She had always been a rage-fueled blunt instrument of destruction.

"Yeah?" I replied.

"What now?"

I brushed my fingers slowly across Jude's arm from the crook of the elbow to the wrist, her skin still warm with the illusion of life.

"I want my gun back," I muttered. "And I want someone to pay."

"Nooooo!" Jude screamed, bolting upright.

"Jesus," Melissa exclaimed.

"Noooo!" Her eyes opened wide, darting around the room. She dug her fingers into my arm. "Where...uh..."

I grabbed her shoulders tight and forced her body square to mine. She fought against me, her muscles wired and tight like coils of steel. Jude finally recognized me, the silver flecks in her eyes glinting in the artificial light.

"It's okay, Jude," I said softly. "We're here. We're all here."

Jude focused on me, her eyes still threatening to dart away at the slightest sound. I continued to speak softly, her head cocking to the side slightly with each syllable. Slowly, her frame loosened and the tension in her body bled away. Her core relaxed and she slumped against me, exhausted from the intense exertion of the last few minutes. Her arms wrapped around my waist and she started to weep.

"It was terrible, John," she whispered so only I could hear her, intentionally or not. "Nothing but black. Worse than death."

I hugged her and pressed her tight to my body. She responded in kind, burying her face into my chest. I kissed the top of her head and ran my hand down to her neck. Her breathing slowed and her arms went from being a vise-like crushing force to a soft caress. I would have stayed in the embrace until the world eventually crashed down on us.

The world already has.

Shut up, Bob. You're ruining my moment.

Apologies.

It was finally Jude who pushed herself away from me. She placed her hands on my chest and looked up at me. Those silver flecks were both beautiful and terrifying. She tapped her hands against me and looked at me with an intense gaze and a pained smile. "Did I hear something about payback?"

59

Take Two Aspirins

+81 Days – 1723 hours
00:00:00

"You designed this thing?" Jude asked Westsmith with a scowl, pointing to her neck.

Westsmith nodded.

"I thought you were crazy," Melissa added.

"I am crazy," Westsmith confirmed. "Clinically, at least. That's what the doctors told me, anyway."

"Is this thing dead?" Jude asked. "Or do I still have to worry about being decapitated from an explosion?"

"It's disarmed," Westsmith said. "Eventually, the nano-metals will dissolve."

"What about what the capsule was carrying?" I asked.

Westsmith looked at the medical staffers still in the corner, most of them now sitting against the wall instead of trying to phase through it. They stared at us outright now with more of a medical curiosity than fear. It must be true men and women in the trauma field were extremely adaptable. When he turned his gaze back to me, his eyes were sharp and dark. "At this point the compound the old man administered is inert."

Why are her eyes silver, then, if the serum is inert?

"Actually, Alvarez administered it," Jude pointed out.

"No one takes a shit without the old man saying it's okay to do so," Westsmith said, responding more to everyone in the room than just to comment on Jude's point.

"What did he want with you?" I asked.

Westsmith shrugged, but his face said he knew exactly what they wanted with him. He turned to the medical staff in the corner. "Carl, what does the old man want with me?" The lead surgeon looked up at us from his not-so-comfy seat against the wall. "Carl?" Westsmith coaxed.

The surgeon glared at Westsmith. "Can't you just leave us alone?"

"I could," Westsmith replied, walking over to the doctor. He looked down at the surgeon and suddenly straddled his lap. "But then I couldn't have as much fun with you."

Dr. Carl Firestein, his technicians and fellow doctors around him, all glared at Westsmith. His antics didn't seem to be unexpected by the surgeon or his staff, but from the looks on their faces they certainly didn't have patience for them. Westsmith put his arms around Dr. Firestein's neck and kissed him under the ear. He whispered something to the surgeon and was rewarded with a curt nod and a darkened stare. The ever-present smile washed off Westsmith's face. He pulled their foreheads together with his interlocked wrists. The surgeon tried to break his hold, all the while twisting his face away. Westsmith's biceps flexed as he easily kept Firestein's brow touching his.

Westsmith leaned back on Firestein's lap, pulling him away from the wall with him. With a clucking sound of his tongue off the roof of his mouth, Westsmith drove Firestein's head into the wall tiles. There was an audible crack, the entire section of wall behind him seeming to shudder. Westsmith sprung up off Dr. Firestein's lap while the surgeon doubled over and grabbed the back of his head. The tile had a concave crater complete with ceramic cracks and a small red splotch at its center. Westsmith left the staffers and stormed through the center of the theater to us.

"And?" I asked, not willing to get into a debate about his methods or his relationship with the remaining R&R medical staff.

"It's not what I thought," Westsmith admitted, "but it's not important."

"Seems like it is," Melissa added.

"Just need to talk to the old man, is all," Westsmith advised. "I'll clear it up with him personally."

"And," I asked with a shrug, "where do we find him?"

"In the highest spire of the highest castle, of course."

Why does that sound so familiar?

Because it was the same thing you said to me during our wild goose chase at the museum.

Wiser words had never been spoken. Bob stood next to Dr. Firestein, watching the surgeon cradle the back of his head. *I have no doubt.*

"How do we get there from here?" I asked.

Westsmith's grin had returned. "You just need the magic words."

60

Abracadabra

+81 Days – 1737 hours

Westsmith had gone back to chat with the medical staff while we stood in the center of the theater between the gurney and the restraint chair. Even though Dr. Firestein held the back of his head, he and several of the other staffers nodded at his questions. I couldn't hear him, not because of the distance but because of a ringing in my ears. Shaking my head didn't seem to do anything to diminish the din.

"John." I did hear Jude clearly.

"Yeah?"

"Did I die?" she asked. I looked at her face, the silver in her eyes sparkling as she cocked her head.

"I don't know," I answered as honestly as I could. "We didn't have you on any monitors."

"Westsmith listened to your heart," Summer chimed in. "He used the heart thingy you put in your ears."

"That's a stethoscope, hun," Melissa educated her niece.

"Okay," Summer replied.

"He didn't seem too concerned about what he heard," I admitted. "Williams gave you a shot of adrenaline and you opened your eyes all on your own."

"Ok," Jude said. "It seemed like I was in the dark."

April spoke up. "This whole place was pitch black."

Holly voiced her agreement with a solid woof. She didn't want to be left out of the conversation. Jude scooped the dog up in her arms and nuzzled into the dog's fur. Holly closed her eyes and stretched out her neck to allow for maximum affection. Jude bounced the dog in her arms like a mother soothing a newborn back to sleep. Holly relaxed her body, lapping up every scratch and cuddle. A lovable distraction, Holly had quickly stopped Jude's line of questioning about her time on the table.

Westsmith returned. Behind him, the surgeons, nurses, and technicians were pulling themselves and each other up off the floor, tip-toeing over the bodies of the soldiers. Dr. Firestein and two of the nurses gingerly extracted ARs from the soldiers, passing them to the others.

"Don't forget the spare magazines," Westsmith reminded them. Firestein nodded with understanding and annoyance, his face twisting with a scowl.

I guess surgeons do not want to be told what to do.

Do any of us want to be told what to do?

You? Absolutely not!

After Dr. Firestein and his people grabbed as many weapons and magazines as they were comfortable with—some of the technicians looking miserable with a weapon in their hands—they walked over to the railing of the lower gallery. They nodded to us before stepping around the bodies at the bottom of the steps and walking single-file through the gallery and out the back. Within a minute, they were gone and we were left alone in the operating theater with dozens of cooling bodies for company.

"Okay, Copperfield," Melissa said to Westsmith. "What're the magic words?"

"Fear not," Westsmith replied, the laugh coming back into his voice. "We will be in the presence of greatness in mere moments." He walked over to the bloody splotch on the wall. Feeling around the cracked tile, he pressed his fingers into one three up and two to the left. It relented to his touch, depressing an inch into the wall. A six-foot tall panel swung into the wall.

Another thing definitely left out of the blueprints.

61

Glass Houses

+81 Days – 1753 hours

Westsmith picked up a sidearm from the soldier closest to the secret panel and tucked it in the back of his pants. He slipped into his discarded T-shirt top with some effort, then recovered his backpack from where it had been leaning against the wall. One of the soldiers must have brought it in after they stole him away from us. He tested the bandage around the pulp of his fingers until he was satisfied the wrap would hold. I was surprised he wasn't glaring at me for the damage I had caused him.

"I'm lucky they didn't cut the shirt off me," Westsmith said to himself as he disappeared through the hidden passage. "No way I was going to walk around like a flabby John McClane." No one responded to Westsmith's movie reference. Maybe Sean would have snickered at the quip, but we would never know.

We hesitated and looked at each other before finally following the former R&R tech into the space behind the wall, spreading out along a ten-foot square steel-grated deck. My brain needed a minute to comprehend where we were. We were in a spacious atrium, several stories in height and lined with massive mullions, supports, and tempered tinted glass. We were standing under the skin of the outer shell of the building–

–like maggots skittering our way under the hides of carrion.

I ignored Bob. It wasn't difficult since the atrium had a spectacular view of the Manhattan skyline. The dark towers of Midtown were back-dropped by fierce and threatening dark clouds.

Even without life or lights, they carried with them a sense of majesty—the echoes of an empire not quite on the verge of winking out of existence. The tinted transparent skin curved to give us a view of the retreating sun to the west, its waning rays only breaking through the clouds when the storm allowed. It was a tease. The sun continued to burn, but no longer with the strength to make the world believe it had any power left. It was the end of the day.

A steel staircase ran along the inner wall, hugging the exposed concrete and joining to grated deck landings above and below us. These observation decks also definitely hadn't been included on the floorplans I had memorized while isolated in my R&R concrete prison.

Apparently, secrecy knows no bounds.

The secret rooms off the official floorplans reminded me of the notorious H.H. Holmes who thrived in the era of the Chicago World's Exposition. The murderous charlatan had built a hotel of horrors for his own sadistic gameplay. He had employed several contractors, each only knowing a specific piece of the architectural and structural design. He had compartmentalized the information so no one person knew the whole truth.

"Christ," Westsmith said. "This is always an awesome sight."

We stared at the marvels the minds and hands of men had built. An island full of steel tributes dedicated to the ancient gods of ego and accomplishment. The angry dark storm clouds hung low on the cityscape and the industrial port of New Jersey across the Hudson River, the gods showing their dissatisfaction with the blood, sweat and sacrifice their ungrateful subjects built to honor them. Actually, it was probably truer men built these buildings to spite the gods… or become them. Melissa could only nod, no sarcastic words able to find a foothold on her lips.

The sun peeked through a break in the clouds for a moment before being swallowed up again. Lightning crackled across the sky, spreading millions of volts—like probing fingers—to the rooftops along the buildings to the west. The strikes sparked off of whatever conductive material they could find on their way to the earth.

Westsmith left us to marvel at the view, climbing the exposed staircase up to the next observation platform. We eventually followed him, Holly sniffing around the first step and growling before her anxiety of being left behind prompted her to bound up the steps after us.

"How do you know about this?" I asked, still miffed at the incomplete structural drawings.

"I was a golden boy," Westsmith answered, stealing glances at me as well as the wonders of nature and engineering around us. "When the old man takes a shine to you, you take advantage of the perks."

"So, you're an engineer?"

"More like a crazy inventor." He laughed loudly, as if to prove he did, at least, embody the crazy part. "I wasn't in Creedmoor by chance, you know."

I had no doubt.

Agreed.

"Agreed," Melissa muttered behind me so her voice only carried to me.

Jude herded Summer and April up the stairs behind us. They alternated between gawking at the view beyond the several stories of glass and where to put their next step. Holly brought up the rear of our column, sniffing each riser before hopping up onto the step itself.

"When you get in the old man's good graces," Westsmith said

without prompting, "he opens up the world to you. When you fuck up one time, he shows you a grand vista from the top of a mountain before he pushes you off the cliff."

"He's a peach," I said.

"He won't be in a few minutes," Westsmith muttered. "The motherfucker was looking to kill me. Me!"

"I guess you ain't the golden boy anymore, huh?" Melissa taunted.

"Nope." Westsmith went back to his strange giggle again. "The good sergeant here is, though."

"John?" Jude asked.

"Me?"

"Well," Westsmith said as he turned back to us from the top step before the observation deck. "It certainly couldn't be the sergeant on the floor of the elevator, now could it?"

I continued climbing until I was one step below Westsmith. With the difference in height, I was looking at him eye-to eye. "What did you say?" He opened his mouth and closed it again, seeing the hate harbored in my eyes for him. Just another thing added on top of the severe contempt I had for Roanoke & Raleigh and for the man who ran the corporation like the planet was just another Petri dish.

"I have offended you," Westsmith said in earnest. "I'm sorry."

How could he be so brilliant but, yet, so socially awkward?

He is probably retarded.

He could be autistic. Or have something like Asperger's Syndrome. Or be a savant.

Or he could be a sociopath.

I was sure the label of sociopath was aptly fitting.

"Come on." Westsmith ran across the observation deck to get to the next flight of stairs. He shrugged out of the backpack. He hooked it in the elbow of his bandaged hand, and unzipped it and rooted around inside it with his good hand. We made it to the grated deck in time to see him start up the next flight. I hurried after him, receiving a backpack flung at my face for my efforts. I slapped it away as the others crowded in behind me, regretting it as soon as the scent of almonds hit my nose and my stomach growled for a moment.

The wall of glass started to close in on us, angling toward the inside wall and observation decks as we climbed. Above us, the glass and steel disappeared behind a massive cantilevered concrete and steel girder ceiling.

"Looks like the last flight," I commented.

Holly limped as her paws pressed against the bumpy edges of the steel risers. She whimpered and whined, but continued to hop up onto the next step after us as soon as April's feet left them. I went back down and scooped her up from where she had paused to sniff at a piece of wire coated in a blue sheath of rubber. Once off the ground and in my arms, she started wagging her tail and licking my neck.

The others waited at the top of the stairs until I got there. Westsmith danced from foot to foot at the other end of the deck, his foot propping open a heavy glass door. His smile wrinkled high up in his cheeks, but the goodwill of his upturned lips never reached his eyes. "Let's go see the old man!" He couldn't contain his manic enthusiasm. "He is going to be thrilled to see us."

62

Membership Has Its Privileges

+81 Days – 1806 hours

We went from an eight-story glass walled view of the darkening city to a two-story ultra-modern office suite. Recessed on the opposite wall of the lobby space, a massive salt-water tank was filled with fish obliviously swimming through the rock formations. The floors were a dark stained wood, on the verge of being black. The walls were bright white—and not an eggshell or off-white color usually lumped into the same conversation as being white. This was a stark white, almost difficult to look at with the addition of white LEDs shining down from high hats gridded all through the blocky aluminum frame drop ceiling. The floating ceilings were rectangular and suspended from the tresses by braided steel cables, overlapping each other as they moved from functional space to space. The vents and electrical junction boxes above the drop ceilings had all been painted black to visually blend the HVAC and mechanicals into the structural roof.

I put Holly down. She bounded across the shiny marble floor before skidding to a bumping stop against the far wall. Westsmith casually strolled through the outer office. We followed as we moved from a large empty semi-circular commons room to a narrower reception area, complete with an aluminum tube-framed glass-topped desk, and a black ergonomic office chair pushed in under it. No paper, no drawers, no computer. April stopped at the desk, putting a hand on the glass top to steady herself as she adjusted the back of her sneaker. The glass came to life with color, showing a

293

holographic display of a virtual keyboard and a screen full of floating folders.

"Cool." Summer went over and tapped on an icon. The folder exploded into a new screen with dozens of documents. Summer reached her finger out to touch one of the files.

"Don't touch anything," Melissa warned her.

"Leave it alone, girlie," Westsmith ordered, having had to come back to see why we were not matching his enthusiastic pace through the suite. "Some things are better left undiscovered, if you know what I mean."

Summer slowly shook her head confirming she indeed didn't know what he meant, but pulled back her hand anyway. April wrapped her arm around her and led her back toward Melissa.

"Told you to leave stuff alone," Melissa said.

"State of the art," Jude commented absently, swiping her hands above the graphical display embedded in the glass top. After a moment, the glass went clear again.

"Thirty second sleep mode," Westsmith said. "Only the best tech for the old man."

"And this is his office?" I asked.

"This?" Westsmith scoffed. "Nah. This is the personal office suite above his everyday office. Where he can lord over all of his kingdom." Curved walls led to a long corridor directly behind the reception desk. At the far end was a set of brushed steel doors with an R engraved high in the center of each one. Was Dick holed up there? Westsmith nodded, as if knowing my thoughts. "That's the old man's lair. You ready to slay the dragon?"

"I just want my Glock back."

Obsessive much?

"Well," Westsmith said with a perplexed look on his face and shrug in his shoulders. "If that's what gets your junk fluttering, so be it."

"You sure he's there?" I asked.

"It's the only place he would go," Westsmith answered with confidence, his chest puffing out. "Why go to a lame office when you can go to your private suite."

"It is pretty sweet," April agreed, her hand tracing the medical tape holding the gauze and bandage onto her grazed neck. It had held up well.

Shaking his head at April, but satisfied Summer wasn't going to touch any more of the office's tech, Westsmith turned about and headed straight down the center of the corridor toward the steel doors. I moved down the hall after him, clearing the open lounge areas on either side of the hallway. The floor plan was open enough to keep blind spots at a minimum. Westsmith centered himself in front of the ten-foot doors and took a door handle in each hand. He exhaled slightly and turned down the levers, pushing both doors open like a sheriff entering through the bat-wing doors of a rowdy saloon.

"What's up, old man?" Westsmith's voice boomed as he entered the office.

The doors started to swing back into the frame. Before they closed, I propped my leg against one of them and scanned the inner office. Dick sat at a large glass desk at the opposite side of the room in front of a massive floor-to-ceiling view of the city. The floor changed from hard marble to a plush white carpet. Westsmith walked with purpose across the twenty-meter deep room.

Jude and the others stopped beside me at the threshold. Melissa looked at me with conflicted eyes, wanting to go on but needing to stay behind to look after Summer and April. She nodded at me before shouldering the Benelli and corralling the girls back toward the lounges. Holly looked up at me. Her tail swished side to side slowly for a moment. When she didn't get a response, she sat back up on her hind legs and woofed playfully.

"Go," I said, nodding toward Melissa. She tilted her head to glance at the retreating women, still balancing on her back legs. After licking her chops and nose, she plopped down on all fours and trotted after them. I looked at Jude. "Stay here."

"Yeah, right," she retorted. "You stay here." She brushed past me with the AR at a full draw, stepping through the doors into the executive office and clearing the right flank. I followed her lead and entered into the belly of the beast.

63

Daddy Issues

+81 Days – 1833 hours

We approached Dick from three directions.

Westsmith had walked toward him using the most direct route while Jude and I flanked him from either side of the suite. Dick sat behind his transparent desk with his fingers interlaced on its surface, looking at us with mild interest. A single freshly sharpened yellow no. 2 pencil sat in a perfect perpendicular position in front of him. My Glock also lay on the desk in front of him, within his easy reach.

"You wanted to cut me open?" Westsmith asked with a tone of incredulity, his hands balled into fists. "Me?"

Dick didn't take the bait, instead waiting until Westsmith was standing in front of him to answer. He spoke softly and evenly, "Xavier, you have always been very important to me."

"As a lab rat, maybe," Westsmith scoffed.

"You were always brilliant as a scientist, Xavier," Dick said. "Haven't I always praised your good works and rewarded you accordingly?"

"Wow!" Westsmith exclaimed. "Being able to stand next to you and watch the sunset while listening to you prattle on about the future of genetics and how you were going to change the world. Yeah… a great reward."

Dick frowned slightly, not because Jude and I had our weapons pointed at his head from less than three meters but because I think Westsmith's words actually stung him a little bit.

"And injecting me with a fucking tracking device? Another

great reward?" Westsmith spat out.

"Purely for your own safety," Dick countered.

"Really? I thought I was going crazy! The constant itch and beeping."

"It is highly unlikely you knew about the tracker," Dick said, shrugging, "or heard any beeping."

"He had it taken out by one of the doctors at the hospital," I told Dick. "We had to track him a completely different way because of it."

Westsmith grinned. "See? Validation!"

Dick put his interlaced fingers to his chin. "Interesting."

"And," Westsmith said, looking to continue his laundry list of slights, "what about all this shit I can do?"

"What… shit?" Dick asked, his mouth detesting the fact he has to repeat such vulgarity.

"Really? You kidding me?" Westsmith threw his clenched fists into the air.

And waved them around like he just does not care.

"I don't believe I am," Dick said, his hands back on the desk.

"You think being able to order these dead things around is normal?"

"That," Dick replied, pausing to mull over his next words, "was another reward for your service and loyalty."

"Did you put that shit in my food? In my water?"

"You are very melodramatic, Xavier."

"It's not like you wouldn't contaminate the city water supply if you felt it was necessary," Jude commented. She tightened the rifle into her shoulder.

"It *was* necessary," Dick said simply. The old man tapped his well-manicured fingers on the glass, his patience for his decisions being questioned—and being talked down to—quickly coming to an abrupt end. He slowly pushed his chair back and stood, smoothing out his tie and buttoning his jacket.

"Obviously," he stated, "Xavier and I have much to discuss about how I have cast such injustice upon him."

"Fuck, right, you do," Westsmith said, his fists now on the tabletop.

Ignoring Westsmith for the moment, Dick continued, "What can I do for you two, Mr. Walken and Ms. Sawyer?"

Jude didn't answer, but clenched her teeth together. She wanted retribution for the mental anguish she had endured. She knew, however, shooting him outright wouldn't make her feel any better... at least not in the long term. Although, she didn't seem to have had any regrets about putting a bullet in Debra's face back at the museum.

"I want my gun back," I said while Jude stewed through her conflicted feelings.

Dick's smile turned up at my comment, but halted its curl when he looked into my eyes. "I assume the arrangement we had agreed upon has been retracted, then?"

"Correct," I replied, never wavering in my glare or the barrel of the AK.

"Fine," he conceded. "Obviously, this gun means much more to you than as a trophy for me, so you are welcome to take it back. I know it was a gift."

Dick apparently knew more about me than I thought. I clenched my teeth and lowered the AR long enough to grab the Glock with my left hand. I clumsily holstered the weapon, realizing how much I had missed its familiar weight against my chest. The Glock was back where it belonged. It was home again.

"Ah," Dick clapped his hands together twice. "A happy man once again. For future reference, please remember my agreeability today." My continued glare was my answer.

"I'm so glad the Sergeant is happy again," Westsmith agreed. There was a tone under his words catching my attention more than the words themselves. "What about me?"

"Well, if there is nothing I can do for the lovely Ms. Sawyer. What *about* you, son?"

"Where's my happiness?" he asked, his words choking on a closing throat. "What about my happiness, Dad?"

Dad? What the fuck?

"Didn't I give you everything?" Dick asked undaunted. "An education. A job. Life. My name?" His last words boomed through the office suite.

Jude repositioned her grip on her weapon, darting glances at me. The end of the gun sights wavered between Westsmith and his dad as the two men argued.

"Sergeant Walken," Dick said. "I am afraid I never formally introduced myself to you. I am the last remaining living senior executive at Roanoke & Raleigh. I am the man whom you and Ms. Alvarez met in the Middle East. It was my department's work with an outdated experiment from the 1940s and 50s leading to the rise of the undead you have nicknamed FRACs. I was the one responsible for contaminating as much of the water supply to the majority of the population, here and abroad, as possible. "My name is Nicholas Westsmith," the old man, formerly known as Dick, said, "and I am the man who failed to stop the world from ending."

"Boo-fucking-who," Xavier spouted. "Poor old man feeling bad about the fucking undead apocalypse he wrought upon us." Xavier's right fist went up again. He had had them clenched for the entire time we were in the office suite. Now he opened his mangled bandaged hand to show it was empty. He gestured to his other hand and opened his pinkie and ring finger.

I recognized the device in his hand instantly. It explained the stray wires I had found on the steps and the faint whiffs of almond puffing out from his backpack. Westsmith the Elder was responsible for the flowers while the younger had brought the nuts.

"What is that?" Jude asked, her weapon shifting toward Xavier.

"Dead man's switch," we all answered her at the same time.

My weapon came up, just as Jude's had, but if Xavier wasn't bluffing then my threat of force was hollow, at best. The elder Westsmith turned his back to all of us and looked out on the Manhattan skyline and the deepening clouds.

"Don't test me," Xavier threatened. Xavier thrust his fist at his father, showing he meant business. The light on the top of the switch pulsed green.

Ignoring his son, Westsmith spoke to me, "Do you think my son could have placed enough explosives throughout this structure to bring it down with all of us in it?"

I thought back to the wood crates of plastic explosives and back to the floor plans I had studied in my sub-basement concrete prison. The right explosives against a few select structural supports would do plenty of damage. Whether he had enough time to plant enough C4 to do the job with the push of a button... "I don't know."

Mr. Westsmith nodded to my best guess. "So, my son is crazy and smart enough to have pulled off this stunt, but is he crazy enough to think it will make a difference?" With amazingly quick reflexes for an older man, Mr. Westsmith pulled a Beretta from the back of his waistband, spun around and held the pistol on his son.

Xavier laughed. He laughed so hard he doubled over and started to cough. Once he got himself under control again, he stood red-faced and wiped the tears from his eyes with his bandaged hand. "You need me, old man. Firestein told me what you needed me for. I don't think you are going to sacrifice me after all the resources you used to bring me in."

"Xavier," the old man said with a shrug, "I can always find a suitable heart. Maybe there's a cloned one gestating somewhere right now. You were never my only option, son." With those words, the Beretta boomed as it discharged with a flash. The bullet found Xavier's forehead, who let out a quiet "oh" before sinking to his knees.

"No!" Jude yelled.

Xavier fell forward. I rushed to him. His face bounced against the deep white carpet, his right hand under his body. I buried my hand under him, running it along his arm and closing my fingers around his hand as tight as I could. I flipped Xavier over and, as slowly and carefully as I could, opened his fingers while putting mine in their place. After getting a strong firm grip on the dead man's switch, I lifted his thumb away with my left hand.

"Jesus Christ," I said to a deity I didn't believe in, but whom I hoped was listening and believed in me anyway. The light had gone from a pulsing green to a solid red.

From far off came several faint booms—like rolls of thunder—one after another.

64

Tremors

+81 Days – 1855 hours

"What have you done?" Jude yelled at the surviving senior Westsmith, another tremor shaking the floor under our feet with tiny vibrations. The glass panels reverberated, sending back their own sounds of distress. Jude trained her weapon at the old man. Nicholas Westsmith looked at the end of Jude's barrel for a moment. He calculated Jude's intent before dismissing her as a valid threat to his well-being.

"Guess we both misjudged my son's ability," Westsmith said to me.

"You might have. I didn't misjudge anything," I replied. "I only questioned whether he had time to plant enough explosive and charges. Is the building going to come down?"

"It's difficult to say," Westsmith said with a shrug. As if in answer, the lone pencil on Westsmith's desk rolled to the right. It fell off the edge and embedded itself point first into the carpet.

Holly rushed in with a throat full of barks. Melissa and the girls burst through the door behind her. Summer clung to her aunt's waist while April held onto the doorframe as if the office was going to suddenly tip over sideways. Melissa was forced to shuffle along with the weight of her niece.

"We got smoke coming out of the elevator shaft," Melissa warned us. "That rumble was no fucking thunder."

Summer buried her face into fabric of her aunt's tactical vest.

"Sorry for my language, sweetie," Melissa apologized to her, then directing her next comment to us. "Jesus! What happened to Westsmith?"

The pool of blood under Xavier's head had expanded on the floor as it soaked into the carpet in an almost perfect circle. His face looked peaceful, his smile still on his face but softer and lacking the manic hard lines he forced to his lips in life.

"And where the hell is Dick?"

Jude and I looked back at the desk at the same time, our weapons swinging toward the transparent and empty surface. The pencil still stood up at an almost perfect perpendicular angle to the floor where it stuck in the carpet.

But the old man was gone.

65

Tipping Point

+81 Days – 1907 hours

"Great," Jude muttered. "Just fucking great."

"Language!" Melissa chastised.

Summer still clung to her aunt with two fingers wrapped through one of Melissa's belt loops. April held her other hand, a strange game of tug-o-war taking place. Holly bounded around Summer with playful barks as she enjoyed Summer bouncing between her aunt and April.

Although there were no more explosions, there were still tremors under our feet. Some of the vibrations were seen in the rattle of picture frame glass or from the multi-story glass skin held in place on the elaborate tube steel structural grid.

"He really was a dick," she said.

"He still is," I confirmed. Westsmith had vanished almost effortlessly, on par with Bob's spectral departures. Neither of us had noticed him slip away. I went to the expanse of glass behind the desk. There didn't seem to be a way for Westsmith to make an exit without passing us. I walked to the exposed concrete and steel column framing the panoramic view on the right side and slapped its porous surface. It seemed solid enough.

We really must go, Sergeant. While the urgent message hadn't come from Bob, the soft feminine bodiless voice was right. We needed to get out of this building.

Was the floor listing?

We retreated to the spacious lobby. Nothing was rolling around the floor, even the reception chair remained under the transparent tech desk. Jude covered our rear, looking back at the Westsmith lying dead on the carpet and the desk the other Westsmith had left behind.

"Weren't those tanks full when we got here?" April asked.

The fish continued to make their way through the coral formations and seaweed, ducking in and out of the natural caverns housed in the massive tank. The water level had gone down from the top edge while we had been in Westsmith's office. The water hadn't leaked out through a crack or splashed out over the top of the Plexiglas. It was tilting toward the back of the tanks behind the wall, keeping its equilibrium even if the building wasn't.

"We need to get lost. Now." We backtracked to the multi-story atrium. The view to the city streets was decidedly more difficult as the angle of the sightline of Manhattan Island was tipping upward toward the dark evening clouds. As we rushed down the stairs, we had to press our left hands into the wall in order to keep our balance. Once we made the turn at the deck of the next lower level, Melissa scooped up Summer and April grabbed Holly around the belly.

The structure groaned in protest.

I wasn't sure how Xavier did it or where he planted the explosives, but the building was destined to come down. It might topple in an hour or a few minutes. We didn't have the luxury of waiting around to find out, making our way back to the operating theater in record time.

Several of the surgical support machines and monitors had rolled toward the railing of the gallery. The surgeons and their staff had been smart to evacuate when they had, the space empty except for the equipment and more than a dozen dead members of the two R&R security teams.

"How we getting out?" Melissa asked, panic settling into her voice.

"John will find a way, Aunt 'Lissa," Summer said.

Yes, John will find a way. I turned toward the voice at the rear of the gallery. The young girl from the screened-in room in the beachfront dreamscape facing a blank Atlantic Ocean had returned. When she registered I had seen her, she turned and walked out through the double doors into the white corridor.

66

Just Talkin' About Shaft

+81 Days – 1919 hours

We pressed on into the corridor. I led the way for the others, none of them knowing I was simply following a long blond-haired ghost girl. In life, the girl had found me on a different island a lifetime ago… back when we made believe the world might have a chance to return to its former self.

"Maybe we should have stayed closer to the outside," Melissa speculated. "Easier to get out."

"Filled with shattering windows able to slice us to ribbons," I answered, envisioning hundreds of shards of mirrored glass impaling all of us.

The girl—not a child, but not yet a young woman—continued through the corridors with a distinct purpose, backtracking our steps. Her nightgown flowed behind her as if a gale wind was whipping through the gossamer material.

"The freight elevator is this way," Jude realized. "Wouldn't they have locked it down again?"

"The squad who collected you and Melissa from the observation gallery brought you down through the elevator, right?" I asked rhetorically. "Odds are they wouldn't have bothered locking it again. Plus, Westsmith was a bit busy to be manning the controls."

The girl looked over her shoulder and smiled. *You got it in one, Mr. Walken.*

Where's Bob? Why aren't you ever together?

She shook her head, still smiling and heading through the white

corridor with the waist high black stripes on each wall. We passed
the two sentries we had dispatched earlier while getting out of the
elevator. She stood to one side and pointed at the call buttons.

I pressed the down arrow. The button lit up. Even with the
fluorescent bars and recessed LEDs flickering and dim, it was a
good sign the power was still on. After several seconds, the whirring
of motors resulted in a soft chime.

"You sure about this, John?" April asked. "What if the power
goes out?"

The doors choose that moment to open.

Sean was still lying in his own blood. While there were a couple
of boot impressions at the still tacky edges of the crimson pool, Sean
had otherwise been left undisturbed. Summer burst out in tears and
wrapped both arms around Melissa's waist, burying her face into her
aunt's belly. April covered her mouth and took a step away from the
elevator. She made a muffled moaning sound and shook her head.
Holly whined and tried to escape April's arms. Luckily, April
continued to hold the dog tight under one arm.

The blonde girl stood to the side of the open doors. She peered
into the elevator, looking at Sean sympathetically.

You do need to hurry, Mr. Walken.

The building trembled in support of her words.

"Let's go," I ordered. "We can't wait."

Jude ushered April and Holly into the car, carefully blocking
April's view of Sean with her own body. They moved to the far
corner next to the car control panel.

"Melissa," I said.

She nodded and shuffled Summer into the car as well. I entered
last, standing in the same spot where Xavier had stood before he and
his backpack of death had been taken away by his father's security

forces.

I nodded to Jude, who pressed the L button. The doors started sliding together, separating us from the sweet young face of the young girl. She was only able to nod once and raise her hand enough to start a parting wave before the doors closed completely.

The soft mechanical voice of the elevator confirmed our destination. There may have been a bit of a British accent in the woman's voice I hadn't noticed before. Apparently, there were other speakers than the one I had destroyed with Melissa's Benelli.

The elevator started its smooth descent.

The low tones of smooth instrumental jazz played around us. It was easy to hear since none of us breathed a word. Besides the music being pumped into the car, the only other things flowing were tears down their faces. Me, included.

The score was unknown to me. Again, Sean would probably have known its composer or songwriter. But, instead, he stared up at me from the diamond plate floor of the elevator… just another casualty of a war he never signed up for. My waging of a losing war against the dick named Nicholas Westsmith. I was always several steps behind the old man. And, now we just need–

The car trembled, a loud shriek of metal echoing all around us. Jude flattened her hands on the walls around Melissa and the girls, protecting them from being jostled.

The elevator continued its descent. The unknown, but soothing music still played. The building groaned and creaked around us. Banging sounds came from above. All eyes went to the ceiling of the car as something knocked on its roof. Melissa raised her shotgun. I drew my Glock since the AR was less maneuverable in the confined space.

Another knock. This time, Summer let out a nervous squeak

before clamping her hand over her mouth. The control panel ticked off each floor as we passed them. 101... 100... 99...

The car seemed to distort.

While the blood from Sean's head was drying, two red trails still managed to weave their way around the raised diamond plates as they crept toward Jude and the others. Melissa stared at the blood with wide eyes as she pressed against the control panel. 89... 88... 87...

More bangs on the roof of the car. A snap. Followed by the sound of a metal whip cracking. The elevator accelerated. I braced myself in the corner to keep from sailing across the car and crashing into the others. Jude was doing her best to keep the others boxed in, the tilt of the car making it easier for them to rest against the no longer vertical wall. 62... 60... 57...

"Shit!" Jude shouted, the elevator continuing to speed up in its descent.

All of the cables holding the car must have been severed. We were in freefall. 55... 50... 45...

The little girl had led us here.

You have led us here, John. Bob's voice pressed into my brain. *Do not blame a little girl for your decisions.*

The elevator felt like the Demon Drop at Cedar Point. My stomach lurched into my throat, the muscles in my arms straining to pin me against the corner of the car. 38... 31... 24...

With the electricity waning, there might not be power to operate the automatic brakes to stop us. Or, at least, slow us down enough to be able to walk away from our descent. The elevator tipped over more. I was above the others now. Shrieks of metal grinding against metal filled the car. I gritted my teeth. If I had tried to cover my ears against the noise, I would dislodge from the corner and fall on top of the others.

Sean's body slid across the floor, quickly overtaking the slowed paced of the two rogue blood trails and dragging a grim wash of red under him. He slapped against the wall, his cheek pressed against the brushed aluminum of the doors.

We were seconds away from the bottom, with only the springs to catch the elevator. It might keep it intact but the sudden stop would likely maim or kill us.

"Jude–," I started. She looked over her shoulder at me, a tear running down her cheek. The muscles in her neck and shoulders stood out from the exertion.

The building was falling down in earnest now. Debris banged against the roof of the elevator. Part of a steel girder frame impaled the center of the car, embedding into the red floor where Sean had fallen after being shot.

The lights flickered and went out. They didn't come back on. The car buckled and twisted. The shrieking got louder.

SLAM!

We came to a somewhat abrupt, but not maiming, stop. It wasn't the bottom. We didn't stop because of any safety braking protocols. The sub-basement springs didn't catch us. And, while the car had stopped, we still felt rumbles and vibrations. The shrieks had been replaced by deeper moaning.

Lights flickered to life again. The others were pressed against the control panel, Jude struggling to keep her weight off them. Sean's body had rolled onto the doors, his eyes staring lifelessly at me—always staring at me. I aimed my feet and dropped to the opposite side of the doors.

Damn, my neck ached.

The rumbling slowed, then eventually stopped. The elevator lay on its side, tipped at an obscene eighty-degree angle. Debris tapped against the elevator. The car itself was creaking in protest. It didn't help the metal rod had pierced through the center of the cab, already damaging the integrity of the enclosure. Even the best constructed elevators—this one included at the top of the list—weren't designed with roll cages and thick solid steel shells. It didn't bode well for how long we had before the elevator shaft imploded or the cab was crushed under the weight of the crumbling building.

A ticking sound started. It was rhythmic and mechanical. After several seconds, the LED recessed lights fluttered back to life.

"Thank the Lord," Melissa griped, holding Summer tight.

Amazingly, Jude still had her arms spread out against the walls above Melissa and the girls, using her body as a protective cage.

"I think you can give yourself a break, Jude," I advised.

Her shoulders flexed and she pushed off from the door, rolling against the corner next to Melissa.

"You okay?" I asked.

Jude rolled her neck around and rounded her shoulders. "A bit sore," she confirmed, "but everything seems good."

"That's a relief," I said.

"Melissa?" Jude asked, touching her arm.

Melissa winched. "Shit. I don't think so."

"Broken?" Jude asked.

"Hopefully not," Melissa grumbled. "Hurts like a sonofabitch, though."

"Auntie!" Summer's voice rang out as a muffle from Melissa's belly where her face was buried.

"You good?" Melissa asked her niece.

"You mean, besides not being able to breath or see good?"

"Yeah, sweetie," I said with a smile. "Besides that."

313

"Besides that," Summer replied, peeking her face out from her aunt's stomach, "I'm great."

Melissa hugged her tight with her good arm.

Summer reached out an arm and lightly tapped April on the thigh. "You good?"

All she got as a response was a groan. Jude looked over Melissa at April. "Shit, girl. You okay? I thought I had you covered." April groaned again. While Melissa held Summer tight to her body, Jude crab walked over them to get closer to Summer. "It's okay, sweetie. I'm coming."

Straddling April at the waist with her feet on the doors, Jude put her hands high on April's arms close to the shoulders. April twitched. "Sorry. Sorry." Jude hissed an inhale, sympathizing with April's pain. "Come on. Let me turn you over and get a look at you."

April tensed up for a moment before grunting and relaxing. Jude put a hand under April's body on her chest, braced her right leg, whispered to her it was going to be okay, and started to roll her over. April let out a gurgled scream. Blood spurted up in Jude's face and chest. A piece of ragged and gnarled metal had pierced through the doors and had impaled April in the middle of her chest.

"Jesus!" Jude arched her face back away from April and pushed her hands against the wound at the same time. April screamed again.

Holly whined. She had been caught under April's body, lying on her side against the doors. I pulled her out by her scruff and hooked her under my right arm while twisting around to get my hand onto April's chest to assist Jude in plugging up the entry wound. Her screams only got louder, her arms flailing and flapping against Jude. April's now slick fingers grabbed at whatever fabric she could, trying to get up to Jude in her panicked and shocked state.

I dropped Holly to the free corner of the cab. She whimpered in pain. Now with two free hands, I pressed one into April's wound and the other into her chest at the collarbone in an attempt to pin her against the doors and to keep her from worsening her injury. She grabbed at me.

"Hold on!" Jude shouted. "Hold on!"

The pain in my neck increased as I pressed April into the doors. The ticking of the LED lights quickened. April shouted and snapped at me. The lights flickered, brightening for a second before they went out. Before they did, they reflected off the gold flecks in April's eyes.

Shit! April had turned.

Summer screamed in terror. I pushed Jude away against the floor—now the wall—and grabbed April by her shirt. I pulled her close, her teeth snapping and her bloody arms sliding against me as her fingers tried to find any purchase on the back of my neck, holster straps, or shirt.

"I'm sorry," I whispered, her teeth chattering a couple inches from my face. I lifted her off the metal and thrust her back down. The lights came back on. The twisted metal killing April pierced through the back of her neck and out through her mouth. Blood spurted out from her lips, staining her face and my shirt.

Melissa and Summer cried as they held each other. My heart thudded in my ears. April's aura darkened to a cool charcoal. The smell of copper filled my nostrils. A metallic taste drifted and sat on my tongue. Holly whimpered again. I now sensed the pain of her broken front leg. Jude reached out a hand to the center of my shoulder blades, her fingers touching me so lightly I may not have even realized it had my senses not been amped up from the experience.

I slowed my breathing in an effort to drop my heart rate. It was an ingrained sniper trick or, maybe, just something I had just honed over the years on my own. The thudding in my ears slowed and then stopped.

Unfortunately, hearing the pulse of my heartbeat lessen was not better than the sound it was replaced by. The blood from April's body pooled against the elevator doors. As it gathered at the threshold, I could hear pings as the blood made its way between the doors and dripped onto another piece of expose metal.

67

Bottoms Up

+81 Days – 1943 hours

The lights continued to flicker. There was no telling how long the elevator's emergency batteries would hold out, especially assuming we lost our connection to the building's generators—if they were still functioning. If the batteries died and the lights went out again, I didn't think Summer would fare very well.

Sean and April were crumpled up on the floor. Jude helped me move both of them against the right side of the doors before scooping Holly up into her arms. With the elevator almost on its side, there wasn't much room on the other side of the doors for Melissa and Summer to stand without either of them pressing the buttons on the call panel. Jude and I stood on the doors, trying to keep from smearing the blood in the middle where the two doors met. Holly whimpered in her arms. Jude rocked her gently back and forth, the dog licking her own nose nervously.

"We gotta get out of here," Melissa advised, her voice cracking. She cleared her throat to force it away.

I didn't know if her claustrophobia extended to enclosed spaces without a water component. I certainly didn't see water becoming an issue here, although the water standpipes did run parallel to the elevator shafts. If the tanks holding the water for the building's gravity feeds cracked, they might be another issue.

As if in response, the building groaned and the pressure inside the elevator car seemed to increase. The top of the car—the other dented doors now acting as the ceiling—pushed down an inch or

317

two. We all looked up without breathing, waiting for the inevitable collapse to crush us all. After an endless series of minutes where we only sipped in the most necessary of breathes, we exhaled our relief and resumed breathing evenly again as it was evident we had earned a reprieve from becoming pulpy remnants squashed between steel.

"Did I mention we need to get the fuck out of here?" Melissa reiterated in a stronger fashion. Summer didn't correct her aunt's choice of words, instead making sure to hug her as tightly as she could with her face buried against her in an effort to block out the sight of the bloody bodies in the car with us.

"I hear you," I confirmed. "The lights and the structural integrity of this place aren't going to hold out forever."

"So, how do we get out?" Jude asked me.

"We can pry open the doors."

"Ain't going to be easy to pry them open with shrapnel through the door," Jude advised. "And who knows what's pinned against the other side of the ones above us."

"Yeah," I said, pointing up. "The other doors won't give us much leverage, either."

"… a hatch?" Summer mumbled from behind her aunt's body.

"Hush, sweetie," Melissa said to soothe her. "It'll be okay."

"But, Aunt 'Lissa," Summer said, poking her face out from her aunt's body. "Isn't there always a hatch? All the movies have a way out through the ceiling."

Jude and I looked at the ceiling. It was easy since we could stare straight ahead at it. The recessed LEDs winked at us, inviting us to take a closer look. The brushed bronze panels with the gold accents didn't give away any easy secrets, making it difficult to tell if there was a maintenance door in the elevator at all. Jude tucked Holly more tightly under her arm and touched the metal ceiling with the four recessed lights. The panel was raised away from the true ceiling of the car, a six-inch jet-black edge around the perimeter with its own flickering hidden light bars. The metal beam impaled through the ceiling was the only thing hanging from it.

"It seems to be one piece," Jude said. She pressed her fingers against the surface in different spots, receiving a hollow thunk as the metal popped back into its original position. "Great idea, sweetie, but I don't think this elevator comes with a trapdoor."

"Stupid, dumb elevator." Summer wrinkled up her face and pouted out her lower lip. "We ain't never getting out of this fucking elevator." None of us corrected Summer's language. In fact, I thought I saw the tiniest glimmer of pride in Melissa's eyes and the upturn of a smirk on her lips. What I saw for sure was Melissa patting her niece's arm and giving her another hug.

There were some elevator designs which allowed for maintenance access from each floor instead of via the elevator itself. With everything in this building designed with cost as no object, it wouldn't have surprised me they would tack on the extra expense of "per floor" access. It was ironic we happened to be in one of the few elevators not designed for the egress we needed.

This entire building reeks of difficult access.

Where were you, Bob?

He stood sideways in the elevator, his feet planted to the actual diamond plate floor *I am sorry, John. I figured you had your hands full without me distracting you.*

Well, the little blond girl managed to make an appearance.

And where is she now?

She led us to the elevator and we left her in the lobby of the 132nd floor.

So, she told you to take the elevator?

319

Yes.

And how is that working out for you?

Going great, so far. Thanks for asking.

That is very evident.

"John," Jude said, rubbing her neck with a frown on her face. "What are you thinking?"

Yes, John. What are you thinking?

"We either pry open the doors above us," I replied, "or we tear open the ceiling. If there is no hatch, the doors are the best bet."

"Well, then," Jude said with a shrug. "Let's get this show on the road. Or at the very least, get us outside this elevator."

"Aye, aye," I replied, grabbing the metal impaling the car through the ceiling. It had narrowly missed Sean's body. Pulling back, the spear of metal shrieked against the former ceiling. I gritted my teeth and felt the metal start to bend. Suddenly, it snapped off from the ceiling, a ready-made crowbar. I thrust it in the seam between the doors above me and pulled.

"John," Jude said.

"Gimme a minute," I huffed. "It's coming."

"That's what he said," Jude laughed, and then shouted. "John!"

"What?" I snapped, irritated I had only managed to open to doors an inch before they slapped shut again. I looked at Jude with a flash of anger. She stood there with one hand on her hip, pointing to the old ceiling. When I had dislodged the metal bar, the hidden hatch had been free to pop open.

"See?" Summer said with pride. "I told you there was a hatch!"

68

Shear

+81 Days – 2007 hours

The elevator shaft was very disorienting. Instead of looking up at how far the shaft went in order to get to the top floor, I stood on the cracked concrete wall with the open hatch at my back and a dark tunnel broken up by flickering light ahead of me. Of course, it didn't denote the way out. The steel cables lay at my feet, now severed completely from their motors. I peeked around the elevator car itself. The tunnel ran for over a hundred meters under the elevator car before it dropped off. Blackness swirled around at the end. Was the sentient mist back, even though Xavier was dead? I exhaled and worked my way around the steel tracks holding the elevator in place.

"What's out there?" Summer called out, a little full of herself since she had been the one to mention the elevator had a ceiling maintenance access point.

"Stay put, kiddo," I called back. "Gimme a minute here." I walked on the outside of the rails where I could. It seemed strange to walk on the actual doors to each floor. The emergency lighting was still working in the shaft, luckily working on battery backups instead of being hardwired into another electrical source.

The black continued to swirl at the far end of the shaft. I pulled my Glock and continued. The angry mist roiled but didn't advance into the shaft. After another thirty seconds, I realized why. The mist hadn't relegated itself to the end of the tunnel with any sense of preoccupation or disinterest. It wasn't even the sentient mist at all. The end of the tunnel wasn't filled with malice… it just ended. The building had toppled over as was obvious by the shaft-turned-tunnel. But what I hadn't realized until now was the building had sheared clean off its base. The tunnel ended, revealing the low-formed, dark storm clouds above Manhattan's night sky.

I stepped to the edge. Open air extended for a hundred meters below me until it reached what was left of the atrium. The bodies we had encountered before were now hidden under tons of concrete, steel and glass. The columns I had admired on our way in were sheared off testaments to what was once award-winning architecture. Massive chunks of broken building piled up along what used to be the perimeter of the property—and beyond. I could only assume the rest of the building had fallen straight down Park Avenue.

The jagged remains of the guts of the building under me would make it nearly impossible for even me to scale down to the atrium below without gear. Going back through the shaft to pry open doors would be fruitless since the resulting lobbies were all crushed under it.

The skies rumbled, the gods distraught over the toppling of one of their earth-bound titans. A flash of lightning crackled across the skyline, quickly joined by several more. One sparked off a taller downtown building antenna a moment before raindrops pelted my face.

"I guess it was too much to hope for a quick exit," Jude said, stepping up to the edge beside me.

"When does *easy* ever happen to us?" I asked.

"Never seems to be in the cards for us, does it?"

"Nope. How you feeling?"

The rain came down harder, dotting the dusty concrete. Jude took a step back into the shaft but put her palm out to catch the

322

raindrops in her hand. She closed her eyes and smiled as she wiggled her fingers in the rain. She remained motionless way for a minute as the raindrops splattered off her palm, until a low moaning chorus interrupted her respite and soured her smile. She opened her eyes, sighed, and responded with, "Never time to just be, is there?"

"Not anymore, it seems," I answered.

"The rain feels so good on my skin. It's been a long time." Flashes of lightning lit up the sky, followed a second later by a low rumble of thunder. Light bounced off the shaft walls. We looked back toward the elevator. Melissa and Summer peeked back at us from the far edge of the car. "Thoughts about how we're getting out of here?"

"Might have to go up." I turned away from the edge, walking ahead of the rivulets of water making their way into the gloom of the shaft.

"Go up to get down," Jude said with understanding, peering over the jagged edge. "Wonderful."

We walked back and sidestepped our way to the top of the elevator car. Melissa flashed the light into our faces for a moment, temporarily blinding us both. When she realized her error, she turned the beam upward. The light splashed off the walls to give us additional light to see by. Summer sat against the elevator with Holly lying next to her. The pooch's chest was rising and falling rapidly, her tongue hanging out and her tail between her legs. Summer lightly stroked her on the head in an effort to comfort her.

While the elevator shaft was dry and free of FRACs, it was no place to be holed up indefinitely. I left the others and climbed back inside the elevator car. The recessed lights, while weak, were still working. I hooked my fingers through Sean's tactical vest and slid him from the corner to the center of the door serving as the elevator's floor now. I took all of the spare magazines he still had on his person. There wasn't much else to take. I took a knee next to him, crossed his arms over his heart, and closed his eyes. I would have whispered a prayer on his behalf, but I was sure anything I would come up with would have been from some trite half-remembered Sunday School drivel.

"You did good, soldier," I finally said. "I know they will welcome you into Valhalla with open arms."

Ooh-rah. Bob agreed solemnly.

I put my arms under April's body and slid her over to lie next to Sean. I also put her in the same pose, not really understanding the reasons why, but needing to formalize their death in some ritualistic way. I wanted to feel like I accomplished something and providing them—and me—a sense of closure. "You can see Lenny again," I told her, patting her arm before standing. "At least there's that."

I thought you didn't believe in God. Bob didn't say it with any twinge of sarcasm, his tone more inquisitive and interested in my state of mind.

"I don't know if I believe in anything anymore," I answered aloud. "Except death."

Death is always a constant.

"Without question."

"John," Jude's voice carried over from outside the hatch. "I think we need to get moving. Melissa is getting a bit anxious."

"Ok. One sec." There was nothing more to do for Sean or April. Both of their deaths had been senseless, one an act of malice and the other bad fortune. Both deserved better than what they got while under my leadership.

I exited the elevator, all eyes on me as my boots splashed on top of a widening trail of water heading past us toward what used to be the top of the building. Melissa's eyes darted from me to the water, careful to keep herself and Summer as far away from it as she could in the tight space.

"We really can't get out through the atrium?" Melissa asked quickly.

"It's a sheer drop," I said with a shake of my head. "We don't have the equipment to repel down or even lower down Summer or Holly. It's not advisable."

"So, the better bet is to walk a hundred stories in the hopes we can get out at the top?" Melissa asked. "What makes you think the rest of the shaft isn't collapsed?"

"In this case," Jude chimed in, "the devil we don't know may be the better choice. Can't hurt to scout it out."

Melissa looked at the quickly expanding water across the grooves in the shaft. She shifted from one foot to another, forcing Summer to loosen her grip on her aunt's thigh.

"Come on, Auntie," Summer spoke up. "It'll be fine."

"Says you," Melissa muttered in response.

"Yep. Says me. I haven't been wrong yet!" Summer grinned.

"The girl does have infallible logic," Jude commented.

"Then let's get on with it." Melissa glared at the water, swallowing hard and gripping her Benelli and her neice as if her life depended on it.

69

Urgent Care

+81 Days – 2025 hours

The storm could be felt through the slain structure, the rumble of thunder vibrating through cracks in the concrete. Puffs of dust swirled through the beams of our rifle mounted tactical lights. Melissa had her shotgun. Jude carried the AR she had picked up from the soldier in the operating theater. I resorted to my Glock, liking the smaller weapon in closed quarters.

Holly licked my face, her tail brushing against my side in spite of the pain she was in from her injured front paw. Jude had adeptly created a splint for the dog from two short metal rods and a strip from her left sleeve. I hitched the pooch up tighter into the crook of my left arm, scanning the shaft ahead.

The water continued to rise, flowing as quick currents in the channels of the overturned sidewalls of the shaft. It hadn't gone beyond the grooves yet, but it was threatening to do so. The water in the enclosed space made Melissa anxious, keeping the pool of her light focused on the flowing rivers. Every far-off splash snapped her tactical light away from the rivers long enough to scan deeper into the blackened shaft.

"It's just concrete falling into the water," Summer surmised.

"That's not helping," Melissa muttered. "Not at all."

Our progress was marked by stenciled numbers denoting the floors. A three-foot-tall 32 spray-painted between the grooves at our feet. The shaft, so far, had survived the building's fall fairly well. There were obvious and expected stress fractures in the concrete structure, but the building's designers must have put special care into the survivability of the elevator systems.

Maybe the executives felt they were too important to have to take the stairs in an emergency.

Maybe.

Or, maybe they were just fat and lazy.

Nicolas Westsmith struck me as someone who would turn his nose up at executives who just let their status and position carry them through their careers. He was the one in the field who had injected me and Rosalita, so he certainly had no problem getting his hands dirty.

Also makes for someone who does not tend to delegate the important tasks.

Probably true. And I was sure he had used his attitude to his advantage to wrest control of R&R. It was doubtful the executives had been aware of Westsmith's ultimate plans. It was one thing to develop military-grade weapons from the DoD's Red Communist Army's undead soldiers research. It was another thing altogether to develop a failsafe involving the contamination of the world's bottled water supply once Pandora's Box was opened.

He probably gave the bottled water directly to all of the senior members of the company when the shit hit the fan.

We passed the three-foot-tall 46. Holly whimpered softly under my left arm. Jude, bathed in the light of her weapon, gave Holly a sympathetic frown and a pout of her lips.

"Oww!" Summer cried. "You're hurting me, Aunt 'Lissa!" Both Jude and I swung our lights over to Melissa and her niece. Melissa had her fingers around Summer's wrist in a vise-like grip. Summer tried to pry back a few fingers by wedging her own fingers under them, but Melissa didn't relent.

"Melissa," Jude called out.

She didn't answer, simply staring into the darkness ahead with her free hand holding the shotgun tightly with white-knuckled fingers. I walked over to her, stepping through the water rising over the grooves and pooling out a foot in either direction. The water between the grooves had joined together, cleaning the dust and some of the smaller debris as it flowed ahead. Grabbing Melissa's wrist, I pressed down until I saw a grimace come to her lips. She blinked and looked at me. "Ouch, John."

"That's what Summer said, too," I replied.

She looked down at Summer. The little girl was still trying to wrench her wrist away from her aunt's grip, tears forming in the corner of her eyes. A look of horror swept over Melissa's face and her fingers sprang apart. Summer grabbed her own wrist and pulled it to her chest.

"I'm so sorry, Summer," Melissa said, and then begged, "please forgive me." The wounded Summer looked up at Melissa—her eyes half hidden as dark sockets—and slowly nodded her acceptance of her aunt's apology. "Ok." Melissa nodded back. "Ok."

I kept hold of Melissa's wrist. "You going to get your shit together?"

She looked me square in the eyes. It wasn't anger residing there, but an abundance of fear. "I'll try."

"Try harder and get your head in the game," I said. "We don't have the luxury of carrying your weight. Your actions affect more than just you."

"Yeah. Ok." Melissa nodded with realization, looking back at Summer. "Sorry, sweetie."

"It's okay," Summer said without much conviction. "Let's just go."

"Now you're talking," Jude agreed. "The girl is always right."

"She is," I said.

Summer beamed again, feeling important and the center of attention.

Melissa walked ahead with her Benelli pointing the way, her boots splashing through the water having nearly found its way to the corner of the walls. She didn't slow down as she disappeared beyond a cascade of water from a gaping fissure above us. The shaft suddenly angled downward, the flow of the water speeding up as a result. The sound of the water echoed loudly through the tight column of concrete.

"It sounds like a waterfall," Summer said.

"Yeah. Right?" Jude replied. "Must be raining up a storm out there, huh?" She emphasized the word *storm* for the young lady.

"You're corny," Summer said with a laugh.

"What did I say?" Jude said with mock surprise.

I walked past the water wall on the left side where it was dripping the least and followed the trail Melissa's tactical light was leaving. Holly slowly shook her head to shed off the wetness sprinkling down on her. Jude and Summer brought up the rear, Jude hunching over the young girl like a human umbrella. Our footfalls became splashes of water as we trudged our way across a 59 sitting under an inch of wavering water. Melissa stared at another large dry fissure above us. She pointed her Benelli at the crack, circling it until she was satisfied nothing was going to spring out at us.

"It's big enough for us to get through," Melissa assessed.

"Looks like it," I agreed.

Jude and Summer arrived, looking on as Melissa and me stared at the hole. I handed Holly off to Jude and holstered my Glock after pulling the tactical light off its rail. I ran the light along the opening before clenching the light in my teeth. Squatting down, I leapt up the three meters to the opening.

"Jesus Christ!" Jude exclaimed. "That's a crazy vertical leap."

"One of the perks of being a super soldier?" Melissa said aloud.

I didn't answer as my fingers fought to find purchase on the dusty aggregate, working my way slowly up another meter into the crack until my fingers found the far edge of the wall. Finally, I pulled myself through the fissure, only resting when I could sit on the other side of the concrete.

The sideways elevator shaft had been disorienting, but my brain had quickly gotten used to the simple linear geometry. Up here— with the lobby's oak reception desk jutting out from a wall of marble several meters above my head—it felt like I was in a surreal Tim Burton movie or an M.C. Escher sketch. Behind the desk was a raised brushed aluminum sign with the words knocked out to spell out Medical Center. The corridor from the elevator to the lobby looked like a vertical cave shaft. The steel and black leather chairs— designated for the asses of guests waiting for personnel working on this floor—were a mangled mess beside me. One of the legs of a couch had embedded itself several inches into the dark paneling. Architectural and golf magazines lay open to random articles and advertisements like tents pitched in a summer campground.

There would be no easy way to climb up to the reception desk. I stood, took a deep breath, bent at the knees, and propelled myself upward toward a long crack in the concrete wall. My fingertips were barely able to engage, but I gritted my teeth and pulled myself up enough to allow for the tips of my boots to find purchase against the wall. I repositioned my body to where the wall and the floor met, pressing my hands and feet outward to wedge myself into the corner to work my way up.

The lobby widened, allowing for me to climb up onto the wall to rest. If I worked my way to the reception desk, I would be able to get myself up to the hallway immediately above it to the left. From there, if the floorplan followed the same layout as the other floors, the first office would lead me to an outer window.

I stood up on the wall—still finding it strange to acknowledge the fact I was standing on a wall—and took several steps back before launching myself at the side of the reception desk. Instead of grabbing onto the back edge, I kicked off the side face and twisted my body to grab at the frame of the hallway doorframe. I got both hands on the edge of the doorway, but only managed to keep one set of fingers from slipping off. I grabbed the metal hard, distorting the steel as I squeezed it. My body swung back and forth as my other hand fought for purchase. After a few seconds, I was finally under control again.

As hoped for, a row of offices stacked up above me to my left. I hefted myself up through the doorframe to the now horizontally oriented window mullions. While the Marine Corps had conditioned me for such exertion, my enhanced strength and stamina was the most useful. I was surprised, though, to feel an ache in my shoulders and neck. Although, it had been awhile since I had free climbed.

Peeking inside, I saw the desk, chair, and what seemed like a quarter ton of books, office supplies, folders, and papers had all slammed into a heap against the lower wall. Beyond the mess was a dark roiling sky and pelts of rain against the window. I was almost there. All I needed was a way to get the others up to me. Looking at the hallway above me, I smiled as I spotted the one thing perfect for getting us out of this hell hole.

The coil of fire hose behind emergency glass several meters above me looked out of place in such a modern building design. I guess R&R would rather isolate water damage than spray down an entire floor with an overhead sprinkler-based water suppression system. It was only a matter of finger strength and balance to hug the mullions and door openings to make my way up to the fire hose box.

Once at the box, I ripped open the door and pulled out the brass nozzle. The white nylon canvas hose unrolled behind it, cascading toward the lobby with the nozzle bumping against the walls and floor as it descended. Finally, the hose couldn't be unrolled any farther, the connection to the spool and the brass fitting to the water supply keeping it secure to the wall.

I tested my weight on it. While the assembly groaned a little, it held. I put my full weight on it, switching both hands to the hose. Descending hand over hand, I made it quickly back down to the elevator bank. Back at the fissure, there was still excess hose piling up on around the snarl of chairs and buckled elevator doors.

My side shot out a sharp pang of pain. When I pulled my hand away from it, blood came away, too. Fuck it all. I was never going to heal if I kept tearing open the wound. Even though my body had rejected the pellets, it still needed way more downtime to recover fully on its own, enhanced healing or not.

Plus, my shoulders and neck were still on fire from the climb.

Something huge fell to the concrete next to me with a splat. One of the surgeons from the operating theater—the head surgeon, Firestein—raised his ruined face at me with a snarl. His cheek was flayed open, revealing a mouth of expensive capped teeth. His eye socket was crushed, the eyeball itself punctured, flat, and hanging by the optic nerve. He reached out blindly around him with the one arm not broken in the fall, curling his fingers around my ankle.

He shouldn't be able to sense me.

332

Maybe it is the blood he senses.

"Wonderful," I snarled back at the doctor. A well-placed stomp to his face helped to loosen his grip. A second kick finished him off completely.

The sound of rushing water came through the crack from the shaft below. It almost drowned out the additional moans and growls echoing from above me. Another body fell from the hallway above, landing on top of the surgeon's body. This time, it was one of the technicians. He survived the fall in much better condition, quickly reaching out at me. I stepped back, pulled my tactical knife, and drove the blade into the back of his exposed neck. His face dropped to the surgeon's shoulders.

More groans from above.

Rushing water from below.

I shimmied into the fissure and pulled the technician's body over it to mask my smell and plug up the crack. I felt another FRAC fall onto the other two, using them as a safety net. Fuck! I dropped back into the shaft, creating a splash when my boots landed in two feet of water. "What the hell?" I exclaimed, staring at how high the water had risen since I had left.

"You okay?" Jude asked, her tactical light pointed at my chest. Holly was cradled in her other arm with her paws over her shoulder.

"We have to go," I ordered. "Now!"

"What happened?" Jude

Summer stood to one side by herself, shivering as the water was flowing past her lower thigh. "Where did Melissa go?" I asked. "Did she go back to the elevator?"

"No," Jude said with a shake of her head. "She went the other way."

"Why the fuck would she do that?"

"To prove she wasn't useless," Summer answered before slapping a hand over her mouth and pointing above us with the other.

"Great God Almighty…" Jude whispered the start of a prayer.

As the snarls and a couple bloody arms worked their way through the fissure above us, it was clear working through a fear of water in a confined space was going to be the least of Melissa's worries—and ours.

70

Raging Rapids

+81 Days – 2100 hours

"How long has she been gone?" I asked Jude in a whisper, not seeing any light bouncing across the walls further down the shaft.

"A couple minutes after you left," Jude replied.

Summer muffled another yelp as a second hand stretched through the fissure. With the shaft a three-meter square, it would be an amazing feat if one of the surgical FRACs managed to grab one of us. It wouldn't take long, though, for one of them to fall through the crack by chance. Three thumps later raised the percentage considerably as the chorus of moans and snapping teeth was joined by more of the undead operating staff. Concrete dust and pebbles started to sift down from the crack and the surviving FRACS starting clawing their way around the edges.

Jude was down a free hand by carrying the injured Holly. The dog couldn't be let down on the floor with the water level as high as it was. Her leg wouldn't hold up for long if she needed to swim to keep her head above water. And while the wide-eyed and shivering Summer was keeping it together pretty well for a young lady, the water was now nearly to her knees.

A belly flop splash from behind me. Followed by a gurgling snarl. The reanimated anesthesiologist—proving to be more clever than the surgeons—struggled to his feet. He splashed back down to his hands and knees in the rushing water once before staggering upright again. He cocked his head, trying to pinpoint something of interest above the sound of water. With Jude, Holly and Summer behind me, I pulled the tactical knife and swung it into his ear, knowing it would be more difficult to shatter through the top of his still solid skull.

"Move," I told the others, flinging the doctor wannabe FRAC into the wall to remove his head from my blade.

Jude took high steps to keep from making splashing noises. I swept Summer up into my arms, pulling her out of the water altogether. She wrapped her arms around my neck and held on tight with her head buried in my chest.

Snarls echoed around us as we moved farther into the shaft and into deeper water. More minor splashdowns came with a frenzy of renewed growls. I hoped they were just concrete chunks dislodging from the shaft walls and falling into the water instead of a pack of frenzied FRACs, but neither option boded well for our continued survival.

"Melissa," I called out as loud as I dared. The sound carried over the water and bounced off the walls in both directions.

We passed the 65th floor with no sign of Melissa. The water continued to rise. I hoisted Summer up a bit more in my arms. She definitely wasn't a kid anymore. Jude had stopped her attempts of high stepping in favor of just pushing through the water with grim determination.

The snarls multiplied. They were louder but didn't seem to be any closer. The echoes of the rushing water and their own growls disoriented them and kept them from targeting our location. A huge sideways 70 was painted on the walls, the number at our feet no longer visible under a meter of dark water—now up to my waist.

"Melissa," I called out louder. As soon as I let her name escape my lips, the FRACs matched it with a frenzied guttural response. They were closer than before. Even with all of the noises bouncing off the water and walls, the FRACs' predatory instincts and heightened senses still gave them some primal advantage when hunting. Or, maybe fighting against the current wasn't preferable to going with the flow.

A true life lesson.

Not now, Bob.

As you wish.

At the 77th floor, we had to walk under another crack in the shaft. This one wasn't filled with FRACs but with a curtain of water.

"Christ," Jude muttered. She hugged the wall where there was a gap in the falling water. "The rain must be torrential out there."

In answer, a booming and extended rumble of thunder shook the building. The snarls behind us turned into high-pitched yelps. They were less than ten meters behind us. I followed where Jude had slipped past the waterfall. Beyond the crack the downward angle of the shaft increased another five degrees. The water was deeper still, its current stronger and quicker. Jude was forced to use the wall for balance. I used my legs to break up the current of water in an effort to make her progress easier.

Just beyond the 80th floor, the structure of the shaft had degraded severely. Huge chunks of the meter-thick walls had fallen, causing an obstacle course of rock and rapids. The shaft looked less like it was designed for an elevator and more like an underground river suited for spelunkers or competitive kayakers.

"John," Jude said, moving from the wall to a chunk of concrete jutting out of the water to rest. "I need a minute."

I nodded.

The snarls continued behind us, masked somewhat by the splashing of the waterfall. Three chunks of concrete lay ahead of us. One of them moved. Jude and I both turned our lights on it. Melissa sat in the river with her legs braced on the concrete in front of her. The water broke on her hunched back, diverting to crash against the concrete on either side of her before it rushed past to the shaft beyond.

"Melissa?" Jude called out tentatively from her own chunk of rock. She didn't respond.

I sidestepped against the wall, hugging Summer more tightly in case Melissa wasn't... Melissa anymore. I moved next to her and shined my tactical light on the side of her face, knowing full well my finger had moved from the Glock's guard to the trigger. Melissa held her arms high across her body, her Benelli held tightly against her shoulders. Even drenched, it was obvious she was weeping.

"Melissa," I said softly, but with the same authority I had grown accustomed to hearing by one of any number of instructors I had trained under in the Corps. "We need to go. Now."

She took a deep breath but didn't move.

"You're going to die here unless you get to your goddamn feet," I ordered.

She continued to inhale deeply, shivering as she drew in breath. "What's the point?"

"What's the point?" Jude reiterated, anger starting to creep into her voice. "We got fucking FRACs ready to chew us up!"

"There's always going to be something trying to kill us," Melissa said, resigned to letting the water erode her away.

"So Summer doesn't matter?" I asked, my own anger starting to paint the edges of my vision a soft rose color. "How about I put a bullet in her head so she doesn't have to suffer anymore."

"You wouldn't," Melissa challenged me.

Summer stiffened in my arms, her grip around my neck loosening as she arched away from my body. I continued to hold her tight as I moved the light and the barrel of the Glock away from the aunt and toward the niece.

"No," Jude and Summer said in unison. Summer started whining as she slapped me against the chest and face.

Holly barked her disapproval. The sharp noise got Melissa to actually look at Summer. The bark also increased the moans of the FRACs behind us. Soon, it wouldn't matter how much water was raging between the undead and us.

"You wouldn't," Melissa repeated, now a little unsure of her conviction as she caught the color change of my irises. She struggled to her feet, the current pressing her farther between the concrete chunks in front of her. She brought the shotgun around and pointed it at me. "You better not."

"Or what?" I challenged her. "Your threats are weak at best. You shoot me and Summer catches some of it. You won't survive without me while we're in this tunnel." I regretted my choice of words, but they were necessary. I wasn't upset at the fact Melissa's teeth gritted and her jaw clenched. She still held her Benelli on me, her hand steady. I wanted her angry.

Doctor FRAC lunged through the water wall. Melissa shifted the shotgun's barrel. BOOM! The doctor's head evaporated completely from his body, the flesh and bone disappearing into thin air. She pumped another round into the chamber as the FRAC dropped under the surface of the water. She gave me a glare. "I hate you."

"Good," I replied.

71

Darkness Falls

+81 Days – 2109 hours

It seemed we had been moving in the current for days. Now, we waited in the dark with our bodies braced in the rapids with frazzled nerves and aching muscles. The anticipation of more FRACs bursting through the waterfall as we stood there with our weapons trained on the falling water seemed way worse. The water was cold. The sound of it cascading through the fallen concrete into the shaft was near deafening, causing enough white noise to cancel out everything else. Its rhythm was soothing, but its echoes forced us to be hyper-vigilant. We wouldn't know when the FRACs were close enough to attack us. The plus side was the walkers wouldn't be able to pinpoint our location easily, either.

The water was rising to my waist, forcing Jude and I to hike up the girls in our arms. Holly whimpered as she was readjusted. Jude whispered reassurances into her floppy ear while holding her AR steady as a rock like an extension of her own body. Melissa stood on the other side of the shaft, her shotgun barrel scanning the width of the space. Water still streamed down from her hair, but the tears of shame and despair had dried up… at least, for now.

"Are we going to die?" Summer whispered into my ear.

"Not today," I assured her, my heart pounding in a way reflecting the rest of me didn't necessarily agree with the confidence and conviction of my statement.

A lump broke through the waterfall. We all followed it with our lights and barrels as it floated downstream through the center of the river until it got caught up against the same concrete chunks Melissa had braced herself against only a few minutes ago. The FRAC was one of the nurses from the operating theater. Melissa looked at us from behind her weapon, cautiously approaching the body while trying to maintain her balance in the rapid's level current. Once she was within range, Melissa poked the back of its neck with the barrel of the Benelli. The body submerged for a second before bobbing back to the surface. It must have caved in its skull when it fell through the fissure.

Melissa looked at me and shrugged.

"Knife," I mouthed, pointing to the handle of my tactical knife. Melissa nodded and switched her shotgun to her off hand. She drew her knife. I pointed my light at the body still caught against the concrete.

She drew back the knife.

A second FRAC, a male nurse, lunged out of the water beside her.

Melissa pivoted, unable to get her finger on the trigger of the gun. She planted the knife into the walker's chest before falling back into one of the exposed concrete chunks. The soggy walker pressed into her.

I didn't have a shot keeping Melissa out of the sight line. And, Summer was still in my arm.

"Save her, John," Summer cried. I lowered Summer into the water. Jude widened her stance to brace herself so Summer didn't get swept away.

High-stepping and putting away my Glock, I reached Melissa just as the wet nurse lunged at her neck. I grabbed the nurse's scrubs and pulled him away, the knife still in his chest. Nurse FRAC snarled to me for pulling him away from his next meal. I reached

341

around and pulled out Melissa's knife and drove it up into the soft palette of his jaw. The nurse chewed on the blade for a moment until I twisted the blade and severed the base of the brain at the back of his throat. He dropped like a stone with a resounding resounding splash into the water. This time, the body floated past Melissa and disappeared in the current.

Whoops echoed off the walls. I turned back to the water wall with Melissa directly behind me, drawing my Glock again. One of the surgeons burst through the water, launching at me with amazing speed. He was in midair when he hit me level with my chest and snapped at me. He shouldn't be able to see me! My finger twitched and I fired an errant shot over his shoulder, luckily hitting a second technician in the teeth as he walked through the waterfall at a slower pace.

Beams of light bounced around the shaft.

The FRAC grabbed me by the shoulder straps of my tactical vest as he pushed his feet into my belly—essentially standing on my chest. He lunged his teeth forward toward my neck. I tried to break his hold, his grip like steel against my failing straight arms. He bent over my chest, pulling himself toward me with more strength than I could muster against it. He forced my arms to bend at the elbows, extending his neck to mere inches from my face.

A loud sharp bark reverberated throughout the shaft. The surgeon FRAC arched his back and whipped his head around in search of the noise. His nostrils flared, the former human reverting to his base animal instincts to ferret out his prey. He perched on my chest like a hunter sitting on a rock scanning the prairie.

With him distracted, I twisted my body and slammed him into the closest outcropping of concrete. His skull cracked. He bellowed in anger and pain, renewing his iron-like grip on my tactical vest. I thrust him onto the concrete again, narrowly missing being caught in the face by a sheared off piece of rebar. He howled and snapped his teeth in the air.

A chorus of howls replied to him from beyond the water wall. Fuck. As Dr. FRAC whipped his head around—searching for the pain bringer—I realized he hadn't seen me at all. The echoes of sound were messing up his ability to hunt, forcing him to lash out at anything in his way. Melissa standing directly behind me didn't help my case. I had been just an object in his way.

Still unable to pry his grip off my vest, I grabbed his shoulders and drove him into the concrete chunk again. The rebar impaled him, coming bloody and slick through his cheek right of his septum. His grip loosened, then his arms fell away to dangle at his sides as his last growl died in his throat.

In spite his death, a FRAC choir sang on as more of the undead sought us out. I waved the others to move deeper into the tunnel. I needed them behind the fallen concrete. I needed room to work. "Get back," I ordered them.

Melissa struggled to get across the shaft, using the concrete for balance. Once she made it over to Jude, she picked up Summer and they all moved as a group hugging the wall to keep from getting caught up in the current. Once they braced themselves against a twisted mesh of rebar several meters behind me, I refocused my attention to the groans and snarls beyond the water wall. I braced myself against the largest of the fallen concrete chunks. The impaled surgeon was to my left, the catch-up technician to my right.

The Glock was drawn. I took in a long breath before letting it out slowly. My heartbeat softened. The water falling through the crack in the shaft slowed as if someone was turning off the faucet. Around me, the splash of water quieted. The water wall parted like a curtain.

Two grinning walkers shambled toward me—or, at least, they moved with the current. I squeezed the trigger. Blood sprayed back into the water curtain and instantly disappeared into the falling stream. The walker, however, continue to walk forward until it realized it was dead again.

Doctors are always such overachievers.

He pitched forward and splashed face first into the water.

The other walker, a nurse with a huge gaping wound in the center of her stomach, lumbered and splashed through the river. She wasn't accustomed to keeping to her feet with so much force on her legs.

Returning to life is like being born again. Well, not born again like a Southern Baptist. More like a calf being birthed.

I drove my tactical knife through her left eye. She stood there for a moment, before sliding off the blade and dropping into the river.

She chose wisely.

She floated downstream toward the others, getting caught up against the same chunks of concrete. Another body bumped against me. As it passed me, it reached out and wrapped its arms tight around my knees. I lost my balance and fell into the chest-deep water. Jacques Cou-FRAC clawed his way on top of me like a spider, knocking the breath from my lungs. I dropped to the deck under the water, pressed down by his weight. Bubbles escaped my nostrils as I drifted into the other bodies against the concrete.

Shit! I had no leverage and no air in my now burning lungs. Through the ripple of the water I could see another FRAC joining the one already on my chest. They snapped at each other, climbing over me and pushing me deeper into the current against the debris.

344

The light on my tactical light winked out. I was cast into darkness. My head felt heavy... and light. I couldn't pry the FRACs off me. Another joined them. More weight pressing on my body. I was buried under bodies and under water.

I lifted the Glock out of the water. And fired. There was a flash. More weight on my body. Not less. The dark was darker.

I fired again. Muted howls. More weight. My hands were numb. Did I still have my gun? Flashes flickered in my vision. What remained of the breath in my lungs bubbled from my lips.

Darkness knocked. And I answered.

72

In a White Room...

unknown

The sparse white five-meter square room was startlingly bright. I sat in one of four available hard white plastic chairs—each centered on a wall. There was no art on the walls or any other furniture in the space. There were no magazines to read. No reception window to look through. No door to stare at in hopes my name was on the verge of being called next.

The recessed ceiling lighting was too bright for the cube, its brilliance reflecting off the walls harshly enough to cast the illusion I was floating inside the white space. In the sea of white, a dark slit emerged in the middle of the room. As it widened and solidified, I realized it wasn't a slit at all, but a familiar form.

Good evening, John.

"Is it?"

Are you referring to the time or the quality of it?

"Either?" I shrugged. "Both?"

Bob stood in the center of the room with his hands clasped in front of him, seeming to float a quarter inch above the floor. *Be thou the rainbow in the storms of life. The evening beam that smiles the clouds away, and tints tomorrow with prophetic ray.*

"Quoting Lord Byron, now?" I asked. "It didn't answer my questions."

Didn't it? I had figured it would be thought provoking, at the very least.

"I'm in a white room," I pondered.

With black curtains.

"Cream, too?"

I like to stay relevant.

"I don't think Cream and Lord Byron are even close to being considered relevant these days."

Everything is relevant these days, John.

"Not sure how."

There is nothing in the world now, John. All you have are those things you remember from 'before'. All of history is now relevant.

"It's highly unlikely we're going to go another hundred years at our current rate."

The Gaunt Man moved to the chair opposite me in this cube disguised as a waiting room. He smoothed out his skinny tie and unbuttoned his jacket before hiking the pleats of his dress slacks and sitting down. He crossed one leg over the other and cupped his hands over his knee.

So, why bother to go on?

I opened my mouth but quickly realized I didn't have a good response. 'Why go on', he had asked so simply as he sat across from me. It was a good question. Bob seemed to think so, at least, as he held my gaze with a soft smile and his head slightly cocked to the left awaiting my answer. "Pressing forward is my natural state, I guess."

So, you are saying you are like a shark.

"You have all the answers so I don't need to answer you, right?"

How long have you known me?

"Too long."

And have I not always been inside your head?

"I prefer not to think so."

But, you know so.

"Maybe that's why my decision-making has been so shitty lately."

The space I take up in your head has no bearing on the decisions you have made, John. You let Ms. Alvarez lead because you had no other choice. Lives hung in the balance.

"And how many lives were lost anyway?"

The Gaunt Man leaned forward, his plastic molded chair creaking as he did so. *You are a Marine. You have seen war. This is just another type of war. You had better come to terms with it.*

"And if I don't?"

Well, the Gaunt Man sat back, *in that case, the next lives lost will be on you.*

"So comforting," I complained, already feeling the heavy weight of the dead on my shoulders. They hung from hooks in my mind and my heart.

It sounds like you have already given up.

I ignored his last jab, instead blinking several times to adjust my eyes to the continued brilliance of the room. "What is this place?"

Do you like it?

"It's a step up from the hospital gurney. And quieter than the room by the ocean."

Bob looked around and nodded, *I would agree with that. A little bit more confining, though. And nothing seems to be falling off the walls.*

"Is that how you measure the accommodations? By the amount of falling debris?"

Bob shook his head. *The fact nothing is shaking or cracking in this room is a bad sign, regardless of how pleasant it appears.*

"Why is it bad? It's quiet here. Serene, even."

Ahh, serenity now. So you... the epitome of serenity.

"Maybe," I said with a lilt of anger creeping up from the back of my throat, "Maybe I deserve a little serenity."

Bob laughed heartily, slapping his hands on his thighs. I thought he was being sarcastic, but he continued to bellow even as he had to draw a finger under his eye to wipe away the tears forming there. *Oh, John. You are really so rich. Thank you for making my day.*

"I'm happy to entertain you," I replied. Bob was pissing me off now with his cackles, even though they were tapering off. He gazed at me with his dark, almost black eyes, and burst into another fit of laughter. Great. The sight of me was a joke, something to be laughed at.

The lights flickered for a moment before coming back stronger and brighter. It hurt to look at anything except Bob. He continued to laugh, now holding his arms across his stomach. My stomach twinged, but not from laughing. I pressed my hand into my side as a sharp pain—like a dagger—shot through me.

I pulled my hand away to see blood on my palm. It was in stark contrast to the white walls and floors. I stared at my hand, breathing through the pain. Several drops of blood fell from my fingertips and splattered on the pristine floor next to my foot. The small cast-off drops seemed to float in the white, expanding on their own to connect with each other into a larger single splotch. I looked away, but all I could see was red. The walls were still bright, but now seeped in a dusty rose color.

A low rumble vibrated through the chair and my feet. I stood and braced myself against the wall. Bob leaned forward with a sneer on his face. He was no longer laughing. The Gaunt Man mirrored me, standing and kicking back the flimsy chair. He launched at me. His fingernails became talons, embedding into the plaster walls on both side of my head. His eyes were jet black and his teeth had grown to a razor's edge. He licked his lips with an alien split tongue and closed to within a few inches of my face.

You're a pathetic loser, son, he growled in a familiar voice now his own. *You won't amount to anything.*

My anger rose. I glared at him and he glared back. I pulled my Glock and shot him in the chest. Three times. He didn't shrink away or fall to my feet.

That's all you got? Fucking, scared little boy. Did you piss yourself already?

"Fuck you!"

Why? You're already fucked.

I straight-armed my fists into his chest. His claws lost their grip from the wall, dislodging and hurling him into the center of the space. He skidded to a stop against the opposite wall. Clicking his talons against the floor, the Gaunt Man tensed his shoulders and lunged at me again. While he was in midair, I drove a boot into his face.

The room shuddered. Shit! That felt good.

The Gaunt Man dropped to the floor, spitting out blood across the tiles to mix with the blood I had already spilled. His grin widened, showing his new feral teeth. He skittered at me on all fours. I stepped forward and swung a boot into him like connecting with a kickball. His jaw crunched.

The walls cracked, letting darkness in.

The Gaunt Man wouldn't relent. He kept coming at me, in spite of a broken jaw, a burst left eye, and severe facial hemorrhaging. I kicked him again. Plaster fell off the walls, revealing the laths underneath. The oxygen bled out of the room like we were in a compromised space shuttle airlock.

The Gaunt Man tackled me. I drove both fists like an axe handle into his shoulder blades. He slammed onto the tiles, sending spider webs of cracks out to every wall. He rose to his feet, staggering as the blood and pus dripped from his ruined face. The white predatory grin remained.

Why do you bother? You won't ever amount to anything!

The lights flashed like lightning, accompanied by a boom of thunder a second later. I couldn't get enough air into my lungs. With the last of my reserves, I pulled back my fist—feeling every muscle in my body tense and coil—and swung at the Gaunt Man. My fist connected with his jaw.

His face imploded in a spray of blood.

The walls tore away into the darkness.

I gulped my last breath, feeling absolutely alive.

73

Baptism

+81 Days – 2130 hours

A deafening boom followed a wavering flash. Then another.

My lungs burned as no oxygen had come to relieve them of the stagnant carbon dioxide filling them. My arms and legs were pinned. I couldn't twist my body or move my head.

Another blast. More weight dropped onto my chest, forcing me to exhale the last bubbles from the lower tunnels of my lungs into the water above me. My pulse raced. The primitive brain screamed at me to get oxygen from somewhere.

More lightning and thunder erupted. An additional weight collapsed across my legs. On the verge of passing out, I suddenly felt the bodies slowly slide off. I used the last of my strength to lift three bloated dead FRACS off of my chest.

Hands grabbed at me. I slapped against them while they tried to drag me up. I broke the surface of the water, gulping in as much air as my lung could take. Pushing the reaching arms and one of the oozing floaters away, I wrapped my arms around one of the concrete outcroppings.

"Jesus Christ," Melissa yelled. "How long were you under?"

How long was I under? I shook my head, having no idea how to answer.

"Duck!" Melissa fired the Benelli at the water wall left of me. I twisted around quickly enough to see the water blow in a circular pattern back for a moment before it was as if the cascade had ever been disturbed. A second later, a body fell through to our side, splashing down in the water and drifting through the current to bump against a dozen bodies surrounding me.

Jude stood against the far wall of the shaft, her eyes darting back and forth along with the barrel of her AR. She fired at the waterfall as a woman in scrubs parted the water. She didn't react as the bullet found her brain, only standing under the water for a moment more before slowly slipping under the rising river.

"Where's Summer?" I asked with a gasp.

"Still behind us," Melissa replied, her eyes and gun barrel never straying from the water wall.

"The FRACs came through," Jude added. "We thought we lost you."

"Good thing we're great shots," Melissa said. "It was like a rugby scrum on top of you."

"Sure you're okay?" Jude asked.

I could breathe, even though my lungs still ached. Nothing seemed broken or bruised. My side continued to seep blood through my soaked clothes. "Yeah," I replied with a nod. "Thanks for the save."

They both nodded back, still keeping their guns high and their attentions to the roar of water behind me. The water was now almost chest deep. There was no way we were going to get deeper into the shaft. I stepped toward the falls, partially seeing my reflection in the water.

There were no growls or snarls. I didn't sense any of the undead. Stepping past the fissure and falling water, I raised my Glock. My tactical light was broken. I only had the light from Jude and Melissa behind me, and my enhanced night vision, to see what may be ahead in the shaft. The water level was lower beyond the crack, the shaft at a slighter angle. Four or five forms swayed back and forth several meters away. I put the front sights on the top of the closest shadow and squeezed the trigger.

Click. I pulled the trigger again. Nothing.

I released the magazine into my free hand. Empty. I felt around for any spares. Nothing. I reached for my tactical knife in its nylon sheath. Gone.

Jude and Melissa had put themselves in harm's way to save me and protect Holly and Summer. I had failed to protect them… again. One shortcoming to be erased right now.

I balled up my fists and sloshed forward. The undead reacted to my splashing at them, their eyes darting toward the noise and their lips curling back to reveal their blackened gums and still white teeth. Their nostrils flared as they smelled the diluted blood dripping from my side.

The closest one reached out at the disturbed water. I grabbed her wrist with my right hand and pulled her to me, delivering a haymaker punch to the side of her head. Freshly dead, her skull was still like hitting a brick wall. Regardless, my punch shattered her bone into bigger fragments driving into her brain. She still grabbed at me. I punched her again, this time my knuckles actually indenting the side of her head. A third punch was enough to make her flecked eyes drift up and her legs buckle.

Two of the other FRACs double-teamed me as their arms wrapped around my elbows. In their rush to tackle the noises, the walkers could only snap at thin air, as they were confused as to what was moving around near them. They sensed my blood, but didn't actually see me. Before they could escort me into the jaws of their remaining brethren, I swung my arms together. The water helped to quickly lift them off their feet, bumping them together with enough force to dislodge their grips on me.

They snarled at each other in what seemed like annoyance or a vie for dominance over their prey. I grabbed the opposite sides of their heads. Letting out a roar, I slammed their skulls together. What resulted was a dull, but sickening crack. One of their eyes—closest to the impact—filled with blood. They didn't relent snapping at anything making noise or moving. Their fingers dragged on my shirt, catching against the straps of my tactical vest. Instead of pushing them away, I drove my forehead into the red-eyed FRAC's face. The red rapidly spread to his other eye. He staggered against his partner, getting more teeth snaps and a nip on the cheek in return. The nip didn't matter as Red Eye fell to the deck and floated downstream.

Nip/Tuck FRAC continued to clench my tactical vest, the remaining two still two meters away. I pushed his shoulder down and away, sliding my arm around the back of his exposed neck. I grabbed the waistband of his wet scrubs and lifted his body completely out of the water. When he was inverted vertically, I snapped his body downward while holding his neck tight.

The human body can only withstand so much. Dead human bodies—animate or inanimate—can withstand a bit more. But, in either case, his spine couldn't handle the extreme whiplash and nerve severing I had just administered. A loud snap sounded a moment before Nip/Tuck belly smacked into the water, his head dangling at an obscene angle.

Only two FRACs remained, stalking slowly toward me as they trudged their way through the water. The muscles in my cheeks hurt. It wasn't from the head butt or the any other physical exertion. It was from the huge grin plastered on my face.

74

End of Innocence

+81 Days – 2200 hours

My arms were bloody, dragging down at my sides like they were laden with bags of lead weights. I splashed into the water wall, happy to use it to rinse off the gore and stench of the dead. Once through the cascade, I opened my eyes. Melissa and Jude stared at me with their weapons pointed at me.

"Goddammit, John!" Melissa yelled as she snapped the barrel of her shotgun up toward the roof of the shaft. "We could have killed you!"

I dragged the last two FRACs along with me, not sure why I still had a hand on either of their collars. I let go and their bodies floated toward Melissa. Her shotgun followed the closest of them until they bumped against the concrete and swept around it through the rapids to head downstream.

"Bodies coming, Summer," Melissa called out. "Don't be scared."

As the echo of her words diminished, Summer could be heard to say, "Scared? You kidding me? Yeah, right!"

Kids these days. Am I right?

I ignored Bob, although I sent a silent nod of appreciation to him and his strange conversation in the white cube waiting room. I looked through the wavering beams of the remaining tactical lights. Jude held her AR in a full draw. Her eyes were sharp and she had the appearance of looking well rested.

Melissa looked ready to drop, the area around her eyes puffy from lack of sleep. Her shotgun was cradled in her elbows, too heavy to hold at the ready anymore. She sighed and worked her way around the fallen concrete. She stumbled as she navigated into the quicker current, but quickly got a hand out to steady herself. It was a miracle she didn't drop the Benelli into the water altogether, but she hugged it tight with her free elbow to keep it pressed against her chest. "I'll be back in a sec."

We both nodded, although Melissa didn't see our gestures of consent in the scarce light. I trudged over to Jude. She bent her elbow and aimed her AR at the ceiling. The beam from the tactical light bounced off the ceiling, casting us into a pool of luminescence.

"How's it going, soldier?" she teased, knowing soldiers weren't Marines. Marines were Marines. Ooh-rah.

I looked into her eyes. The silver hadn't diminished but it also hadn't spread any further across her irises. The flecks shimmered as they caught the light bouncing off the concrete ceiling. Wrapping my left arm around her waist, I drew her close. Her trigger hand was now caught against my chest, the business end of the AR dangerously close.

"Slow down, cowboy." Jude chuckled softly. She stepped back and slung her rifle, dropping all of the light we had been under. The silver in her eyes continued to shine. She gave me a cocked smile. "Now what?"

I pulled her against me again, her free hand landing on my chest. She gazed up at me with those brilliant eyes. Her hand patted against me—perhaps impatiently.

"Well?" she asked in the dark.

I pressed her body into mine and kissed her. She closed her eyes and parted her lips. Her hand found its way from my chest to the back of my neck, her fingers running through my hair. There was urgency to our kiss. As if the world could end tomorrow—or had already ended. She pulled me toward her, too, using a good amount of strength to press our lips together. It was as if she wanted us to meld into a single being. The heat radiating from her body was a pleasure to be bound to. Eventually, she softened her grip at the back of my neck, letting her fingers drift to my cheek as she pulled her lips away to look at me. I instantly missed her heat.

"Thank you," she said. As a typical man, I was hard-pressed to know what she was thanking me for. It seemed silly to be thanked for a kiss. I smiled and nodded. I wasn't sure she saw me in the dark, but her fingers could feel the lift in my cheeks and the drop of my chin.

Out of the black, she licked me.

Holly. Not Jude. Melissa had brought her back upstream since the FRAC threat had ended. Holly started at the corner of my lips and moved in a straight line across my scruffy jawline to the opening of my ear canal. Holly did whimper softly from way back in her throat, but was content enough to clean as much of my face as her rough tongue could reach. Jude scooped the furry critter away from Melissa. Holly continued to use her tongue to wash my face.

"Gross," Summer said as she also emerged from the dark, her arms suddenly wrapping around Jude's waist.

Melissa quickly pried Summer away from Jude and picked her up out of the water. "We need to get to higher ground."

The water had risen another half foot. Melissa and Summer's lips had turned blue, both of them shivering from the cold of the rain water. We were lucky the heat of the summer night was keeping the air temperature comfortable.

"Agreed," I answered, not feeling the effects of the cold water. Jude seemed unaffected, too. A lone floating FRAC drifted past us and got carried away in the deepening current. "I think we can get back to where we started now."

Melissa, with Summer in her arms, splashed over and hugged her body against the wall behind Jude. I led the way as we skirted the edge of the water wall and slowly fought against the slowing current. It was a while, almost a half hour before we managed to see the original crack where I had ascended to find a way out, thanks to Jude's drawn sidearm and functional tactical light.

The water level was still above the knees here. Which was much more tolerable for us adults. It was still almost waist deep for Summer who Melissa had to put down to rest her arms and back. I would have taken Summer for her but I had another task to complete.

The crack had grown wider. Very obvious claw marks raked against the sides and edges. Two arms still hung from the opening, the lifeless curled fingers whittled down to the bone.

I expected them to twitch, even scooping up water with my hands and splashing them to coax them to move. Nothing happened. They were dead again.

"Head back to the elevator," I said. "The water will be lower and you can rest inside the car if you want." The three of them stared at me. I knew what they were thinking. "I know," I acknowledged. "But it's your best chance. We need to rest up because we aren't out of the woods yet."

Miles to go before we sleep.

Exactly.

"Do what you have to do, John," Jude agreed. "We will do the same."

"Yeah," Melissa said, less onboard than Jude was about seeing the bodies of Sean and April again. "Summer and I may stay outside."

"You decide," I conceded to Melissa, and then to Jude, "but I need to borrow your tactical light."

"Figures," Jude replied. "We'll get by. We have Melissa's light." She dismounted the tactical light from her AR and handed it over. I took it with a nod, our fingers touching for a moment. We smiled at each other before withdrawing our hands.

"You're welcome to make the climb yourself," I offered.

"Nope." She shook her head. "Us poor little girls can't do man-sized things. Come on, 'Lissa, let's leave the man to his manly work."

I flashed Jude's tactical light back at her, the smile evident across her lips. The light caught Melissa's eye roll, too.

"Good luck, John," Summer cut in.

"Thanks, kiddo," I replied. "See you in a minute."

"A few minutes," Jude amended.

"Yeah," I agreed. "A few minutes."

Jude hitched up the tired Holly and threw a wink my way. Without another word or look, the four women in my life splashed away toward lower tides and higher ground.

I looked up at the dangling arms. Crouching down, I leapt up and grabbed two of them, swaying myself up hand over hand. Luckily, their shoulders were locked against the other side of the crack. The fact they were freshly dead meant they would be able to support my weight. Otherwise, the bones would have shattered and the arms would have detached from the sockets, sending me ass first back into the water.

Once I secured my grip on the other side of the crack, I hoisted myself up easily through it. It was obvious to see why all the expired medical personnel hadn't escaped through the crack. One of them, a woman, had her skull crushed. While there wasn't any debris evident, my guess was one of the others who got through to the shaft had landed a knee or shoulder into her upon landing. The other dead FRAC, a male nurse with a "Just Do It!" tattoo inked on his bicep under his torn sleeve, stared at me with his mouth agape. A piece of rebar had impaled his head like a pike, entering through the soft tissue under his chin, visible in his open mouth, and disappearing into his brain. The steel only came back into view once it spiked through the top of his head. Sitting on the edge of the fissure, I counted five bodies used as a cushy landing pad for the others.

Such touching sacrifices.

As usual, I ignored Bob's intermittent commentary. Flashing the tactical light upward, I spotted the fire hose I had unrolled. The end of it had been buried under the bodies around the fissure. I grabbed the hose and pulled. It was still anchored tightly to the water connection and shouldn't break away its mounts from my weight.

So, I climbed.

75

Fireman's Carry

+81 Days – 2254 hours

It didn't take long to climb up the hose, disconnect it and let gravity do the work to send it coiling down through the fissure. Climbing down without the aid of the hose was a bit more work, adding a few scrapes to my arms and a few additional bloody tears to my already brutalized side. Once back in the elevator shaft, I wound the hose across my body like a bandolier until the brass nozzle slapped heavily against my hip. It was heavy, making my side ache.

I guess you will need to work on your core.

"Well," I answered sarcastically, "when my muscles are whole again, I'll try to set aside time to add more lunges and crunches into my daily routine."

Maybe Pilates, too.

"Of course." I waded toward the elevator with the weight of the hose threatening to sink me into the water. The building vibrated through another bout of thunder. I could only imagine what the lightning show looked like accompanying it. We wished for rain and we got exactly what we had asked for.

Be careful what you wish for, as the saying goes.

"You are so wise, Bob," I said aloud.

A very astute observation, Sergeant.

"That's me. Astute."

Thunder rumbled through the structure again. Water rushed at me with a renewed purpose. The rain must be coming down even harder now. Or more cracks in the structure had just developed. At any rate, we would be out from under the Roanoke & Raleigh deathtrap soon. After a couple of minutes, I realized the light in the tunnel wasn't coming from just Jude's tactical light. The new light source was darting about from behind the black block silhouette of the elevator car, creating a dim aura—like the center of a full eclipse—around it. The murmur of a trio of familiar voices also came from beyond the elevator. I couldn't tell what was being said, but there was a burst of sudden laughter.

A flash enveloped the space.

"Christ!" Jude said.

"Is the rain ever going to let up?" Melissa replied.

"Probably not," Jude teased.

"I like the lightning, Aunt 'Lissa."

"I know you do, hun."

As a treat for Summer, lightning flashed again. She squealed her delight. More thunder ripped through the shaft. The surface of the water trembled with tiny ripples radiating out from the walls. Another wave of water rushed at me, slowing my progress.

"Should we get inside the elevator?" Jude asked the others.

"I'd prefer to stay out here," Melissa answered, an edge to her voice. "Summer doesn't need to see that again."

"Sean and April ain't coming back," Summer told her aunt. "But I can stay out here and watch the rain, right?"

"Sure, sweetie," Melissa said. "Whatever you want."

I squeezed between the elevator car and the shaft wall, whistling to alert the others to my return. I would hate to get a face full of lead from a nervous and reactive shotgun blast.

"The conquering hero," Jude announced. "And, you bring with you our salvation. It seems everything is water-related today."

"It does, doesn't it?" I nodded. "Ready to go?"

"No time like the present," Melissa said, slapping the water continuing to rise. She raised her hand to the light. "I'm getting wrinkled."

"Auntie," Summer said with conviction, "you've been wrinkled since as long as I can remember."

76

Where the Sidewalk Ends

+81 Days – 2337 hours

We splashed toward the light... and, by that, I meant the now constant flashes of lightning creating a square of brilliance at the end of the broken elevator shaft. The shaft shook from the thunder, the surface of the water trembling in ever overlapping ripples. Small pieces of loosened concrete splashed down around us. The dust-thickened air forcing us to cover our mouths.

It was a strange empty feeling, the absence of water weighing down our every step. It had tapered down to a trickle by the time we reached the edge of the tunnel the sheared building had created. The others stayed far enough back into the shaft to keep from being rained on, finding a newly fallen slab of concrete to rest on. Summer sat on Melissa's lap while Holly rested against Jude's chest.

The rain pelted against my face as I ventured to the edge. Even with my vision and the assistance of Jude's tactical light, the way down hadn't gotten more accessible. Since my last visit, numerous waterfalls had been created, probably making the available footholds more slippery. Luckily, we had the fire hose. I would lower each of them down to the atrium individually.

A crimson and white wraith suddenly slapped at my face, wrapping itself wetly across my body. I fought against it until I was able to get my arms up to peel it away. I had fought for my country, but never against the American flag. It whipped in my fist as the gale tried to peel it away from me. I scrunched the soppy material into a wet ball and tossed it toward where the others were sitting.

"Seriously?" Jude asked, wiping her arm where the flag had splashed water on her.

"Yep," I called back. "We need a sling for the mutt."

"Good thinking," she admitted. Holly snored lightly in her arms.

"Get some rest," I ordered. "We aren't getting out until morning."

"What?" Melissa asked with grin. "You're going to let a little rain stop you? A building collapse and FRACs are fine, but get a little wet and you shrivel up like a delicate flower?"

"You found me out," I replied.

She laughed good-naturedly—a sound I don't recall ever hearing out of her in the entire time I had known her. It was a good sound. And it was infectious—no pun intended. Summer started to giggle, maybe more from exhaustion than from the actual humor of it. Jude smiled. Holly opened and rolled her eyes around, but was too content in Jude's arms to join in. I felt my cheeks harden, the corners of my lips curling up.

I backed away from the edge, getting under the cover of the shaft out of the direct force of the driving rain. Sliding down the wall opposite the others, I bumped onto the floor and leaned my head back. The hose was still wrapped around my body, an adequate comfort I hugged my arms around. I closed my eyes, knowing sleep would continue to be a fleeting thought, but hoping to shut my brain down for a minute or two.

77

Gravity of the Situation
+82 Days – 0637 hours

The desert dunes fell away as the team headed over cobalt blue water. The slap of rotors and the roar of diesel engines didn't distract from the beauty of the warm Mediterranean. The pilot spoke to me through the earphones.

"I never get over how amazing this course is," the voice crackled.

"It is something to be thankful for," I replied into the headset. "Without a doubt."

A sudden pop led to a series of alarms in the cockpit and a trail of black smoke fuming from the tail rotor.

"We got a problem here, Sergeant," the pilot called back, his panic heard both in the headset and above the roar of screeching metal. "We're going to have to ditch…"

"…Walken," another voice said. "Wake up, John."

I may have uttered a whine as I hugged the fire hose wrapped around me, but I opened my eyes anyway. "Let me sleep."

"You can sleep when you're dead," Melissa said in a hushed tone from the familiar slab of concrete. Summer lay across it, her knees pulled up to her chest and her thumb in her mouth.

It was a quarter to seven in the morning. Shit! I had managed to sleep six hours. What a foreign concept. I stretched out my arms, wide awake and alert.

"You were out cold, Marine," Jude stated. "I guess even you

have to sleep sometime."

"I guess so," I replied. "How about you? You sleep well?"

"On and off," Jude said. "Holly was restless and whimpering so I tried my best to keep her comfortable."

The end of the shaft was visible enough in the morning hours, in spite of the continued rain and the stream of water passing over our feet. Behind us, the water rippled and reflected the faint light as the shaft had filled up with water enough to obscure the elevator car.

"Pretty soon, we're going to be exposed out to the edge with no place to stay dry," Jude said. "I can't believe it's still raining."

I couldn't recall the last time we were dry. Even with the shaft providing cover and the fallen concrete slabs giving us perches to get our feet out of the water's flow, none of us had dried out during the night. "I'll lower people down now that we have the light," I told her. "Maybe get us into someplace dryer and warmer for a bit."

"It's the best idea I've heard in a while," Melissa chimed in. "Let's get that on the docket, yeah? Summer is shivering being out here in the open. There's only so much body heat to go around."

Jude turned back to me. "We need to take care of Summer and Holly, John."

I stood up, lifting the hose over my arm and head and letting it fall to the wet concrete. I grabbed one edge and wrapped it around the exposed rebar of the concrete chunk I had fallen asleep on. After tying it tightly, I gave it a good yank. The hose didn't give, the tug tightening the knot I had already made. Good. I unrolled the coiled-up hose as I walked it to the edge. Dropping what was left, I picked up the end with the brass nozzle. "Okay, who's first?"

"Melissa," Jude announced the order. "So there is someone down at the bottom to catch Summer."

"Agreed," Melissa said, checking how many shells she had

remaining in the Benelli. She did the same to the Beretta she had confiscated last night. "Let's get this done."

I wrapped the business end of the hose around Melissa's chest and tied it tight enough under the armpits to warrant a dirty look from her. I pulled the knot again to make sure friction would be working for us, not against us.

"Try to use any outcroppings to control your descent," I instructed her. "I'm going to be lowering you as slow as I can, but you may still twist around when you don't have anything to anchor you. Ok?"

"Ok." Melissa nodded, her face tensed up and her forehead furrowed to say she wasn't okay.

I walked her to the sheer edge. "Ok. Face me."

"Don't you dare fucking push me off this thing!"

I wrapped the hose over my arm and held her by the shoulders. "Just look for foot and handholds where you can to keep from spinning around. If you end up without anything to grab, keep your arms in to keep from rotating. Understand?"

She nodded she understood, in a rational way, but the pinpricks of her wide eyes told me a different story. Regardless, when I let go of her tense shoulders and braced myself with the fire hose in my hands and around my waist, she grabbed the end of the hose tied around her chest and started to lean back.

"Keep your eyes on me," I advised.

Melissa nodded and complied. The hose went taut. She leaned back more, her legs straight and stiff. When her chest moved to even with the bottom edge of the shaft, her eyes started to dart away from me and to her new surroundings.

"Do you have any place to get a footing?" I asked.

She frantically looked around, the hose already starting to sway from her movement. "A couple spots... but not many."

"Do your best, Melissa," Jude said, having crept to the edge for a better look.

"Yeah, yeah," Melissa grumbled, striking out a foot into an outcropping of metal to slow her sideways swing.

I continued to let out lengths of hose hand over hand. Jude peered over the edge to serve as my spotter. Melissa shouted out colorful expletives as the wind whipped against her, the rain pelted down on her. The speed of her descent caused her to bump against parts of the sheared off building where they jutted out. After ten minutes, I knew Melissa had touched down in the atrium because Jude held up her closed fist and I felt slack in the hose. A minute later, the hose yanked three times in my hands and I started to reel it back up.

The building rumbled. It was still raining, but with none of the lightning Summer had enjoyed so much. No lightning meant no thunder. The vibration in the structure had come from something else.

I redoubled my efforts to quickly bring the hose back up. The nozzle did get caught a couple times, but each time I let out a length of hose to let it dislodge from whatever it got caught on. Once the brass nozzle came into view and dangled at the end of my hand, I looked back at who was next in line to be lowered down.

"Come on, Summer," I said softly. "Let's get you down to the ground floor."

She hurried over to me and raised her arms in the air. I wrapped the hose around her little chest and tied it tight enough to keep it from slipping past her armpits but loose enough for her to breathe without discomfort.

"I'm going to lower you as even–," I started.

"And slowly as you can," Summer finished for me. "I'm ready to go, John. Anchors aweigh!"

"You're awesome, sweetie," Jude commended her.

"Without a doubt," Summer replied. "Ready, John?"

I smiled. Now I was taking orders from a 12-year-old. "Yes, ma'am," I replied. "Hold on tight."

She winked at me and almost hopped backwards off the edge with a big grin on her face. She was easy to lower, being a third the weight of her aunt. I think I even heard a squeal drift up on the wind. Melissa's voice was definitely audible over the storm as she sent up fretted instructions to her niece. Summer, in typical fashion, replied with mock disdain and, I'm sure, a few eye rolls and heavy sighs.

Suddenly, the line went slack way before the full length had been let out. "Jude, what's happening?"

"I don't know. She's under a shelf of concrete. I can't see her."

I pulled in the slack, plus another foot of hose. Summer's weight was still on the end.

"She's caught up!" Melissa called up.

I lowered the hose until I felt the slack then pulled up again. I repeated the action twice more.

"Wee," Summer squealed. "Keep doing it!"

Jude chuckled. I smiled and joined in with Jude's mirth as I lowered the line, this time Summer descending at a nice even pace without the hose getting caught up again. When I felt the familiar slack in the hose, I knew Summer had touched bottom.

A minute later, Melissa called up, "Ok!"

I pulled the hose back up while Jude went to go retrieve the cast aside flag. She wrapped it around her and made a knot dripping water as she pulled the ends tight. Once tied, the flag made a nice sling.

When she went to get Holly, I stopped her. "I'll take Holly. You need to pay attention to the climb down." She looked at me with a stare telling me she was perfectly capable of carrying Holly with her. My stare back told her I wasn't asking her opinion on the matter. In the end, she took off the flag-turned-dog carrier and dropped the sloppy patriotic fabric it at my feet. She came back to the edge and faced me. I tied the hose around her like I had with the others, taking care I wrapped it over her breasts and under her armpits without too much physical contact. I tied the knot.

"Ready, soldier?" she teased, the water from the tunnel splashing around her feet and cascading off the edge. It misted into the air as it caught on the heavy wind. She leaned in and kissed me on the lips, gave me a wink and a smile, and leaned back before I could properly reciprocate her affection. She was almost horizontal and even with the bottom of the shaft before she started to step down and out of sight. I let out the hose a foot at a time, allowing Jude enough time to find places to brace herself.

The building shuddered. More water found its way to the edge, dumping a rush on Jude's head.

"Hey," she called out.

To my left, the concrete split into a crack a couple inches at its narrowest.

Shotgun blasts sounded from below.

Holding the hose tight, I inched to the edge to see Melissa dispatching a trio of FRACs in the atrium below. Summer clung to the back of her left leg. Several FRACs milled around the perimeter of a low wall of rubble, swaying back and forth as they tried to figure out a way around or through the debris field.

The water rushed past the back of my legs as another quake rocked the structure. The end of the shaft tilted downward. The river had reversed itself, now flowing toward the edge. The crack in the shaft wall beside me had widened and had been joined by others. Jude was still only halfway down to the atrium, a hundred meters of air and numerous impaling possibilities between her and the rubble below. Now, the water was falling with force on top of her.

More gunshots.

I lowered out more hose. Or, should I bring her back up? Slabs of concrete splashed into the river beside me, one chunk knocking into my shoulder and forcing me to my knees. I lost my grip with my left hand, the hose sliding through my fingers. Fuck! I redoubled my grip with my right hand. My left arm was limp against my side. I slowly got my feet under me, turning my body, stepping over the hose to put it at my back, and slipping it under my useless arm to use my waist as a brake. I loosened my grip and tightened it again, letting out lengths of hose as evenly as I could.

The shaft pitched forward again, the concrete shuddering as the water rushed off the edge. The current of the water threatened to take me off my feet. Metal groaned and glass shattered from the structure under me.

A shotgun blast, followed by a scream. Was it Melissa or Jude? A higher popping sound from a Beretta.

I still had fifty meters to let out before Jude was safely on the ground. Was the ground even safe anymore? I could see more of the atrium as the sightline from the elevator shaft changed. There were FRACs milling around in the streets beyond the debris, their bodies twisting and contorting as they zeroed in on the gunshots.

Squeeze. Release.

My lame arm tingled, needles prickling through the shoulder and bicep while blood streamed down to numb fingers from a gash in the meat surrounding my rotator cuff.

Squeeze. Release.

The water hammered against my calves, desperate to carry me with it as it raced to the edge to become a waterfall. I leaned back to better brace myself.

Squeeze. Release.

Still twenty meters of hose to let out, leaving three stories of air and twisted metal and glass between Jude and the ground.

Squeeze. Release.

My grip failed me. Hose rushed through my fingers. A scream from below. I pinned my dead arm against my waist. Hose still raced out. I jammed my body against the crumbling wall of the shaft. The hose was pinned between my body and the wall. My heart pulsed in my head and throat. Taking in a ragged nervous breath, I flexed my fingers for a proper grip on the hose again. Ten meters of hose left.

"Jude?" I called out. All I received as a response were gunshots. "Jude!" I yelled louder. I let out more hose. More water rushed past my legs. Metal strained and concrete crumbled. Glass shattered with a massive pop. The shaft pitched forward, showing Melissa and Summer standing on a mound of concrete with FRACs crawling around at the base of the hill in a waist-deep pool of murky water. Jude was still hidden under the lip of the shaft.

A wall of water slammed into my back. It was a freight train. My feet lost contact with anything solid. The hose raced out, Jude the weight at the end of it. More pops. Someone screamed. A sharp bark echoed from behind me. The shaft was gone.

Heavy chunks pummeled my back. The steel, glass and concrete groaned its last death throes. The water had finally beaten me, sending me into open air. Gravity took over, always winning the war of falling bodies.

I was lost to it. We were all lost.

Day Zero will continue…

BAD COMPANY

OTHER BOOKS BY CHARLES INGERSOLL

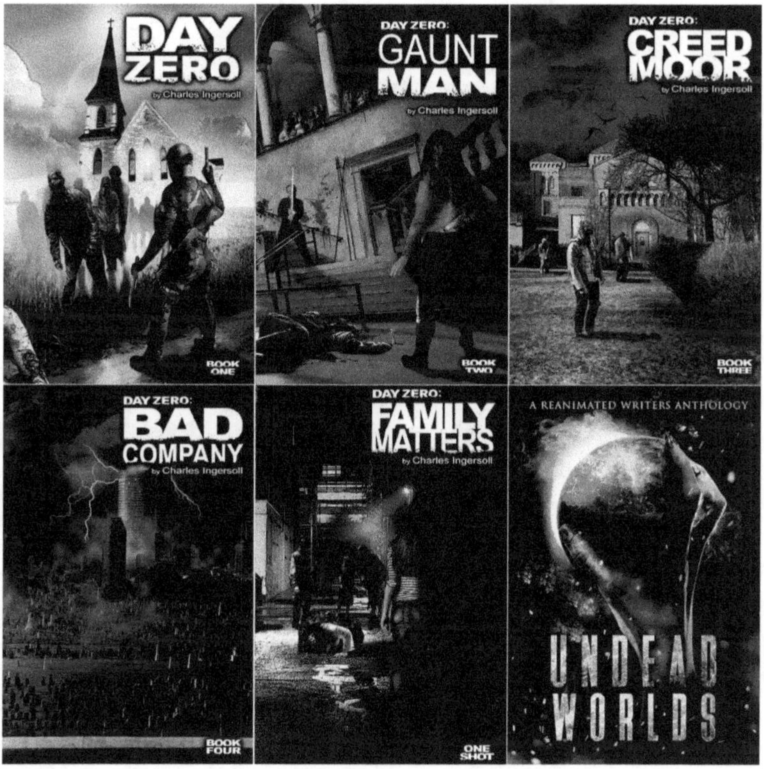

All titles available in paperback and in most places
where you enjoy downloading eBooks!

ABOUT THE AUTHOR

The love of zombies was in my blood immediately after watching George Romero's *Night of the Living Dead* at a far too young and inappropriate age. That feeling never faded, festering for forty years before the fever finally broke and beckoned me to write my own "Great American Zombie Novel". One story became a second. Two stories became an ongoing series.

I love comic cons, cosplay, movies and television, guns, the Marvel Cinematic Universe, and the supernatural. I currently reside in what the South Carolina locals call the Upstate with the two real loves of my life, my very own real-life Jude (Judy) and a certain fur baby canine named Holly—both straight off the pages of Day Zero universe.

A special *thank you* to my partner in crime, and to everyone who chooses to support my work to ensure my zombie universe doesn't die a horrible death.

LEARN MORE AND BE SOCIAL

To find more information about Charles Ingersoll and the *Day Zero* zombie survivor apocalypse book series, please follow on:

Facebook @ https://www.facebook.com/dayzerozombies/

Twitter @ https://twitter.com/dayzerozombies/

Instagram @ https://www.instagram.com/dayzerozombies/

Website: http://www.dayzerozombies.com

bit.ly/dayzerozombies